"Come warm yourself at the fire," Drew said, feigning indifference.

Roslyn obeyed with obvious reluctance—and then jumped when he reached up to touch her hair. "What are you *doing*?"

"Taking down your hair. It's still dripping wet. You need to dry it if you hope to get warm."

She stood stock-still while his fingers searched for the pins that held up the heavy gold mass, then smoothed the damp tresses down her back. "There, that should help."

"Thank you," she murmured, glancing up at him.

Drew sucked in a sharp breath. The light thrown by the flames cast a golden glow over her beautiful face. She was temptation itself, and he wasn't able to resist.

Slowly he lifted his hand to her face, letting his thumb trace her jaw. When he moved his fingers to her lips, she drew in a sharp breath, too. "You promised. . . ." Her protest was no more than a whisper.

His smile was tender. "I said I wouldn't ravish you, and I won't." *But ravishment implies lack of consent,* he added silently to himself, *and I promise your consent won't be lacking.*

By Nicole Jordan

The Courtship Wars:
TO PLEASURE A LADY
TO BED A BEAUTY
TO SEDUCE A BRIDE

Paradise Series:
MASTER OF TEMPTATION
LORD OF SEDUCTION
WICKED FANTASY
FEVER DREAMS

Notorious Series:
THE SEDUCTION
THE PASSION
DESIRE
ECSTASY
THE PRINCE OF PLEASURE

Other Novels:
THE LOVER
THE WARRIOR
TOUCH ME WITH FIRE

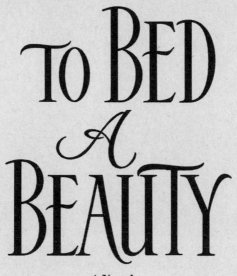

TO BED
A
BEAUTY

A Novel

Nicole
Jordan

BALLANTINE BOOKS • NEW YORK

Copyright © 2008 by Anne Bushyhead
Excerpt from *To Seduce a Bride* copyright © 2008 by Nicole Jordan

Published in the United States by Ballantine Books, an imprint of The Random House Publishing Group, a division of Random House, Inc., New York.

BALLANTINE and colophon are registered trademarks of Random House, Inc.

This book contains an excerpt from the forthcoming book *To Seduce a Bride* by Nicole Jordan. This excerpt has been set for this edition only and may not reflect the final content of the forthcoming edition.

ISBN 978-0-7394-9282-6

Cover design: Carl D. Galian
Cover illustration: Aleta Rafton

Printed in the United States of America

To my oh so wonderful partners in crime:
Sandra Anglain Chastain, Ann Howard White, and
Patricia Lewin.
You guys are just the very best!

Chapter One

❧

How astonishing that a gentleman would ask a perfect stranger to become his mistress without so much as an introduction.

—Letter from Miss Roslyn Loring to Fanny Irwin

London, June 1817

"They say he is a marvelous lover."

Unable to ignore such a provocative comment, Roslyn Loring reluctantly shifted her gaze across the crowded ballroom to scrutinize the tall, lithe nobleman who had just entered.

She had never met the handsome, rakish Duke of Arden, although she'd heard countless tales about him. He was the picture of a wealthy aristocrat—his fair hair gleaming amber under the chandeliers' light, his commanding, elegant form garbed in a black domino, the cloaklike garment his only concession to costume for the masquerade ball.

He wore no mask, so his striking features were clearly visible. And his attendance was obviously welcome to everyone but *her*. Immediately he became the intent focus of a bevy of beauties, all eager to attract his notice.

"What makes him so marvelous?" Roslyn asked, intrigued despite her regret at the duke's unwanted arrival.

Her friend Fanny Irwin smiled. "His amorous skills, my dear. It is said he has the power to make women weep."

Lifting an eyebrow behind her own mask, Roslyn pursed her lips wryly. "Why in heaven's name would making women weep be a coveted skill?"

"Weep with *rapture,* my dear. Arden is extraordinary because of the exquisite pleasure he can bring a woman."

"I cannot imagine."

Fanny responded with the musical laugh that had helped make her one of London's most sought-after courtesans. "I should hope not, since you have no experience with carnal matters. But it is a rare man who is concerned with his paramour's satisfaction, or who will see to her pleasure even before his own. That kind of lover is priceless."

Roslyn's gaze narrowed thoughtfully. She was here tonight in order to gain a measure of experience, yet she had no desire to begin with the duke. Arden was a close friend of her new guardian, the Earl of Danvers, who had recently become engaged to marry her elder sister Arabella. Roslyn didn't wish for the duke even to *see* her, since she was courting scandal attending a notorious Cyprians' ball. She expected to make his formal acquaintance at her sister's wedding in a fortnight, and it would never do to have him recognize her.

No doubt his grace would disapprove of her brazen excursion into the glittering realm of the demimonde. According to Arabella, Arden had been severely critical of his friend's betrothal, skeptical that Lord Danvers could have fallen in love with the eldest Loring sister so quickly or so wholeheartedly.

Viewing the duke now, Roslyn had little trouble understanding his cynical response. His lean, chiseled features were remarkably handsome but rather proud; his bearing much as she would have expected from an aristocrat of his consequence—refined, commanding, a bit imperious. But a duke of Arden's extensive wealth and power had the right to arrogance, Roslyn supposed.

That he was reputed to be such an extraordinary lover, however, quite surprised her.

Her musings were interrupted as Fanny continued her frank observations. "Not that I have any *personal* knowledge of the duke, I want you to know. He prefers to keep one mistress at a time. Doubtless that is why he has come tonight—to choose a new mistress."

"What happened to his last one?" Roslyn asked, interested in learning all she could from Fanny.

"Possessiveness, my dear, which is a cardinal sin if you mean to keep your protector content. Particularly for a nobleman like Arden, who can have his pick of females."

He did seem to be examining the merchandise, Roslyn saw as the duke casually scanned the ballroom. Just then his gaze lit on her and paused in obvious interest. Reflexively, she took a step backward, feeling the sudden urge to hide. She had come incognito, the upper half of her face concealed by a mask, her own pale gold hair covered with a powdered wig and wide-brimmed bonnet.

But perhaps it was her uniqueness itself that attracted his attention. Although her décolletage was much lower than she liked in the costume she had borrowed from Fanny, she was dressed rather modestly as a shepherdess, while most of the other females here were scantily clad in the alluring costumes of Greek goddesses or Roman slave girls or Turkish harem beauties. Fanny had come as Cleopatra, which complemented her exotic features and raven hair.

When Roslyn saw that Arden's focus remained fixed on herself, her heart skipped a beat. Even at this distance, she could feel the impact of his penetrating gaze.

"He is looking directly at me," she murmured, half vexed and half concerned.

"That is hardly surprising," Fanny said in amusement. "Your combination of elegance and innocence is a novelty at a fete such as this. You are a rare English rose compared to the more exotic blooms for sale here."

Roslyn slanted her friend an exasperated glance. "You know very well I am not for sale."

"But *he* does not know it. Arden naturally assumes you are here to display your wares and sell your services."

"Well, I am not. I only came to find out how your colleagues comport themselves with their patrons."

"You should be flattered to pique his grace's interest," her friend remarked, teasing.

"Good heavens, I am not flattered, Fanny! Rather I am alarmed. I don't dare let Arden discover my identity. I will have to face him across the church aisle in two weeks, and I don't want him bearing tales about me to my new guardian. I think I should find a potted palm to hide behind. Look . . . he is moving this way!"

Taking another step backward, Roslyn slipped behind a marble column. Fanny joined her there, laughter lurking behind the eyeholes of her mask.

"You may cease laughing, traitor," Roslyn muttered. "It is not *your* reputation at risk."

"No, I suppose not, since I gave mine away several years ago." Fanny's expression suddenly sobered a little. "It is just as well that you have no interest in Arden, Roslyn. He may be a magnificent lover, but he reportedly has no heart. And you only want a man who is capable of falling in love."

"Yes, exactly."

She intended to make a love match someday, and cynical, rakish dukes were not known for contracting matrimonial unions for any reason other than their duty and convenience.

Canting her head slightly, Roslyn peered beyond the column. "Blast it, he is still headed this way." More urgently, she glanced behind her at the rear entrance doors. "I cannot stay here. There must be someplace I can take refuge until he quits the ball."

"There is a gallery at the rear of the building with numerous alcoves where couples may be intimate, but they shouldn't all be occupied yet, since the night is still relatively young. Why don't you seclude yourself there for a time? Arden never remains long at these events. I will find you once he leaves."

"An excellent idea," Roslyn said, turning quickly.

"Don't run," Fanny advised. "That will only arouse his primal male urge to pursue fleeing prey."

Forcing herself to pause, Roslyn threw an arch glance over her shoulder. "I have no intention of becoming any man's prey. And if he should speak to you, Fanny, you cannot give me away."

Her friend affected a mock wounded look. "I'll have you know, I am the soul of discretion. In my profession, a guarded tongue is worth more than gold. Now go! He will forget all about you if he cannot find you. And if he persists, I will attempt to mislead him."

"I wish you will send him to the devil," Roslyn muttered as she moved away, vexed at having her plans for the evening spoiled by Arden's unexpected presence. She was here to learn the secrets of attracting a gentleman's ardor, and being forced to hide herself away would hardly help her attain her goal.

Keeping her head bent low to prevent her bonnet from being tracked, Roslyn skirted the crowd and slipped out the rear doors, only to find herself in a dim corridor. When her eyes adjusted, she made her way down the hall to an even dimmer gallery that apparently ran the width of the building. The yearly Cyprians' ball was a public assembly, but for this occasion, all the rooms save the main ballroom had been poorly lit, the better for trysts and assignations.

As Fanny had advised, Roslyn found numerous empty alcoves stationed along either side of the gallery. Slipping into the last one on her left, she let the velvet draperies fall closed behind her, yet she could still see well enough in the moonlight flooding through the floor-length window at the rear of the alcove.

Too restless to sit, Roslyn disregarded the welcoming chaise longue and instead pushed open the window. The June night air was cool and damp compared to the stuffy, perfumed warmth of the ballroom, and with a sigh of resignation, she stepped out onto a narrow balcony, prepared to outwait the duke.

"Devil take him," Roslyn muttered another recrimination at the vexing nobleman. "Why must he appear just when the ball was getting interesting?"

She'd had high hopes for the evening. Until now she had never mingled with a company of lightskirts, and she was fascinated by what she had seen and learned thus far.

Indeed, until recently, Roslyn had rarely mixed with any sort of society during the past four years. Instead, she'd lived quietly in the country—at Danvers Hall near Chiswick, some half dozen miles west of London—with her sisters and their curmudgeonly step-uncle and guardian, the Earl of Danvers, who had grudgingly taken them in after their parents mired them in shame and scandal.

Four years ago their mother had run off with her lover to the Continent. Then their libertine father had promptly gambled away the last of his fortune and been killed in a duel over his mistress, which had ruined any last-gasp chances the Loring sisters had of making good marriages.

They had endured with fortitude the disgrace and rejection and poverty that followed. They'd even found a way to earn their own livings so they would no longer be at the mercy of their miserly step-uncle for mere sustenance. With the support of a wealthy patroness, they had started a successful academy to teach the daughters of wealthy merchants and industrialists how to be proper ladies and compete in the lofty, disdainful world of the ton.

But the lack of matrimonial prospects had struck Roslyn the hardest. Of the three sisters, she was the one who still secretly dreamed of marrying for love and having children. Although her birth and breeding were impeccable, being penniless and tainted by her parents' scandals severely limited her choices.

Even more detrimental were her looks. She was widely considered the most beautiful of the three sisters, to her immense regret. Her golden hair and fine-boned features along with her tall, slender build made her seem deceptively delicate. That appearance of fragility, combined with her family's disgrace and the lack of a strong male protector, had left Roslyn vulnerable to the unwanted advances of disreputable rakes and roués, and she'd suffered more than one mortifying proposition that entailed sordid debauchery rather than respectable marriage.

Just remembering now made her shiver.

Clenching her jaw, Roslyn stepped closer to the balcony railing to gaze down at the nearly empty lane below. She would never settle for becoming some man's mistress. Nor would she ever marry for any reason but true love.

Which is why you resolved to take control of your own fate and find a husband who could share that elusive ideal.

Before she could act on her resolve, however, her pitiful prospects had improved significantly. Several months ago, their elderly step-uncle passed away and the new Earl of Danvers, Marcus Pierce, assumed their guardianship. Loath to be saddled with three impoverished almost-spinsters, Marcus had declared his intention of finding husbands for them all—which had precipitated a spirited battle with the eldest, Arabella, over their independence and resulted in an unexpected love match between her and Marcus.

Roslyn was overjoyed for Arabella . . . and grateful for her own sake as well, since Marcus had generously granted his two youngest wards their legal and financial independence so they could choose their own futures.

Roslyn had known exactly what future she wanted, only she wasn't quite sure how to achieve it. Thus, she'd called on the experience and expertise of her childhood friend, Fanny Irwin, a once genteel young lady who had left home at sixteen to become one of London's most celebrated Cyprians.

When they first broached the subject last week, though, Fanny had responded with consternation. "Surely you are not planning to take up the life of a courtesan, Roslyn?"

"No, not at all."

"Good, because I have no intention of corrupting you."

Roslyn smiled. "I don't wish to be corrupted, Fanny. I simply want to learn your secrets . . . specifically how to make a gentleman enamored of me."

"Whatever for?"

"Because I hope to make a respectable marriage before long, but I want my husband to love me first. It seems clear that gentlemen commonly fall in love with their mistresses but rarely their wives, so I concluded I should study the experts to learn how a mistress arouses a man's ardor."

Fanny stared at her for the space of several heartbeats before breaking into laughter. "I forgot how scientifically minded you are, my dear."

"I am that," Roslyn agreed amiably. "But regrettably, I haven't the faintest notion how to go about developing the skills necessary to engage a man's heart. And you are the most successful of all the Cyprians I know."

"I am the only Cyprian you know," Fanny returned wryly.

"True, but I could probably find someone else willing to instruct me."

She gave a grimace. "Arabella would have my head if I allowed you to go to someone else. Do you have a prospective target in mind for your husband?"

"Actually I do. The Earl of Haviland. Do you know him?"

Fanny pursed her lips. "I have made his acquaintance. Haviland recently came into the title, along with a significant fortune, did he not?"

"Yes, and his country villa marches with Danvers Hall."

"Is he in the market for a bride?"

"Rumor claims so."

"And you wish to be considered a candidate for his hand?"

Unable to control her blush, Roslyn nodded. "From what I've witnessed these past few months, I think Haviland could make a good husband for me. We have begun a friendship, and I believe he feels a certain . . . fondness toward me, which I hope can blossom into something much stronger. But I don't have faith that I can win his heart fully on my own."

Fanny's expression grew thoughtful. "Aren't you setting your sights rather high, Roslyn, hoping to make a love match with Haviland? There are other alternatives, you know. Despite your family's history, you are the daughter of a baronet in addition to being one of the most exquisite beauties in the country. And even at two and twenty, you are hardly on the shelf. Now that Lord Danvers has settled such a generous sum on both you and Lily, you could likely choose from any number of suitors and contract a perfectly satisfactory marriage of convenience."

"*No,*" Roslyn replied almost vehemently. "The last thing I want is to marry for convenience. You know what my parents' convenient union was like." Remembering, she couldn't repress a shudder. She had loathed the pain her parents had delighted in causing each other. "I want true love in my marriage, Fanny. Nothing else will do."

Fanny looked at her with amusement and admiration. "So let me see if I comprehend. You are harboring a secret passion for a neighboring earl, and you wish to learn how to make him fall in love with you?"

"Precisely," Roslyn said. "And if anyone can instruct me on how to achieve it, it is you. Will you help me, Fanny?"

"Yes, I suppose so. If nothing else, it should prove highly diverting. Do your sisters know of this scheme you have hatched?"

"Not yet."

She hadn't confided in anyone but Fanny. Arabella would understand, of course, but at the moment she was immersed in wedding plans and reveling in the glow of first love. Roslyn wanted nothing to spoil her sister's hard-won happiness.

Her younger sister Lilian was a different matter altogether, since Lily had sworn off love and marriage and fully expected Roslyn to do the same.

Roslyn hated to disappoint her sister, but it was *her* life at stake after all. And the outcome was too important to leave purely to chance. Thus, she'd sought out Fanny.

But now, to her dismay, her education had been rudely interrupted by the Duke of Arden's unwanted arrival.

Muttering another mild imprecation under her breath, Roslyn reached up to press her fingers against her temple. Her head was beginning to throb under the weight of her wig and bonnet, and the suffocating mask was rubbing a raw spot on her left cheek.

At least she could mitigate some of her suffering by removing the offending bonnet and mask.

Roslyn untied the ribbons beneath her chin and slid the bonnet off, then loosened the strings of her mask and drew it down. As the cool night air fanned her face, she gave a sigh of relief . . . until a low, masculine voice spoke behind her:

"So this is where you are hiding yourself."

Gasping in startlement, Roslyn whirled and promptly dropped her bonnet when she recognized the tall, imposing nobleman standing there. His broad, domino-clad shoulders filled the narrow embrasure, while his amber hair glinted more silver than gold in the moonlight.

Alarmed to see the duke, she fumbled to replace her mask, hoping he hadn't been afforded a clear glimpse of her face. "How you startled me . . ." she exclaimed too breathlessly as she finished tying the strings.

"Forgive me. It was the least of my intentions—to discomfit a beautiful woman."

Roslyn's gaze narrowed through her mask. His tone

was mild, languid even. If he was attempting to flatter her, he wasn't making much effort. But perhaps he was merely playing an expected game, spouting compliments he thought she wished to hear.

There was nothing languid about the warm glance that raked over her figure, however. Instead his eyes showed pure male interest—and had the deplorable effect of making her pulse race.

"I am Arden."

"I know who you are, your grace," Roslyn said rather crossly. He was Andrew Moncrief, Duke of Arden, known as "Drew" to his intimates. And she had seldom been less pleased to see anyone in her life.

His eyebrow lifted at her tone. "Regrettably, I do not know *you*, my lovely Incognita. I would have sought an introduction, but you fled the moment you spied me. And Fanny suddenly made herself scarce before I could even discover your name."

Having no valid defense, Roslyn remained mute. When the duke stepped forward and bent to retrieve her dropped bonnet from the balcony floor, she would have retreated except that the railing was at her back. Trapped, she was forced to endure his scrutiny. He stood watching her in speculation, holding the ribbons in his long fingers.

Roslyn stared back, unable to help herself. It was too dark to be certain, but she thought his eyes were green. A deep, vibrant green. And this close, his lean, aristocratic features were even more sensually compelling than at a distance. His nearness, as well, had a devastating effect on her composure.

He spoke before she could gain control of her

whirling thoughts. "I congratulate you, sweeting. Your ploy worked."

"My ploy?" she repeated, puzzled.

"You hoped I would pursue you here, and you succeeded. I was intrigued enough to follow you."

He thought she had purposely lured him here to the alcove? "It was no ploy, your grace. I found the ballroom overly warm and came here for a respite."

One corner of his mouth twisted sardonically. "How convenient that you chose a location so well equipped for an assignation," he said, nodding at the chaise longue behind him. Before she could protest, he went on. "You must be new to London. I would certainly have remembered had I seen you before now."

Roslyn hid her wince of dismay. She hoped his memory was not so keen when she encountered him at her sister's wedding in a fortnight. "Yes, I am new to London. But I promise you, I did not lure you here for an assignation."

And she had no intention, either, of prolonging this unwanted encounter. Murmuring a polite "thank you," Roslyn retrieved her bonnet from his grasp and tried to slip past him.

The duke, however, reached out to curl his fingers lightly around her wrist. "One might think you are actually eager to avoid me."

"One might."

"Why?" His tone held surprise and genuine curiosity.

"I dislike the way you are inspecting me, as if I am merchandise to be purchased."

"I stand corrected." His lips curved in a rueful smile that was slow, sensual. "I don't think of you as merchandise, I assure you."

It was impossible to ignore that captivating male smile, and Roslyn suddenly understood why females pursued Arden in droves. "Then you will pray excuse me," she said, her voice more uneven that she would have liked.

Pointedly, she glanced down at his imprisoning grasp, yet he didn't release her. "Are you currently taken?"

She blinked. "Taken?"

"Do you have a protector yet?"

He was asking if she was currently employed as a lightskirt, Roslyn realized. She considered saying yes, but then she would have to come up with a name for her nonexistent patron, and Arden would very likely see through her lie. "No, I have no protector."

"Then why don't you simply name your price? I dislike haggling."

She stared up at him. "Are you asking me to be your . . . *mistress?*"

His smile turned bland. "Unless you have another proposition in mind? Yes, I am asking you to be my mistress, darling."

Roslyn knew her jaw had dropped inelegantly, but she couldn't help it. It shocked her a little that he would offer such an intimate position to a perfect stranger. "We are complete strangers, your grace. You know nothing about me."

"I know enough to find you lovely and desirable. What more is necessary?"

"I could be a vicious harpy, for all you know."

"I am willing to risk it. A thousand pounds a year during pleasure. Half that should we decide to part ways sooner."

When Roslyn remained gaping with astonishment,

he cocked his head and nodded briefly, as if coming to a decision. "Very well, two thousand. And of course I will pay all your expenses . . . a house and carriage plus an allowance for clothing and jewels."

Roslyn couldn't help being amused. It seemed an outrageous sum to offer an untried courtesan, although she knew Fanny made several times that amount. "How can you be certain I am worth it?"

Appreciative laughter lit his eyes as he gave a casual shrug. "Your beauty is alluring enough to satisfy my discriminating tastes. Anything else you need to know I can teach you."

Roslyn's own amusement faded as anger pricked her. Arden had unwittingly struck a raw nerve. He couldn't know that her beauty—or more precisely, being coveted solely for her physical attributes—was a painfully sore point with her.

She also realized it was ridiculous to resent his quite generous proposition, since she was here tonight pretending to be a Cyprian. But after the other shameful offers she had already received over the past four years, she couldn't respond with equanimity.

"I believe the proper response is to thank you for your generous offer, your grace," she said coldly, withdrawing her wrist from his grasp, "but I must decline."

His eyebrow shot up at her wintry tone. "It is common practice to feign reluctance in order to increase your price, but you will find that I dislike coyness."

Roslyn bristled. "I do not *have* a price, nor am I trying to be coy. I simply have no desire to have you for my lover—despite your vaunted reputation."

His eyes narrowed. "Did Fanny say something to give you a fear of me?"

"No."

"If you need to assure yourself of my qualifications, I would be happy to demonstrate."

"I don't need a demonstration. I don't doubt your expertise in the least."

"Then perhaps we should test *your* skills." Before she could do more than draw a breath, he stepped even closer and cupped her face in his hands. "Kiss me, love, and show me your charms."

His bold gesture caught her completely off guard. Roslyn went rigid with dismay as the duke bent his head and captured her mouth with his.

It was a startling kiss, not only because of its unexpectedness but because of the effect it had on her entire body. His lips moved over hers in a sensual exploration that was tender and arousing and wildly exciting.

She had been kissed before, but nothing whatever like this. Her skin suddenly felt covered in heat, as if she were standing too close to a fire.

Her heart was pounding when he finally shifted his caresses away from her mouth. His lips brushed fleetingly along her jaw to her ear, where they lingered. "You taste like innocence," he murmured, his voice surprisingly husky. "It is a charming act, but entirely unnecessary."

"It is no act," Roslyn replied shakily. "I am not experienced."

He drew back enough to study her, his gaze skeptical. "I much prefer honesty."

Roslyn stiffened. "You don't believe me?" she asked in a warning tone.

He reached up with his fingertips to trace her lips

beneath her mask. "Let us say I am willing to be convinced. Come here, my sweet. . . ."

He bent to her once more and kissed her again, this time more passionately. Alarmed by her own response, Roslyn tried to retreat, but Arden pulled her fully against his body, letting her feel the hardness of him, the vitality.

Stunned by his devastating sensuality, Roslyn whimpered, amazed that she could be so aroused by a man's embrace. When finally he broke off the kiss and raised his head, she looked up at him in an unfocused daze.

His smile was rueful. "I confess . . . most women don't have this powerful an effect on me. You feel it, too, Beauty, don't deny it."

It was true, she had never in her life experienced anything like it—this lightning bolt of attraction that sparked between them. This devastating heat and desire. This yearning.

Not that she would ever admit it to *him*.

Struggling to regain a semblance of composure, Roslyn cleared her throat.

"Indeed?" she managed to say with a blithe laugh. "Your arrogance is astonishing, your grace."

It was obviously not the response he expected, and Roslyn pressed her point. "Your vanity is vastly over-inflated if you think I am eager to leap into your bed."

The slow, charming smile he gave her was impossibly wicked, impossibly seductive . . . and sensual enough to bewitch a saint. "A bed isn't necessary. We can make use of the chaise longue behind us." He waved in the general direction of the alcove. "And at the same time we can remedy the fact that we are strangers."

"I have no desire to become better acquainted with you."

"Perhaps I can change your mind."

He raised his hand, his warm fingers tracing a path from the hollow of her throat to the swells of her breasts, which thrust prominently upward in her shepherdess costume.

"Your grace . . ." Roslyn began in protest, but he stole any further words away with another kiss, claiming her mouth with tender possessiveness. When he cradled her silk-clad breast in his palm, the brazen shock of it rendered her immobile. She wore no corset beneath her low-cut bodice, so she could feel the heated pressure of his caress through the fragile fabric.

A rush of excitement swept her senses; fire radiated from the hand that held her throbbing breast and from his lips that were plying hers with such expert skill.

His mouth continued to hold hers effortlessly as he stroked the bare skin above her bodice with his fingers, dipping down into the valley between her breasts. Then his hand curled over the low neckline and lightly tugged, sending the mounds spilling out of her gown.

Roslyn gasped as the cool night air brushed her exposed flesh, but she couldn't manage a word of rebuke, not even when the duke's sensual kisses ended and he drew back.

His eyes darkened as he gazed down at her nakedness, surveying the ripe firmness crested with dusky nipples.

Her breathing suspended, Roslyn remained speechless as with his thumbs he traced slow circles around the hardened peaks. A low moan was dredged from her throat while the ribbons of her bonnet slipped through her nerveless fingers.

At her response, he took the weight of her breasts in his hands and tugged the nipples to taut attention with lingering caresses, pinching lightly with his fingers, soothing with his thumbs.

Roslyn pulled in a deep, shuddering breath, finding it impossible to move. His masterful hands knew just how to arouse, to excite, to delight.

"Your grace," she finally repeated in a shaken voice.

"Hush, let me pleasure you."

She tried futilely once more to resist, but his arm came around her, locking her lightly to him. Bending her backward a little, he lowered his head to her breast, closing his mouth over the distended tip.

The shock of sensation was overwhelming. Her knees had felt unsteady before, but now they nearly buckled. Thankfully he supported her as he suckled the pebbled bud.

Roslyn shut her eyes helplessly. She felt her pulse pounding in her throat as sweet pleasure seared her. His mouth was burning hot, devastatingly wicked, his tongue laving, swirling, circling . . . coaxing, *demanding* a response from her.

His sensual assault was all male, primitive and commanding, and roused a primal feminine need in her that she couldn't deny. Her body came alive for him just as he intended. She had never been kissed this way, never been touched this way.

When he drew her nipple between his teeth, biting down lightly, the delicious eroticism further weakened her, further thrilled her. When he soothed the aching crest with his tongue, with his lips, a fresh shiver of delight rippled down her body, making her spine arch.

He took advantage of her helplessness. Still nipping and nibbling, he eased her thighs apart, wedging his knee between hers. Her stomach clenched in a tight knot of sensation as his powerful thigh pressed through her thin gown, against her woman's mound. She wore small panniers on her hips, which puffed out the sides, but there was little barrier in front to protect her from the intimate knowledge of his body. She could feel his maleness, the hard, swollen arousal that pressed teasingly against her abdomen.

Her head swam, drugged with the heady sweetness. A spiraling pleasure spread into the very depths of her, turning her body boneless and inciting a deep throb between her legs. In the hollow of her secret flesh, a moist heat seeped.

She almost cried out in disappointment when the duke finally ceased his ministrations. When his hot mouth left her breasts, she opened her eyes to discover she was clinging to his shoulders.

She felt the cool night air tingle across her wet nipples, along with the sensual rasp of his voice as he murmured, "I could show you pleasure you will never forget."

She believed him. Then he lifted his head, and she met his dark gaze. His eyes were smoldering, intense, triumphant.

Seeing that possessive look made heat flood Roslyn all over again. It was all she could do not to melt into his arms once more. Indeed, it took all her willpower to push her palms against his broad chest and stand upright on her own.

Her wits were still scattered, her heart still hammering hard against her ribs, but she forced herself to inject a faint note of scorn in her voice as she determinedly replied, "I am afraid your offer isn't tempting enough. If I wish to find a protector, I can do better than an arrogant lord who thinks he need only to snap his fingers to have women fall swooning at his feet."

Her mocking declaration had the desired effect of making him release her entirely. Grateful for her success, Roslyn stepped back, fumbling with her bodice, trying to repair her wanton disarray.

Drawing the silk up to cover the throbbing peaks of her breasts, Roslyn managed to school her expression to cool dispassion as she surveyed him. "Do me the kindness of believing my sincerity, your grace. I do *not* wish you to follow me again."

His expression of disbelief was priceless, she thought, stifling a shaky laugh. She supposed it was a victory of sorts—leaving the elegant, imperious Duke of Arden with *his* jaw hanging down.

Deciding not to push her luck, however, Roslyn turned on weak limbs and moved past him through the window, stepping down into the curtained alcove. She felt a trembling sense of relief when he didn't follow her, yet she was still breathing hard, her heart thudding as if she had run a great distance, her body overheated.

Leaving the alcove, she hurried along the darkened gallery, making her escape like Cinderella fleeing the ball at midnight. It wasn't until she reached the far end that she remembered dropping her bonnet again.

But she wasn't about to risk retrieving it. She had to find Fanny and tender her excuses. She was going home to Danvers Hall at once. It was too dangerous for her to remain at the ball any longer. Indeed, she was foolish to have come in the first place, Roslyn admitted.

And yet . . .

She paused as she reached the ballroom doors. She could still feel the burning imprint of the duke's mouth on hers, still feel his lips suckling her aching nipples. She would never forget his incredible kisses, his erotic caresses—

Have you completely lost your wits? a scolding inner voice finally intervened.

Stepping into the ballroom, Roslyn blinked in the bright light. She was utterly disgusted with herself. She had set her sights on another nobleman entirely. She couldn't possibly be attracted to the arrogant Duke of Arden!

Even so, she couldn't help but feel a twinge of regret that she would miss the opportunity he had offered her, to have him demonstrate his amorous skills. Undeniably it would have been an eye-opening experience, to spend one night in his arms.

Her sense of the absurd returning suddenly, Roslyn shook her head wryly. She had spent the last four years fending off unwanted advances, and she was too much of a lady to change that now. Not to mention that becoming Arden's mistress for even one night would totally ruin her as a prospective bride for any other gentleman.

Just then, she spied Fanny dancing with an armored

knight. Ignoring the laughter and gaiety emanating from the crowd, Roslyn plunged into the throng.

She had no doubt now that Arden was a marvelous lover. A pity she didn't dare risk examining his expertise more closely for herself.

Chapter Two

❧

Some noblemen are so swelled with their own conse-quence that they expect the opposite sex to fall swooning at their feet.

—Roslyn Loring to Fanny Irwin

Chiswick, June 1817

It was a perfect day for a wedding—the morning sky bright with hope and promise. Yet Drew Moncrief, Duke of Arden, could summon little enthusiasm for the occasion as he waited with his two closest friends before the church entrance.

Primarily because he believed the groom was making an irrevocable mistake.

Lounging against a pillar on the church portico, Drew watched as Marcus, the new Earl of Danvers, restlessly paced the drive below in anticipation of the bridal party's arrival.

"Devil take it, Marcus, will you calm down, man?" Heath Griffin, the Marquess of Claybourne drawled from his own similar position on the portico. "Your nerves are seriously wearing on mine."

"He's suffering from a case of bachelor terrors," Drew murmured with sardonic amusement. "I told you he would succumb."

Marcus cast the two of them a dismissive glance. "It

isn't fear, it's impatience." But to satisfy his friends, he climbed the short flight of steps to rejoin them on the portico. "I want an end to this waiting so I can make Arabella my wife. This last month has been interminable."

Marcus and Miss Arabella Loring, the eldest of his three wards, had been officially betrothed a month ago, but now the moment finally was at hand. The village church was filled to overflowing with guests and flowers. The vicar was standing by to conduct the ceremony. And Marcus looked the part of the noble bridegroom—blue superfine coat, gold embroidered waistcoat, white lace cravat, and white satin breeches.

Drew, who was dressed similarly for the occasion, let a sad smile curve his mouth as he shook his head. "I never expected to see you so hopelessly besotted, my friend."

"Your time will come someday," Marcus predicted in a sage tone.

Drew flicked an imaginary speck of lint off the lace of his cuff, his half smile turning to one of pure cynicism. "Oh, I will eventually do my duty and wed to carry on the ancestral line, but I won't ever lose my head over a woman as you have obviously done."

"I don't know," Heath interjected. "I think it would be intriguing to find a woman who could make me lose my head."

His blithe tone, however, suggested that he wasn't entirely serious. While Heath loved the fair sex in general, he was convinced he would never encounter the woman who could cause him to willingly relinquish his cherished freedom and settle down in staid matrimony.

Drew was even more determined to retain his bachelorhood, as Marcus knew very well.

"Before meeting Arabella, Drew, I was nearly as cynical as you," Marcus remarked amiably. "I fully understand your reticence to marry. You see all eligible females as the enemy."

"They *are* the enemy. I have yet to meet the eligible female who doesn't view me as prey."

"Arabella's sisters won't. You will find them refreshingly indifferent to your rank and consequence."

Drew's gaze narrowed on Marcus. "You aren't possibly thinking of playing matchmaker, are you?"

"I wouldn't dream of it, old sport," Marcus said jovially. "Even if Arabella's middle sister does have the qualifications to make an admirable duchess."

Drew uttered a mild curse at the deliberately provoking jibe, while Heath laughed out loud.

His eyes glinting with amusement, Marcus ended his baiting. "Never fear, Drew. I know nothing I could say would persuade you to give love a chance. But if you are supremely fortunate, you will discover the joys for yourself."

It most certainly wouldn't be with Marcus's wards, Drew rejoined silently. He was determined to steer clear of the two remaining Loring sisters.

Just then they finally heard the sound of carriage wheels announcing the bride's arrival. Shortly, three vehicles swept up the drive. Drew recognized Arabella Loring in the first one, but not the two young ladies who accompanied her.

Beside Drew, Heath straightened, his gaze focused on the beauties sitting with Miss Loring in the open barouche. "Those are Arabella's sisters?" he asked Marcus.

"Yes. The dark-haired one is the youngest spitfire, Lilian. And the blonde is the lovely Roslyn."

Drew's eyes suddenly narrowed as he caught sight of the golden-haired Roslyn. There was something vaguely familiar about her . . . the graceful shoulders, the elegant bearing, the slender, delicate figure with the high, ripe breasts. And her face . . . He had glimpsed those perfect, fine-boned features in the moonlight not so very long ago.

Drew slowly straightened from where he was leaning against the column, his stomach muscles clenching in recognition. *What in blazes?*

At his irrepressible start of surprise, Marcus smiled with knowing amusement. That, however, was the last consideration he gave his friends for some time. As soon as the cavalcade rumbled to a halt before the front entrance, Marcus bounded down the steps and went to meet his bride and her sisters.

He assisted first Miss Roslyn and then Miss Lilian from the barouche, then offered his hand to Arabella. Accepting it, she stepped down into the circle of his waiting arms, her expression radiant with love as she gazed back at him.

But while Marcus only had eyes for his bride, Drew couldn't take his gaze off the fair-haired Roslyn. He would never forget that exquisitely memorable face, even though he'd been afforded only a fleeting glimpse of it in the moonlight.

She was the same woman. The mysterious beauty who had turned down his offer the night of the Cyprians' ball.

Hell and the devil!

She kept her eyes carefully averted from him as she stood to one side, waiting for the rest of the bridal party to alight from the other carriages. But when Drew slowly descended the church steps, she stole a glimpse at him. The faint blush that stained her cheeks would have confirmed his suspicions, yet he didn't need that telltale sign to know he wasn't mistaken.

Miss Roslyn Loring indeed was his mystery woman.

She was currently garbed in an Empire-waisted gown of rose-hued silk, not a provocative shepherdess's costume. But her distinctive loveliness couldn't be disguised by a wig or a mask. And even if he hadn't seen her entire face that night, he would recognize that luscious mouth anywhere. He had kissed that delicious mouth, tasted those ripe breasts, felt that slender, arousing body pressed against his. . . .

His loins stirring in remembrance, Drew slowly advanced upon Roslyn, while annoyance and anger warred with surprise inside him. The elusive Cyprian who had left him intrigued and enchanted that night was not only a genteel lady, but *the ward of his best friend*.

What the devil had she been doing at a notorious ball for lightskirts? Was she merely kicking up a lark or searching for more sinful pleasures?

Whatever her purpose for attending, it could have spelled disaster for him. He damned well would have compromised her if they'd simply been discovered alone together in such a place. And if he had succeeded in actually seducing her as he'd wanted . . . It didn't bear thinking on.

Drew clenched his jaw. At least her identity explained

why she had run from him the moment she saw him—because she didn't want him to recognize her later. At his approach now, Roslyn pressed her lips together stoically, apparently resigned to formally meeting him.

He was saved from having to request an introduction when Marcus stepped forward to present the bridal party: Arabella's two sisters, her mother and stepfather, and some of her close friends and neighbors, including the patroness of the Freemantle Academy for Young Ladies where all the Loring sisters taught.

Drew was interested in only one person, however. He stopped before Roslyn, deliberately holding her gaze as he took her gloved hand to offer her a bow.

At the contact, tension, hot and rapid as summer lightning, arced between them. Giving him a startled look, she withdrew her hand quickly, while Drew cursed under his breath. His damned loins had tightened in response to merely touching her. Utterly inappropriate, given her status, but the instantaneous spark of desire he'd felt for her that moonlit night was still deplorably potent.

He kept his own expression cool when he said, "You look familiar, Miss Roslyn. Have we met before?"

Her chin lifted slightly at his mocking query, yet she didn't reply directly. "I believe I would remember meeting you, your grace."

Her voice held the same honeyed warmth he recalled, but Drew fought the allure, just as he tried to ignore her startling beauty. In the morning sunlight, Roslyn looked fresh and lovely as a dew-speckled rose. Of course, the last time he'd seen her, she had looked deliciously wanton.

When her gaze dropped to his mouth, he knew she

was recalling precisely what had happened between them that night, as he was.

Her eyes were blue, he noted—a warm sky blue—while her face was a classically shaped oval.

"I'm certain we must have crossed paths before," he mused.

"Surely you are mistaken."

At her prevarication, his patience faded. Lightly grasping her elbow, he urged Roslyn aside a few paces, so as not to be overheard by her relatives and friends. "Does Danvers approve of your dangerous escapade?"

The flush returning to color her cheeks, she conceded the futility of denying their meeting any longer by giving a small sigh. "Lord Danvers doesn't know about my escapade . . . and I don't intend to tell him."

"Why not?"

"Because I don't wish to distract him when he and my sister are celebrating their nuptials."

Drew favored her with a piercing look that had been known to make most mortals quake. "I expect an explanation, sweeting."

Roslyn arched a slender eyebrow. "Do you indeed?" When he remained sternly silent, she responded pleasantly, "My reasons are my own, your grace, and none of your affair."

"Perhaps so, but when the ward of one of my closest friends is offering herself for sale, I think he has a right to know about it."

Roslyn's blue eyes flashed at him. "I am not in that particular trade, I assure you."

"You will understand if I take leave to doubt you."

"You may doubt all you like, but my conduct still is not your concern."

"But it is definitely your guardian's concern. And I collect I have an obligation to tell him about your subterfuge."

"Oh?" Her gaze was a challenge. "Are you in the habit of bearing tales then, your grace?"

"Are you in the habit of kissing perfect strangers?"

That took her aback. "*You* kissed *me,* you should recall."

"But you allowed it."

"I couldn't very well protest without giving myself away—" Roslyn stopped suddenly and took a deep breath, then managed a disarming smile. "I don't intend to spoil my sister's wedding, and I won't allow you to do so, either. Perhaps you would condescend to continue your interrogation at some more convenient time?"

Drew felt a surge of annoyance tinged with amusement at being so summarily dismissed. "You may count on it, Miss Loring. We shall resume our discussion after the wedding service."

Her smile never faltered. "I fear I will be extremely busy afterward. We have six hundred guests attending the wedding breakfast, and I am responsible for seeing that everything runs smoothly. Now, pray excuse me, your grace. The ceremony will be starting shortly."

Surprised to discover that he was enjoying sparring with her, Drew was reluctant to let her go. "Allow me to escort you to your seat."

"I can manage on my own, thank you."

"One might think you are eager to avoid me," he said dryly, repeating the words he had used when she had tried to escape him on the balcony.

Her answering smile was just as wry, although more

charming. "One might indeed. It is perfectly understandable why you are so full of your own consequence, your grace, but you shouldn't expect every
woman to fall at your feet. I certainly won't."

Leaving him standing there staring after her, Roslyn
turned to accompany her sister Lilian into the church.
Drew eventually followed them up the front steps and
along the center aisle to the front pews, which held
the only remaining empty seats.

To his surprise, he recognized Fanny Irwin among
the honored guests on the bride's side. He hadn't expected to see a famous courtesan sharing the family
pew.

The sisters embraced Fanny warmly and then settled
beside her. Drew took his own place on the right side
of the aisle, next to Marcus's younger sister, Eleanor,
and her elderly aunt, Viscountess Beldon.

When Eleanor caught Drew watching the opposite
aisle, she leaned toward him to whisper over the hushed
murmurs of the crowd, "You remember when we first
met Arabella, she told us that Fanny was their longtime friend? Well, Fanny remained loyal to them during all the years of scandal, and they aren't going to
snub her simply because she is no longer received in
polite circles."

"There is a vast difference," Drew remarked in an
under voice, "between supporting a friend and courting notoriety."

"I beg your pardon?" Eleanor asked.

"Never mind, love." He didn't intend to discuss the
last time he had seen Fanny Irwin. But it seemed curious that Marcus would allow her intimate connection
with his wards to continue.

Drew knew all about the Loring family scandals, which had undeservedly made the sisters social pariahs. He also knew that Marcus had done his best to improve his wards' standing in society, but those efforts would only be undermined if Roslyn's brazen antics became known.

She was half turned away from him now, and Drew found his eyes fixed on her slender back, a variety of emotions warring within—curiosity, pique, disapproval. He was intrigued and perturbed at the same time.

"Roslyn is quite beautiful, is she not?" Eleanor whispered. "She would be considered an Incomparable if not for the disgrace her family suffered."

She was indeed beautiful, Drew had to admit. Her hair was pale gold, the color of fine champagne. And with her tall, willowy figure and exquisite features, she was as lovely and delicate as gilded crystal.

Eleanor evidently took his silence as agreement. "You cannot tell simply by looking at her, but Roslyn is the most clever and studious of the three sisters."

"Studious?" Drew replied with skepticism.

"Yes, indeed. She even knows Latin. She has read nearly every tome in her late uncle's library, and Marcus has begun sending her books from his own library in London. Her delicacy gives one a false impression. Lily, on the other hand, is quite the hoyden. She is the passionate one in the family."

Heath joined them just then, in time to overhear Eleanor's last remarks. Bending closer, he murmured with amusement, "Marcus was right, Drew. Miss Roslyn looks suited to the role of duchess."

"Stubble it, you old bleater," Drew murmured.

Despite their attractions, he wanted nothing to do with marriageable young ladies of the Loring sisters' ilk. For much of his life he'd been hounded and harassed by avaricious mamas and daughters who had only one goal in mind—the taming and matrimonial capture of a wealthy duke. The thought of being shackled for life to that sort of covetous, grasping female made him shudder.

Roslyn Loring might not be so material-minded, but he most certainly didn't want to find himself strangled in the parson's noose with her as his wife, which likely would have happened had he made love to her that night.

Drew was vastly relieved by his near escape from potential disaster. Because of his mistaken assumption regarding her identity, he might have been honorably compelled to offer for her hand in marriage.

Indeed, if Roslyn hadn't been so set on escaping him, he might have thought she'd purposely contrived to entice him out onto that balcony. It wouldn't be the first time a scheming husband-hunter had plotted to entrap him by luring him into a compromising situation.

But whatever her reasons for attending the Cyprians' ball, he intended to discover them. If his friend's ward was courting trouble and risking scandal, or worse, actual danger, Marcus needed to know about it.

His thoughts were interrupted as the bride and groom took their places before the altar. A hush fell over the crowd, and a moment later, the vicar began the service.

"Dearly beloved . . ."

Drew sat back in his seat, girding himself to endure

the proceedings. He did *not* like weddings. In fact he loathed them, for they signified the entrapment of a man in marriage. And this particular wedding was especially regrettable, since Marcus was shackling himself to a young lady he had known for a ludicrously short period of time. Marcus had been a devout bachelor before meeting Arabella and completely losing his head over her, swept up in an infatuation.

Drew shook his head. He cared deeply for his friend and hoped he wouldn't be bitterly disappointed in love, but suspected it was inevitable.

As the vicar prosed on, he found his gaze straying across the aisle to the lovely Roslyn. She sat tall and straight, watching the ceremony with solemn interest.

Eventually his thoughts drifted back to the night they met. He remembered her scent, soft and tempting. He remembered the feel of her in his arms, her sweet, tentative response when he kissed her the first time.

Perhaps she truly was as inexperienced as she'd claimed. If so, that explained why she kissed so innocently.

She'd responded fervently to their second kiss, though, and to his more erotic ministrations afterward. He was an expert at reading his lover's responses, and he could tell she wasn't feigning passion.

He'd responded with an unanticipated fervency of his own, Drew acknowledged. He rarely was that swiftly, that intensely, attracted to any woman. In truth, he couldn't remember ever feeling such a sudden fierce spark of desire as he had that night. The urge to sweep Roslyn up in his arms and carry her to the nearby chaise longue had been overwhelming. He'd wanted to make love to her for hours, to arouse her to pleasure and to experience his own, to prove to her they could have a supremely enjoyable liaison while it lasted.

Thank God he had taken it no further.

But how damned ironic that the first woman he'd been interested in for months was off limits. Roslyn Loring was completely untouchable. No honorable gentleman would pursue her without marriage in mind. And he had no intention of winding up here in this church with her.

She had remained in his thoughts for days afterward, however. Hell, she was still captivating his thoughts. He couldn't forget her lush nakedness, her sweet, ripe breasts. Couldn't forget how her dusky nipples had felt in his mouth, how they tasted. . . .

The ceremony was thankfully brief. A short while later, Marcus was given permission to kiss his bride, which he did with obvious tenderness.

Beside Drew, Eleanor sighed and wiped a tear from her eye.

Seeing her action, Heath leaned over to tease her. "For someone who has jilted two suitors, Nell, you are strangely romantic."

"Simply because *I* don't wish to wed doesn't mean Marcus shouldn't. He and Arabella are made for each other."

Drew refrained from scoffing, but barely.

Eleanor saw his expression and eyed him curiously. "You don't believe they are in love, do you?"

"I believe Marcus *thinks* he loves her, which is not the same thing at all."

Heath's mouth curved. "Such a cynic."

Drew smiled. "Just so. But I've never seen a union

that was formed so precipitously last beyond the first flush of infatuation."

"Neither have I," Eleanor said wistfully, "but I know they must exist. All the poets say so."

She rose then and went to join her brother, where she gave him a long and heartfelt embrace. Heath and Drew followed but contented themselves with shaking hands with Marcus.

For once, Drew kept his cynical thoughts to himself. Through much of their boyhood and all of their adulthood, the three of them had been inseparable, having attended Eton and Oxford together and then come into their vast fortunes and illustrious titles the same year. Like Roslyn, Drew didn't want to spoil the momentous day for Marcus, even if he was troubled by his friend's reckless rush into matrimony.

Nearby, the Loring sisters were engaged in an emotional embrace of their own, their tears and smiles a clear indication of their fondness for one another.

Shortly, however, the vicar intervened and urged the newly wedded couple to the rear of the church to sign the documents officially making them man and wife.

Meanwhile, the guests spilled out of the front entrance, most heading for their carriages. The company would repair immediately to Danvers Hall for the wedding breakfast—although breakfast was a misnomer, since the festivities would last all afternoon and evening, culminating with a grand ball.

Marcus had warned that the guest list would be huge, for he wanted much of the ton to take part, to pave the way for his bride to be received in the highest circles. Marrying an earl would go a long way toward restoring Arabella's tainted reputation, and by association, her sisters', but Marcus was set on having her fully accepted as his countess.

Drew was *not* looking forward to the wedding celebrations any more than the wedding. Heath had escorted Eleanor and her aunt, Lady Beldon, to the church and would return them to London this evening once the ball ended, but Drew had brought his own carriage so he could leave early if he wished to.

Yet now he had to deal with Miss Roslyn Loring.

He glanced over the crowd as he descended the front steps, searching for Roslyn. He wanted to get her alone for a private word, but it didn't appear as if that would happen anytime soon, since she stood with Arabella, who was surrounded by well-wishers, including their once-estranged mother.

After fleeing to the Continent, the scandalous Lady Loring had eventually married her French lover and was now simply Mrs. Henri Vachel. Rather admirably, Marcus had recently arranged for the sisters to be reunited with their mother, and for the moment at least, her disgrace was apparently forgiven.

While Arabella spoke to her, Roslyn was engaged in animated conversation with Fanny Irwin, as well as a fellow teacher at the academy, Miss Blanchard, and the academy's matronly patroness, Lady Freemantle.

Standing beside Roslyn also was a dark-haired gentleman whom Drew recognized as the Earl of Haviland. When he saw her laughing up at Haviland, Drew's eyes narrowed.

Eleanor joined him just then and saw where his gaze was fixed. "Are you acquainted with Lord Haviland?" Eleanor asked.

"We have met briefly at various clubs."

"I should like to meet him. He is said to be a very intriguing man. Supposedly he was a brilliant spy for Wellington and was repudiated by his family for such ungentlemanly behavior. But he was compelled to return home last year when he inherited the title. His country villa is adjacent to Danvers Hall."

Which explained why Roslyn was on such good terms with him, Drew thought. They were neighbors.

Or perhaps *more* than neighbors, if her laughing demeanor was any indication.

At the sight of her gazing up so admiringly at Haviland, Drew felt an odd little kick to his stomach. Yet he promptly dismissed the sensation.

He was merely feeling impatience, nothing more. He wanted this interminable day over with. And before it ended, he wanted to question Roslyn Loring about why she had attended an infamous Cyprians' ball without her guardian's knowledge or approval.

To Roslyn's relief, the wedding breakfast and ball proved a splendid success. She was chiefly responsible for overseeing the lavish celebrations, a daunting challenge for the sheer size alone. An army of servants had prepared frantically for days, ensuring that Danvers Hall sparkled and the grounds gleamed.

The enormous throng of guests appeared to be enjoying themselves, if their laughter and gaiety was any indication. The crowds had spent the afternoon feasting at banquet tables beneath colorful tents, playing various games on the lawns, boating on the River Thames behind the manor, and strolling in the terraced gardens.

In the past half hour, the merry company had removed indoors to the ballroom and parlors to partake of dancing and cards. Roslyn had watched with delight as Marcus led out Arabella for the opening quadrille, but when the orchestra struck up the first waltz, she settled gratefully in a chair in the far corner of the ballroom. After the frenetic activity of the past few weeks, she was glad for the respite.

She was gladder still to have avoided the Duke of Arden thus far. Thankfully, her hostess duties had kept her occupied and afforded them no opportunity for private conversation. She didn't want to be alone with Arden so he could grill her about her attendance at the Cyprians' ball a fortnight ago.

She'd felt his eyes fastened upon her more than once during the course of the afternoon. Those vibrant green eyes were cool and critical, and Roslyn had done her best to ignore him. Yet he clearly comprehended her tactics. Moments ago when he'd spied her across the ballroom floor, he had offered her a smile filled with lazy charm, but his keen gaze promised an eventual accounting.

Roslyn was remembering that unnerving look when Fanny settled beside her. "You appear spent, my dear."

Roslyn smiled. "I am indeed a little weary, but any discomfort I feel is utterly worthwhile. I have never seen Arabella so happy."

"I know." Fanny gazed wistfully toward the ballroom floor where Arabella was waltzing with her new husband. "I'm thankful that you and your sisters allowed me to take part in the celebrations."

"You didn't expect anything less, did you?"

"No." A trill of Fanny's musical laughter followed. "You all place such high value on loyalty and friendship that you are willing to flout society for my sake.

But I only hope your defiance doesn't prove too detrimental to your own matrimonial prospects."

Roslyn shrugged. "Frankly, I don't want any husband who cannot value loyalty and friendship as I do. And Lily doesn't wish to wed at all, so the issue of your jeopardizing our matrimonial prospects is immaterial."

The two women shared a moment of amiable accord before Fanny spoke again. "You aren't dancing?"

Roslyn's smile turned to a wry grimace. "My feet hurt too much in these new slippers. Marcus insisted on funding completely new wardrobes for us all, and I had no time to break them in."

"I noticed you haven't spoken to the duke since the church service."

The observation elicited a rueful sigh from Roslyn. She'd given Fanny an abbreviated recount of what had happened the night of the Cyprians' ball, although leaving out the fact that she'd shared more than a kiss with the duke. "No, we haven't spoken, but I must eventually, I suppose. Arden has demanded an explanation and threatened to tell Marcus if I don't comply. He thinks I have betrayed his friend's trust, which isn't quite true, since when I attended the ball with you, Marcus had already granted us our legal independence from his guardianship and I was no longer technically his ward."

"Why don't you simply tell Arden the truth? Your motives were not so devious, after all."

Roslyn laughed outright. "I doubt he would understand my desire to make Lord Haviland fall in love with me. And the less I have to do with the Duke of Arden the better."

Her lips pursing in amusement, Fanny waved a hand airily down the sidelines. "Clearly not everyone feels the same as you do."

Following her gaze, Roslyn saw Arden in conversation with a half dozen of the other wedding guests. Not surprisingly he was the center of attention—and not merely because he was a scion of the nobility. His magnetic, commanding presence drew the eye. That, along with a breathtaking virility, made every member of the female sex take notice.

"The ladies are obviously eager to shower him with attention," Roslyn agreed.

"Not just the ladies," Fanny countered. "The young bucks in London all try to mimic his sporting exploits. And he is well respected for his political views by the Whigs and many of the Tories as well. Arden takes his seat in the House of Lords quite seriously."

She raised an eyebrow. That the duke was a sportsman was obvious, to judge by his well-muscled shoulders and limbs, but that he would be interested in governing the country did indeed surprise her.

Roslyn shook her head. "No doubt he is a perfect paragon, but he is a trifle too arrogant for my tastes. The night of the Cyprians' ball, he clearly expected me to fall swooning at his feet."

"Arrogant, perhaps, but handsome, you must admit," Fanny prodded.

It was true, Roslyn thought, the duke was devastatingly handsome. His hair was dark blond, a rich shade of amber, and he had the aristocratic, beautifully carved features of a fallen angel.

But physical beauty had never impressed her much. Appearance had little to do with the true measure of a man. She herself had been misjudged far too often because of her looks, for many people automatically assumed she had no brains or substance of character.

Indeed, Roslyn had always seen her beauty as something of a curse. And she suspected Arden might have been subjected to a similar prejudice. With his dark gold hair, his lithe elegance, his polished address, he was the model of masculine perfection. Roslyn had to admit, however, that she found his sardonic smile more appealing than any of his other physical attributes, since it made him seem a little less perfect and more human.

Of course, she had experienced several of his other devastatingly masculine attributes firsthand. She could remember with startling vividness the hardness of his body, his magical hands, his hot, searching mouth. . . .

Scolding herself, she sat up straighter in her chair. She had vowed to drive those erotic images from her memory and never dwell on them again.

Unquestionably, however, she wasn't the only female here tonight to find Arden appealing. One of the most flirtatious and troublesome pupils at their academy, Miss Sybil Newstead, was gazing up at him admiringly—ogling him, in fact—and hanging on his every word. Yet when the girl brazenly reached out to touch the sleeve of his elegant coat, he slowly lifted an eyebrow and stared down at her clutching fingers until Sybil snatched her hand away.

At the deep flush staining her cheeks, Roslyn couldn't help but smile at how his cool hauteur had depressed the little hussy's pretensions.

"You should take note of her miscalculation, Roslyn," Fanny remarked sagely. "There is an art to dealing with experienced noblemen of Arden's stamp, and that bold young minx is an utter novice."

"I am very much a novice also," she said thoughtfully, "despite what you have tried to teach me."

Fanny's mouth curved in a teasing smile. "Perhaps you should ask the duke to advise you. If you could learn to attract a man like him, you can be sure the ploys would work on Lord Haviland."

Her suggestion made Roslyn laugh again. "I cannot imagine the illustrious Duke of Arden sinking so low as to help me capture a husband." Her friend was jesting, of course, although no doubt Arden could teach her more than a thing or two about the attributes he found desirable in a mistress.

She was precluded from further considering the possibility when her sister Lily joined them.

"Please, you have to save me," Lily lamented, sinking into the seat next to Roslyn.

"Save you?"

"From Winifred's infuriating attempts at matchmaking. I vow she is driving me to distraction."

By Winifred, she meant Lady Freemantle, the patroness of their academy.

"What has she done that is so terrible?" Fanny asked curiously.

"She is set on throwing me at the Marquess of Claybourne."

Fanny's brows drew together. "How so?"

"She practically begged him to dance with me and then prosed on and on about what an exemplary young lady I am. His lordship could scarcely keep a straight face."

"That is a crime indeed."

"It is no laughing matter, Fanny!" Lily said in exasperation. "It is utterly mortifying to be dragged before an eligible nobleman and exhibited like a heifer at a fair." Lily shifted her attention to her sister. "I came to warn you, Roslyn. Next, Winifred will be trying to arrange a match for you with Arden, for she hinted as much."

The prospect of enduring Winifred's machinations unsettled Roslyn, while Fanny found it highly amusing. "I doubt she will have much success," Fanny said. "Matrons have marked Arden as a target for their unwed daughters for years. He's been chased mercilessly by designing females of all ages since he left off short coats, yet no one has come close to catching him. Trust me, he is aware of every trick and stratagem. Not even Lady Freemantle could ensnare the elusive duke unless he wishes to be caught. Or the marquess either."

"Even so, I don't mean to let her carry her wretched intrigues any further," Lily declared.

Roslyn quelled a smile at her sister's earnestness. Lily would rather have her fingernails torn out than play the mating game that was eagerly embraced by most young ladies of quality.

"It would be impolite," Lily added, "to abandon the celebrations before the late supper is served, but afterward . . . I hope to convince Tess that we should leave early. I trust you don't mind, Roslyn. I will be happy to return tomorrow to help you put the Hall to rights again, but you will have to excuse me tonight."

The two sisters planned to spend tonight at the house of their close friend, Tess Blanchard, to give the newlyweds privacy on their wedding night. It would only be for this one night, since Arabella and Marcus would embark on their wedding trip tomorrow morning. "I don't mind if you go home early with Tess, Lily, but I will need to remain until the last guests depart."

"Perhaps you can ask Winifred to take you to Tess's in her carriage. Her ladyship will stay till the last dance, if I know her."

"Winifred won't mind, I'm certain," Roslyn said. "But you and I should say farewell privately to Arabella before you go."

"Of course." Lily offered her a smile of gratitude and relief and then rose to her feet. "Pray excuse me. I need to find Tess and ask her to sacrifice for me just this once. She was so looking forward to this evening, and I hate to spoil her enjoyment. But now the pleasure is entirely spoiled for me, too. At least Tess will likely sympathize with my plight, since she has been the victim of Winifred's maddening matchmaking schemes before."

Fanny rose also. "I had best go myself, since I have promised dances to several gentlemen, and I cannot afford to disappoint them. May I bring you some punch or a glass of wine first, Roslyn?"

"Thank you, no, Fanny. I need to check in on the kitchens shortly to be certain the preparations for supper are proceeding smoothly, but for the moment, I only want to sit quietly."

When her sister and friend were gone, Roslyn found her gaze returning to Arabella and Marcus. Along with utter delight, she felt a wistful stab of envy at their remarkable happiness.

Oh, she enjoyed her current life, to be sure. Even before Marcus's generous settlement, the income she earned from teaching at the academy had given her adequate financial freedom. And preparing young girls to become refined young ladies who could compete in the glittering world of the ton was very rewarding. Yet she felt something vital was missing in her life. Her sisters were infinitely dear to her, but they couldn't fulfill her yearning for love . . . for a husband and children of her own.

And now that Arabella had found happiness in marriage, Roslyn's resolve was only bolstered. She wanted to find that kind of true love for herself.

Roslyn hoped it would be with Rayne Kenyon, the Earl of Haviland. The black sheep of his illustrious family, Lord Haviland had unexpectedly inherited the title and fortune last year, which made him an extremely eligible bachelor, despite his nonconformist nature and his distaste for the trappings of the peerage.

As a rebel, he had more in common with Lily than with herself, Roslyn knew. In looks he was also very different from her. He was tall, as she was, but dark-haired, and handsome in a harsh sort of way, with a bold, masculine virility that commanded attention and respect. Yet Roslyn found herself attracted to his rugged appeal, as well as his forthright manner and his wicked sense of humor.

Because he disdained the frivolity and supercilious pretenses of the ton, Haviland had never bothered to learn the exalted social graces expected of an earl. Yet for his family's sake, he had begun making an effort to establish himself in society.

It was his regard for family that had most impressed her. She'd seen his affection for his nephews recently when he began teaching them to swim next door. And he was quite busy these days, squiring his elderly grandmother around London. Such kindness was just the quality Roslyn wanted in a husband.

More important for her, Haviland was said to be in the market for a bride, although chiefly at his grand-mother's urging.

Roslyn's gaze moved over the ballroom, uncon-sciously watching for Lord Haviland. She didn't see him among the dancers. Perhaps she should go in search of him. . . .

Roslyn looked up just then to see Winifred bearing down upon her with the Duke of Arden in tow. De-plorably, her heart skipped a beat at the sight of him. But then she pressed her lips together in vexation. Af-ter Lily's warning, she knew precisely what Winifred intended. Regrettably, though, there was no escape.

Rising to her feet, Roslyn stood reluctantly waiting for her ladyship's assault.

A large, ruddy-faced woman, Winifred had a boom-ing voice and accent that betrayed her lower-class ori-gins, but she was a kind soul and very well meaning. She'd been their dear friend and supporter for four years, ever since the disgraced Loring sisters had come to live at Danvers Hall with their step-uncle. In fact, she had been more of a mother to them than their real mother.

The summer previous to their arrival, Winifred had been widowed, a misfortune that had left her heartbroken—which was rather odd considering that hers had been an arranged marriage where she had wed far above her station. Her father, a wealthy in-dustrialist who'd made a vast fortune with his manu-facturing and mining enterprises, had purchased a baronet for her in hopes of elevating his daughter to the gentry.

Seventeen years later, Sir Rupert Freemantle had unexpectedly suffered heart failure, yet Winifred still wore the willow for him. She was dressed in the height of fashion now, but her gown of lavender crepe was the color of half-mourning. And she rarely was seen without a certain silver-enameled brooch pinned over her ample bosom in memory of her late husband, for inside was a miniature portrait of Sir Rupert. To anyone's knowledge, Winifred had never considered remarrying, even though she was barely middle-aged now, no more than forty.

She was fingering her brooch absently when she reached Roslyn. "There you are, my dear," Winifred exclaimed jovially. "Why are you hiding yourself away like a wallflower? You should be dancing." Without waiting for a reply, Winifred gestured at the nobleman beside her. "Allow me to present the Duke of Arden. His grace will make you an ideal partner, so I have brought him to you."

Trying to hide a wince of embarrassment, Roslyn offered Arden a polite curtsy, then murmured in an exasperated undertone, "Winifred, I am certain his grace can find his own dance partners."

"But none as beautiful or charming as you, dear. The duke will be well pleased to become better acquainted with you."

Since the music had just ended, her ladyship's voice carried over half the ballroom. Roslyn felt color flood her cheeks at her friend's obvious attempts at matchmaking. Lily was right; it was indeed mortifying.

She stole a glance at the duke. His expression was

enigmatic, so she couldn't tell if he was feeling the same vexation that she was at being cajoled to dance with her.

Indeed, he was all politeness when he bowed and said, "Will you do me the honor of dancing with me, Miss Roslyn?"

Roslyn managed a strained smile. "You are all kindness, your grace. But I was just on my way to the kitchens to confer with our housekeeper about the supper buffet. I hope you will understand if I beg to be excused."

"Why does that not surprise me?" he replied, a gleam in his green eyes that said he knew very well why she didn't wish to be alone with him.

Winifred looked unhappy, but Arden merely shrugged his elegant shoulders. "By all means, don't let me keep you from your duties."

"Thank you, your grace."

Curtsying again, Roslyn turned away and tried not to hurry from the ballroom as she'd done the night of the Cyprians' ball, yet she could feel his penetrating gaze boring into her back all the while.

Chapter Three

✣

I find it vexing that the duke condemns me for being a "designing female" even when I have no designs on him.

—Roslyn to Fanny

Drew's eyes narrowed as he watched Roslyn Loring walk away from him. He was not accustomed to being dismissed, as he had been each time they met.

His pique must have been obvious, for Lady Freemantle gave him a troubled look. " 'Tis right sorry I am, your grace. Roslyn truly is a delightful girl. She is just quite busy this evening, seeing to all the countless details required in putting on a gala like this. She is an excellent hostess, Roslyn is."

Drew wiped his annoyance from his expression and offered her ladyship a polite smile. "I understand perfectly, my lady."

"I will be happy to find you another partner—"

"Pray, don't trouble yourself," he said quickly. "I prefer to find my own dance partners."

"As you wish, your grace," the dame said with a strained smile before taking her leave.

Drew was under no illusions, however, that Lady Freemantle had abandoned her attempts at matchmaking. Her presumption would have irked him had he not desired to have Roslyn to himself for a few moments.

He could almost have laughed at her uninventive excuse to avoid speaking to him alone. Not that he disbelieved her about needing to see to the supper preparations. He'd watched Roslyn all afternoon as she mingled with the crowd, quietly and efficiently overseeing the wedding breakfast and the ball that followed. She was charming and gracious to the innumerable guests, anticipating their every need.

She was just as charming to the army of servants while marshaling her forces like a female general. The staff seemed eager to do her bidding, and as a result, the wedding celebrations had come off without any apparent hitches.

As if to prove his point, a footman materialized at Drew's elbow to offer him a glass of champagne. Drew accepted it and sipped, admiring the quality as he absently scanned the dancers waltzing around the ballroom floor.

Roslyn Loring was no doubt as excellent a hostess as Lady Freemantle avowed, he reflected. In that respect, she reminded him of his mother, the widowed Duchess of Arden.

At the thought of his illustrious mother, Drew grimaced. It was utterly unfair to compare the two women. Like the duchess, Roslyn was every inch the lady, elegant to the bone, yet she likely had more warmth in her little finger than his coldhearted mother did in her entire body.

Just then the music ended. With a sigh Drew set down his glass on a side table and stepped onto the ballroom floor in search of an elderly matron to charm. He had promised Marcus he would do his duty and dance with all the older ladies here, particularly the influential leaders of society, to help persuade them to support the new Countess of Danvers.

Sometime this evening, he would seek a dance with the bride herself and try to mend his fences with her. He and Arabella had not begun their acquaintance on the best of terms, since he'd been certain Marcus was making a grave mistake in marrying her.

But for the sake of their long friendship, Drew was prepared to grin and bear the choice Marcus had made—and hope it wouldn't end in sorrow and resentment when the first flush of love wore off.

An hour later, he also managed to secure a dance with Fanny Irwin. When he quizzed her about the Cyprians' ball, however, Fanny suggested that he ask Roslyn directly about her attendance.

Then Fanny hesitated. "If I may be so bold, your grace . . . Perhaps it might be best if you leave her alone. She is an innocent compared to you, not in your league in the least."

Drew's eyes narrowed on the beautiful courtesan. Telling a man he couldn't have something was certain to provoke just the opposite reaction, and Fanny well knew it, despite her ingenuous, wide-eyed look.

"I might say the same of you, Fanny, darling," Drew responded. "It hardly reflects well on you, to be leading an innocent young lady astray."

Fanny smiled at that. "I assure you, I did not do the leading. Roslyn knows her own mind, your grace."

At her wry tone, Drew found himself searching the crowd again for the subject of their discussion, just as he'd done all day. Truthfully, he couldn't understand his fascination with Roslyn. She was not his preferred style. He usually liked more curves in a woman, more earthiness. Her delicate beauty belonged more to a gilded figurine, except that he knew firsthand that she was warm, enticing flesh and blood. She had certainly enticed him that night, in part because of her elusiveness.

Suddenly he spied her dancing with Lord Haviland. She was gazing up at the earl, smiling softly, and the sight made Drew's gut clench unexpectedly.

She'd never given *him* that lovely smile, and he found himself craving it. Entirely absurd, since he had no interest in pursuing her himself. No, he was merely irritated that she had accepted Haviland's offer to dance after so pointedly refusing his own.

His jaw tightened imperceptibly—but Fanny was a perceptive woman, in the business of understanding men. "They are friends, your grace. Haviland is their closest neighbor."

"So I was told," Drew said, feigning indifference.

After the set ended, though, he made it a point to seek out Haviland and renew their slight acquaintance.

Following an interval of small talk where Drew learned more about the earl's background and family circumstances, Haviland asked how he was enjoying the celebrations.

"Well enough," Drew replied, "given that I generally loathe weddings."

Haviland grinned. "I understand the sentiment. I always feel as if my cravat is too tight. Gatherings such as this are not my forte, either, particularly since I came into the title. It's rather unnerving, facing packs of young ladies and their mamas on the prowl, eyeing me as if I were their matrimonial prey."

It was Drew's turn to grin, since he fully appreciated the earl's situation. A wealthy peer who still possessed his hair and teeth and faculties was a grand prize on the Marriage Mart.

When he suggested they leave the ballroom and repair to one of the cardrooms, however, Haviland expressed regret that he had a prior commitment. "I have an engagement in London later this evening that I cannot miss, but I would be pleased to take you on some other time . . . perhaps at Brooks?"

Drew agreed they should meet at the gentleman's club in London sometime in the near future. He was surprised to discover that he liked Haviland, which was probably why a short while later, he paid attention when he saw the earl take his leave of Arabella and Marcus and then exit through the French doors at the rear of the ballroom. Since Haviland lived a short distance from Danvers Hall, Drew supposed he planned to walk home across the estate grounds rather than take the trouble of hailing his carriage.

But when Drew saw the familiar figure of Roslyn Loring slip out the doors immediately afterward, he felt his jaw harden reflexively. Wondering at her intent, he found his footsteps carrying him to the nearest entrance, which offered a side view of the terrace overlooking the gardens. There he hesitated, watching.

Haviland had paused to wait for Roslyn, and when she reached him, she stood gazing up at him, making a breathtaking picture. The sun was setting, turning her hair to gold flame and illuminating her ivory complexion with an ethereal glow.

Drew felt his breath falter at the stunning sight. If

Haviland was half a man, he would be just as bowled over, Drew knew. And if *he* were half a gentleman, he would leave before interrupting a romantic tryst.

Yet he couldn't force himself to turn away. Instead his gaze remained riveted on Roslyn Loring as she offered her lovely smile to another man.

A trifle breathless from hurrying by the time she caught up to Lord Haviland, Roslyn was pleased when the earl turned and flashed her a welcome smile.

"I looked for you to say farewell, Miss Roslyn, but I was unable to find you."

"Regrettably I had another matter with the staff to attend to."

"Please accept my compliments on an enjoyable evening," he said with a formal politeness worthy of his new rank as he bowed over her hand. "Organizing such a large celebration must have been difficult."

To her chagrin, Roslyn felt herself blushing. "The size *was* a little challenging," she began, then abruptly chastised herself for sounding inane. It was absurd how she sometimes grew tongue-tied around Haviland, no doubt because she was so eager to make a good impression. "I am glad you came today, my lord."

"So am I. And I regret that I must leave so early, but I must be in London within the hour."

Roslyn found herself regretting that he released her hand. "Your relatives expect you tonight, I believe you said."

Haviland's grimace held rueful amusement. "Lamentably, yes. My grandmother is holding a poetry reading and has requested my appearance. I would rather swallow a flaming sword than be subjected to her notion of entertainment—pedagogues and literary pretenders reciting bad poetry—but I feel obliged to attend."

"Perhaps it will turn out better than you anticipate."

"It will likely be pure torture." He hesitated, surveying her thoughtfully. "You don't find these social functions painful, obviously, so perhaps you might help me. You know that I am holding a ball of my own next week?"

"Yes, my sisters and I received your invitation."

"Might you be willing to advise me in hosting mine? The denizens of the ton—particularly my august relations—will be expecting a disaster, and I would very much like to prove them wrong."

"I would be happy to help, my lord."

"Shall we meet tomorrow to discuss it, then?"

"Yes, if we can arrange it for the afternoon. Arabella and Marcus will have left on their wedding trip by then."

"Very well, I will call upon you at three o'clock, if that's agreeable."

"Very agreeable, my lord."

"Until then, Miss Roslyn," Haviland said with another bow.

She watched, smiling, as he turned away and descended the terrace steps two at a time, heading toward his own nearby manor.

Roslyn felt like hugging herself. She wanted very much to help the rebel Lord Haviland prove his detractors wrong. Yet she was just as pleased to have the opportunity to spend more time with him, since she hoped to show him that she could make him an ideal wife.

She was still smiling when she turned back to the house, but her footsteps faltered when she happened to glance toward the side entrance door. The Duke of Arden stood there in the shadows, one shoulder casually propped against the lintel.

Her smile fading, Roslyn halted. "How long have you been lurking there, your grace?"

"Long enough to observe your encounter with Haviland. I saw you follow him and was curious to know if you intended an assignation."

Her chin came up. "Has no one ever told you it isn't gentlemanly to eavesdrop on a lady?"

"Has no one told you it isn't ladylike to chase after a gentleman?" Stepping out of the shadows toward her, Arden made a tsking sound. "Such forward behavior. I expected better of you, Miss Roslyn."

She could see the gleam of sardonic amusement in his green eyes and had to bite back a retort. Even though she longed to set the duke back on his heels, she managed a sweet smile instead. "If you overheard our conversation, then you know there was no assignation. I merely wished to say farewell to a friend before he left for the evening."

"Haviland looks to be more than a friend to you."

"He is also our nearest neighbor, and a man I respect and admire," she said coolly, although why she felt she had to defend herself to this provoking nobleman, Roslyn had no idea.

"And you mean to aid him in hosting his upcoming ball?"

"Of course." When Arden moved closer, she thought of retreating a step, but she held her ground. "If I can use my particular talents to advise him, I will. When he was younger, Haviland left home in search of adventure and was never forgiven by his family. Since returning, he has not been well received in their elite circles, but he's attempting to rectify matters and fulfill the obligations of his new title."

"You seem eager to attract his goodwill," Arden mused.

"Perhaps I am," Roslyn said lightly, "but what of it? My affairs really are not your concern, your grace."

"Except for the matter of your conduct a fortnight ago," he drawled. "I am still waiting for an explanation."

The duke's sharper tone made Roslyn recall his threat to tell Marcus about her impropriety.

"Ordinarily," Arden continued, "your indiscretions would not concern me, but in this case, there would have been the devil to pay had we been discovered together. I might have been obliged to marry you to make amends."

Her eyes widened, then narrowed in understanding. "Is *that* why you are so vexed with me? Because you feared the repercussions if we were found together?"

"In large part." His mouth curved wryly. "I wanted you as my mistress, sweeting. A wife is another matter altogether."

Roslyn couldn't help but smile. "Yet I hardly deserve all the blame, your grace. You were the one who propositioned *me,* I seem to recall. I did not seek your attention."

"You should have stopped me before I kissed you."

"I was too startled at being assaulted."

"*Assaulted?*" he repeated, his eyebrow arching.

"Perhaps 'assaulted' is an exaggeration, but you could have taken me at my word when I declined your offer to become your paramour."

His lips twitched. "I suppose I should beg your pardon for that."

Her own smile turned rueful. "Well, I suppose you were justified in thinking I was that sort of female."

"Indeed," Arden said dryly. "Particularly since the annual Cyprians' ball is held precisely for the purpose of conducting such transactions, and since I first saw you in Fanny Irwin's company. The last thing I expected to find there was a virginal innocent. Believe me, I'm not in the habit of seducing genteel young ladies. In fact, I avoid them like the plague."

"Well, thankfully nothing came of it, so you may congratulate yourself on your narrow escape. You are quite safe."

He cocked his head. "Did you never consider that I might be concerned for *your* safety?"

"No," Roslyn said curiously. "Why should you be?"

"You put your reputation at risk, and possibly yourself. You could have been truly assaulted that night. Had I been a man who wouldn't take no for an answer, it would have ruined you."

"I assure you I have learned my lesson, your grace. From now on I will be entirely satisfied with secondhand knowledge."

"Secondhand?"

Roslyn considered him for a long moment. Judging by his current tone, the duke was prepared to be reasonable. If he understood why she had attended the ball . . . She took a slow breath, deciding to give him a frank explanation.

"If you must know, I asked Fanny to invite me that night so I could observe her success with her patrons. She has a remarkable talent for making men fall in love with her, and I hoped to learn her secrets."

When Roslyn saw his eyebrow lift in surprise and skepticism, she plowed ahead, even though embarrassment stained her cheeks at having to confess her plan to a nobleman as imperious and arrogant as Arden. "You see, I want to make my own future husband fall in love with me, and observing courtesans at work seemed the best way to accomplish it."

"I'm afraid I don't see," the duke said slowly.

"Well, you must admit that gentlemen fall in love with their mistresses far more often than with their wives."

"I won't dispute that, but what of it?"

"I wonder why that is. How do women like Fanny arouse a gentleman's ardor? They must have some significant knowledge that genteel ladies do not. Knowledge that Fanny has promised to teach me."

Arden simply stared at her. "So you are scheming to find a husband," he finally said.

Roslyn was rather taken aback by his derisive tone. "I wish to find love in marriage, not merely a husband."

"And I presume Haviland is the husband you have in mind?"

"Well . . . yes," Roslyn admitted.

"And you intend to entrap him? Rather cold-blooded of you, is it not, sweeting? And to think I had decided you were an innocent, not a designing female."

"I am *not* a 'designing female,' as you put it," Roslyn

replied stiffly. "Nor am I cold-blooded in the least. I hope to make Haviland fall in love, not entrap him."

"Isn't it the same thing?"

"I don't believe so, your grace." Roslyn's own gaze narrowed. "But perhaps you wouldn't understand, since Fanny tells me you are reputed to have no heart."

Arden took a step closer, studying her intently, before finally shaking his head. "Of course I have a heart." Surprisingly, his tone turned more amused than caustic. "I am kind to children, animals, the elderly. I just don't believe in love."

"Your cynical view is not surprising, I suppose, considering how often you have been targeted for matrimony."

"So you see why I might feel sympathy for Haviland? I would no doubt be doing him a favor if I warned him of your scheme."

Dismayed to think Arden might spoil all her plans, Roslyn searched his face. His eyes contained a gleam of mockery that made her suspect he was teasing her. "Please . . . you cannot tell him."

"Oh, I won't. That wouldn't be gentlemanly of me."

"And you won't tell Marcus either about what I was doing that night? I don't want to worry him when he is preparing to leave for his wedding trip with my sister."

"I don't want to worry him, either," Arden agreed dryly. "I have no desire for him to discover that I tried to seduce his ward, however unwittingly."

"I am not technically his ward any longer. He drew up a contract, granting us our legal independence."

"So he told me, but he still would not be happy to

learn of our prior encounter. I might end up facing him over pistols at dawn, God forbid. So you may count on me to keep your indiscretion a secret. I suppose your crime was not so terribly egregious, after all. And the danger is over now."

Roslyn breathed a sigh of relief. "Thank you. I know I acted foolishly. And I promise I won't be attending any more notorious functions like that again."

"I will let it pass if you will."

"Agreed, your grace. Indeed, I would prefer to forget that night ever happened."

"Oh?" An odd little smile touched his lips. "Do you think you can forget?"

"I suppose not. No one has ever . . ."

"Ever what? Tried to seduce you?"

Roslyn wrinkled her nose in amusement. "Oh, several have tried, but they never succeeded. I have never allowed any man to . . . to kiss me as you did." *Or touch me like that,* she couldn't help thinking.

"I am gratified," he said in that dry-as-dust tone.

When a silence fell between them, Roslyn suddenly became aware that dusk had fallen during the time they'd been talking on the terrace. She could hear the strains of music spilling through the doors from the ballroom, could smell the sweet scent of roses from the gardens below. With his face in shadow, though, she had trouble making out the duke's expression.

Then he took a step closer, and she recalled the last time she had encountered him alone . . . what had happened between them.

He was gazing down at her mouth, and Roslyn found herself staring back at his, remembering how those sensual lips had kissed her breasts, suckled them.

A hot, biting arc of awareness flared between them.

As if he was remembering, too, his voice lowered to a husky murmur. "You shouldn't make a practice of being alone with a gentleman after dark."

"I know." Her own voice was unsteady—and that was before he reached up to lightly touch her jaw, stroking with a fingertip.

Roslyn knew she should pull away, yet she couldn't move. She stared up into his unforgettable eyes, wondering if he intended to kiss her again. The very air seemed to crackle all around them. She moistened her lips, half in dread, half in anticipation.

Then suddenly the duke dropped his hand. "You had best return to your ball."

Roslyn curled her hands into fists and struggled to breathe evenly. "Y-yes, your grace." Shaking herself, she started to move past him but then stopped. "Thank you for being so reasonable," she said, her tone conciliatory.

His mouth twisted, but he didn't reply, so Roslyn turned away.

Drew watched her go and then stood there on the darkened terrace long after she had slipped through the ballroom doors.

He didn't feel particularly reasonable. Instead he felt . . . sexually frustrated. He had been the one to end their encounter this time, but it had been unaccountably difficult.

The damnable truth was, the spark he'd felt that night for Roslyn Loring was still there between them.

Drew cursed beneath his breath. She was a forbidden temptation, one that aroused all his most dangerous instincts. He'd had the strongest urge just now to draw her into his arms and make love to her right there. Her supple body had beckoned him, her innocence had dared him. In her elegant silk gown, Roslyn had looked remote, untouchable, yet he knew better. He'd seen a glimpse of the real woman before this. The woman whose untutored passion had set his blood racing.

He hadn't imagined her wild, sweet responsiveness that night, or the way she had set him alight. He was still unsettled by the disturbing potency of that encounter.

Even now her delicate scent filled his nostrils, the same fragrance that had haunted him for days after the Cyprians' ball. And earlier this evening . . . seeing the evening sunlight catch her hair, caress her face, had taken his breath away.

He wasn't just merely appreciative of her perfect beauty, though. There were other things he couldn't forget about her. Her eyes, her lips, her breasts. Her voice—velvet, warm, honeyed. He hadn't liked her using that soft, warmhearted tone with Haviland.

Drew shook his head abruptly. He couldn't possibly be jealous. He never became possessive over a woman, never felt any such heated emotions. He couldn't refute Roslyn's allegation about his lacking a heart. He'd been raised by his haughty, aristocratic parents to be emotionally detached and had never seen any reason to change.

Oh, he'd experienced infatuation before, but he had never fallen in love. He didn't think he was even capable of it. And while any number of women had professed to love him, he knew the attraction was as much for his immense wealth and vaunted title as himself.

His own attraction to Roslyn Loring was inexplicable, since he'd had more than his fair share of beauties. No doubt his trouble was merely physical, Drew reflected. It had been too long since he'd enjoyed the services of a mistress.

A self-mocking smile curled his mouth. *And perhaps the trouble is that you've finally met a woman who clearly isn't interested in you.*

He had never found himself in such a novel situation. It was amusing really. He'd always earnestly avoided designing females, and Roslyn Loring was certainly a designing female of a sort. She just didn't have designs on *him*. If he were a vain man, he might be insulted.

But she didn't want him; she wanted her neighbor. She was also right on that one account. Her pursuit of Haviland was none of his own affair.

Remembering, Drew felt his smile fade. He was oddly disappointed in Roslyn. Admittedly she wasn't quite like the usual scheming husband-hunters he'd encountered in the past. She claimed her motives were a bit purer, that she was after love, not fortune and title. Even so, she was still on the hunt for a husband— the very kind of mercenary female that made him shudder.

On the other hand, he was grudgingly impressed by her honesty. In fact, he could actually admire her initiative and her boldness, even if he couldn't like her purpose.

Recalling her goal of finding love in marriage, Drew made a scoffing sound and abruptly turned back toward the house.

He had no desire to return to the ball, however.

Instead, he meant to find Marcus's study and indulge in a very large brandy . . . until he could politely take his leave and return to London, where he would try to forget that the most beautiful of the three Loring sisters even existed.

Chapter Four

❧

I concede I may have misjudged the duke. He has
more substance than I gave him credit for.

—Roslyn to Fanny

Roslyn felt tears of happiness blur her vision as the
Freemantle barouche carried her away from Danvers
Hall. She and Winifred were among the last to leave,
since she had stayed behind to direct the household
staff and spare Arabella the task, and Winifred always
delighted in closing down a ball.

Two hours earlier, the sisters had said farewell privately to each other. It was a poignant moment, full of
love and tears. This was the last evening they would
really be together as sisters, the three of them standing
against the world. Now that Arabella was married,
she would have a doting husband to love and care for
her.

A half hour after that, Lily had left to spend the
night with Tess. It was well past midnight, however,
before the enormous crowd of wedding guests took
their leave and the long line of carriages thinned out.

Most of the remaining family and close friends had
departed moments ago, heading for London. The Marquess of Claybourne had escorted Marcus's lively sister Eleanor home, along with her aunt, Lady Beldon.

Fanny was accompanied by one of her wealthy gentleman friends. And their mother, Victoria, had left with her French husband, since the Vachels planned to stay in the town house of Henri's English relations for another fortnight before returning to his home in France.

As Roslyn stood in the entrance hall, saying a final good-bye to the bride and groom, she had spied the Duke of Arden behind her. But she hadn't wanted to suffer another encounter with him, so she embraced Arabella and Marcus warmly and then hurried down the front steps to the waiting barouche to join Winifred, who had kindly agreed to drive her to Tess's.

Settling back against the velvet squabs, Roslyn gave a sigh of weary contentment. She had promised Arabella she would oversee running the estate and the academy while the newlyweds were on their wedding trip, yet she couldn't imagine encountering any trouble. The summer school term had already begun, so most of their pupils had gone home and classes for the rest would be minimal. And now that the wedding was over, Roslyn was looking forward to a few weeks of peace and quiet and the hope of making Lord Haviland fall madly in love with her—or at least the opportunity to nurture the intimacy of their burgeoning friendship.

Winifred heard her sigh and responded with a pleased sigh of her own. "It is good to see Arabella so happy."

"It is indeed," Roslyn agreed softly.

"I vow your mother is happiest of all," Winifred expounded. "Victoria was vastly relieved to see at least one of her daughters well married. She feared the scandal she caused would destroy all your chances for decent futures."

It very nearly had, Roslyn thought before giving a light shrug. She had never allowed herself to bemoan her fate, and she wouldn't start now. She was glad, however, to finally have some brighter prospects for her future. "It is all over now, Winifred."

"Not by a long chalk, my dear." Shaking her head smugly, Winifred chuckled. "It is only beginning for you and Lily. I have high hopes that you will both be able to make good matches now."

Trying to hide her exasperation, Roslyn returned a bland smile. "You know Lily's feelings about marriage."

"She will change her tune if she meets the right man."

Roslyn remained skeptical, doubting that her high-spirited younger sister would ever alter her opinion about matrimony. After the acrimonious example their parents had set, Lily had vowed never to be subjected to the kind of battles they had waged against each other for years.

Roslyn was just as fiercely determined never to be locked in a hostile marriage of convenience, which was why she had sworn she would never marry without love. She had no desire, however, to be the target of Winifred's meddlesome assistance, any more than Lily did.

"Perhaps so," Roslyn said pointedly, "but Lily will have to make her own decisions about marriage without any outside interference, no matter how well intentioned."

At that arch reference to her matchmaking efforts, Winifred looked a trifle guilty. "I just want you both to be happy."

"I know, Winifred, but you must allow us to be responsible for our own happiness. . . ."

Her words trailed off when she became aware that the carriage had begun to slow. Moments later she heard a shout from outside.

"Hold there, I say!"

"What the devil?" Winifred muttered.

Just as puzzled, Roslyn peered out the window. There was enough light from the carriage lamps to make out the mounted horseman by the side of the road. Her heart started thudding in alarm when she realized the rider was masked and armed with a pistol.

"Stand and deliver!" he commanded, waving his weapon at the coachman.

The two ladies looked at each other in shock and dismay as the barouche lurched to a shuddering halt.

"I believe we are being held up," Roslyn murmured.

"And me wearing all my best jewels," Winifred said worriedly.

When the highwayman shifted his aim toward the rear of the coach, Roslyn knew he was addressing the footman perched up behind the boot.

"You there, fellow, climb down and open the door!"

The servant must have jumped down from his perch since shortly the door swung open. Through the opening, she could see their assailant more clearly as he sat upon his bay horse. He was ginger-haired and wore a dark coat, but despite his smallish build, the pistol in his hand looked large and deadly.

The footman obviously thought so, too, for after letting down the step, he raised his hands high and sidled away from the door, keeping a wary eye on the weapon.

"Now come out, your ladyship," the brigand called.

He was ordering them out of the carriage, yet

Winifred seemed disinclined to obey. "I will not!" she exclaimed mutinously.

"You will, or I'll shoot your man here."

The highwayman's voice was surprisingly unsteady but determined enough to suggest he would carry out his threat if thwarted.

"We should do as he says, Winifred," Roslyn said, not wanting to risk the servant's life.

Gathering her courage, she stepped down first, then assisted Winifred. As she turned to face the highwayman, Roslyn drew her cloak a bit tighter around her silk-clad shoulders. The June night was warm enough, yet she couldn't help shivering at the danger they faced.

"What do you want, sir?" she asked, trying to keep her own voice calm.

"What do you think I want? Your money and your jewels."

Her reticule was looped around her wrist, but it was empty except for a bit of pin money. And she had no jewels other than a lovely pearl necklace and earrings given to her by Marcus. Winifred, however, was practically dripping in diamonds.

The highwayman seemed to know it, for he only had eyes for Winifred.

"Hand over your jewels, Lady Freemantle," he demanded, brandishing his pistol.

He sounded rather nervous, or at least he didn't seem to be enjoying his villain's role. Roslyn wondered vaguely if this was his first foray into crime. Regardless, she thought it wiser not to argue.

When she reached up to remove her pearl necklace, though, the thief shook his head. "Not you, Miss. Her ladyship's is all I want."

Scowling, Winifred fumbled with the clasp of her diamond necklace, but the fellow again shook his head. "Give me the brooch first."

"What brooch?"

"The one pinned to your bodice under your shawl."

Roslyn wondered how the thief knew what Winifred was wearing under her satin shawl and decided he must have seen her earlier this evening. Winifred, however, was evidently unwilling to hand over her prize possession, for her spine went rigid. "I won't give it to you!"

"Damn and blast it, do as I say!" he demanded.

"You needn't curse at me, you devil."

When he aimed his pistol at Winifred's ample chest, his hand shook, as did his voice, yet the dame seemed finally to realize the danger. "No, please, take all my other jewels. Just leave me this piece."

Hearing the tremor in her friend's plea, Roslyn understood. Winifred would dislike surrendering her expensive baubles, but she positively couldn't bear to part with her brooch, since it held a miniature of her late husband.

Seeing Winifred's distress, Roslyn stepped forward protectively, hoping to reason with the highwayman to leave the brooch. "Surely you could be content with her diamonds. They are far more costly. The brooch is not particularly valuable. In fact its value is mostly sentimental."

"No matter, it's the brooch I want. Now give it to me!" he insisted, just as they heard the rattle and accompanying thud of hooves of an oncoming carriage and team behind them.

The highwayman froze. Another vehicle was bowling down the dark country road, Roslyn realized.

When it rumbled to a halt behind the barouche, she recognized Arden's coach from the ducal crest emblazoned on the door panel.

Cursing, the highwayman clenched his horse's reins, sending the animal prancing as he debated what to do.

While his attention was thus distracted, Roslyn acted on sheer instinct: She slipped her reticule off her wrist and threw it with all her might at the footpad's face.

At the same time she lunged toward his horse, hoping to seize his weapon and possibly disarm him.

The unexpected blow made the highwayman flinch violently and jerk his pistol upward, causing it to discharge harmlessly over Roslyn's head, yet with a report loud enough to frighten not only his mount but the Freemantle team as well.

To her horror then, the highwayman abruptly fumbled in his coat pocket and pulled out another pistol, which he started to point at her.

Roslyn halted in her tracks, just as his attention was captured again by the shout Arden gave behind her. The duke had leapt from his coach and was sprinting toward them, his own pistol drawn.

When the brigand swung his weapon toward the new threat, the duke took aim and got off a deterring shot first.

The thief cried out in pain and slumped forward, clutching his right arm. Awkwardly then, he whirled his horse and galloped away, apparently having lost his combative appetite.

Watching the fleeing bandit disappear into the darkness, Roslyn felt weak with relief—and so apparently did Winifred, for the older lady sagged against the barouche.

Concerned, Roslyn went to her side and took her arm to support her heavy weight. "You weren't hurt, were you?"

Winifred shook her head while clutching her brooch possessively. When the duke reached her side, she said in a trembling voice, "Thank you, your grace. You saved us. I thought that cutthroat might murder us."

"He didn't seem intent on murder," Roslyn said, trying to calm her friend.

"No?" Arden's tone held a hard note of skepticism. "Then why did he shoot?"

"Because I threw my reticule at him."

"Indeed."

He was eyeing her narrowly, Roslyn saw. "I hoped to wrestle his pistol away from him," she explained.

"That was foolhardy of you. You could have been killed."

"I decided it worth the risk. He was so agitated, I didn't think his aim would be very accurate."

"Which made him all the more dangerous."

Roslyn grimaced impatiently. "We shouldn't be standing here debating, your grace. We should ride after him."

The duke's mouth curled sardonically. "And what do you expect to accomplish in the dark?"

"We could at least attempt to find him."

"Her ladyship's servants could search the country-side tonight, but it would be pointless. He'll be long gone by now."

"So we should simply do nothing?" Roslyn asked in frustration.

The duke's eyes, cool and green, met hers. "A thorough search can be conducted in the morning. I wounded him, so there may be a blood trail to follow. But for now there is nothing to be gained by trying to chase after him."

The duke directed his gaze toward Winifred's coachman, who was still attempting to calm his jittery team. "You will take her ladyship home and see to her safety."

"Aye, yer grace."

Roslyn wanted to argue, yet she knew Arden was right. It was pointless to search for the wounded highwayman until morning.

"I *would* like to go home," Winifred murmured in a weak voice.

She looked about to swoon, which alarmed Roslyn even more than the holdup had done. Her friend was one of the strongest women she knew and never succumbed to the vapors.

"You need to sit down, Winifred," Roslyn urged, guiding her to the door of the barouche.

Arden helped her inside, then handed Roslyn up beside her.

He was about to step back to allow the footman to close the door when Winifred leaned forward to address him. "Please, will you accompany us, your grace?" she implored. "I would feel ever so much safer with your presence." When he hesitated, Winifred patted her bosom with a fluttery motion. "Please . . . my heart is beating so hard, I think I might faint."

Roslyn shot her friend a highly suspicious glance. Winifred had never before suffered heart palpitations either, and the possibility that she was feigning weakness in order to secure the duke's time and attention was too strong to dismiss.

Arden, however, nodded in polite agreement, perhaps

because he was too much of a gentleman to question her motives. "Let me direct my coachman to follow us."

Roslyn was not overjoyed that the duke would be riding with them, for she'd expected to be rid of him by now. Yet she could hardly object when Winifred claimed to need his comforting presence to soothe her frayed nerves.

When he turned away, Winifred sagged back against the seat, fanning herself weakly. In the glow from the interior lamp, her complexion was as ruddy as ever. Her voice, too, was steadier when she said, "You were very brave, my dear. I am grateful that you tried to save my brooch, but it wasn't worth your life. I am so thankful you weren't shot—and that Arden was there to rescue us."

"I am as well," Roslyn murmured.

The duke returned just then and climbed in to sit opposite them. He was still armed, she saw as the barouche began moving.

"I always carry a brace of pistols when I travel," he said, seeing the focus of her gaze.

"Thank heavens you did," Winifred said. "You are a capital shot, your grace, and quite heroic. Was he not, Roslyn?"

"Yes, indeed," she admitted reluctantly.

His mouth curved. "You managed to stay calm, I noticed, Miss Loring. Some young ladies would have given way to hysterics."

"I am not the hysterical sort."

And yet she was more unnerved by the holdup than she'd realized. They all could have been injured or worse. Roslyn felt herself shudder, remembering how the bandit had threatened to kill Winifred's footman. No doubt she was suffering from a delayed reaction, but she was indeed grateful for the duke's presence.

"Bloody coward," Winifred muttered, "accosting two unarmed ladies." She glanced at Arden. "I hope you will stay the night at Freemantle Park, your grace. We need you to protect us."

"I had already decided as much."

Roslyn shifted uneasily in her seat. "Surely it isn't necessary to impose on his grace."

His eyes held a gleam of amusement. "Are you so eager to be rid of me?"

She felt herself blush at his perceptiveness.

"Someone," Arden continued, "must organize a search and speak to the local authorities tomorrow. Perhaps set up a watch to try and prevent future robberies. You have a bailiff or a steward, my lady?"

"A bailiff."

"Then I will meet with him in the morning and make arrangements."

Roslyn still was reluctant to involve the duke in their affairs. "You needn't put yourself to such trouble."

"I have no wish to tell Marcus about the attempted robbery, do you? If I handle the matter, he won't need to know."

She hesitated, acknowledging his point. If Marcus thought there was a highwayman at large threatening the district, he would likely postpone his wedding trip, and Arabella deserved to enjoy her newfound happiness uninterrupted.

"I suppose not," Roslyn finally said. "But still—"

"I will deal with it," Arden stated, cutting off any

further protest. There was an implacable note of finality in his tone, as if he was unaccustomed to having his decisions questioned. But he *was* a duke, after all.

"Now tell me what happened tonight," he suggested. "What exactly did our highwayman say and do?"

Roslyn gave a brief account of the attempted robbery, and Winifred chimed in with a detail or two.

"I could scarcely believe it was happening," the elder lady added at the last. "Ours is a very quiet neighborhood. And this is not the main road to London."

"I think," Roslyn said slowly, "that he waited for us to leave Danvers Hall and then followed us."

Arden's interest sharpened. "Why do you say so?"

"Because he knew precisely what jewels Lady Freemantle was wearing. He must have seen her earlier today."

"Or perhaps he was informed by someone who did see her," Arden observed.

"But it *is* curious that he only wanted her brooch."

"Brooch?"

Winifred drew aside her shawl to display the piece. "This was the only item that devil demanded. I can't imagine why he would want my brooch."

"Did either of you recognize him?" the duke asked. "Anything familiar about him? Any identifying characteristics?"

"Not that I noticed," Roslyn said thoughtfully. "Although I realize now that he was surprisingly wellspoken."

His speech was not of the lower classes, Roslyn was certain. In fact, Winifred's accent was much rougher than the brigand's.

"Well," the duke said, "we can do our best to find him, but I doubt we will have much luck."

Roslyn had to agree. Finding a small, red-haired, well-spoken footpad who had tried to rob Winifred would likely be impossible. The only detail that might lead to his identification was that he was likely wounded, perhaps in the arm, but they couldn't even be sure of that.

Falling silent, she settled back against the squabs, wondering how the special evening had suddenly turned so grim.

Drew was regretting the turn of events almost as much as she. This was precisely what he had hoped to avoid—becoming further entangled with Roslyn Loring. He would rather be halfway to London by now. Yet he couldn't leave the ladies without protection. And he owed it to Marcus to stay and see to matters.

Barely an hour before, he'd promised his friend to keep an eye on the two younger Loring sisters. He and Heath had remained late at the ball in order to say farewell to Marcus and share a brandy to mourn the demise of his bachelorhood, even though Marcus had soundly rejected their condolences and claimed to be wildly content with his love match to Arabella.

Drew found himself swearing at the wretched timing. It was the devil's own luck that the highwayman had struck so soon after his making that promise.

He had to admit, however, that Roslyn had borne the danger with aplomb. He'd been impressed by her courage and resourcefulness, even if it *had* sent his heart to his throat to see her in danger of getting shot. Most females of his acquaintance would have fainted dead at the threat.

Simply because he could admire her mettle, however, did not mean he wished to spend the night with her under the same roof. He didn't want to be tempted by her, or to be subjected to Lady Freemantle's annoying attempts at matchmaking. But it looked as if he would have no choice.

When the coach drew up before the Freemantle mansion, her ladyship wouldn't hear of Roslyn going on to stay with her friend, Miss Blanchard, and insisted she remain at the Park to provide solace and company.

Roslyn's cheeks colored with chagrin, Drew noted, and she sent him an embarrassed glance, yet she didn't argue with her friend, merely nodded with a wry sigh of resignation.

Lady Freemantle seemed to have recovered from her weakness as she swept into her entrance hall, where she was greeted by her butler. The elderly servant looked distressed when she quickly explained about their frightening experience, but she assured him that the Duke of Arden would handle matters.

"The duke and Miss Loring will be our guests for the night, Pointon," she added. "Show them to the green parlor, if you please, and bring them refreshments while you attend to their accommodations. His grace has no luggage, but I believe passable attire may be found for him in Sir Rupert's wardrobe."

"As you wish, my lady."

"Oh, and his grace wishes to speak to our bailiff in the morning. Will you have Mr. Hickling summoned at the duke's convenience?"

"Yes, my lady."

"Thank you, Pointon. And please send a footman to

Miss Blanchard's house to let Miss Lily Loring know her sister will not be coming this evening." Lady Freemantle turned to Drew then with an apologetic smile. "I hope you will forgive me, your grace. I am still feeling rather faint and believe I must retire to bed. Roslyn, I trust you to entertain my guest. At the moment I am still too unnerved to be a hospitable hostess."

Roslyn did protest at that. "Winifred," she began, her tone tinged with vexation.

Her ladyship held up a hand. "You should have a glass of wine, my dear. I'm sure your nerves are a trifle distraught after that dreadful upset. I will see you in the morning."

With that, Lady Freemantle turned to ascend the sweeping staircase, leaving Drew alone with the butler and a very irritated Roslyn Loring.

Chapter Five

✣

I agree wholeheartedly with Lily: Winifred's match-making endeavors are maddening! But at least I was able to turn her meddling to my advantage.

—Roslyn to Fanny

Roslyn gritted her teeth, trying to hide her mortification. Initially she'd been alarmed by Winifred's uncustomary feebleness, but now she was simply vexed, since it was clear that once again her ladyship was attempting to throw her at the duke's head.

She sent him a fleeting look of apology, hoping he was astute enough to realize that she had played no part in her friend's machinations, but his look was inscrutable.

Removing her evening cloak, Roslyn handed it to the butler. "I will direct his grace to the parlor, Pointon, if you see to the other arrangements."

"Very good, Miss Loring."

Silently then, she led the way down the corridor to the green parlor while Arden followed. It was an ostentatious room that bespoke wealth if not good taste. Although there was no fire in the grate, a lamp burned dimly on the mantel.

Crossing to the lamp, Roslyn turned up the flame before facing the duke with a rueful grimace. "I feel I must apologize for Lady Freemantle, your grace. She is evidently set on matchmaking, but you needn't feel threatened. You are in no danger from me."

An ironic smile played across his lips. "I remember. You have set your sights on Haviland."

Roslyn felt color rise to her cheeks. "Well . . . yes." She gestured toward the brocade couch. "Please, make yourself comfortable. Pointon will bring you wine shortly."

With a polite curtsy, she started to leave, but Arden's amused drawl followed her. "You needn't run away again, Miss Loring."

Her gaze snapping back to his, she halted, nettled by his provoking tone. "I am not running. I am *walking* to the library to fetch a book to read, since I am too agitated to sleep."

His penetrating glance surveyed her. "Eleanor told me you are bookish." When that elicited no response, he said more pointedly, "Stay and have some wine. You look as if you could use it."

Roslyn hesitated. Winifred had been right on that score at least; she *was* still shaken by the attempted robbery.

Pointon entered just then with a tray containing a decanter of wine and two crystal wine goblets. When the duke instructed him to leave the tray on a side table, the butler did as he was bid and bowed himself out.

"Sit down, Roslyn," Arden ordered as he went to the table to pour them each a glass of wine.

Roslyn didn't protest. Deplorably, her hands were trembling. Sinking onto the couch, she clasped her fingers together and gave a small laugh. "It is foolish to be so missish. The peril is long passed."

"It isn't foolish at all," the duke replied. "You could have been shot tonight."

She glanced up at him as he carried her glass over to her. "Have you ever shot someone before?"

"Once, to foil another highway robbery. I was more successful that time."

"You were successful this time. The thief didn't make off with Winifred's jewels as he intended. She would have been devastated to lose her brooch—although I doubt she is quite as distraught as she claims."

Arden settled beside her with the fluid elegance that characterized all his movements, making Roslyn suddenly very aware of his proximity. She quickly took a sip of wine to distract herself. "It was kind of you to remain here tonight to solace our nerves, but you needn't become any more involved in our affairs."

He gave a shrug of his lithe shoulders as he relaxed back against the couch. "Marcus would never forgive me if I let harm befall you when I could have prevented it."

At his casual movement, Roslyn shifted uncomfortably in her seat. She couldn't help remembering the feel of the hard-muscled body concealed beneath that impeccably tailored coat. She drank another swallow of wine, trying to discipline her wayward thoughts. "You are not responsible for my welfare, your grace."

"I know. But I still plan to remain here for a day or two."

She managed a wry smile. "If you stay, her ladyship's matchmaking will only get worse."

"Don't concern yourself. I've had ample experience foiling eager matchmakers." His tone was still amused, but an undercurrent of cynicism had crept into his voice.

"I can imagine," Roslyn replied, before returning to the problem of the holdup. "So you mean to meet with the bailiff, Mr. Hickling, tomorrow morning?"

"Yes, to have him begin a search for the highwayman."

"I would like to be present." When Arden raised an eyebrow, Roslyn expounded. "I saw the culprit up close, so I can offer the best description. And I know most everyone in the district and where to search." She paused, gazing down at her glass. "The real truth is, however, I would like to feel as if I am contributing. I don't like feeling so helpless."

Arden nodded as if he understood. "You are welcome to join us, sweeting. But only if you promise me never to challenge any more armed bandits. You should allow me the chance to play the hero."

Roslyn shot him a sharp glance before realizing that he was baiting her in a deliberate attempt to take her mind off the robbery. "You *were* rather heroic tonight," she admitted lightly, making an effort to quell her disquiet.

"So were you."

"You said I was foolhardy."

His slow grin was irresistible. "That too."

Roslyn smiled back at him. The wine was succeeding in relaxing her somewhat, so she wasn't quite as unnerved by Arden's nearness. But it still was deplorable the way her pulse reacted to him. It was a purely physical response, of course. Her emotions were not engaged in the least. She wasn't even sure she *liked* the duke. She certainly couldn't deny her attraction, however.

She was glad when he changed the subject, even though the one he chose was just as provoking.

"Marcus told me of your bluestocking tendencies," Arden said, studying her. "And Eleanor says that you read Latin. I confess I find it surprising."

"Why?" Roslyn queried. "You don't believe women should be educated in masculine disciplines?"

"No, I just wonder at your having such an unusual interest. You don't look to be the scholarly type."

Her smile this time was cool. "Many people mistakenly leap to that conclusion. They take one look at me and assume I don't have a mind. You did yourself the night we first met. Your proposition was based entirely on my appearance."

"Not entirely. Your wit appealed to me, too."

She laughed at that. "You had no chance to determine my wit before you offered to make me your mistress."

"I believe the circumstances justified my assumption about you," Arden said amiably. "I thought you a courtesan."

"But even men who know that I am a lady rarely look beneath the surface."

"So you consider your beauty a disadvantage rather than an attribute?" he clarified, his tone skeptical.

Her smile turned strained. "It frequently is. No woman wants to be plain, of course, but beauty can make one a target for the worst sort of reprobates."

"Marcus said a wastrel recently pursued you."

Her brows drew together as she eyed Arden. "You

seem to have discussed a great deal about me with Marcus."

"Not a great deal. He volunteered the information several months ago when he was lamenting inheriting responsibility for you and your sisters."

Roslyn squared her shoulders. "Well, I have been propositioned too many times for comfort. But *I* intend to do the propositioning this time."

The gleam of amusement in Arden's eyes only deepened. "And your proposition entails marriage."

"Indeed. I intend to find a husband who can love me for myself, not for something so superficial as my appearance."

She stared at Arden defiantly, expecting him to say something cutting, but he merely took a swallow of wine.

"Why choose Haviland?" he finally asked.

"Because I think he would make an ideal husband for me."

The duke responded with a sardonic lift of one eyebrow. "How so?"

"For one thing, he doesn't see me as a featherhead or an object to covet. And I sincerely like him. He is intelligent and kind, and he shares my sense of the absurd. What's more, he enjoys children and treats his elderly grandmother with affection. He doesn't feel compelled, either, to prostrate himself before society's dictates, which could prove beneficial for me. Given Haviland's rebellious streak, he should be more amenable than most noblemen to having a countess tainted by family scandal."

"It isn't just his wealth and title that appeal to you?"

Roslyn shook her head firmly. "Wealth and title don't make a man admirable, your grace. Lord Haviland gave up an exciting career to fulfill his familial obligations. I admire his willingness to sacrifice, to put his responsibilities over his own personal desires."

"You expect me to believe you aren't the least interested in his fortune?"

She eyed the duke with exasperation, realizing he was determined to think the worst of her. "You may believe whatever you like, but I don't consider wealth a qualification for happiness, at least not if one has enough income to subsist on." She gave a wry smile. "Four years ago the issue was in question. I thought I might have to accept a marriage of convenience in order to protect my sisters. We were penniless and disgraced and dependent on our step-uncle for our very existence. I was prepared to marry to spare my sisters having to do so if necessary. But thankfully Arabella soon hit upon the idea of starting our academy, and Lady Freemantle willingly funded the endeavor. She employed us to design the buildings and curriculum. And once our doors opened seven months later it allowed us the financial independence to choose our own futures."

"But Marcus has provided amply for you now. I understand that you needn't marry at all if you don't wish to."

"But I *do* wish to marry. I don't want to go through life as a spinster. I want a family . . . children."

Arden's mouth twisted. "How positively dull that sounds."

Roslyn smiled. "Perhaps so, but I expect I will cherish it."

"Passion isn't a requirement in your marriage?"

She felt her face warm. "Passion would be agreeable but it isn't critical. What I want more is fidelity." When he raised an eyebrow, waiting for an explanation, she gave him one. "You may have heard that my father had countless mistresses. He made my mother's life miserable . . . left her so hurt and humiliated that she took her own lover. I could never accept such blithe attitudes toward affairs and infidelities in my marriage. A husband who loves me will be less likely to stray from the marriage bed."

"And you think you can make Haviland fall in love with you?"

"I hope so. I would never marry him otherwise."

Drew stared at her for a long moment, taking in her earnest expression, the solemnity in her blue eyes. The sincerity in her arguments rang true, he conceded. Perhaps Roslyn Loring was not really as mercenary as he'd presumed. She simply had developed a logical, rational plan to go after what she wanted.

He had to admire her determination to take charge of her own fate, at least.

"You have obviously given this careful thought," he finally said.

"I have," Roslyn agreed, her beautiful features relaxing.

Tearing his gaze away, Drew drained his wineglass. He couldn't imagine why an image of vulnerability kept flitting through his mind when he looked at her, since Roslyn seemed to be one of the more capable women he had ever met. Perhaps because Marcus had told him how she'd had to fight off more than one eager admirer. Her exquisite beauty, combined with her lack of fortune and her former guardian's indifference, would make her the target of rakes and scoundrels. Which was why she had reacted so scornfully to his own improper offer, Drew suspected.

Feeling rather contradictory emotions toward her, he rose and crossed the room to refill their wine-glasses. When he returned, he handed Roslyn hers but remained standing.

She thanked him and then offered him a rueful smile. "I hope you will forgive Lady Freemantle for her plotting. She means well. Now that Arabella is wed, she hopes to see Lily and me well settled. But her desire to matchmake is not driven by any avaricious motives. Winifred really is a romantic at heart."

"As are you, it would seem," Drew replied, his tone sardonic.

"Yes, and you are a complete cynic," Roslyn said sweetly. "I can comprehend why, since so many women have hounded you, trying to ensnare you in matrimony. But I trust you will acquit me of having designs on you." The teasing light in her eyes brightened. "You needn't worry, your grace. I have no intention of joining the leagues of love-smitten females in a contest for your hand."

Drew gave a rough chuckle. "They are hardly love-smitten. Obsessed with rank and fortune is a more apt description. They all see wealthy members of the peerage as potential marks."

"I assure you, I do not. I have absolutely no desire to marry you—*or* to become your mistress," she added, amusement dancing in her eyes.

He couldn't help but grin. "Your adamant rejection that night was rather insulting to my vanity."

Her laugh was soft and light. "I doubt your vanity suffered too greatly. You expected me to leap at your offer, I know, but my refusal was no reflection on your qualifications as a potential patron."

Bemused, Drew watched as she raised her glass to her lips to drink. He wasn't sure at what point he had let himself be charmed by Roslyn Loring, but he was—intensely. Despite his determination, he found himself enchanted by her warm character and lively wit.

Her eyes were still warm, he noted, but her gaze turned thoughtful as she contemplated him over the rim of her glass. "Perhaps we could simply be friends. My sister is married to Marcus now, so we may be seeing more of each other in the future. And I don't wish there to be any awkwardness between us." An elegant dimple flashed in her cheek. "You can treat me as you do Eleanor, as a younger sister."

He couldn't possibly think of this woman as his sister, Drew reflected. Not after kissing her the way he had, after tasting her delectable body the way he had. Not with the powerful lust he still felt for her.

And yet he was surprised to find that he could relax in her company. Perhaps it was because she didn't toady to him as most everyone else did. Or perhaps he was just no longer concerned that she might try to trap him in marriage.

"Friends it is," he said, raising his glass in salute.

They both drank to the agreement, before Drew settled in a wing chair across from her. "So tell me about your husband-hunting plans. You mean to assist Haviland with his ball next week?"

"Yes," Roslyn answered. "Before my mother left

us, she taught me a good deal about running a genteel household and hosting social entertainments. I believe I can help his lordship make his ball a success."

"And after that?"

"I'm not certain, but I will need to decide soon, since Haviland plans to remain here at his country villa for only a week or so after the ball to hold a houseparty for his relatives. Fanny promised to advise me, but I've had no time to give it much consideration with all the preparations for the wedding." Roslyn cocked her head, her eyes still glimmering with laughter. "To be truthful, Fanny suggested that I ask you to instruct me. I think she was jesting, but the idea has merit."

"Instruct you on what?" Drew asked warily.

"On the tricks a mistress uses to make her protector enamored of her."

He nearly choked on his wine. "That is hardly a topic for a proper young lady to be discussing with a gentleman," Drew rasped.

Roslyn laughed again. "Now who is being missish, your grace? I think we have already gone well beyond the bounds of propriety, don't you? A little further won't hurt."

"You are actually serious."

"Yes, of course. It is brazen of me, I know, but I have a great deal at stake, so it would behoove me to use any resources I can find. You are an acknowledged expert in mistresses, so I should like to hear your views on the subject."

Drew frowned. "I doubt my views could help you."

"Will you allow me to be the judge of that?"

He stared at her a long moment before giving in. "What do you want to know?"

"To begin with, why do you even employ a mistress?"

"For the usual reasons. Entertainment, companionship, pleasure."

"So what makes you choose one over the other? What qualities do you look for? I suppose beauty is a chief requirement?"

Drew gave the question some thought, trying to remember his criteria for his last inamorata. "Beauty is desirable, but I mainly want one who is undemanding."

"Who isn't possessive? Fanny said that was what made you give up your last mistress." When his eyebrow shot up, Roslyn smiled. "I am not asking to know the intimate details of your affairs. My question is purely academic—so I won't make the same mistake with Lord Haviland. What else appeals to you in a mistress?"

She wasn't going to relent, Drew realized. With mingled feelings of admiration and resignation, he settled back and stretched his long legs out in front of him. "I want one with enough wit to carry on an intelligent conversation. And, of course, she must be skilled at lovemaking."

That last qualification made Roslyn blush, but she pressed on. "Yet there must be more to making a man become enamored. According to Fanny, a good mistress knows how to drive her protector a little wild and even enslave him."

"And you want to enslave Haviland."

"I don't wish to go *that* far with the earl, merely rouse his ardor. I think you could advise me on how to achieve it."

Drew found himself unable to stifle his amusement. "You truly are unique, Miss Loring."

She wrinkled her nose at him. "I doubt you mean that as a compliment, but no matter. I don't mind that you have a low opinion of me, as long as you are willing to help me."

He didn't have a low opinion of her in the least. On the contrary, he was intrigued by her, even fascinated. He also liked that she was so refreshingly honest. But that didn't mean he wanted to have anything to do with helping her snare Haviland for her husband.

When he hesitated, she made a *tsk*ing sound. "I think you must be afraid of me."

"Afraid of you?"

"Yes. You are still concerned about compromising me. But I told you, you needn't worry. I wouldn't marry you under any circumstances."

"I am not afraid of you, darling."

"Then you should have no objection to teaching me what I need to know. You are reputed to be a magnificent lover. I would think you would want to prove it."

His body's response to her lighthearted words was quick and intense: His loins abruptly tightened.

"Are you challenging me, Beauty?"

"I believe I am."

Her musical laughter rippled through him. Drew stiffened, not liking the way arousal made itself felt in his groin.

When he didn't automatically take up her challenge, she took another tack. "Don't you realize it is in your self-interest for me to attach Lord Haviland?"

"How do you conclude that?"

"So Lady Freemantle will cease hounding you. As

long as you stay here, she will keep pushing us together. But we can foil her efforts if I acquire Haviland as a suitor. She won't want to spoil my chances with him if he is truly courting me."

Roslyn's disarming smile affected Drew more than he cared to admit. She was intent on getting her own way with charm, much like Marcus's minx of a sister. He could see Eleanor making such an outrageous request of him.

"You want me to tutor you in how to captivate Haviland so he will be eager to court you?"

"Yes, and so I can make him fall in love with me. I would be very grateful. And you would be doing Marcus a favor. He would be pleased if I could secure the earl for my husband. Marcus wanted to marry us off to perfect strangers, you know, when he first assumed our guardianship."

Drew shook his head in wry disbelief. "I must be daft to even consider it."

"But you want to," she pressed.

He couldn't respond with a denial. He had to admit he sympathized with her situation. Roslyn hadn't deserved the difficulties she'd faced for the past four years. And it was certainly true that Marcus wanted to see her wed so he could cease worrying about her.

"I will have to give it some thought," Drew said at last. "I am no authority on feminine arts of seduction."

"But you know what appeals to you . . . how a woman could captivate *your* interest."

I know how you *could captivate my interest,* Drew reflected silently. Judging from her wide-eyed innocent look, though, Roslyn had no idea how lascivious his thoughts were just now. How he wanted to lay her down and remove her gown very slowly, kissing each luscious creamy inch of her body. . . .

Drew shook himself, focusing on her request. His mouth curled sardonically as he debated. He recognized the irony of helping a scheming debutante lure a man to his matrimonial doom when he himself had always been so set against marriage. Yet it was a novel prospect, teaching a proper young lady to be an ideal mistress. Besides, if he had to remain in Chiswick to keep an eye on the Loring sisters because a highwayman was menacing the district, instructing Roslyn would make the time pass faster.

He had no intention of going beyond the bounds of real propriety, of course, for in all honor, he couldn't compromise the ward of his best friend without unwanted consequences.

To his surprise and amusement Drew found himself nodding. "Very well, I will give it a shot."

Roslyn offered him a brilliant smile that made him blink with its sheer beauty. "*Thank* you, your grace. I think I can manage to sleep now."

I am glad one of us can, Drew thought dryly. The image of Roslyn sleeping—her lovely body nude, her hair streaming across a satin pillow—played havoc with his loins.

His gaze settled on her ripe, tempting mouth, and his pulse quickened further as he fought the fierce urge to kiss her. There was a rational explanation for the rapid beating of his heart, for why this woman set his blood racing. It was pure lust of course.

The affliction would pass, he was certain.

Yet his fingers itched to free her golden hair from the confines of its elegant coiffure, to free her body from the confines of her stylish ballgown. He could picture taking her right here on the brocade couch, could imagine her coming alive in his arms, all yearning hunger. The thought of being inside her, that first thrust, made his groin ache. He wanted to bury himself in all that unawakened fire. . . .

The erotic image shattered when Roslyn set her glass down on a side table and rose to her feet. "Good night, your grace. I will see you in the morning when you confer with Winifred's bailiff."

Drew rose politely as well and bowed, ignoring the frustrating ache in his loins. "Good night, Miss Loring."

He watched as she turned away, his gaze drawn to the graceful sway of her hips as she left the parlor.

Blowing out a slow breath then, Drew ran a hand roughly through his hair. He couldn't believe he had actually agreed to give her lessons in how to arouse a gentleman's ardor. Especially when she presented such a powerful temptation to *him*.

But he could manage it, Drew told himself. He would be charming, distantly polite, even friendly.

Even so, he knew that keeping his hands off Roslyn would prove to be a severe exercise in self-control.

Chapter Six

✤

The art of flirtation is more difficult to master than I expected.

—Roslyn to Fanny

Roslyn rose early the next morning, eager to set in motion the search for the highwayman. To her surprise she found the duke already up before her, meeting in the study with the Freemantle bailiff.

Mr. Hickling expressed alarm at the danger she and her ladyship had faced during the holdup, but Roslyn assured him they hadn't suffered any lasting damage. When she described the place where the coach had been waylaid, he recognized it at once, since it was close to the farm belonging to his eldest son. Hickling took his leave shortly, promising to conduct a thorough search of the area.

When he was gone, Roslyn surveyed the duke. He hadn't yet shaved, so his jaw was shadowed by stubble, making his lean, aristocratic features look a trifle rugged. Yet he still managed to give the appearance of lithe elegance. Except for missing a cravat, he wore the same formal attire as he'd worn to the wedding, probably because the late Sir Rupert Freemantle was smaller of shoulder and much larger of girth.

Roslyn herself had changed into a modest muslin

round gown. She felt Arden's perceptive gaze survey her in turn.

"Did you have trouble sleeping?" he asked, his tone sympathetic.

"A little. I kept seeing that pistol pointed at us every time I closed my eyes."

"The dark images will pass eventually."

"You sound as if you speak from experience."

"I do." Arden glanced at the ormolu clock on the mantel. "I didn't expect you to rise so early."

"Nor I you, your grace."

Amusement flickered in his eyes. "No doubt you presumed I would laze abed till noon."

"Many noblemen of your stamp would."

"You have a rather low opinion of me, don't you, darling?"

Roslyn laughed. "You are improving upon better acquaintance, I must say."

Arden grinned. "Considering where I started, I should be gratified."

Pointon appeared at the study door just then to announce that breakfast awaited them. When they moved to the breakfast parlor, Winifred was already seated at the table, her plate piled high from an array of dishes on the sideboard. Evidently her hearty appetite had remained unaffected by the previous night's traumatic events, Roslyn noted.

When she inquired how Winifred was faring, her ladyship smiled. "Well enough, my dear. But I am so very grateful to the duke for electing to remain with us for a few days." She favored Arden with an even brighter smile while Pointon served her guests coffee. "It is comforting to know that you will be here to protect us from a vicious highwayman, your grace. Although we are less than an hour's drive from London and close enough that you could return home each night, it will be more convenient if you billet here at Freemantle Park. And of course," Winifred added, "you cannot stay at Danvers Hall while the new earl is gone, since Roslyn and Lily will be unchaperoned. Pointon will send to London for fresh clothing for you."

"I have already made arrangements, my lady," Arden replied mildly, apparently prepared to put up with her overbearing supervision.

Winifred proceeded to chatter on about how splendid the wedding had been, as if she was determined to forget the holdup had ever happened. Since Roslyn was of the same mind, the conversation remained light all through breakfast.

When her ladyship had exhausted the topic of nuptials, she proceeded to question the duke about his interest in governing the nation, but Arden replied that most of his work was done for now. Parliament had adjourned for the summer, and many of the noblemen in the House of Lords had left the heat of London for their family estates.

At the conclusion of breakfast, Winifred adopted an innocent look. "Perhaps you would like to see the Park, your grace. Roslyn can show you before she returns home to Danvers Hall this morning. Roslyn, my dear, why don't you take his grace to the charming little folly by the lake?"

Roslyn shared a brief glance with the duke, who was barely stifling his amusement. But she didn't protest, since showing him over the estate would allow them to escape Winifred's watchful eye, and she wanted a measure of privacy so she could continue the discussion they had begun last night.

"The grounds are indeed lovely this time of year," Roslyn murmured. "Just let me fetch my cloak, your grace." The sun was out, but the June morning would be a trifle cool.

When she had retrieved the garment from Pointon, she found the duke awaiting her in the entrance hall. She led him through the house to a side door, and once outside, she stayed to the gravel path so the dew wouldn't stain her slippers.

The park boasted beautifully landscaped lawns and gardens. In the distance atop a rise, she could see the folly that overlooked the ornamental lake, and she headed that way.

"I don't suppose you have changed your mind about me tutoring you," Arden began as they walked.

"No, I have not," Roslyn replied pleasantly. "I would very much like you to advise me on the feminine arts of seduction."

"I was afraid as much."

"Have you given any more thought to my questions?"

"Yes, sweetheart."

She glanced up at him expectantly. "I am all ears, your grace."

"I expect I should start with the easiest question—you asked me what appeals to me in a mistress. I thought of several more attributes I find favorable."

"And those are?"

"For one thing, a good mistress doesn't complain about neglect from her patron if he visits her infrequently."

"Her time is at his disposal, you mean?"

"Yes. And she doesn't overspend her allowance, running up huge bills at the modiste and milliner, or press him for more jewels."

Roslyn nodded thoughtfully. "It seems entirely reasonable that a patron wouldn't appreciate extravagance."

"Yes, and if he chooses to give her gifts, they should be at his discretion."

"In other words, if she wants him to lavish gifts on her, she should make his generosity seem like his own idea."

Arden's mouth curved at her teasing remark. "Just so. And she should want him for himself, not his wealth—or at least give the appearance of it."

Not replying, Roslyn cast a sideways glance at the duke. He seemed to have a great deal of experience being pursued for his wealth. It was obviously a sore point with him, much the way her appearance was with her. She had no doubt he was seen as a great prize, yet she knew very well his attractions were due to more than his fortune or his exalted title. In looks alone, he was far superior to other noblemen.

Against her will, she found her gaze lingering on him. His fair hair glimmered amber in the sunlight, while his features held an austere masculine beauty.

Admittedly, she herself felt a fierce attraction toward him, despite her determination never to be swayed by appearance. Yet she had discovered there was much more to Arden than met the eye. Despite his aristocratic elegance, he had a commanding look, a virile vital energy that suggested he was a man of substance. And his exhilarating charm and stimulating wit kept her on her toes—

Roslyn shook herself as they reached the folly, a small, circular edifice built of gleaming white marble resembling a Grecian temple. The folly had no walls, merely a roof supported by thick columns, while the open interior was adorned by marble statues and supplied with benches. She mounted the three steps and settled on one of the benches. Arden followed her inside but remained standing.

"What else does a successful mistress do?" she asked, determined to ignore his appeal.

"From what I've witnessed, she makes her patron the sole focus of her attention. She should occasionally flatter him and express admiration—but again, she must seem to be sincere. And she should at least appear to listen to what he says."

Roslyn lifted an eyebrow in amusement. "So she should compliment and admire him and hang on his every word, even if she finds little admirable about him and nothing interesting in his conversation?"

"Even so," Arden replied, his own tone edged with humor. "And as I said last night, she should see to his physical comfort and pleasure."

Roslyn couldn't help blushing a little. "We needn't go into detail about the carnal side of an affair, your grace. I will take your word for it."

Arden's eyes gleamed. "Your modesty is showing, love."

"I expect it is. It is a curse to have a complexion that displays embarrassment so easily."

"Then suffice it to say, she must leave him physically satisfied. But she should also keep the relationship purely on a physical level. A good mistress doesn't become overamorous or let her affections become engaged. She never lets emotion get in the way of a business transaction, and she certainly never expects love to be the outcome."

Roslyn couldn't help but smile as she contemplated the duke. "I can clearly see that *you* would not want something so bothersome as love to interfere with your pleasure. Fortunately my situation with Haviland is not a business arrangement, so it won't matter if my affections are engaged by him, as long as it is not one-sided."

"True, but a mistress is making a contract for services rendered."

"I understand. As you said last night, you want your lover to be undemanding."

"But the reverse is also true. Fidelity is crucial. The worst offense she could make is to let her attention stray to another man while under his protection. She must have eyes only for him . . . which leads me to my first lesson. In order to begin a dalliance with Haviland, you need to learn how to conduct a subtle flirtation."

"So how do I manage that?"

"I intend to teach you. The surest way to kindle his interest is to speak to him with your eyes."

"My eyes?" She shook her head in amusement.

"You can communicate a great deal with just a glance."

"Such as?"

"Such as the fact that you are interested in him, that you find him appealing. Gaze at him a long moment. Flutter your eyelashes at him a little."

"How fascinating."

The duke ignored her impudence. "And then there is your mouth."

"I cannot wait to hear this one," she remarked dryly.

"This is gravely important, darling," Arden chided, his tone laced with mocking amusement. "If you mean to ridicule every suggestion I make—"

"No, please . . . my apologies. Do proceed." Roslyn disciplined her expression to soberness, even though it was hard.

"As I was saying, you need to draw his attention to your mouth. Purse your lips into a pout. . . . Subtly touch your fan to your lips, that sort of thing. Just make it provocative."

Roslyn laughed out loud at that. "I am sorry, but I find it hard to credit that a man with any claim to intelligence would fall for batting eyelashes and pouting lips."

Arden gave her a stern look. "Do you want me to continue or not?"

"Yes, of course."

"Then behave yourself, Beauty. Now show me a pout."

Roslyn tried to comply. She pursed her lips into a moue while glancing up at him through her lowered eyelashes. Arden responded by dropping his gaze to her mouth . . . which was precisely what was supposed to happen. But then she spoiled the effect when she couldn't hold the pose; unable to keep a straight face, she broke into laughter again. It was all too absurd.

"This may be impossible," she finally said when her laughter subsided.

Arden didn't scold her as she expected. Instead he regarded her with a tolerant look, clearly amused to watch her efforts. "Hopefully you will get better with practice."

"Perhaps I should forget all about this."

"Are you giving up so easily, sweetheart? I never would have supposed you to be a quitter."

Roslyn lifted her chin at his challenge, no doubt as he intended. "Of course I am not a quitter. But I just find it hard to believe this will work."

"You don't have to take my word for it. You can apply to Eleanor for confirmation. She is two years younger than you but has far more experience with the courting game. You are a mere babe compared to her."

She didn't know Marcus's sister well enough to quiz her on such a delicate topic. "I think perhaps I had best rely on Fanny."

"But I am available now." Leaning back against a column, Arden crossed his arms. "You need to try again with me before you have to face Haviland this afternoon. I will be your test subject."

"Really, this isn't necessary, your grace. I have already put you to enough trouble."

"You wanted to learn how to seduce a man, didn't you?"

"Yes, but—"

"Then do it. Stand up, angel. Pretend I have walked into a room and spied you. What is the first thing you do?"

Roslyn brought her hands up to her suddenly flushed cheeks. "I haven't the faintest idea."

"Have you observed your pupil, Miss Newstead? Mimic her actions."

She could do that much, Roslyn thought, recalling how Sybil Newstead had tried to catch the duke's attention last night at the wedding ball.

Obediently she rose to her feet. Then taking a deep breath, she pasted a teasing smile on her lips and slowly crossed the folly in front of him, swaying her hips in a brazen display of coquetry. When she reached one side, she paused to flash him a flirtatious glance over her shoulder before sauntering back across the marble floor.

It encouraged her to see the duke watching her avidly. Throwing her heart into the role, Roslyn tossed her head and made a moue, then primped her hair and smoothed her skirts just as she had seen Sybil do a hundred times.

Arden threw back his head and laughed. "I daresay that's a fair imitation of the little minx."

"I am gratified you appreciate my efforts," Roslyn murmured.

"Now make it much more subtle."

She made another effort, this time toning down her performance, her movements more hesitant and sensual.

Arden nodded in approval. "Not bad for a novice. Now, come here."

"Why?" Roslyn said pertly.

He grinned. "Because you need more practice."

She did as he bid, moving to stand before him. "What next?"

"Look into my eyes. Pretend that I am the only man you could ever be interested in."

Roslyn locked eyes with him . . . and promptly felt her breath falter. The deep vibrant green held her spellbound. It was a mere glance, yet time seemed to stop. And just like before, a sizzling spark of awareness arced between them.

Fighting the power of it, Roslyn struggled to catch her breath. The sparks didn't mean a thing, she told herself. The duke was merely giving her a lesson in dalliance. To construe anything intimate or sexual in it was ridiculous.

Then her gaze dropped to his mouth, that firm, sensual mouth that had shown her such pleasure a fortnight ago. She felt the strongest longing to kiss him—and an even more powerful craving to have him kiss her the way he had that night. The temptation of that warm, sensual mouth was nearly impossible to resist.

Jerking her scandalous thoughts to order, Roslyn tore her gaze away and stepped back. Chastising herself for her inexplicable reaction, she cleared her throat that had suddenly grown dry and made a supreme effort to pretend indifference. "Thank you, your grace. I believe that is enough instruction for one day. You have given me ample ideas to practice on the earl this afternoon."

Arden's gaze had turned enigmatic, she saw, but then his mouth slanted sardonically. "I expect a report on your success, sweeting. It should prove highly interesting."

"Very well. I owe you that much."

Relieved that he didn't press her further, Roslyn turned away. She had imposed on the Duke of Arden far enough. It was high time she went home and set in motion her campaign to win Lord Haviland.

Thankfully there were no more chances for intimacy with the duke before Roslyn took her leave of

Freemantle Park. By the time she reached home, Arabella and Marcus were gone, having set out an hour before on their wedding trip.

The butler and housekeeper were supervising the servant staff in cleaning up after the ball. After conferring with the Simpkins, Roslyn settled in the morning room to begin cataloging the vast array of wedding gifts the guests had sent to the Earl of Danvers and his new countess.

She had made good progress when a short while later her younger sister entered. A frown drew down Lily's mouth while her cheeks were unusually flushed.

"Whatever is wrong?" Roslyn asked in concern.

"Nothing that I care to discuss," Lily replied cryptically. She surveyed Roslyn intently. "What about you, Rose? Tess and I were appalled to get your note this morning explaining why you stayed with Winifred last night. We called at the Park, but you had just left, so Winifred told us all about the highway robbery. It sounds as if you were very brave."

"I was frightened out of my mind," Roslyn replied dryly. "But at least no one was harmed."

"Except for the brigand. I understand Hickling has initiated a search for a wounded man."

Roslyn nodded. "Yes, although we don't hold out much hope of finding him." She eyed her sister again, noting that Lily's normal high spirits were nowhere in evidence. "Are you certain you are all right? You look as if something has upset you."

"I am not upset. I merely have a touch of the headache, and having Tess drive me home in her gig didn't help."

"Why don't you sit down and have some tea? Mrs. Simpkin just brought in a fresh pot."

"You always think tea is such a great restorative," Lily complained, although she sank down beside Roslyn on the settee. "A dose of Marcus's brandy would be more helpful."

"It is far too early for brandy—not that a lady should even be drinking anything so potent."

"You sound just like Arabella."

Roslyn fixed a stare on her younger sister. "Arabella is concerned—and rightly so—that you've turned into a little hellion."

Shaking off her dark mood, Lily managed to grin. "I know. But I have no desire to pretend to be a lady."

"You are a lady all the same. And if I remember, you don't even like brandy."

"True. But I am told that it might help with my throbbing head." Flashing a rueful smile, Lily leaned forward to pour herself a cup of tea. "You see, I got rather foxed last night at the ball. I should know better, since spirits make me tipsy, including champagne. But I drank three glasses of it because I was feeling sad at losing Arabella, and now I am sincerely regretting my indulgence."

"Is that all that is wrong, Lily?"

Surprisingly, her cheeks flushed a deeper pink. "Well, perhaps not *all*. Winifred is still driving me to distraction with her maddening attempts at match-making."

"I know," Roslyn agreed wholeheartedly. "I was her target last night and again this morning. You were right about her wanting to pair me with Arden. It was mortifying in the extreme."

"Well, I don't intend to remain here to become Winifred's hapless victim," Lily said decisively. "I mean to go to London and stay at Fanny's boarding-house. She has room, and she has asked my advice in dealing with two of her friends who run the house. I don't know if I can help them, but I would like to try."

Roslyn stared at her sister in surprise. "You intend to hide in London in order to elude Winifred's match-making schemes? Are such drastic measures really necessary?"

Lily grimaced. "I am beginning to think so. If I can't be found, then I needn't worry about any unwanted suitors, do I? I cannot stay in Chiswick, obviously. And no one will think to look for me at Fanny's place, including Marcus, thankfully. You know he would not approve of my intimacy with her particular friends." Lily's tone suddenly became more cheerful. "I have it! You can tell Winifred and anyone else who inquires that I have gone to Hampshire to visit friends at our old home."

Roslyn's brows drew together in a puzzlement. "Why would you want her to think—"

"Please, Rose, just humor me this once."

Wondering if she should be concerned, Roslyn searched her sister's face. "Lily . . . is there more you aren't telling me?"

"Not at all. Don't worry about me, dearest. It is noth-ing I cannot handle." Lily smiled reassuringly before adding under her breath, "I simply have absolutely no intention of allowing any man to court me."

Roslyn would have prodded her sister further, but Lily clearly didn't wish to discuss the subject. And since she was perfectly capable of knowing her own mind and dealing with her own problems, Roslyn decided to focus on her own immediate affairs—chiefly preparing for her three o'clock meeting with Lord Haviland to discuss his upcoming ball.

When Roslyn finally finished her appointed task of itemizing wedding gifts, she started making lists of the countless details that needed to be decided on in order to conduct a ball of large magnitude.

At half past two, she went upstairs to change her attire with the help of their lady's maid, Nan. Making use of the new wardrobe Marcus had funded, Roslyn donned a stylish gown of blue jaconet that was the same color as her eyes. Then she returned downstairs to the small salon, where she intended to receive her guest, since it was much more informal and comfortable than the drawing room, which had been totally refurbished by Arabella in the past month.

Roslyn felt a measure of excitement as she waited for the earl to arrive, but she forced herself to keep from glancing out the window more than once every few minutes. Instead she went over in her mind the techniques of flirtation that Arden had taught her this morning . . . eyes, mouth, flattery. . . .

She found herself smiling anew while wondering if his tricks would have any effect on Haviland. She hoped so. She would sometimes daydream of the earl, imagining how their courtship would go. He would be irresistibly drawn to her from the first, and in a very short time, declare his love and ask for her hand in marriage.

Perhaps, Roslyn ruminated, she had concocted a mere fairy tale, but if she could kindle his desire for her in any way, she was willing to exert her best effort, including developing her skill at coquetry, despite the fact that she was not really cut out for such pretenses.

Haviland arrived promptly at three, but to her surprise, he was not alone; when he was shown into the salon by Simpkin, he was accompanied by the Duke of Arden. The two noblemen seemed to be on amiable terms, although they claimed to have met at her front door.

Roslyn looked a question at Arden, wondering why he had chosen to call at this precise moment when he knew she had an appointment with the earl.

"I thought you might like a report on the search for our highwayman," he answered without prodding.

Haviland's heavy eyebrows drew together sharply. "What highwayman?"

He had not yet heard about last night's holdup, so Roslyn was required to relate the events.

"What is being done about it?" Haviland wanted to know.

The duke answered for her, telling him about the search the Freemantle servants had conducted this morning. "They canvassed the district for the brigand, but found no traces of blood anywhere, or any real clues to follow. He could have taken refuge anywhere, even as far as London."

"Perhaps we should have armed footman patrol the roads for the next few nights," Haviland suggested.

"It is already being done," Arden replied.

"Good. And we should alert the local citizens to be on the lookout and to keep their possessions well guarded. I don't want to alarm anyone unnecessarily, but they should take precautions."

Simpkin arrived with the tea tray just then, and Roslyn invited the earl to sit beside her on the settee. If she expected Arden to take his leave, however, she was disappointed, for he settled comfortably in a wing chair and showed no signs of retreating. And as she poured for the gentlemen, he changed the subject to the earl's ball, which vexed and dismayed her more than a little. She had hoped for some time alone with Lord Haviland and had not expected to have an audience.

But since the duke apparently intended to give her no choice, Roslyn summoned a smile and asked Haviland what plans had been made for the ball.

"My housekeeper has already arranged for flowers and musicians and more serving staff, but she would be grateful for your advice on the menu, since she has never been required to feed such distinguished company. There will be a dinner beforehand for two dozen guests, and a late buffet supper at midnight. And I would welcome your help with the social niceties— where to place the reception line, how to seat the guests by rank, that sort of thing."

"I would be happy to help," Roslyn said. "It would be best if I inspected your house and met with your butler and housekeeper. And I should like to see the guest list."

"I have brought it with me." Haviland drew out a sheaf of papers and handed it to her.

Roslyn glanced down the long list, which contained some two hundred members of the ton, many of whom had attended the Danvers wedding celebrations. When she was finished, the duke surprised her by asking to see it.

"I can probably assist in this respect," Arden said, "since I'm acquainted with a good number of the ton."

Roslyn handed it over without demur. No doubt he *could* help, since he moved in the highest circles of society and knew everyone of consequence.

While he perused the list of guests, she picked up her own list of requirements for a successful ball and began to review the various categories with the earl to make certain they had been properly considered. Haviland moved nearer to her, the better to see, and bent his head close to hers.

The intimate position would have offered Roslyn the perfect opportunity to initiate her intended flirtation with him—if not for her keen awareness that they were not alone. The duke was watching her too closely for comfort, which made her exceedingly self-conscious. Yet whenever she glanced up at Arden, he merely raised an innocent eyebrow and sipped his tea.

When eventually she narrowed her eyes at him, he merely smiled, his gaze gleaming a challenge, as if daring her to order him out.

His presence flustered Roslyn so that she could barely concentrate on the plans for the ball. When she was done reviewing her lists with Haviland, she set an appointment for eleven o'clock the following morning to inspect his house for herself and meet with his upper servant staff. A few minutes later he rose and took his leave after thanking her sincerely.

When he was gone, Roslyn turned to Arden with an undisguised look of exasperation. "What do you mean, your grace, intruding on us that way? I had hoped for privacy with Lord Haviland."

His expression remained mild in the face of her

obvious pique. "I wanted to see you employ your new skills on him."

"So you came to critique my performance?"

"And to observe so that I could offer you pointers." He shook his head ruefully. "I admit I was not impressed by your lackluster attempts at flirtation, darling."

His remark provoked her even more. "How could you expect me to flirt with him with you watching my every move?"

The duke settled back in his chair. "You shouldn't let yourself be discomfited. Conducting a dalliance under public scrutiny is all part of the game."

Roslyn's hands went to her hips. "It is *your* scrutiny that discomfits me."

"Why? I am merely your tutor."

Her frustration only rose. "I asked you to help me, not hinder me! Why did you even come here today?"

Arden shrugged. "Would you believe boredom? I found myself at loose ends, cooling my heels at Freemantle Park with nothing to do. And I decided that watching you with Haviland might prove entertaining."

"So you decided to use us for your own personal amusement?" Roslyn asked dangerously.

His expression sobered. "Not entirely. The truth is I wanted to escape Lady Freemantle before I throttled her. Her enthusiasm for conversation is enough to drive a saint mad. But you are right to be annoyed with me. Pray accept my apologies."

Somewhat mollified by his explanation, Roslyn felt her ire fading. The duke had only remained at the Park out of chivalry. She couldn't blame him for wanting to escape Winifred.

"I understand your impatience with Lady Freeman-tle," Roslyn said more softly. "She does tend to get a bit giddy when she has a captive audience. But it is because she is lonely—a widow with no children or family relations. And she has few friends in the neighborhood because of her lower-class origins."

"But you understand why I might want to take refuge here?"

"Yes, and you are welcome here, of course."

"Thank you, Beauty."

She gave him another exasperated look. "I wish you would not call me that, your grace. You know my feelings on the subject of appearance. You needn't keep reminding me of mine."

His mouth curved. "You will have to become accustomed to an occasional endearment if you mean to become more intimate with Haviland."

"How can I become more intimate when you won't allow me the chance?"

"Point taken. Very well, it won't happen again."

"I trust not. I begin to believe I can do better on my own."

He raised an eyebrow. "Are you saying you no longer want my advice on how to win Haviland?"

Roslyn hesitated. "No, I am not saying that at all. But you needn't be so . . . provoking."

"Fair enough. Sit down so we can discuss your performance. You fell short in several areas, I'm afraid."

Reluctantly Roslyn returned to the settee. "What was wrong with my performance?"

Clasping his fingers over his stomach, Arden surveyed her thoughtfully. "For one thing, you were too businesslike just now. You should make an effort to be more feminine with Haviland. Strive to be a little less dictatorial and managing."

She frowned. "But Haviland seems to esteem my management skills."

"Do you want him to see you as his majordomo or as his potential lover?"

"His lover, of course."

"Then leave the generalship to his servant staff. For a moment or two there, you were so commanding you reminded me of my mother."

"You have a mother?" Roslyn asked archly.

He grinned. "What did you expect? That I was hatched?"

"I would not be surprised."

His grin took on a satirical slant. "My mother is a dragon, but I'm told I came into the world in quite the usual way."

Roslyn heard the sharp note in his tone at the mention of his mother, but she was more interested in returning to the subject of her deficiencies with Haviland. "Where else did I go wrong?"

"You might want to temper your frankness a little. Some men may find your brand of forthrightness off-putting."

"Do you?" she asked curiously.

"No, but we're not concerned with my likes. Haviland will respond better to a sweeter tone. And whatever you do, don't flay him with your sharp tongue."

Disheartened, Roslyn sank back against the settee. "I am not likely to flay Haviland. More often I find myself at a loss for words with him."

"Somehow that surprises me," Arden said dryly.

"Well, it is true."

"I suspect you are too eager to earn his good opinion, whereas with me, you have no compunction at telling me off to my face."

"Because I have no desire to impress you."

"So quit trying so hard with Haviland. Simply be yourself. You are charming and personable enough to let your natural self shine through."

She stared at him. "Merciful heavens, I believe you just complimented me."

"I suppose I did."

His green eyes glimmered at her, making her pulse quicken. Shaking herself, though, Roslyn managed a smile. "Well, thank you for the lesson, your grace. I will try to do better next time."

"If you like, I will call on you tomorrow morning before your meeting with Haviland and give you another lesson."

"I would appreciate that. For now, however . . ." Bending, she gathered up her lists and stood. "If you will excuse me, I still have a great deal to do. But please make yourself at home for as long as you like. If you care for more tea—or something stronger like wine or brandy—just ring for Simpkin."

Politely rising to his feet as she left, Drew found himself grinning ruefully at having been dismissed once more. But he could not have expected a warmer welcome from Roslyn when he'd intruded on her privacy so flagrantly.

He'd answered her question truthfully; escaping Lady Freemantle was the chief reason he'd come here when he was clearly unwanted. Boredom was also a part of it. And curiosity. He had wanted to see how Roslyn would behave with Haviland, to discover how far she would take her campaign.

But once he was here, some perverse part of him wanted to provoke her, to rouse that flash of passion in those blue eyes.

An even more idiotic part of him had wanted to pull her into his arms and kiss that lovely mouth, to make love to that alluring body. . . .

Drew laughed softly as he remembered her response to his careless endearment when he'd called her "Beauty." Roslyn was absurdly prickly on the subject of appearance—a unique oddity in his experience. He'd never before known a woman to complain about being *too* beautiful.

He certainly couldn't fault her for her extraordinary beauty. Admittedly he derived pleasure from simply gazing at her; he was a red-blooded man, after all.

But Roslyn was also unique in other respects. He found her innocence rather endearing after the calculated arts his former mistresses employed. Her smile was fresh and honest, not sophisticated and cynical. He hated to see that freshness ruined by the scheming games played by the femmes fatales she was attempting to mimic.

Drew abruptly shook his head. He had fulfilled his promise to her for the time being. How she applied his advice was really not his concern.

He had no reason to remain at Danvers Hall any longer, either. In fact, there was nothing more he could do here in Chiswick at the moment, Drew decided. He might as well take himself off to London for the evening and spend a few pleasant hours at his club.

Or better yet, resume his search for a mistress. If he was able to lose himself in a lush female body, then perhaps he wouldn't find the lovely Roslyn Loring quite so damned appealing.

Chapter Seven

Your list is highly enlightening, dear Fanny, even if I have some doubts about my ability to follow your counsel.

—Roslyn to Fanny

For her lesson the next morning, Roslyn awaited the duke in the library, since she felt most at ease there and thus should be better able to hold her own with him there. Reading had always been her favorite pastime, the library her refuge and her haven whenever the tribulations of life became too difficult.

She was curled up on a cushioned window seat—her preferred spot because it offered both comfort and ample light—when Arden was shown into the room. He was dressed much less formally today, his buff riding breeches and burgundy coat more appropriate to the attire of a country gentleman, but the superb London tailoring only emphasized his devilish virility.

Setting aside her history tome, Roslyn rose to greet him, then watched as Arden glanced appreciatively around the library. Every wall was filled floor to ceiling with gleaming walnut shelves of leather-bound books.

"Impressive," Arden murmured, inspecting the titles on the nearest wall.

"What is impressive?" she asked curiously.

"That you would have tackled a collection of this size. Eleanor said you had read most of the volumes here."

"Except the ones in Greek, since I never learned. Regrettably I was never able to attend university because I wasn't born male."

Arden gave her an amused look. "You actually wanted to learn Greek?"

She felt her cheeks warm but lifted her chin. "It would have been helpful to know the original language of the classics. As it was, I had to rely on translations."

Not replying, he moved on to the next section. "Judging from the titles here, I would say that significant thought went into compiling this collection."

Roslyn smiled at his surprised tone. "It did. My step-uncle was a skinflint except when it came to his books. His scholarly bent was the chief thing I admired about him."

"From what I hear, there was little else to admire about the late Lord Danvers," the duke said dryly.

"Yes, well. . . . It isn't polite to speak ill of the dead, but he was very . . . disagreeable."

Roslyn crossed the room to a chair and invited Arden to have a seat on the sofa opposite her. "I am happy to report that a letter from Fanny arrived this morning. She made out a list of suggestions for me to consider."

"Regarding tricks of the mistress trade?" he asked as he settled on the sofa.

"Yes, or rather, her advice on how to captivate a gentleman."

"What does she have to say?"

Drawing out three close-written sheets from the pocket of her skirt, Roslyn decided to read parts of Fanny's letter aloud so she could question the duke about the effectiveness of some of the techniques.

"Her first recommendations have to do with physical appearance . . . grooming, clothing, hairstyles . . . which we needn't go into. Then—"

"Why not? You could use some improvement in that area."

"Perhaps," Roslyn retorted, "but I believe Fanny's counsel will be sufficient on such intimate subjects as my personal grooming. Now where was I? Oh, yes. After that she discusses how to attract a man's attention in other ways. She begins by saying 'It is imperative to be a good listener.' "

Arden smiled. "I already told you as much."

"I remember." Roslyn let her gaze sweep further down Fanny's list. "She also says a woman must learn to exchange witty banter, but not so witty as to intimidate her potential patron. To quote: 'Her purpose should be to make him feel clever, never dull and insipid.' "

"Quite wise," Arden agreed. "He will preen his feathers if he feels clever."

Roslyn shot the duke an amused glance. She wouldn't have to work to make *him* feel clever, since he had a sharp mind and was rarely without a quick comeback.

Returning to her list, she read the next recommendation. " 'Make him feel strong and powerful, as if he is the most important person you have ever known. In short, make him feel like the most fascinating man alive.' "

"Your friend Fanny is highly perceptive. Does she suggest *how* to make him feel fascinating?"

"Not really, only that she should make him the sole focus of her attention, which is precisely what you advised."

"Has Fanny any advice other than what I suggested?"

"There are several ideas regarding the woman's behavior. For one thing, she suggests being a little mysterious. 'If you have secrets,'" Roslyn quoted, "'he will be eager to ferret them out.'"

"What sort of secrets?"

"She doesn't say. But I suspect she would agree with you—that honesty and frankness are not the best policy."

Arden nodded. "What else?"

"'There are times when she should remain a little elusive. She should make him pursue her in order to spark his interest. Under no circumstance should she appear to chase him.'"

"I agree. Even if you *are* chasing him, you cannot let him know it, since that's the fastest way to drive him away. Pray continue."

"'Sometimes,'" Roslyn read, "'you should make him wait for your favors, to rouse his . . .' never mind."

"Rouse his what?" he prodded.

"'His lust to a fever pitch,'" Roslyn said hurriedly. Knowing Arden's eyes would be gleaming with laughter, she carefully avoided his gaze as she moved on to the next item. "'Strive to be unforgettable. Be different from anyone he has pursued before. The trick is to make him think of you frequently, to yearn to be with you and only you.'"

"That seems excellent advice," Arden observed.

"Yes," she replied, perusing the last page.

When she folded the list and returned it to her pocket, he raised an eyebrow. "Is that all?"

Roslyn felt her face warm. "No, but the rest has to do with physical aspects of attracting a gentleman's ardor."

"I should very much like to read it," he said innocently.

She gave him a sharp glance. "No doubt you would, but it is too risqué for me to discuss with you."

"Your modesty is showing again, fair charmer."

She ignored the endearment, just as she ignored his provocative tone. "The question is, how do I apply Fanny's advice in my dealings with Lord Haviland? Her suggestions all seem rather abstract."

"True, but you are getting ahead of yourself."

"What do you mean?"

"You cannot overlook the physical aspect of seduction. It is much too important."

Vexingly, Roslyn felt her blush increase. "I don't intend to ignore it, your grace. I merely would rather discuss such details with Fanny."

"You should call me Drew. If I am to be your tutor, we can dispense with the formalities."

Certain she didn't want to be on such intimate terms with him, Roslyn shook her head. "Thank you, but the formalities will do perfectly well."

"As you wish," he said amiably, but then he held out his hand. "Come here, sweetheart."

Giving him a wary glance, she hesitated. "Why?"

"Because I mean to give you your next lesson."

Suddenly recalling their situation, Roslyn checked the clock on the mantel. "I doubt I have time for another lesson. My appointment with Lord Haviland is set for eleven."

"We have plenty of time for this. You are only going next door. Now come here."

His charming smile did nothing to reassure her, but she obeyed, albeit reluctantly. Rising, Roslyn moved to sit beside him on the sofa, holding her spine stiff.

"Closer," the duke ordered. "This won't hurt, I promise."

That is what worries me, she thought nervously. She was afraid his demonstration would be too pleasurable, not too painful. But she shifted closer so that only a few inches separated them. "Now what?"

"Give me your hand. I want to show you one of your most effective feminine weapons—the power of a simple touch."

Roslyn's brows snapped together. "Is this really necessary?"

"It's not only necessary but important. You need to learn just how arousing a careless brush of fingertips on bare skin can be."

"Can't you just explain it to me?"

"Not effectively. There are some things that must be experienced."

"Very well then," she said, holding out her hand.

His fingers curled over hers, letting her feel their warmth. Then turning her hand over, he slowly began to stroke the center of her palm with a fingertip.

Roslyn's breath caught in her throat, and it was all she could do not to show it. She stared down at their joined hands, wondering how he managed to infuse such sensuality into a mere touch.

"When you are with Haviland, you should contrive to touch him occasionally," Arden murmured.

"Why?" she asked, striving to keep her voice even.

"In order to increase his awareness of you."

There was no denying her awareness of the man beside her; she was maddeningly conscious of his body next to hers. Yet she was determined to pretend indifference to him, despite the arousing effect he had on her senses. There would be no repetition of that awkward moment in the folly yesterday when she had longed to kiss him.

His stroking fingertips skimmed over the heel of her palm to her wrist. "Make it seem accidental if you can. Just graze his skin with the slightest pressure. He will feel it, believe me."

She had no trouble believing him; even that light caress left her breathless.

Then Arden shifted his attention further upward, letting his fingers glide along the sleeve of her gown to her elbow. The glancing touch sent pleasure rippling all the way up her arm and down again to her breasts, assaulting Roslyn with a potent memory of their passionate encounter on the balcony during the Cyprians' ball. A heated tremor eddied deep in the pit of her stomach at the remembrance.

"See how powerful a mere touch can be?" he asked, his gaze locking with hers.

"Yes . . . I see."

"You should consider it a chief weapon in your arsenal."

His caress was indeed a weapon, Roslyn realized; a weapon of sensual enticement. It ignited an explosion of sensations in every part of her. And that was even before he brought his hand to her face and grazed her jawline with his fingertips.

Her pulse became a rapid tripping as he traced her cheekbone with his thumb and down over her lower lip.

The erotic gesture reminded her of the fantasies she'd woven of the duke's hands and mouth after that first stunning experience with him. She hadn't been able to forget his expert ministrations.

But of course, Roslyn thought as she struggled to calm her racing heartbeat, a legendary lover like Arden would know just how to make the most of a simple touch. He was clearly a master with women. His skilled hands knew just where to linger, how to arouse.

As if to prove that very point, his fingers curled beneath her chin and slid down to the hollow of her throat. A tremor coursed downward between her legs in liquid warmth, shocking her with its strength.

Roslyn tried to swallow as slowly Arden ran the back of his hand down her throat to her collarbone and then lower to the neckline of her gown. When his fingers hovered over her bodice, her mouth parted in a breathless protest. . . .

And then suddenly he stopped. To her vast relief, his hand fell away.

There was an unreadable light in his eyes as he scrutinized her. "There," he said casually, "that should give you some indication of your power."

The careless remark was like a douse of chill water.

Stiffening, Roslyn forced a bland smile. "That was very . . . educational, your grace. And now I had best try to put your instruction into practice."

"Yes, you should go now. You don't want to keep Haviland waiting."

Smoothing her skirts, Roslyn rose and made her way to the library door, where she risked a backward glance at the duke. She couldn't tell at all what he was thinking, though; he hid his thoughts so skillfully behind that lean, handsome face.

"Won't you wish me luck, your grace?" she asked, deliberately imbuing her voice with a note of flirtation.

His mouth twisted in an ironic half smile. "I doubt you need any luck, sweeting. You're sure to be a success if you apply the arts you've learned. I expect a report when you're done. I shall wait for you here."

"As you wish, your grace."

When she was gone, Drew blew out a long breath as he fought against his maddening feelings of desire and his even more irrational pique. Admittedly Roslyn's appearance of cool serenity irked him. He had to be losing his touch with the fairer sex if she could remain so unaffected when he was throbbing with heat from such a simple encounter.

"Hell and the devil," Drew swore at himself. "You were a fool to become so involved with her."

His lessons in seduction had unexpectedly backfired on him, he realized. He'd craved to take his instruction much further just now. He'd wanted Roslyn to touch him in return, wanted those delicate hands caressing his own body, drifting over his bare skin. . . .

It had required supreme willpower to draw away from her. Just that brief physical contact had left him in a state of severe sexual frustration.

Drew grimaced, feeling his erection straining painfully against his breeches. The innocent enchantress had no idea how powerfully she aroused him. The damnable truth was, he wanted her. More than he could remember wanting any woman. And he was beginning to be positively haunted by visions of bedding her.

He muttered another mild oath. His loins were aching, no doubt because he hadn't sated his lust in the scented arms of a courtesan last night as he'd expected to. When it came right down to it, the thought of taking his pleasure with a voluptuous tart had held little appeal, especially when he kept comparing all the Cyprians he knew to Roslyn's elegant, regal beauty.

But his decision to abstain last night had left his control with her this morning tenuous at best.

His jaw taut, Drew closed his eyes. He would have to assuage the painful pressure in the privacy of his bedchamber tonight, he knew. If he didn't give himself relief soon, he might very well lose control with Roslyn and do something they would both regret.

Even now he couldn't restrain his lascivious thoughts about her, couldn't help picturing her there with him. His imagination insisted on undressing her . . . stripping her gown away and baring her exquisitely lovely body . . . laying her back against the sofa.

She looked wildly desirable, her golden hair spilling over her shoulders in a pale, tawny mane, her ripe breasts beckoning, her creamy thighs parted in invitation. In his fantasy he covered her with his body and sank into her, thrusting deep and hard. He could almost feel her inner tightness, her sleek warmth as her sheath clenched and shivered around him. . . .

Grinding his jaw in frustration, Drew rose abruptly. He couldn't explain why Roslyn filled him with such hunger, but he was not about to let his lust for the woman run away from him.

"You would be mad to cross that line," Drew muttered to himself.

Still aching and restless, he took a turn around the library, yet his thoughts remained on Roslyn. She was supremely dangerous to him, but not only because he felt an extraordinary attraction to her. It was because she managed to get beneath his guard so easily. Except for Marcus's sister Eleanor, he had never been able to relax around a genteel young lady. He was always on the defensive, alert for matrimonial traps. But being himself with Roslyn felt entirely natural.

And so did his fierce sexual urges.

Giving in to them, however, was strictly forbidden. Not only was she under Marcus's protection, Drew reminded himself, but he had promised to help groom her to ensnare the affections of another man.

He suddenly frowned at the inexplicable twinge of jealousy that stabbed him. He had no right to be jealous. And in truth, he was eager to help her win Haviland as a suitor as soon as possible, so she would cease plaguing his own thoughts, and worse, his fantasies.

It might take some time, since Haviland appeared to view her as much as a cordial neighbor as a potential bride. Roslyn's affections weren't fully engaged yet, either, she had admitted so. Drew had carefully scrutinized her response toward the earl yesterday. While she'd been perfectly amiable, there was little sign they were more than friends, although she hoped for so much more.

Wondering what success she was having at the

moment, Drew strode to the window to look out, even though the landscaping prevented him from seeing the earl's estate next door. He was impatient for her return, yet she had barely been gone ten minutes, and would likely take a good while longer.

Chiding himself for even caring, he glanced down at the window seat where Roslyn had been sitting upon his arrival. When he picked up the heavy tome she'd been reading, his mouth curved at the title. . . . Volume VII of William Cobbett's *The Parliamentary History of England*.

Drew shook his head in mingled amusement and admiration. The contrast between Roslyn's delicate beauty and her scholarly mind was highly intriguing.

He'd always valued intellect and education. Marcus and Heath were his closest friends in large part because their minds were sharp enough to keep up with his. At university, he'd been the studious one. And his library at his London town house was even more extensive than this one. So he couldn't help but be pleased to find a woman with a thirst for knowledge as great as his own.

Remembering Roslyn's complaint that she had never been permitted to learn Greek, Drew found himself grinning. She was certainly not simply a beautiful featherhead. Rather she was extremely well read and well educated, with a sparkling intelligence that presented a challenge even to a man of his intellect.

In fact, he'd already read the twelve volumes of Cobbett's *History* that had been published to date and had a standing order with the publisher for future volumes. But he settled in the window seat with Volume

VII and lounged back, prepared to pass the time reading until Roslyn's return.

Perhaps she *should* have been born male, Drew thought, still amused, although it would have been a damned shame to waste all that remarkable beauty. A beauty she didn't even appreciate.

Chapter Eight

❧

Why do I feel such a vexing attraction for one man when I know I want another one entirely?

—Roslyn to Fanny

Roslyn returned home an hour later, disgruntled and severely disappointed in herself. She would rather not have to face the duke, but she found him awaiting her in the library as promised.

"So how did your seduction go?" he asked when she entered.

"Not as well as I hoped." Moving across the library, she sank heavily into a chair.

Arden left his place at the window seat to resume sitting on the sofa. "That's all you mean to say? Did you attempt to apply our advice?"

Roslyn summoned a wry smile. "Oh, I tried. But I was too self-conscious to be very successful."

The duke regarded her curiously. "But you contrived to touch Haviland?"

"Yes." *But it didn't work.* At first she couldn't bring herself to be so forward as to accidentally caress Haviland, or even to flirt with him. Her efforts felt too calculating. But just before she left, she'd let her fingers brush the earl's as she handed him her notes about the ball.

"And?" Arden prodded.

"And nothing." Roslyn made a face. "He didn't appear to feel anything at all."

"Perhaps you weren't overt enough."

"Perhaps." Yet she didn't believe that was the case. She hadn't elicited any reaction from Haviland whatsoever. Even more troubling, she hadn't felt the expected spark between them, either.

What vexed her most, however, was that while she was trying to kindle sparks in the Earl of Haviland, all she could think about was the flaming response that the Duke of Arden had ignited in her so effortlessly earlier this morning when he'd conducted his demonstration of the effectiveness of touching.

"You will have to be less subtle next time," the duke advised.

"There may not even be a next time," Roslyn said crossly. "We have already decided on all the details relating to the ball, such as where to place the flowers and musicians and reception line."

Arden gazed at her with amusement. "Then invite him over for luncheon or tea tomorrow."

"On what pretext?"

"I'm sure you can think of something. Tell him you want to learn more about his family, the haughty relations he wants to impress. Or you can discuss taking protective measures against the highwayman."

Roslyn frowned. "We held that discussion today. Haviland means to have armed grooms patrol the roads during his ball to thwart any holdups like the one Lady Freemantle and I suffered, even though there has been no further sign of the highwayman since."

"Good," the duke replied. "It will be best if he

assumes responsibility for the safety of the district. I plan to return to London tomorrow, since Lady Freemantle seems fully recovered from her ordeal."

Roslyn roused herself from her morose thoughts long enough to offer him a faint smile. "I wish to thank you again for staying to comfort her. It was very noble of you."

Arden grinned. "Indeed it was. So what do you mean to do about Haviland? Are you certain you even want to continue your campaign to win him?"

"Yes," she said stubbornly. "I am certain."

"Perhaps he isn't the right husband for you after all."

"Perhaps not, but I mean to discover that for myself. I still have hopes he can come to love me."

Arden cocked his head, surveying her. "Why this insistence upon marrying for love? Members of our class usually settle for marriages of convenience."

Roslyn couldn't hide her wince. "Because I don't want to end up like my parents. They were bitter enemies who relished hurting each other."

"Most ton marriages are not much better," Arden said sardonically.

"You are far too cynical, your grace."

"And your notions about love are far too idealistic."

Roslyn raised an eyebrow. "You think true love is merely a fairy tale?"

"Isn't it?"

"I don't believe so. I've never experienced genuine love myself, but I know it exists. My friend Tess Blanchard loved her betrothed very deeply before he was killed at Waterloo. And my mother found love with her second husband."

The duke shook his head. "Neither case is representative of genteel British marriages. Your friend's betrothed died, and your mother married a Frenchman."

"Arabella and Marcus certainly love each other."

His mouth curled, but he held his tongue.

Even so, Roslyn protested his skepticism. "You have seen them together. You cannot dispute how ardently they feel for each other."

He shrugged. "They fancy themselves in love for now, but I doubt it will last. I've witnessed too many couples profess to be madly in love until the first flush of lust wears off. Then they are left with nothing more than boredom—or worse."

Roslyn gave him an arch smile. "I would not expect your sentiments to be any different. Merely because you are reputed to be a marvelous lover does not mean you know a thing about love."

"Indeed, I don't. And I don't wish to know, either." His expression remained bland as he studied her. "It surprises me, though, that with your experience, you still believe you can make a love match. You said your parents' marriage was a battleground?"

"Yes. When I was young, they fought all the time." Even now their animosity was still intensely painful for Roslyn to remember, but she managed a shrug. "That, no doubt, is why I became 'bookish,' as you termed it."

"How so?"

"Books provided me an escape. During my parents' fights, I would hide in the library among my beloved books until their battles ended, cowering like a timid mouse."

"I can't imagine you cowering at anything."

Her mouth twisted wryly. "Oh, I did, believe me. I would crawl behind the window seat curtains and try to shut out their conflicts, but I couldn't stop myself from shaking. Sometimes I couldn't even hold a volume still enough to read." Her expression became bleak. "My sisters would usually find me and try to comfort me, but it was something I couldn't control."

Roslyn fell silent, recalling those dark, turbulent years of her girlhood. Both her sisters had worried for her. Lily would slip into the library where she was hiding and hold her hand, offering solace by chattering on about the latest kitten or foal born on the estate farms. Arabella, however, would drag them both out of doors, where they walked or rode for hours, returning only when they could be assured that their father had stormed out of the house and left their mother weeping bitter tears.

Arden remained silent, too, as he regarded her intently. His gaze was unreadable as usual, but Roslyn thought she saw a hint of softness there that seemed like sympathy.

Taking hold of herself, she shook off the uncomfortable vulnerability. She had no need for his pity. Yet the painful remembrance of her parents' unhappy marriage only reinforced her resolve to control her own fate.

"It was a long time ago," she said, forcing a lighter note into her tone. "But perhaps you see why I am determined to make Lord Haviland fall in love with me."

"Yes, I see." Arden slowly rose to his feet. "Take heart, sweeting. All is not lost. I will call on him now and see if I can encourage him."

Roslyn felt a sudden stab of unease. "What do you intend, your grace?"

"Merely to sing your praises a little. Don't worry, I will make it subtle. I need to speak to Haviland on several matters in any case, so he will never suspect my intentions."

She scowled. "I hope not. You said the last thing I should do is let him realize I am pursuing him. It would be nearly as detrimental if he thinks you are matchmaking."

"Matchmaking . . . God forbid." The duke gave a mock shudder. "But I suppose that is precisely what I am doing." He hesitated a moment. "If you like, I'll give you a final lesson before I leave for London tomorrow morning. You still need to work on a few shortcomings."

His provocative tone somehow made her distrustful. "What shortcomings?" she asked warily, trying not to feel insulted.

The smile he flashed her was irresistible. "I will tell you tomorrow."

Roslyn blinked, taken aback by the stunning impact of that potent male smile. The beauty of it made her heart lurch and her stomach flutter—both reactions she had never felt with Lord Haviland.

But before she could reply, the duke spoke. "Shall I see you at ten, then?"

"Yes, your grace."

When he had bowed himself out, Roslyn muttered a soft oath. She shouldn't let herself be so affected by her arousing tutor.

Of course, that was easier said than done. Even

though she'd braced herself against his devastating appeal, she was far more attracted to him than was wise.

She knew better than to fall under the duke's spell. Certainly she would never behave like the leagues of starry-eyed females who pictured themselves as his duchess. So what if his wicked smile set her pulse racing? If his mere nearness heightened her senses? Arden was a practiced lover who could charm and enchant any woman he pleased.

Not that he actually *wished* to enchant her. It was merely a natural skill that he utilized without thought. She would like to have even a fraction of his talent for seduction.

Roslyn felt herself frown. Was that what he'd meant by her shortcomings? Her inability to enchant the opposite sex? She had certainly failed with Haviland this morning.

At the very least she had to overcome her awkward reserve with the earl. That seemed to be her biggest obstacle at the moment—shedding her self-consciousness long enough to try out her newly learned techniques of seduction on him.

But hopefully the duke could show her how tomorrow.

It was generous of him to continue her lessons, Roslyn reflected, especially when he had such a disdain for love and marriage. It was also a little sad that he would never know the joy of a love match, as she hoped to do one day.

Abruptly reproving herself, Roslyn shook her head, determined to put Arden from her mind until tomorrow morning.

As long as he was prepared to help her, his beliefs about love mattered not a whit.

Despite his reluctance to be alone with Roslyn, Drew kept his promise to call at Danvers Hall the next morning. He wanted to get her lesson over with, for the sooner he succeeded in helping her win Haviland, the sooner he could wash his hands of her.

She was in the library again, he discovered when he was shown in by the butler, and she looked pleased to see him.

"Did you call on Haviland yesterday?" was the first question she asked while moving to sit in a wing chair.

"Yes," Drew answered as he settled in his usual place on the sofa. "We mainly discussed plans for his ball. I reviewed his guest list and gave him my opinion of those I knew."

"No doubt he appreciated it," Roslyn replied.

Drew shrugged. "I wouldn't care to be in his shoes, having to perform for the ton like a dancing bear at a fair."

"So do you mean to attend his ball?"

"Yes, I promised to make a show of support. Eleanor and her aunt are invited as well, and so is my friend Claybourne."

Roslyn's brow furrowed. "I trust the highwayman won't strike again that night. It would reflect poorly on Haviland if any of his guests were assaulted." She shuddered. "And I dread to think of someone else being threatened with a pistol, as we were."

"I plan to escort Lady Freemantle to the ball myself," Drew said. "If the brigand was specifically targeting her for the first robbery, as you believe, he may try a second time."

She gave him a fervent look. "Oh, thank you! I have worried about her safety."

"I think you may stop worrying. Haviland is taking extra precautions and has his defenses well in hand. And I will keep in touch with him meanwhile."

"What else did you discuss?" Roslyn asked leadingly. "Did you mention me, perhaps?"

Drew couldn't help but smile at her eagerness. "Only in the most flattering terms. He seems to think very highly of you. But our conversation soon turned to politics. Haviland wants to take up his seat in the Lords when Parliament reconvenes in the fall."

"So he told me. It is one of the things I admire about him . . . that he is not the typical indolent nobleman."

"Was that a gibe at me, darling?"

Roslyn dimpled. "Not really. I understand from Lady Freemantle that you take your ducal responsibilities quite seriously. Your estates reportedly are the model of modern agricultural management, and you are heavily involved in governmental affairs. I admit I find that admirable, even if it surprises me. Many noblemen spend their time in frivolous pursuits."

"I find too much frivolity deathly boring," Drew said quite truthfully. "And I think Haviland is of the same mind. He asked if I would be willing to advise him on the workings of the government, so I agreed. And I offered to lend him my secretary for a time."

"That is extremely kind of you," Roslyn observed. "You make an excellent tutor."

She offered him a warm smile—a smile like a gift. That smile tantalized him against his will, and Drew shifted uneasily in his seat. "I suggested he begin by reading Cobbett's *Parliamentary History*. I plan to send him my volumes."

"I could loan him mine."

"No, you don't want him to think you too bookish."

She laughed. "I suppose not."

Her gaze turned thoughtful then, and she gave him a measuring glance. "I am curious, your grace. If you feel so strongly about your ducal responsibilities, do you intend to marry someday? I should think you would want heirs for your dukedom."

"I will eventually," Drew replied.

"I wondered. You have such an aversion to matrimony, I thought you might have decided never to wed."

His smile was more of a grimace. "I know my duty. And I'm prepared to suffer a wife in order to beget heirs."

"You sound very much like a misogynist."

Drew grinned. "I like women well enough. I just can't bear the thought of being shackled to one specific woman for life."

"It is a pity that marital vows require a man to choose only one wife," she replied, her tone teasing. "I presume you will make a marriage of convenience rather than love?"

"Of course." His reply was bland. "Aristocrats don't marry for love. For members of our class, marriage is a callous business transaction. A cold union of blood and titles and fortune. One that will likely end up proving tedious or even distasteful."

"What a delightful prospect," Roslyn said wryly.

"My ideas for marriage are very different from yours, quite obviously."

"Indeed. You believe in fairy tales."

She smiled. "It is a shame you cannot hope for anything better. But perhaps someday you may encounter a woman you actually wish to marry."

Drew frowned, wondering how he had come to be discussing matrimony. Usually his mind sheared away from the unpleasant subject. Oh, he knew he would do his duty eventually. But he had never given serious consideration to the woman he would one day wed. He only knew he didn't want his duchess to be anything like his mother—a cold, grasping, power-hungry witch who thought only of her own needs and desires.

"Did your parents have anything to do with your aversion, as mine did?" Roslyn asked quite innocently.

His mother had a great deal to do with his aversion to marriage, Drew acknowledged to himself. "I would say so."

"Why?" Her tone was curious. "Were your parents as horribly antagonistic as mine? Did they despise each other?"

"No. They rarely showed any emotion toward each other at all. They considered it ill-bred to exhibit any feelings."

"And they raised you that way?"

Her perceptiveness cut too close for comfort. He'd had a cold upbringing. A childhood barren of affection or familial feeling. "Somewhat," was all Drew could bring himself to say.

"So your parents married for convenience."

"And to perpetuate their illustrious bloodlines.

They both could trace their ancestry back to William the Conqueror."

"I suppose you mean to do the same?"

Again Drew shrugged. "I don't particularly care. But other than carrying on the line, there are few benefits to marriage."

"Do you really think so?"

"Yes. In fact, there are many disadvantages."

"Such as?"

"For one thing, most couples who wed for convenience have little in common, so there is little enjoyment to be found in each other's company."

"Perhaps," she conceded.

"And marriage can be a prime opportunity for boredom. If you're shackled to one wife, you can't easily be rid of her. At least a mistress can be exchanged if you grow tired of her."

Her blue eyes danced with laughter. "That is an advantage indeed. I hadn't considered it."

Drew leaned back in his seat, beginning to enjoy himself. "Marriage can be a breeding ground for hostilities, as your own parents proved."

"That is one point we can agree on, at least," Roslyn said with a shudder. "What else?"

"A bachelor has no family to tie him down, as a married man does. A bachelor can do precisely as he pleases."

"Yes, it would undoubtedly be frustrating to have to consider another person's feelings. It is much easier to be selfish and never put anyone else's happiness before your own."

Drew appreciated her humor, but he pressed on. "A wife may turn out to be a nag," he pointed out. "Or fall into jealous rages if her husband spends his days at his club and his nights in bed with his mistress."

"Could you blame her?"

"Yes. A marriage of convenience is just that—a legal union with no promises of love or fidelity."

"Which is precisely why I would never consider wedding for mere convenience," Roslyn said, leaning forward earnestly. "But there are advantages to be found in a good marriage that I'm certain you have never considered."

"Name one."

"I can name several. The best is that you will always have a companion. Someone to talk to and listen to. To wake up to each morning, and share meals and congenial pursuits with. You are rarely lonely."

Drew relaxed against the sofa back. "Assuming the couple is compatible, which is rarely the case in a convenient marriage."

"In a *good* marriage, they are compatible in most respects and have many shared interests. Moreover, they can have children, a family," Roslyn continued.

"You can have that in any marriage."

"True, you can beget children. But it will hardly be a *loving* family. And keep in mind the most important advantage: A husband will have a hostess for his balls, and his wife will have an escort to various entertainments." She gave a light laugh. "You must admit that Haviland wouldn't be in his current predicament if he were married to me."

"I cannot argue with that," Drew admitted, amused.

"No, seriously . . . a good marriage is based on friendship and affection and perhaps love—even though you don't believe in it."

Drew mentally shook his head. He couldn't imagine his own parents ever having loved each other or even being friends. If his mother had a heart of ice, his father hadn't been much warmer. The late Duke of Arden had been rigid, reserved, aloof—a strict disciplinarian who never showed any signs of affection for a living soul, not even his only son and heir. Drew hadn't grieved terribly when he lost his father eight years ago, for they barely knew each other.

He'd been shipped off to Eton when he was six, where he was fortunate to meet his cherished boyhood friends. Except for Marcus and Heath, he might have turned out very much like his austere sire. Thank God they had saved him from becoming such a self-important stuffed shirt.

Drew summoned a smile. "Not even those possible advantages could tempt me into marriage. I am quite content to remain single."

"Are you truly?" She cocked her head. "A loving marriage can give you satisfaction and fulfillment. Can you say your mistresses give you fulfillment other than the carnal kind?"

No, he couldn't claim that. He'd had a number of mistresses in the past, but those liaisons, while fulfilling sexually, had been only superficial. He had wanted it exactly that way, with no attachment, no bonding, no passion beyond the physical.

"The carnal kind is all that interests me," he answered evenly.

Her expression turned impish. "I sincerely hope Lord Haviland doesn't share your opinion."

"You will have to convince him otherwise—which means you need to work harder at seducing him."

"I intend to," she said sweetly. "Why do you think I have spent so much time learning your techniques? I have every intention of seducing him into loving me."

When she smiled serenely, Drew's gaze was drawn to her mouth. Not only did he feel the fierce urge to kiss her, but he found himself increasingly captivated by the enchanting Roslyn Loring.

Yet she clearly had no such feelings for him.

Her disinterest in him not only irked him but was beginning to be a challenge, Drew realized. It roused the primal urge in him to prove that she wasn't nearly as indifferent to him as she pretended.

Comprehending the danger in succumbing to his urges, however, he consulted the mantel clock. "Enough about matrimony. I suggest we move on to your lesson, for I need to be in London by noon."

He rose and moved to shut the library door. "So we won't be disturbed," he explained before returning to lounge on the sofa. "Tell me about the rest of Fanny's letter. What did she advise you about clothing?"

Roslyn had been pondering the duke's remarks about marriage when he abruptly changed the subject, so it took her a moment to shift her thoughts.

Even then she hesitated, reluctant to repeat Fanny's suggestions, since they entailed making an effort to show off her physical charms. "She merely said I should adopt a more inviting style."

"She's right. That gown you're wearing is attractive enough"—his gaze skimmed down her peach-colored muslin morning dress that was part of her new wardrobe—"but it is a trifle too modest for your purpose. The neckline should be lower to show more bosom, and the waist tighter to emphasize your figure.

Your curves are ample enough, I know firsthand. But with your height and slenderness, you need to highlight the lushness of your breasts."

Unable to stop her blush, Roslyn sent the duke a reproachful look, certain he was enjoying discomfiting her. In return he gave her a smile that was wickedly charming—one that had a deplorable effect on her pulse rate.

"Your hair is another problem," he said, his assessment moving upward from her body to her face.

Instinctively Roslyn raised a hand to her coiffure. She had pinned it into a sedate knot at her nape, a simple style that didn't require a maid's help to achieve. For years the Loring sisters had been too poor to afford servants of their own, and their step-uncle had been too miserly to provide them any. "What is wrong with my hair?"

"It's too severe. You should wear it in a more careless style. Let a few curls frame your face. Better yet, let some tresses hang down over your shoulder. It's most appealing if you look like you've just risen from your bed. That gives a man notions about taking you back there."

"I'm not certain I *wish* to give Haviland notions of taking me to bed," Roslyn said dubiously.

"You need to. He'll be more willing to tie the knot if he believes he won't be getting a cold fish in his marriage bed."

She frowned. "Do you think I am a cold fish?"

The duke's expression turned enigmatic. "I know you are not, but you have to show Haviland as much. Which leads me to my next suggestion. You can do much more with your mouth."

"More than pouting?"

"Yes. Your mouth is full and inviting, but you need to look kissable."

Her eyebrows shot up. "How do I do that?"

"Bite your lips to make them look passion-bruised. Wet them with your tongue. You want to entice your suitor to kiss you."

"Is that why Fanny made me wear lip rouge at the Cyprians' ball?"

"I expect so. And it worked quite well."

"You truly wanted to kiss me?"

"Very much. But you looked the part that night. You were much more approachable than now."

"Approachable?"

She could see the duke almost smile at her peeved tone. "You don't want Haviland to think of you as a delicate porcelain doll but a flesh and blood woman. It's much more enticing to a man."

The furrow in her brow deepened. "I don't really understand the difference."

"Take your friend Fanny, for example. She is considered a beauty, but that isn't what most men find appealing about her. She has an earthy quality that's highly alluring."

"Which I lack."

"But you can make up for it with your actions. You may appear a proper lady of refinement, but you want Haviland to know you have a passionate nature underneath that perfect, untouchable exterior. You must give him the urge to abandon all his gentlemanly discipline and think about bedding you."

"I see," Roslyn said slowly, although she had little confidence that she could pull off such a feat.

"So try looking kissable."

Obediently, she worried her lower lip with her teeth, then wet it with her tongue. "Like that?"

"Yes. But try to be more sultry. Part your lips. Pretend to be a little breathless. And look directly at me. Remember, eyes and mouth are your first weapons."

She held his gaze as she parted her wet lips and manufactured a subtle pant, but it still felt absurdly unnatural.

Arden obviously thought so too, since he shook his head ruefully. "You can do much better than that, darling. Come, now . . . make me want to kiss you."

Despite her determination, the thought of kissing Arden again sent a thrum of excitement shivering across her skin. Purposefully ignoring the wanton feeling, Roslyn tried again to look kissable, slowly licking her lips while trying to appear sultry.

"That's somewhat better," he encouraged. "Just watching you should arouse me."

Arouse the Duke of Arden? Impossible, Roslyn thought with a silent chortle. The techniques of seduction he was teaching her might work on normal men, but not in a million years would she ever believe she could have the same effect on him, especially when he knew exactly what tricks she was attempting.

When she broke off her struggles with a laugh, Arden sank back against the sofa in defeat. "Perhaps you are hopeless after all."

"No, no, I can do it," she asserted, trying to stem her amusement.

"Then show me. See if you can arouse me. Come sit beside me here so you have a better chance."

When he gestured at the sofa cushion beside him, Roslyn hesitated barely a moment before gathering her determination. If she intended to conquer her self-consciousness with Lord Haviland, she would have to become more at ease with the physical aspects of a seduction. And she had a willing subject to practice on right now, perhaps for the last time, since the duke intended to return to London after this lesson.

"Now what?" she asked when she had settled beside him.

He lounged back against the padded arm of the sofa. "I will leave it entirely up to you. What did I teach you yesterday?"

"That I should contrive to touch you."

"So do it."

Reaching out, she let her fingers settle on his hand, which was resting on his buckskin-clad thigh. In response, he slid his hand from beneath hers and placed his on top, covering her fingers and pressing her palm against his thigh. "This is more arousing to a man," he explained.

And to a woman also, Roslyn reflected as her heart gave a leap at the feel of the granite-hard muscles beneath the soft fabric. But she wouldn't let herself pull away. Instead she gazed directly at Arden and practiced her mouth exercises. His eyes lowered to her lips, but otherwise he seemed unaffected.

"Isn't that good enough?" she finally asked.

"You should move closer. Tempt me with your nearness."

She shifted her position and leaned forward so that their mouths were only a short distance apart, which made her excruciatingly aware of his body, especially since she was required to brace her hand against his thigh for balance.

"Now kiss me," he ordered blandly. "You should learn how to do it properly."

Her own gaze dropping from his, Roslyn eyed the sensual fullness of his mouth and felt herself tense. It would be utterly unwise to kiss Arden, even though she longed to. But then she chided herself for being missish. She had already kissed him once before—and allowed much more than that! Letting him teach her to kiss wouldn't be nearly as scandalous, but could be highly beneficial in her campaign to win Lord Haviland.

A deep breath did nothing to calm her nerves, however, and when she hurried to press a quick kiss to his lips before drawing back, his slight frown told her clearly that she had utterly failed to impress him.

"Again, but more slowly," he suggested. "Make it linger. And put your hands on my chest so that I'm aware of you touching me."

His coat was open, so Roslyn tentatively pressed her palms against the lapels of his waistcoat. She had to lean over much farther than was comfortable, yet he didn't intend to help her at all, she realized. He kept his arms at his sides and remained still while she set her lips to his.

The heat of his mouth was highly distracting, so she concentrated on ignoring it as she kissed him with untutored skill. After a long moment, Roslyn pulled back, eyeing him questioningly.

His green eyes had darkened a fraction. "Better, but still inadequate. Use your tongue. That's very arousing to a man."

Leaning forward again, she let her tongue slip inside his mouth to explore the warm recesses. It was highly intoxicating for her, if not for him, and had a profound impact on her senses.

She was more than a little breathless when she drew back. "Are you aroused yet?"

"Not quite. You'll have to be more assertive. Lay claim to me when you kiss me."

"I beg your pardon?"

"Let me show you . . ."

Reaching for her, he lay back and pulled her on top of him, molding her softness to his much harder frame. She could feel the shifting muscles of his chest beneath her palms as their lips melded and he took over kissing her.

Her body softened, yielded to him, as his lips shifted over hers in sensuous coercion. Then his tongue slid inside and found hers, mating with it in a slow, intimate dance. When she gave a soft little sigh, he angled his head and pressed even deeper, exploring, tasting, coaxing.

For a long moment she became lost in the sheer wonder of his kiss, in the lush assault on her senses. The delicious feelings he aroused in her were overwhelming, kindling a throbbing ache between her legs, a fierce yearning. Without conscious thought, she began moving her hips against his, seeking a release she couldn't even name.

When at last he broke off his kiss, disappointment surged through her. She hadn't wanted him to stop. Yet she knew she had affected him this time. She could feel the taut muscled strength of his body beneath hers, and something more—the swollen hardness nestled in the cradle of her thighs.

Somewhat dazed, Roslyn opened her eyes and lifted her head. "There, that aroused you, I can feel it."

"I would say so." His voice was husky and amused as he caught her hand and drew it between their bodies to his groin.

It was shocking to touch the thick ridge of male flesh there; even through his breeches the heat of him was apparent. Yet she also felt a sense of triumph. She had wanted to learn how to arouse a man, and she had succeeded.

Suddenly recalling how improper it was to be fondling a man's body, Roslyn quickly eased her hand from his grasp and made to rise.

"Not so fast, love," Arden murmured as his arms closed around her to hold her in place. "We've barely begun your education in kissing."

Without giving her a choice, he drew her head down again and resumed her instruction. But the tenor of his kiss changed. This one was harder, more powerful. If Roslyn had any thought at all of resisting, he shattered it quite thoroughly, his mouth slowly forcing hers open, his thrusting tongue seizing, claiming.

It was a kiss of possession, devastating, expert. The blatant sensuality of it was stunning as his mouth made love to her mouth, as his hands slid around her hips to capture her more firmly, letting her feel his hard arousal through their clothing.

Yet it was a trap from which she had no desire to escape. Instead, Roslyn kissed him back with an intensity that she would have thought utterly foreign to her nature.

They were both breathing raggedly when it finally

ended. Drawing back, Roslyn stared dazedly down at him.

His eyes were dark and sensual as they surveyed her flushed face. "You look extremely kissable now," he observed in a low rasp.

Roslyn had started to return a diffuse smile when she realized his hands had moved to the back of her gown and were unfastening the hooks. A small gasp escaped her when she comprehended what he was doing, but she made no protest as he pushed down the décolletage and freed her breasts from the confinement of her chemise and corset.

His eyes flashed as he bared the pale mounds to his hot gaze.

Her nerves knotting in near painful anticipation, she held her breath, knowing exactly what came next. She should stop him, Roslyn told herself sternly as he raised her higher to give his mouth better access to her nipples. But she couldn't find the willpower.

Then he bent his head, and her heart leapt. He didn't suckle her as she expected, though. His tongue merely circled one taut aureole, never touching.

Roslyn arched against him, wanting desperately for him to put his mouth there. Instead he merely played with her, his lips nibbling around the aching tip, deliberately arousing but never fulfilling.

"Your grace . . ." she murmured in a breathy plea.

"Call me Drew."

"Drew . . . please."

His hands moving to cup her naked breasts, he pressed his tantalizing mouth closer to her nipple. The first flick of his tongue made her breath hiss between her teeth. Then he drew back slightly to blow a stream of air across the wet bud. The delectable sensation sparked a low heat inside her belly and dredged a trembling pleasure sound from deep in her throat. When she felt the nip of his teeth against the sensitive tip, Roslyn whimpered. Yet he continued to deny her, his lips rubbing and teasing over her breasts.

Finally, however, he drew a dusky peak between his lips. Her hands gripped his shoulders as he sucked the engorged nipple deeper into the moist heat of his mouth, igniting a searing heat deep within her.

His tongue kept laving slowly, and each time he stroked, a new thrill shot through her. Roslyn shivered with heat as his lips suckled the peak to an unbearable tightness rivaling that in her chest. She felt almost faint with delight. She was drowning in sensations. He was a master at giving pleasure, and she accepted eagerly.

How wonderful it felt. How wonderful and thrilling.

When his teeth nipped her again, she moaned helplessly, so caught up in his erotic attentions that she was only vaguely aware his right hand had moved to her bare shoulder. It drifted down her back, caressing the arch of her spine, then lower over her hip and down the skirt of her gown. When he raised the hem, drawing it upward, she felt the sensation of cool air on her legs.

In contrast, his warm fingers fondled her bare thigh, stroking her skin in small undulations, teasing with lazy spirals and slow, erotic touches.

The trembling, shivery ache in her belly heightened by slow degrees, building until his caresses moved to her inner thigh. Then she tensed, wondering what he intended.

His hand had moved upward to cover her woman's

mound. When he cupped the warm, throbbing place between her thighs, Roslyn gave a start and abruptly lifted her head.

He held her startled gaze as his fingers parted the damp curls of her sex. When he began to stroke the wet folds of her flesh, the pleasure of his probing touch took her breath away.

Roslyn shuddered, her heart beginning to pound, yet she was unable to look away; he was holding her captive with the intensity of his eyes as he found the aching nub that was the secret of her femininity. She could feel urgent desire burning through her senses like fire. The powerful sensations centered in the shimmering, heated core of her body, and her hands clenched reflexively, digging into his shoulders.

Then one finger slowly slid inside her hot, slick moistness. The novel, shockingly intimate caress was wholly unexpected.

Gasping, Roslyn jerked her hips away as a feeling of panic suddenly assaulted her.

Her body jolting, she pushed herself off him and stood on shaken limbs, covering her naked breasts with her arms as she stared down at him.

"This was a m-mistake, your grace."

A flame had kindled in the depths of his eyes, but his expression was as cool and enigmatic as ever.

Still dazed, she struggled to restore her clothing to order, feeling like the wanton she knew she had to look.

The duke said not a word as he pulled out a linen handkerchief from his coat pocket. His fingers were soaked with her essence, Roslyn saw to her mortification. The heated flush on her face rose when he wiped his fingers dry.

"I agree," he said finally, his smile sardonic. "This was a mistake."

The husky rasp in his voice stroked her nerve endings, reminding her that she had aroused him almost as much as he had aroused her.

Lord preserve her, Roslyn thought frantically, she had to put an end to this temptation. Certainly she couldn't continue such intimate sessions with him. It was far too dangerous.

"We shouldn't have any further lessons," she said, her voice uneven.

A muscle in his jaw flexed, as if he might object, but all he said was, "Indeed."

He returned the handkerchief to his pocket and stood. When he took a step toward her, though, Roslyn retreated.

His mouth curled. "You needn't fear, darling. My intentions are somewhat honorable this time. Turn around and let me hook your gown. You don't want your servants to see you looking so disheveled."

She didn't want him coming near her again, either, but she couldn't manage the hooks easily on her own.

Reluctantly, she turned her back to him and held herself rigid as he performed the service of lady's maid.

When he was done, he paused with his hands resting lightly on her shoulders. "You should definitely contrive to kiss Haviland. He won't be able to resist you. Good day, Miss Loring."

Roslyn couldn't bring herself to answer or even to look at Arden as he let himself out of the library. When he was gone, she stood there trembling and cursing herself.

How could she have allowed his lesson in kissing to

go so far? She'd lost any shred of common sense the moment his lips touched hers.

She could never let him make love to her. She had absolutely no intention of losing her innocence before her wedding night. She was saving herself for marriage, for a loving husband who would cherish her for the rest of their lives.

Yet she couldn't deny the maddening desire the duke roused in her so effortlessly.

Roslyn shut her eyes, recalling her response to his erotic kisses, how she had come alive in his arms, all yearning hunger. The tremulous pulsing that still heated her body was a clear reminder that she was in deep trouble.

Moving to a chair, she sank down and raised a shaking hand to her temple. Her head still swam with drugged pleasure, her heart still pounded thickly. It was no wonder Arden was renowned as a marvelous lover. She had no doubt that he could make women weep with delight. He had the power to compel any woman to surrender, to *want* his possession. . . .

But a rakish nobleman like the duke was only interested in physical pleasure, not love or marriage or children.

She had absolutely no future with him, and she would be an utter fool to let herself think otherwise.

No, Roslyn vowed. After this, she would keep far, far away from the Duke of Arden. Certainly she would never again ask him to give her any more lessons in seduction!

Chapter Nine

❦

It is appalling to realize how easily he can make me behave like a perfect wanton.

—Roslyn to Fanny

"Where have you been, Roslyn dear?" Winifred demanded over the din of the crowded ballroom. "I expected you an hour ago."

"Some matters at home required my attention," Roslyn replied, which was only partly true. She had arrived late to the Haviland ball chiefly to avoid one particular arousing nobleman. She hadn't wanted to face Arden after their fervent embrace in the library last week.

In fact, she hadn't seen him since, and would have eschewed tonight's ball altogether except that she'd promised Lord Haviland she would attend.

"You missed the reception line," Winifred's raucous voice sounded over the musicians and the throng of guests. "But it is turning out to be a fine party."

It was indeed a veritable crush—a sure sign of success. Roslyn was pleased for Lord Haviland, although she would have preferred less noise and heat. The blaze from myriad glittering chandeliers overhead, combined with the press of so many splendidly garbed bodies, made the ballroom almost oppressive.

Yet before Roslyn could reply, Winifred took her to task. "I am disappointed in you, my girl. First you arrive late, then you hide yourself on the sidelines. That is not what balls are for. You should be dancing."

"It is too warm to dance," Roslyn replied, fanning herself with the gilded fan she wore looped at her wrist.

"Pah," her friend scoffed. "You can bear a little warmth for one evening. But you need a partner." Winifred searched the crowd. "I wonder where Arden is. He was kind enough to escort me here, but then he disappeared into one of the card rooms shortly after we arrived."

Roslyn bit back her exasperation at Winifred's continued matchmaking efforts. "Thank you, Winifred, but I can manage my own affairs."

"His friend, that handsome Marquess of Claybourne, is here also, although I haven't seen him lately. It is too bad Lily couldn't come tonight. 'Struth, I cannot believe she elected to go to Hampshire just now. The marquess is such an eligible *parti*."

Roslyn hesitated to reply. Lily had set out for London last week to stay at Fanny's boardinghouse, but she hadn't wanted their meddlesome patron to know her whereabouts. Lily had no desire to be the victim of Winifred's machinations or to be thrown at Lord Claybourne's head again.

"You know Lily doesn't care for balls, Winifred," Roslyn said carefully. "She would much rather be visiting friends at our old home in Hampshire."

Which was technically true, even if that was merely the fabrication Lily wanted to use to misdirect Winifred.

Roslyn almost wished she had accompanied her sister

to London, for then she wouldn't be bedeviled by a certain other handsome nobleman. As it was, the duke was befuddling her thoughts and playing total havoc with her peace of mind. She didn't want to remember their last encounter, how Arden had kissed her and caressed her and led her into a whirlpool of sensation that left her dazed and aching.

She was rudely brought back to the present, however, when she realized Winifred was speaking again. ". . . you wait here, I will fetch the duke so he can partner you."

Dismayed at the thought of having to dance with Arden, Roslyn shook her head. "Pray excuse me, Winifred, but I had best find Lord Haviland and make my apologies."

Hurriedly she moved away, searching the crowd for the earl. She felt fortunate to spy him at one end of the ballroom, but then frowned to realize he was surrounded by a group of adoring young ladies—her competition, Roslyn surmised.

She had made little progress thus far in her campaign to win Haviland, for he'd spent much of his time in London this past week at his grandmother's behest. In the interval, Roslyn had met twice more with his housekeeper and butler to plan the menus for the evening, but she'd had no opportunity for intimacy with the earl, except when he'd politely brushed a kiss to her fingers upon saying farewell at her second visit. And tonight he was occupied with playing host.

When she drew closer, however, she could see that not all the ladies in his party were young; one was positively ancient. She suspected that was Haviland's elderly grandmother, for whom he claimed to bear a great fondness. When the venerable dame struck him on his arm with her fan, he threw back his dark head and laughed.

Not wishing to attempt a seduction in front of so many witnesses, Roslyn decided to wait to approach Haviland. When she detoured to the refreshment table to find a glass of punch, she passed by the open French doors and caught a waft of cool evening breeze. Wistfully Roslyn wondered how soon she could slip away from the ball. She had walked across the rear lawns of their adjoining estates rather than summon a carriage, not only to spare the servants the trouble, but so she could retreat easily if need be. She couldn't politely take her leave for at least another hour, though.

At the moment, she couldn't even have a comfortable coze with Tess Blanchard, since Tess was pleasantly occupied dancing. A fellow teacher at the academy, Tess had been one of the Loring sisters' closest friends for the past four years, ever since they moved to the neighborhood to live with their stepuncle. And like the Loring sisters, Tess found herself hard-pressed to avoid Winifred's meddlesome matchmaking.

A number of people nodded and spoke politely to Roslyn as she advanced through the crowd, and Roslyn responded with similar politeness. She didn't dislike balls as Lily did—or deliberately flout conventions as Lily relished doing—but she cared little for the shallow trappings of the ton, and the rampant hypocrisy galled her. These very people had gleefully shunned the Loring girls until a few months ago, when their step-uncle died and Marcus had assumed their guardianship along with the title.

The scandals had hurt her sisters even more than herself, Roslyn reflected as she stood drinking punch on the sidelines. Arabella had suffered not only a broken betrothal but a broken heart. And Lily had encased her heart in a wall of ice, determined never to let anyone close enough to wound her. Lily's reckless, devil-may-care manner, however, hid a sensitive, vulnerable nature, Roslyn knew. So if she could protect her younger sister from Winifred's amorous schemes, she would do so. Just as she would protect herself from the Duke of Arden—

Speak of the devil.

Her heart fluttered alarmingly when she spied him across the ballroom. He cut a commanding figure, dressed in formal finery—black coat and gold brocade waistcoat, pristine white cravat and white satin breeches—that accentuated his fair good looks.

Determinedly Roslyn ignored the pleasure rising inside her at the mere sight of him. But when he locked gazes with her, capturing and holding her with no more than a look, she couldn't help remembering the last time they were together. The feel of him lying hard and aroused beneath her. His warm lips that had plied hers to such devastating effect. His skillful hands that had played over her bare skin, searching out her feminine secrets.

A flush heated her cheeks as they stared at each other. He didn't need to touch her now to make her spellbound, Roslyn thought with a sudden breathlessness. The flicker of awareness in his green eyes set her pulse racing deplorably.

It was with supreme effort that Roslyn tore her gaze away now. She felt a wave of gratitude when she saw

Lord Haviland approaching her, and thus was unusually effusive when she apologized for her tardiness.

"Think nothing of it, Miss Loring," the earl said with a smile. "But I was hoping you would come so I could thank you. Your advice regarding my ball was invaluable."

"I was glad to help."

"My grandmother claims to be impressed with my efforts, and she is remarkably difficult to please. I should like to introduce you to her, if you would allow me."

Roslyn glanced back at the elderly lady. "I would enjoy meeting her," she said, feeling a warm little glow at the honor.

When Lord Haviland asked her to dance the next set, she accepted readily and let him lead her onto the floor for a quadrille. She knew she should begin a flirtation with him, yet she was too aware that the duke was watching her on the sidelines. No doubt that was why being this near Haviland didn't affect her pulse rate as she expected, and why she felt no lightning-spark of pleasure at touching him when their hands came together.

Fortunately, Haviland was less tongue-tied than she. When the movements of the dance allowed, he carried on a conversation.

"I must think of some suitable reward for your help, Miss Loring. Will you accompany me on a drive tomorrow morning?"

Roslyn was delighted by the invitation but knew of his plans for a weeklong houseparty. "Are you certain you wish to leave your houseguests? I thought your grandmother and other relatives were staying with you for the week."

"They are, but I will be glad to escape them for a time. My grandmother is one of my few relations whose good opinion I care about, and she will likely remain abed until noon after the exertions of the evening. Her health is not what it was."

"I am sorry to hear that," Roslyn replied politely.

Haviland's mouth curved wryly. "She is not at death's door yet, as she wants me to believe. I think she exaggerates the severity of her spells just so she can make me dance to her tune. She claims she is waiting for me to choose a bride and settle down before she goes to meet her Maker."

Her heart skipped a beat. Did his telling her about his grandmother's desires have any implication for her? "Oh? And do you mean to comply with her wishes?"

The smile he flashed her was very appealing. "It is an ongoing battle, but I expect she will win in the end."

Lord Haviland spoke fondly about his grandmother then, and afterward, Roslyn found it far easier to enter into a lighthearted banter with him, just as she had practiced. And soon she discovered that Haviland was rather skilled at the art of flirtation himself.

When she asked teasingly if his grandmother must approve his choice of brides, he replied with an emphatic no. "Even though I would like to please her, that is one decision I intend to make for myself. But she will be impressed that I am dancing with the most beautiful lady in the room."

Roslyn laughed up at him with pleasure—until she once again saw Arden watching her, his green eyes heavy-lidded and intent. He was leaning one shoulder against a column in a relaxed pose, yet she had the impression he wasn't relaxed in the least. Instead, he looked almost . . . disapproving.

With a slight toss of her head, Roslyn ordered herself to stop dwelling on the vexing duke and returned to her flirtation with Lord Haviland.

His eyes narrowing, Drew watched as Roslyn gracefully moved through the steps of the dance. He felt a lurch in the vicinity of his chest when she laughed up at Haviland.

The two of them made a stunningly attractive couple—the earl's rugged dark looks contrasting starkly with Roslyn's elegant fairness.

She looked regal and enchanting tonight, her pale gold hair coiffed to allow curling tendrils to frame her face. The simple elegance of her gown added to her appeal also, the indigo blue lustring setting off her eyes to perfection and complementing her radiant, glowing skin.

That heated glow made Drew recall the last time he'd been with her . . . her face gently flushed, swollen lips slightly parted, blue eyes dazed as her supple figure sprawled over him. Her loins pressing against his swollen cock had made him ache with desire.

He was hot and hard now, just remembering.

He'd wanted to take her right there in the library. His forbearance had resulted in even greater sexual frustration this past interminable week.

Yet avoiding Roslyn hadn't helped, for she'd begun to invade his dreams. Drew found himself weaving wild, erotic fantasies involving Roslyn wrapped around him in the heat of passion. He couldn't shut them out, much to his annoyance.

He had just clamped his jaw tight when he heard a familiar voice over his left shoulder.

"So the lovely Miss Roslyn has attracted your interest after all," Heath said, clearly amused.

Unable to deny the truth of that observation, Drew made no reply.

"I wondered," Heath went on, "why you would trouble yourself to attend a dull country affair—and I didn't think it was merely because you pledged to defend Lady Freemantle against lurking highwaymen."

Hiding his displeasure, Drew replied blandly, "We both promised Marcus that we would keep an eye on his former wards."

"Not *this* close an eye."

He managed a nonchalant shrug. He hadn't told his friend about his tutelage of Roslyn, and he wouldn't do so now. "Haven't you better things to do than irritate me?"

Heath held up his hands. "Don't take my head off, old son. I just find it humorous to see the greatest cynic in England in an ill temper over a woman."

Drew narrowed his gaze. "Why the devil did *you* come tonight if you find it so deadly flat? Don't you know that Lady Freemantle is lying in wait to snare you in her web?"

The question didn't appear to faze Heath. "I'm not overly alarmed, since the match her ladyship has chosen for me has fled the district."

"The youngest Loring sister, Lilian?"

"Just so. Reportedly the fair Lily has gone to Hampshire."

Drew roused himself from his own dark mood to gibe, "What, did you drive her away?"

Heath's own smile was rueful. "There is that possibility. She is set on eluding me, in any event."

"How astounding," Drew said truthfully. Heath had always been the heartbreaker of the three of them. Adoring women flocked to Heath in droves, enticed by his natural charm. "I've never known a woman to run from you."

Heath's grin turned self-deprecating. "It *is* astounding, isn't it?" He gave Drew a penetrating look. "Is the lovely Miss Roslyn running from you? Marcus suggested she might make you a good match, and you seem to be inching toward that opinion yourself."

Drew's scowl returned. His instinctive response was to accuse Heath of having maggots in his head, but he wasn't so certain it would be true. "You can't possibly think I have matrimony in mind."

"Don't you? Then why have you been watching Roslyn as if you want to carry her back to your lair?"

Had he been that obvious? Drew thought with chagrin.

"Have no fear," Heath said as if reading his mind. "No one else would suspect. I just know you too well."

"You are not helping my temper any," Drew said through clenched teeth.

Heath laughed. "No doubt. But you'd best take care if you don't want to find yourself hanging in the parson's noose. You can't do to her what you're thinking without the benefit of marriage. Marcus would rip you apart, not to mention that your own honor wouldn't allow it."

When Drew all but growled, Heath gave him a friendly clap on the shoulder. "I think I will take myself back to London before you call me out. There's little amusement to be found here, anyway. In truth, I wouldn't mind encountering your highwayman. At least it would liven up my life for a time."

There was little amusement here for him, too, Drew thought as Heath walked away. Seeing Roslyn dance with Haviland was the primary cause, but his dissatisfaction went deeper than that.

The thought of her trying to seduce Haviland, of making love to him, filled Drew with an inexplicable anger. The bald truth was, he didn't want her to become carnally intimate with any other man but him.

He wanted to be the one to introduce her to the secrets of sensuality, to awaken her to passion and pleasure and every other delight to be found between a man and woman.

Which confounded him to no end.

This was the first time in his life he had ever been envious of another man over the fair sex. He was frankly astounded to realize how possessive he felt toward Roslyn.

Worse, he saw no resolution to his cursed predicament. He damned well had no desire for marriage, yet he couldn't deny the primitive, purely masculine urge to "carry Roslyn back to his lair," as Heath had put it. Or at the very least, to hold her in his own arms again.

But then, Drew realized, firmly tamping down his lust, it was perfectly proper for a gentleman to hold a young lady at a ball if he danced with her.

Roslyn did not look happy to see him, Drew noted when he came up to her at the conclusion of the quadrille and interrupted her lively conversation with Haviland to claim her for the next set.

"You don't mind if I steal her away for a dance, do you, my good man?" Drew asked, making the point moot by taking Roslyn's elbow possessively.

The earl gave him a piercing look, but then bowed with good grace. "As you wish, Arden. I don't want to monopolize Miss Loring's time, despite the pleasure it gives me. And I have other guests I must see to."

Drew knew Roslyn couldn't very well argue with him, either, as he led her onto the floor for a waltz.

"What if *I* mind?" she said then, her tone exasperated.

He returned an innocent look. "Do you have some objection to dancing with me?"

"Of course I do. Winifred has been matchmaking again. She sought you out to beg you to partner me, didn't she?"

"Well, yes," he answered truthfully, "but *I* chose to ask you."

"You might have done me the courtesy of giving me a choice."

"You could have refused."

"Not without causing a scene."

"Which you are in danger of doing right now," Drew pointed out, "since the music has begun and we are simply standing here." When she gave a guilty start, he took her hand and drew her close. "Smile sweetly, darling, and look as if you are enjoying yourself."

Roslyn complied, even though the light in her eyes suggested she was ready to do battle with him. Drew smiled to himself. The enjoyment had returned to the evening, unquestionably. In fact, he was enjoying himself for the first time since their awkward parting nearly a week ago.

She fitted into his arms quite well as they settled into the rhythm of the waltz, her steps light and graceful. He wondered if Roslyn would follow his rhythm as well when they made love.

If they made love. Which would never happen without the benefit of marriage, as Heath had rightly pointed out.

"So why don't you wish to dance with me?" Drew asked, determined to confront her misgivings and get them out in the open.

"Our lessons are over," Roslyn replied primly, as if she had rehearsed her answer. "There is no point in us even seeing each other again. Certainly we are not required to dance together."

"It will only help your consequence if you are considered the object of my attentions. You *do* want to impress Haviland's relations, don't you?"

"Yes, of course, but you interrupted a highly promising conversation with him."

"That was precisely my intention."

Her eyes flashed. "Are you purposefully trying to spoil my chances with Lord Haviland?"

"What if I am?"

"You wouldn't . . ." she began, then eyed him suspiciously. "Would you?"

"That would be ungentlemanly of me," Drew equivocated. "But it won't hurt for him to think he has competition."

Her expression was full of irony. "You are *not* his competition. You have made it abundantly clear you aren't interested in love and matrimony."

"But he doesn't have to know that. Take my word for it, a man can become extremely possessive if he thinks someone is poaching on his turf."

Drawing a deep breath, Roslyn made an apparent attempt at composure. "Thank you, your grace, for your concern on my behalf, but I will proceed with my campaign on my own from now on."

"What gratitude," Drew drawled, amused.

"I have already expressed my gratitude several times."

"I told you, I don't want your gratitude."

"Then what do you want?"

You, was Drew's unbidden thought. *I want you.* I want your lovely mouth glued to mine. I want your luscious body writhing beneath mine. I want to hear you gasping with pleasure as I fill you. . . .

Aloud, he merely said, "I want to know why you have been avoiding me so assiduously tonight."

A telltale blush rose to her cheeks. "I think you must know why."

"You're embarrassed by what happened between us in your library last week."

"You are mistaken. I am *appalled* by what happened in our library last week."

"So we kissed. There was no harm done."

"So you say," Roslyn muttered cryptically.

Drew peered down at her. "*Did* I hurt you somehow?"

Roslyn grimaced, then shook her head as if chastising herself. "No, of course not. I just should never have let it go so far." Her gaze narrowed up at him. "Yet *you* bear the greater share of the blame, for you are the expert. You should have stopped me."

"Can I help it if you find me irresistible?"

Her eyes widened as she struggled between vexation and amusement. "Your conceit is astounding, your grace," she finally said. "It was the novelty of the situation that caught me off guard. But now that I know what to expect, I intend to forget the incident entirely, I assure you."

"I can't forget it," Drew murmured truthfully. "And I don't believe you can either. You felt something when we kissed, just as I did."

She refused to acknowledge his assertion. Instead she summoned a serene smile. "You haven't asked me how my seduction of Haviland went this past week."

Drew felt his amusement fade. "Very well, darling, how did it go?"

"Splendidly. I think I have finally gotten the hang of flirtation. Haviland seems to be enjoying it, at any rate. I expect we will proceed to kissing at our next encounter, hopefully tomorrow morning. He asked me to drive out with him then. It is what I have been striving for, and I have you to thank for teaching me."

The lightly taunting words, the challenge in her smile, had a predictable effect on Drew's male pride, and he found himself clenching his teeth again, while his hands tightened reflexively at her waist and around her fingers.

He was vaguely aware that their steps had slowed as the waltz came to an end, yet it wasn't until she spoke that he realized he was still holding her.

"Your grace," she hissed through her teeth. "People are beginning to stare.

Drew released her reluctantly and stepped back. Roslyn offered him a swift curtsy before turning away, a stiff smile pasted on her face that suggested she was struggling for the pretense of civility in front of their audience and trying to hide her eagerness to get away from him.

Drew's brooding gaze followed her as she moved away through the crowd. He could still feel the lithe warmth of her body, could still feel his own arousal at her nearness. Could feel his temper heating anew.

Roslyn not only had ignored his provocative remarks, but had thrown her own back in his face, leaving him with the natural craving to pick up the gauntlet.

Drew swore a low oath under his breath. The turmoil inside him was only growing stronger.

What in blazes was he going to do about Roslyn Loring? She roused a heat in him, a hunger he'd never felt for any other woman. A hunger that was still unsated.

The need to possess her gripped him like talons, along with the even greater need to mark her as his, to claim her before Haviland did.

Yet there was only one way he could have her, Drew reminded himself grimly. By making her his bride.

Was he prepared to take such a drastic step?

And if so, what would Roslyn herself have to say about it?

Her limbs still a little weak from her clash with the infuriating duke, Roslyn made the decision to leave the ball at once. She had accomplished what she intended. She'd danced with Lord Haviland and received an invitation to go driving with him tomorrow. There was nothing more to be gained by remaining.

And there was very good reason to escape—not the least of which was to regain command of her scattered wits. Every time she encountered Arden, he roused more turmoil in her.

How could she have allowed him to rile her into nearly making a scene with half the ton as witnesses, including Lord Haviland and his haughty relations? She had intended to ignore Arden's very existence tonight. Instead she had let him provoke her into an unladylike altercation right there on the ballroom floor.

While it was true the duke could improve her consequence by showing her a measure of polite attention, any more intimate interest would only be detrimental. She couldn't afford to give rise to gossip, not with the scandals attached to her family name. And if anyone discovered what had already passed between her and the duke, it might very well destroy any chance for her to win Haviland's heart, not to mention a respectable proposal of marriage.

When Roslyn had retrieved her silk shawl and reticule from the Haviland butler, she made her way through the house to the rear terrace, where she was taken aback to find Arden waiting for her.

Coming to an abrupt halt, she stared at him in frustration. "What the devil are you doing here, your grace?"

He was leaning against the stone balustrade but pushed away when he saw her. "I thought you might decide to leave early."

"So?"

"So I intend to accompany you home. With a highwayman at large, you should have the protection of an escort."

His offering her protection was like a tiger offering to guard a lamb, Roslyn thought crossly. "Thank you, but I do not need your escort. I am just walking next door, and there are no highwaymen in the gardens."

"Nevertheless, I don't intend to let you go alone."

There was a subtle challenge in his eyes that dared her to refuse him.

She gave in with a sigh. Arden fell in beside her as she descended the steps and set out across the estate grounds, easily matching his long stride to her shorter, more hurried one.

There was ample moonlight to see by, and the July evening held a welcome coolness after the warmth of the ballroom. In the distance, she could hear the rustle of water as the River Thames meandered its lazy path to London at the rear of the estate grounds.

Her unwanted escort remained silent as they traversed the gravel paths. Roslyn made for the side gate that offered entrance to the Danvers gardens. When Arden opened it for her and allowed her through, she wished he would leave her there. But he followed her inside and shut it behind him.

There were few lights on in the house, Roslyn saw, since most of the servants had already retired to bed.

When she reached a side door to the manor, she paused to say over her shoulder, "Thank you for your escort, your grace, but now you may return to the ball with a clear conscience."

His voice, low and intent, came to her. "Roslyn . . . stay a moment."

She turned reluctantly at his request. "Why?"

He didn't answer for a long moment. He simply stared down at her, as if debating with himself.

Roslyn gazed up at him distractedly, wondering how she had managed to end up in a moonlit garden with Arden. She deplored the thrilling, edgy quiver of nerves that being alone with him in the dark engendered in her. She found her gaze dropping to his mouth, that firm sensuous mouth that could kiss so marvelously. . . .

"I don't want you driving out with Haviland tomorrow," he finally said.

"Whyever not?"

"Because I don't want you trying to seduce him when I intend to court you myself."

Her gaze abruptly lifted to his, wide and disbelieving. "I beg your pardon? You intend to *court* me?"

"That is what I said." There was a note of dry amusement in his voice, as if not even he could believe his declaration.

"Court me?" Roslyn repeated. "As in prelude to marriage? That makes no sense. You don't want to marry anyone, you've said so in no uncertain terms."

"So I did. But I have since changed my mind."

"If you are making game of me—"

His mouth curled. "I would never jest about a subject so serious as matrimony. I must wed eventually, and you will do far better than anyone else."

Shocked speechless, Roslyn stared at him, a dozen emotions warring inside her. The chief was disbelief, but that soon gave way to anger.

Arden must have seen her temper flare, for he grimaced. "I phrased my proposal rather boorishly. Let me try again. I would be honored for the privilege of making you my duchess, Miss Loring."

She shook her head wildly. "You wouldn't be honored in the least. And neither would I."

"Don't dismiss the idea out of hand—"

"Of course I will dismiss it! I told you I would never marry without love, and you don't even believe in it."

"I want the chance to change your mind. Love is vastly overrated, and in time, I can make you see it."

The nerve of him, Roslyn thought furiously. Did he honestly believe she would give up her dreams just because a nobleman of his consequence deigned to propose to her?

"I have heard quite enough, your grace."

She turned away, shaking, and made to enter the house, but Arden forestalled her by grasping her arm. When he spun her to face him, the air seemed to crackle all around them. Roslyn was suddenly very aware of the thrum of excitement pounding deep in her stomach.

She swallowed hard. "You have obviously taken leave of your senses."

"Perhaps I have," he muttered in a rough under voice.

"Well, I still have all of *my* faculties. Even if you have convinced yourself for some mad reason that you want me as your duchess, why the devil would I ever want to marry you?"

"Because of this. . . ."

His mouth came down hard to take possession of hers. Roslyn tried to get away, but his hand held her head still while his mouth slowly forced hers open, his tongue stabbing deep in a sensual assault that was dominating, possessive. The unexpectedness of it stole her breath and sent a surge of heat shuddering through her entire body.

Roslyn whimpered. She couldn't resist the strong

arms that crushed her to him. He ravished her mouth, ripped her senses from her.

Her hands crept up to wrap around his neck. The moment she surrendered, his kiss changed . . . softened, deepened, flooding her with longing.

Feeling her willpower slipping away, Roslyn made one last frantic effort to break the spell he was weaving around her. She pushed against his shoulder and tore her mouth away.

"Your grace! Drew . . . we have to stop this!"

"Not yet," he rasped. "I mean to show you one last lesson."

"What lesson?" Her voice was shaky and as hoarse as his.

"Pleasure," he murmured. "The kind of bliss you can find with a considerate lover."

Her stomach clenched with chagrin. "We cannot be lovers—I could never allow it. It would be utterly disgraceful."

"I know. But I'll stop short of claiming your innocence. Hush now," he urged when she would have protested.

He resumed his slow-burning kiss, which had the same effect as before: Her body melted back against his forearm while her mouth opened willingly under his. Roslyn moaned softly. His sensuality was deep and intoxicating and roused a now familiar ache low in the pit of her belly.

She could feel the heat and hunger in him, as well. His arousal was blatant against her abdomen. She shivered with raw desire.

Then one of his hands glided downward and slipped between their bodies. Roslyn stiffened, but his lips made her forget her dismay. A moment later his hand moved between her legs, seeking and caressing.

She tensed, throbbing deep inside, and then gasped when he cupped her woman's mound through the fabric of her gown and chemise. But he went on massaging lightly, stroking, his expert, coaxing touch setting her nerves on fire. When she instinctively pressed closer, rocking her sex against his hand, his kisses shifted from her mouth and trailed along her jaw to her ear.

His breath was a little ragged when he asked, "Can you claim you don't want me touching you?"

She couldn't claim any such thing. She wanted to be touched, wanted him to touch her.

When she didn't reply, he drew back to watch her. His eyes riveted on her face, his gaze smoldered, as his fingers worked their magic. She fought the maddening desire but her body was on fire for him.

"Do you want me to stop?"

"No. . . ."

Her spine arching, she strained against him, helpless to control the quivers that suddenly rocked her body. Quivers that only kept building in ferocity and power. His eyes held her captive with their intensity while explosive pleasure spasmed deep within her. Roslyn bit back her gasping cries, even though she was so weak she swayed against him.

Yet he wasn't finished, it seemed. Not at all. Before she could even recover her breath, he knelt before her. To her shock, he lifted her gown to bare her naked limbs to his gaze.

She clutched his hair as he stroked up the insides of her thighs, his long fingers gentle against her sensitive skin. When he pushed her gown to her waist, she felt exposed, damp with desire. He leaned forward then, and his mouth touched her, the moist heat of it a burning contrast to the coolness elsewhere. Roslyn nearly cried out, yet she clamped her teeth shut, knowing she had to keep quiet for fear of waking the household.

For a time, her soft pants were the only sound in the hushed garden as his relentless mouth plied her sweetly, inciting her to a fever pitch of passion. He slowly lapped at her tender folds, teasing the bud of her sex with erotic strokes until she thought she might faint from the pleasure of it. And just when she could bear no more, he penetrated her deeply with his tongue.

It was too much. The sensation streaking through her was so excruciatingly blissful, her entire body shook.

Her second climax was even more powerful than the first and almost brought her to her knees. As brilliant, bursting lights rocketed inside her, he rose to press his palm over her mouth, stifling her cry of pleasure so that it came out as a keening moan. And when she collapsed against him, Arden's strong arms caught and held her tenderly as his lips brushed soft kisses at her temple.

She clung to him, her heart pounding, her ragged breaths loud in the hushed night.

"Can your earl make you feel such pleasure?" he finally murmured in her ear. "Does he set your body on fire as I do?"

Roslyn hadn't enough energy to shake her head. The earl had never given her such pleasure; with him she'd never experienced anything like what she'd just done with Arden. Her body felt as if it had suddenly burst into flames, while her heart and mind were in similar turmoil. Wonder and amazement at the incredible sensations Arden had made her feel vied with dismay and disbelief that she had let him go so far—and that she had enjoyed it so much.

Dismay won out. Her racing heartbeat slowing, Roslyn groped behind her for the door.

When he started to kiss her again, she averted her head. "Don't. . . . Please, just leave me alone."

Hearing the panicked plea in her voice, Drew stood stock-still for a long moment before his arms reluctantly fell away from her. Freed from his embrace, Roslyn turned and stumbled inside the house, shutting the door in his face.

Drew made no move to stop her as she fled. Instead, he stood there wanting to curse. His arms felt empty, his body hot.

He was aching with more than just sexual frustration, though. The tension knotting his insides had even more to do with his conflicted emotions. He had never felt so torn in his life. His first and only proposal of marriage had been an abject failure—and it was his own damned fault.

He'd decided to stake his claim to Roslyn, whatever it took. Even if it meant having to wed her. But it had been sheer idiocy to blurt out his intentions like that. Not only had he insulted her, but he'd put her on her guard against him.

Her adamant refusal had spurred a fierce need to vanquish her objections. To prove she was attracted to him as well as let her feel real pleasure for the first time. And admittedly, he'd given in to jealousy. He wanted to be the only one who drove her wild, who unleashed that wild, wanton side of her.

She was just as sensual and passionate as he'd expected. Pleasuring her had left him with heat pummeling through his blood—and only strengthened his primal desire to conquer, to seize, to hold.

Drew swore a low oath. His behavior was beginning to border on obsessive. He'd started to act just like Marcus. Call it what you will—infatuation, obsession, madness—but he was infected with the same malady.

Perhaps he *had* gone a little mad, Drew acknowledged. Yet his impulsive proposal was not wholly irrational. After all, Roslyn would make him an excellent duchess. She had the grace and training for the position in addition to the birth and breeding. And he could certainly admire her personal qualities. She was forthright and honest, independent, generous. Her intelligence and sense of humor matched his own.

Yet her most appealing quality was her warm nature. His greatest fear was that he would be shackled for life to some icy noblewoman like his mother, but Roslyn was the antithesis of his bloodless, passionless mother.

And if he must marry someday to carry on his title, he could do far worse. Roslyn was no simpering, vapid miss who would bore him to tears. She would prove a challenge for him, in bed and out.

Now, however, he faced a more immediate challenge—persuading Roslyn to accept his proposal. After tonight she probably wished him in Hades.

The biggest obstacle to a union between them was her vow never to make a marriage of convenience. She feared the bitter antagonism that had characterized her parents' marriage.

They wouldn't have antagonism in their marriage, Drew was fairly certain. They would have friendship and passion, which was more than most genteel marriages had. As for love . . .

Drew dragged a hand roughly through his hair. Roslyn's notions about love in marriage were idealist claptrap, but he knew they were heartfelt.

For a fleeting moment, he wondered if he should attempt to make her fall in love with him, but he rejected the idea almost as soon as it occurred. He didn't want to get tangled up with emotional complications. He certainly didn't want to trick her into believing he could give her what she wanted. When he couldn't reciprocate, it would be highly painful for her.

No, honesty was his best course. Yet he would not only have to convince her of the benefits of marrying him, he would have to overcome her refusal to marry without love.

Turning abruptly, Drew made his way through the dark gardens to return to the ball. He could persuade her to his way of thinking, he felt confident, but he would have to give careful thought to his campaign.

He had never purposely set out to win a woman, but he didn't doubt he could win Roslyn if he truly set his mind to it.

Chapter Ten

❦

Devil take the duke! He has completely spoiled my desire to seduce Lord Haviland.

—Roslyn to Fanny

"Woolgathering, Miss Loring?" the Earl of Haviland said mildly as he slowed his pair of spirited bays to a walk.

Slanting a guilty look at the handsome nobleman in the phaeton's seat beside her, Roslyn shook herself from her brooding reverie. Her thoughts had been so distracted, she'd completely lost track of the conversation.

"I beg your pardon, my lord," she said, her face warming with embarrassment. "What were you saying?"

Haviland's wry smile held a great charm. "Nothing of much import. But you are obviously stewing over some problem. I trust it isn't too serious?"

Not gravely serious, Roslyn thought ironically. *It is only that the plan I so carefully made for my future has splintered in a dozen fragments.*

"Is there anything I may do to help?" Haviland added solicitously.

"Thank you, no. I am just poor company this morning." That much was true, certainly. Her mood matched the weather, which during the night had turned cold and dreary. Casting a glance at the overcast sky, Roslyn drew her pelisse more closely around her.

"Perhaps I should take you home," the earl offered.

She made a determined effort to smile. "No, no, there is no need. Doubtless the brisk air will chase the cobwebs from my brain soon."

"Are you certain?"

"Yes, my lord." She made her smile genuine. "I didn't mean to spoil our outing. This is actually a delightful treat for me."

Haviland was silent for a moment as he directed his horses around a sharp bend in the country lane. "Your preoccupation wouldn't have anything to do with Arden, would it?"

Roslyn tried to conceal her dismay. "Why would you think so?"

"I couldn't help noticing last night that there seemed to be some tension between the two of you. You didn't appear eager to dance with him."

"Because he only asked me under duress."

"Ah, so Lady Freemantle is throwing you together," Haviland observed shrewdly. "She does have a lamentable tendency to play matchmaker."

"Indeed," Roslyn agreed, her tone tart. "It is driving me to distraction—and the duke as well."

"Oh, I don't know about that. I don't expect Arden enjoys being the target of her machinations, but I would say he is interested in you for your own sake. And I think perhaps you are not indifferent to him."

Roslyn couldn't bring herself to lie, so she remained silent. She could feel Haviland's gaze measuring her.

"If you need me to intervene with Lady Freemantle," he finally said, "just say the word."

"Thank you, my lord," Roslyn replied, warmed by his protectiveness.

But her problem was not one Haviland could help her with. She had to deal with this on her own—and she was doing a deplorable job thus far. Her passionate encounter with Arden in the moonlight last night had thrown all her emotions into utter confusion, along with all her best-laid plans.

To begin with, she'd been shocked by his proposal of marriage, even though she couldn't put any real store in it. The duke couldn't possibly want to marry her. And even if he did, she wasn't about to accept. He had proposed for all the wrong reasons—because she would do better than anyone else. What sort of justification was that for marriage? Roslyn reflected with disgust.

If she'd thought for one minute that he could conceivably come to care for her, she might at least have hesitated a fraction of an instant before refusing him. But no, it was impossible to think of the elegant, cynical Duke of Arden losing his head or his heart to her or any other woman. He was the last man who would ever make a love match when he didn't even believe in love.

Yet last night, Roslyn conceded, she'd been forced to admit her fierce desire for him—the illogical, vexatious, maddening desire she'd tried earnestly to deny ever since meeting him. And during a long sleepless night of tossing and turning, she'd had to acknowledge a more profound truth. Not only had Arden shown her the forbidden pleasure that awaited her if she surrendered to him. Not only had he filled her with an anticipation and craving for a passion beyond what she ever imagined. Much worse, he had made her question her own deepest longings.

Did she truly want to win Lord Haviland's heart? Or was it merely a pipe dream that she had built out of an idealistic need for love?

Whatever the answers, she no longer felt in control of her destiny.

She wanted to curse the duke, and yet she couldn't place the blame entirely on him. Her own wanton behavior was inexcusable.

Swearing mentally at herself, Roslyn shook off her dark thoughts and bestirred herself to give all her attention to Lord Haviland. For the next three-quarters of an hour, they indulged in amusing banter with the pleasant intimacy of old friends. It was the most comfortable she had ever been around him.

And that was a big part of the trouble, Roslyn realized with chagrin when his lordship returned her to Danvers Hall and took his leave of her. She felt little of the spark with Haviland that the Duke of Arden kindled in her with only a glance. Every time she was with the earl, all she could think about was Arden.

And her mind kept insisting on comparing the two of them. They were both dynamic, charismatic men, but only one made her blood sing and her stomach flutter. Only one made her lose all her willpower when he merely kissed her as Arden had done last night.

His embrace had been dominantly possessive, eliciting an erotic response in her beyond her control. The experience had shaken Roslyn to her core, and opened her eyes to self-doubt as well.

A doubt that had only been confirmed in the cold light of day. The moment she'd greeted Lord Haviland this morning, she'd understood why her pulse didn't quicken at the sight of him. Why her heart didn't race and turn somersaults in her chest at his nearness.

She felt affection and friendship for the earl, but not much of the delicious thrill she always felt with the duke.

Feeling a deep regret, Roslyn slowly made her way upstairs to her bedchamber. She wished her sisters were here so she could discuss her dilemma with them. Arabella would likely understand and be able to offer sage advice, yet regrettably she was still away on her wedding trip. And Lily was also away, in London.

Besides, Lily would be the last person to ask, since she was so adamantly opposed to marriage. Lily would say that she'd lost her wits—and Roslyn would have to agree. She had just tossed all her long-held aspirations, all her beliefs about what she wanted for her future, out the window.

Fanny would be happy to listen, of course, but Roslyn felt that she'd intruded on her friend quite enough in the past few weeks. And in any case, Fanny was in London, too, nearly an hour away.

Perhaps she should apply to Tess for advice. Tess fully appreciated her desire to make a love match and approved of her interest in Lord Haviland. But what would Tess say about a woman's need for passion in her life?

Roslyn had never let herself dream of having a grand passion in marriage. She'd told herself she would be content with love and affection. But now she was beginning to wonder if she didn't want passion after all.

One thing was becoming certain, though. She would have to end her pursuit of Haviland. It wouldn't be fair to him to continue trying to rouse his interest and affection when she was so attracted to another man. It wouldn't be fair to make Haviland fall in love with her, either, when she might never be able to truly love him in return.

Closing her chamber door behind her, Roslyn took off her half-boots and pelisse and sat upon the bed with her arms around her updrawn legs, her chin resting pensively upon her knees. She wanted to remain there for the rest of the day, stewing over her dilemma, but in a few hours she would have to face Lady Freemantle. Winifred's invitation to tea this afternoon had practically been a summons.

Roslyn had considered declining but knew her friend might show up on her doorstep demanding to know what was wrong with her. And it would be easier to battle Winifred's matchmaking efforts at Freemantle Park when she could threaten to leave.

As expected, Winifred wasn't the least contrite about last night's conniving. In fact, Roslyn learned to her dismay when she had settled in her friend's ostentatious drawing room, the Duke of Arden had been invited to tea this afternoon as well.

"Winifred! You simply must stop this shameful scheming," Roslyn complained. "It is utterly mortifying."

Smiling, the elder woman shook her head. "In this case you are off the mark. It wasn't *my* scheme to invite you both here. Arden himself suggested it."

When Roslyn's jaw dropped, Winifred's smile

broadened. "Don't looked so surprised, my girl. Anyone can see that the duke is taken with you."

"That isn't so."

Ignoring her protest, Winifred glanced out the drawing room window at the gray sky. "I trust it won't rain until after he arrives."

Roslyn found herself gnashing her teeth. She had no idea why Arden would want to take tea with her, but she was very certain she didn't want to see him again. Not after last night.

Did he wish to apologize to her for his scandalous attentions in the garden? Or perhaps he intended to renew his addresses to her, God forbid. He couldn't do either in front of Winifred.

Yet it was more likely, Roslyn realized, that he had arranged a meeting this way so she couldn't refuse his company. At least they would be chaperoned so there was no chance she would repeat her deplorable surrender. Even so, she wondered how she would manage to get through the next hour.

Her agitated thoughts were interrupted when Winifred mused aloud, "It is much chillier than I expected. Would you be a dear and fetch my shawl from my dressing room?"

Roslyn jumped to her feet, eager to have something to do to distract her. "Yes, of course."

She quickly left the drawing room and went upstairs to Winifred's bedchamber. The dressing room door was partially closed, but when she pushed it open, she came to a puzzled halt.

A footman stood there in front of Winifred's dressing table, pawing through her ladyship's jewel case.

He froze at Roslyn's unexpected entrance, then

guiltily dropped the expensive diamond necklace he had been fingering.

Her first instinctive thought was that she'd interrupted a thief trying to steal Winifred's jewels. Yet before she could say a word, the footman suddenly whirled and barreled past her out the dressing room door, his head bent low so she couldn't see his face, only his ginger-colored hair.

Knocked askew, Roslyn nearly fell to the ground, and as she struggled to regain her balance, she realized the thief wore a sling on his right arm.

Good God! He had been wounded, just like the highwayman who had held up the Freemantle carriage last week!

Gathering her scattered wits, Roslyn gave chase, but he had already bolted out of the bedchamber. Picking up her skirts to keep from tripping, she ran after him. By the time she reached the end of the hall corridor, she saw him bounding down the sweeping front staircase.

"Stop him!" she cried out, hoping one of the servant staff would hear her and help her thwart his escape. "Stop that thief!"

Another footman was stationed at his post behind the stairs, along with the Freemantle butler, Pointon, no doubt because they were expecting the duke's arrival any moment. When Roslyn shouted again, both servants recovered from their startlement and bounded after the fleeing thief just as he flung open the front door.

As Roslyn ran down the stairs, they caught him and dragged him back to the entrance hall. At the first contact, he gave a yelp of pain and clutched his wounded right arm, but then erupted in fury, swinging his good arm and delivering a hail of blows against his captors so that he eventually broke free.

Roslyn had almost reached the foot of the stairway when Winifred appeared, the shouts and scuffle having brought her out of the drawing room.

"What in heaven's name . . . ?" Winifred demanded in bewilderment as the injured thief made for the door again. Her words trailed off, though, when she caught sight of the ginger-haired miscreant. She abruptly froze, while her face turned white.

Yet Roslyn was too occupied to pay much attention to her friend. Instead she set out after the thief, reaching the doorway as he charged down the entrance steps. When he turned to his right, racing along the front of the mansion, Roslyn hesitated barely an instant before following, nearly tripping on the steps in her haste.

It registered in her mind that the duke had just driven up in his curricle while a waiting groom had gone to the horses's heads. But she couldn't spare the time to answer when Arden called out to her. She rushed past him and along the gravel drive, watching the thief sprint for the south corner of the house.

Her breath ragged now, Roslyn dashed after him, but when she turned the corner in pursuit of him, she saw with dismay that he had reached his bay horse that was tied to a tree branch. Roslyn muttered an oath as he hauled himself up onto his saddle with his good arm. He was getting away!

Whirling, she ran back to the front of the house. Arden had jumped down from his curricle and was staring at her. "Roslyn, what the devil is going on?" he exclaimed.

"No time to explain!" she cried. "The highwayman . . ."

Without pause, she scrambled to climb up into the curricle's seat and gathered the reins, hoping the duke would forgive her for commandeering his expensive equipage and pair.

"Stand aside!" she ordered the startled groom.

The instant he obeyed and let go the bridle, she snapped the reins over the backs of the spirited grays. The horses sprang forward, nearly throwing Roslyn from the seat.

With a gasp, she righted herself at the same time she heard the duke's own muttered curse over the rattle of carriage wheels. Arden had somehow caught the seat railing and leaped on board the swaying curricle. He was clinging precariously to the side as they bowled along the drive.

Roslyn had difficulty controlling the grays, but she didn't dare stop long enough to let the duke climb to safety. Ahead, the highwayman's bay had broken into a gallop and was racing up the drive.

Arden cursed again as he finally pulled himself into the seat beside her. "Roslyn, for God's sake, slow down!"

"No, I have to catch him!"

"Then give me the damned reins before you land us in a ditch!"

He seized them from her grasp and took control, and in a moment the grays recognized his expert hand and settled into a more even rhythm.

Yet the highwayman was still increasing the distance between them. And before the drive ended, he cut across a stretch of lawn to meet up with the country lane, giving himself an even greater advance.

The curricle lost some speed as Arden negotiated the turn, but then he urged the grays faster. Roslyn clung to the side railing as the curricle bucked and shuddered over the uneven ground. Yet she could tell they were losing the chase.

She was certain of it when suddenly the bay horse plunged off the lane and disappeared into the woods.

Arden slowed the curricle when they reached the path the rider had taken, but the opening in the trees was too narrow for the curricle to negotiate. Having no way to follow, he drew his panting grays to a halt. They could hear the dull echo of hoofbeats growing ever more distant.

"Blast, blast, blast!" Roslyn sputtered, banging her fist on her knee in frustration.

"So explain to me why we were chasing him," Arden said when she finally fell silent. "You believe he was the highwayman who held you up last week?"

"Yes, didn't you see his right arm? He wore it in a sling."

"And you found him in Lady Freemantle's house?"

"Yes. At first I thought he was one of her footmen, but I caught him in her dressing room, in the act of rifling through her jewel case. I don't think he had time to steal anything—he ran from me as soon he saw me—" Roslyn broke off suddenly to point at the lane in front of them. "Why are we just wasting time sitting here? We need to hunt for the thief," she said urgently.

"Just what do you propose we do?" Drew asked, lifting an eyebrow.

"He was headed in the direction of Chiswick. We should at least inquire in the village if anyone has seen him."

She reached for the reins, but Drew held them away. "No you don't. I still haven't recovered from the shock of you absconding with my rig. And I'm damned if I want you risking my horses' lives again, or our own."

He set his pair into a brisk, ground-eating trot, heading toward Chiswick, which calmed Roslyn enough for him to question her about the highwayman.

"Why did you think him to be a footman?" Drew asked as they drove.

Her brow furrowed. "I just assumed so because he was dressed in livery."

Drew shook his head. "He wore a different color livery than the Freemantle servants. His coat was dark blue with gold trim. Her ladyship's colors are burgundy and silver."

"I didn't think of that," she said.

"So why was he in disguise?"

"I'm not certain. Perhaps he thought he could more easily sneak into the house if he could be mistaken for a servant."

"But why take such a risk?"

"Because," Roslyn mused aloud, "Winifred was too well guarded after last night's ball?"

"I suppose that's possible," Drew conceded.

"He must have wanted her brooch. He didn't seem interested in her diamonds this time, just like the last."

"What the devil is so special about that brooch?"

"I have no idea," she answered. "Its value is mostly sentimental since it contains a portrait of Winifred's late husband inside. But I wouldn't think Sir Rupert's likeness would be of any interest to anyone but her."

"Was the brooch in her jewel case?"

"No. After the holdup, she decided to keep it in a safer place, thank heavens. She would be devastated if it were stolen."

"You realize that searching the village will likely be futile? I doubt he will have let himself be seen there— or anywhere else near here for that matter. Not with every farmer and tradesman in the district on the look-out for him."

"I know, but I must do *something*."

"What you should do," Drew muttered under his breath, "is allow me to take you home."

"Don't you want to catch him?"

"Of course. But I dislike the way you keep putting yourself in dangerous, possibly life-threatening situations."

Roslyn turned her head to stare at him. "You can't honestly fault me for trying to prevent him from stealing my friend's prize possession?"

"In fact I do. I admire your determination, but you could have been seriously hurt just now, not to mention that you could have lamed my horses."

"I'm sorry, but I was desperate."

"Have you ever even driven a pair before?"

"No," Roslyn replied a trifle guiltily, "but I am quite proficient at driving one horse since I take out our gig frequently."

"It isn't the same thing. I shall have to teach you how to handle a pair."

"No, you will not! I have had more than enough lessons from you, your grace, thank you all the same."

"Stop addressing me as 'your grace' in that stately tone. We have gone far beyond such formalities. My name is Drew."

"I know what your name is. But that doesn't mean I care to use it."

"Why not?"

"It would signify too much intimacy between us."

He didn't point out that they had already been a great deal more intimate than merely using their given names, since he didn't wish to remind Roslyn of their acrimonious parting last evening. Instead, Drew cast her a sideways glance, surveying her. She had to be chilled. Her afternoon dress of gray twilled silk was not meant to withstand a windy drive on such a stormy day.

He drew the horses to a halt and handed her the reins. "Don't you dare drive. Just hold them for a moment." Taking off his coat, he slid it around her shoulders.

"You don't have much sense, chasing after him without so much as a shawl."

"I don't care about my comfort. I just want to find the thief so he will stop terrorizing Winifred."

Drew bit back the sharp remark that was on the tip of his tongue. It exasperated him that Roslyn would chase after the thief with no thought to her own safety, even though he had to admire her courage and her determination to get to the bottom of the mystery and protect her friend, Lady Freemantle. But he knew she wouldn't rest until she had her way.

In a few moments they arrived in the small village of Chiswick, which boasted a market, a posting inn and tavern, a blacksmith, and a church, in addition to several shops. Drew escorted Roslyn into each one and took over the questioning. But the result was just as he'd expected. No one had seen any sign of the thieving footman; his trail had gone completely cold just like before.

Roslyn was not happy to admit defeat. "This is so *frustrating*," she exclaimed as Drew handed her up into his curricle. "He has escaped twice now."

"I know, but we've done all we can do this afternoon." Hearing a distant roll of thunder, he glanced up at the darkening sky. "I need to return you to Freemantle Park. There's a storm brewing, and we don't want to be caught in it."

"We can't simply give up," Roslyn protested. "I doubt he will stop trying until we apprehend him."

"I'm not giving up," Drew assured her as he turned his horses back toward the Park. "But there are smarter ways to conduct a search than chasing about in this haphazard fashion."

"What ways?"

"We start by identifying the livery he was wearing."

"How can you possibly identify his livery?"

Drew delayed answering momentarily while he urged the grays to a brisker pace. The wind was blustering now and the scent of rain was rife in the air, and he wanted Roslyn safely back before the storm hit.

"I'll hire a Bow Street Runner to investigate," Drew said then. "Think about it. He had to have acquired his attire somewhere. He may very well be employed as a footman in some noble household. And if not, it will still put us closer to discovering his identity if we can learn where his costume came from."

She frowned thoughtfully. "That might indeed work. But I want to speak to Bow Street myself. You have done more than enough already."

"I don't mind in the least."

"Perhaps not, but this is not your problem."

"I am making it my problem."

"Your grace," she said, her tone exasperated, "Winifred is one of my dearest friends, and I wish to handle this problem on my own."

Drew's mouth twisted wryly. "Didn't any of my lessons sink in? Your authoritarian manner is likely to put off your suitors," he chided lightly. "You should be playing damsel in distress instead."

"So you can play the silver-armored knight?"

"Quite. It's good for a man's self-esteem, letting him feel heroic once in a while."

Roslyn rolled her eyes. "There is only one difficulty. I have no desire to attract you—*or* to have you for my suitor."

"I know. Which I find rather amazing. How many women would reject the hand of a duke?"

She gave him a quelling look. "I don't wish to discuss it."

"And I don't wish to discuss my involvement any further. I'll pay a visit to Bow Street as soon as I return to London. Now just say a gracious thank-you, sweeting, and hold your tongue."

"Very well, thank you, your grace," Roslyn said grudgingly.

"That wasn't gracious enough," Drew observed. "I can be of help to you and you know it."

She couldn't help but smile. "Very well, you win. I would appreciate your help."

Drew regarded her with satisfaction. After their tumultuous parting last night in the garden, he wanted very much to have Roslyn smile at him again. "That is much better—"

He had only completed half the sentence when a sudden crack of lightning split the sky on their left, followed swiftly by a ferocious clap of thunder. His high-strung horses shied violently at the boom and lunged forward, jerking the curricle behind them.

Drew swore under his breath and tightened his grip on the reins, struggling to hold the grays, yet it was difficult when a gusting wind began buffeting them. And when a second jagged streak of lightning was accompanied by more explosive thunder, the pair panicked and bolted into a gallop.

It was all Drew could do to maintain control as the curricle went careening down the country lane. He had just started to slow the frightened horses when one of the wheels hit a pothole with a loud crack, jolting the vehicle so hard that both he and Roslyn were nearly thrown from their seats.

Drew caught her and clung precariously as the curricle canted at a dangerous angle. They were dragged behind the racing pair for a hundred yards or more, until at last he managed to haul the horses to a trembling halt.

"Are you all right?" he demanded of Roslyn.

"Yes," she said shakily. "What of the horses?"

Tossing her the reins, Drew jumped down and went to their heads, trying to soothe them. "They're unharmed, but the wheel is shot."

The metal rim had come off and the wooden wheel had splintered in fragments, so that the axle was almost touching the ground. The wheel would have to be repaired before the curricle was functional again.

In any event, outracing the storm was out of the question, for already they were being pelted by stinging raindrops.

He was debating whether to walk back to the village or search for the nearest farm when the heavens suddenly opened up. In seconds they were drenched by a torrent of icy rain.

Drew immediately set to work unharnessing the horses, and when another lightning bolt shook the ground, Roslyn climbed down from the curricle and pointed at a shadowy structure set back off the lane.

"There is a cottage," she shouted. "Can we take shelter there?"

"Better than remaining here," Drew responded over the din. The cottage would offer nominal protection from the lightning and slashing rain at least.

Roslyn helped him to unbuckle the leather straps of the harnesses, but for her safety, Drew led the nervous horses through the deluge.

It was slow going. They could barely see in the downpour, and her shoes were not made for trudging over uneven ground made treacherous with mud.

The lightning struck dangerously close again just as they finally reached the cottage. The small dwelling was built of stone with a thatched roof, Drew saw, and boasted a shed for livestock against one wall.

"I recognize this place," Roslyn shouted again. "It belongs to the Widow Jearson, but she may not be here. I heard she is visiting her granddaughter for her lying-in." Stumbling forward, Roslyn dragged open the door to the shed. "Yes, I was right. She has a pony and cart, but they are both are gone. There is room for your horses, though."

Drew led the skittish grays inside while Roslyn quickly shut the door behind them to keep out the fierce gusts of rain. As he took stock of the shed, she leaned back against the door in obvious relief, her breath a little ragged. Through the dim light slanting through the one window, he could see she was soaked to the skin, with her hair plastered to her head. His coat had been useless in protecting her, but at least she was now safe from the ferocity of the storm.

There was only one stall, but it would serve to hold the horses, Drew decided, and there was even a forkful of hay in the manger to keep them occupied. He removed their bridles and turned the grays loose, but to his surprise, Roslyn followed them inside.

She had rummaged in a cupboard and found some rags, which she proceeded to use to wipe down their soaked hides.

"You don't have to curry my horses, sweeting," Drew said, relieving her of a rag.

She flashed him a damp smile. "I feel obliged, since they suffered enough abuse at my hands for one day. And it won't be good for them to be put up wet."

It didn't totally surprise him that she would place the animals' comfort and well-being over her own, but it did surprise him that a lady of her breeding would know how to properly care for blood horses.

"Where did you learn to groom?"

"My sisters and I had to care for our own mounts for the past four years, since our step-uncle wouldn't let his grooms assist us."

Drew found his jaw tightening at the reminder of the late Lord Danvers. The miserly curmudgeon had treated his step-nieces like supplicants, not only forcing them to work for their livings and become teachers at their academy, but to perform the tasks of menial servants.

"We didn't mind," Roslyn added when she saw his frown. "And Lily thrived on it. She would much rather spend her time in a barn than a ballroom."

When they had finished, the grays not only were much drier but had calmed down significantly. They stood quietly munching hay, even though rain still drummed fiercely upon the roof and outside thunder rolled and lightning crackled.

Roslyn, however, had begun shivering in her wet clothing.

"Let's move to the cottage," Drew said. "It will be warmer there."

"The doors may be locked," she replied skeptically.

"Then we'll break in. You can't stay here in this condition."

Leaving the shed, they made a dash through the rain for the front cottage door, which indeed was locked. Drew had to pry open a window in order to gain access. He climbed inside, then ushered Roslyn in through the door and slammed it behind her.

"I don't think Mrs. Jearson will mind if we take refuge here," Roslyn said breathlessly as she stood drenched and dripping, "but she won't be pleased that we've damaged her home."

"I'll repay her, of course."

The interior was cold and dark, since minimal light

seeped in through the shutters. But it was spotlessly clean and quite comfortable—or it would be once they got a fire going in the hearth.

There were two rooms, Drew saw. The main one that served as living quarters and kitchen, and a smaller one to the rear that was obviously a bedchamber.

"The accommodations are not what a duke is accustomed to," Roslyn said, moving to the kitchen. "Mrs. Jearson is a pensioner of Sir Alfred and Lady Perry—she was nanny to their children, but she has no other income."

"It will do well enough," Drew said with all honesty.

In truth, he was just as pleased that the widow wasn't here. He hadn't planned this debacle, but he was glad to have the chance to be alone with Roslyn. He not only wanted to clear the air between them, he wanted time to persuade her to accept his proposal of marriage.

Drew shook his head in sardonic amusement. The fact that he actually welcomed being caught in a chilling rainstorm so he could further his matrimonial goals was solid proof that he had gone a little daft.

A fire had been laid with logs, so he knelt on the rug in front of hearth to light the kindling, while Roslyn lit a lamp in the kitchen.

The glow helped present the illusion of comfort. The storm continued to lash the small cottage—wind shook the shutters and rain pounded on the roof—but inside the sounds were hushed.

"I don't want to light the stove," Roslyn said while searching through the cupboards, "since hopefully the storm will pass soon and we can be on our way. But I could make some tea at the fireplace."

"Can you?" Drew asked.

"Yes. There is a canister of tea here and fresh water in an urn."

"I meant, do you know how?"

"I am capable of boiling water, your grace," she replied, her tone dry.

His mouth twitched. "I don't doubt you are a woman of many talents," he said as he sat in a wooden chair to remove his sodden boots. "But I wouldn't expect you to know much about cooking."

Across the room, Roslyn shrugged. "We were raised to privilege, but we had to learn any number of new skills once we lost our home and fortunes." Glancing up, she regarded him across the room. "You seem surprised."

He was indeed surprised. He couldn't imagine his imperious mother deigning to make her own tea over an open fire, or grooming her own horses either.

But Roslyn seemed efficient as she filled the kettle and hung it in the hearth to boil.

Then remaining there, she held her chilled hands out before the struggling fire. Even over the snapping flames, Drew could hear her teeth chattering, and she was obviously shivering.

"You had best take off your wet gown," he said casually as he pulled off his second boot and started on his stockings.

She glanced over her shoulder at him, her eyebrow lifted in a perfect arch. "You cannot be serious."

"Do you think I mean to ravish you? When you look as appealing as a bedraggled cat?"

She studied him silently, a worried frown creasing her brow.

Drew kept his expression bland. He had meant to set her at ease regarding his lascivious intentions, but even with her looking like the pitiful victim of a shipwreck, he still felt an uncommonly powerful attraction for her. And seeing her soaked and shivering brought out his protective instincts, along with other less-nurturing urges that were strong and powerfully male.

"There should be some blankets in the bedchamber. You can swathe yourself head to toe."

"Thank you, but I will be fine as I am."

"You would rather freeze?"

"I think perhaps I might."

He shook his head. "Don't be foolish. I have seen your charms more than once, angel. Taking off your gown would hardly be a worse offense."

"Please, do *not* remind me. Last night was a mistake. It should never have happened."

Drew couldn't disagree more. Last night had certainly *not* been a mistake—and he meant to make Roslyn understand that.

"I am crushed," he drawled. "My first proposal of marriage ever, and you fling it back in my face."

"Because you weren't at all serious."

"I beg to differ. I was deadly serious."

Roslyn's short laugh held little amusement. "You were only trying to demonstrate your prowess. You are devastatingly adept at lovemaking, and you wanted to prove how easily you could seduce me. It meant nothing to you."

"That couldn't be further from the truth," he said in a low voice.

Instead of answering, she faced the fire again and

wrapped her arms around herself, trying to stop shivering.

"Roslyn," Drew said again, "go take off your gown before you catch your death. I promise I won't ravish you." *At least not without invitation.*

"No. Last night was bad enough."

"You're afraid Haviland will learn we are here together, but I won't tell him, I promise."

"Haviland, among others. It is highly improper for us to be here alone like this, even if we had little choice."

But Drew's attention was still focused on his rival. "You haven't told me how your drive with him went this morning. Did you even go?"

"Yes, I drove out with him," she said slowly.

"After I specifically asked you not to?"

Roslyn turned her head to stare at him. "You cannot possibly be jealous of Haviland."

He wanted to deny it, but even to his own ears his tone held irritation and impatience. Curse it all, of course he could be jealous. Roslyn wanted another man. Lord, how he hated the idea.

Before he could reply, another wracking shudder ran through her, which only added to his growing ire. When she clenched her teeth together to keep them from clacking, Drew had had enough.

"Roslyn, my sweet, take yourself into the bedchamber and divest yourself of those wet garments before I do it for you."

She eyed him for a long moment before giving an exasperated sigh. "You probably would, wouldn't you?"

"Most assuredly."

She didn't quite stalk into the other room, but she was clearly not happy about having to obey his order.

During her absence, Drew took the opportunity to remove most of his own soggy clothing—his cravat and waistcoat and shirt—and hung them on wall pegs to dry. In the interest of propriety, he left on his drawers and breeches, no matter how cold and clammy they were, and crossed to the hearth to warm his chilled body before the growing blaze.

But even that, apparently, was too risqué for Roslyn. When a brief while later she emerged from the bedchamber with her feet bare and a quilt wrapped around her shoulders, she came to an abrupt halt. Her eyes widened as she surveyed his partial state of undress, the blush staining her cheeks revealing her discomfort.

"I f-found a blanket for you," she stammered. "You should cover yourself."

"I will be happy to."

When he made no move toward her, though, she slowly crossed to him and handed him the blanket. Drew draped it around his shoulders as Roslyn quickly turned away. His loins had hardened at the thought of her naked beneath that quilt, but when it parted slightly, he saw that she'd kept on her chemise, even though the lawn fabric was wet.

She was carrying her sopping gown and other undergarments, however, and hung them on wall pegs before casting him a wary glance as if to ask, "Now what?"

Drew was very aware of the sudden tension in the air, just as he knew she was.

She was also still trembling with cold.

"Come warm yourself at the fire," he said, feigning indifference.

She obeyed with obvious reluctance—and then jumped when he reached up touch her hair. "What are you *doing*?"

"Taking down your hair. It's still dripping wet. You need to dry it if you hope to get warm."

Her indecision was understandable; she couldn't remove the pins from her hair and still keep hold of the quilt.

She stood stock-still while his fingers searched for the pins that held up the heavy gold mass, then smoothed the damp tresses down her back. "There, that should help."

"Thank you," she murmured, glancing up at him.

Drew sucked in a sharp breath. The light thrown by the flames cast a golden glow over her beautiful face. She was temptation itself, and he wasn't able to resist.

Slowly he lifted his hand to her face, letting his thumb trace her jaw.

"I th-think I had best make the tea," Roslyn said shakily.

"The water isn't hot yet."

When he moved his fingers to her lips, she drew in a sharp breath, too. "You promised. . . ." Her protest was no more than a whisper.

His smile was tender. "I said I wouldn't ravish you, and I won't." *But ravishment implies lack of consent,* he added silently to himself, *and I promise your consent won't be lacking.*

"Sit here on the rug," he said aloud, moving his hands to her shoulders to nudge her down. When she complied, he knelt behind her.

Roslyn went rigid. "Drew. . . ."

"Hush, sweeting. Let me warm you." He slid his

arms around her, along with his blanket. "You're half frozen."

Leaning closer, he eased her down so that they both lay on their sides, her head resting on his left arm, his bare chest pressed against her back, his loins cradling her derriere. Although her quilt still separated them, he knew she could feel his body heat.

He felt an inexplicable heat inside him as well, despite the chill of his flesh. It was possibly madness, what he was contemplating, but instinct drove him, not reason.

Gazing into the crackling fire, Drew found himself smiling at the irony. After so many years of eluding matrimony, he was about to make the choice irrevocable. He intended to make love to Roslyn here and now. To claim her for his bride.

His surrender seemed somehow fated, though, and shortly Roslyn would feel the same way. She was willfully deceiving herself, Drew reflected. She felt a mutual passion for him, he was certain of it, even though she stubbornly continued to deny it.

And before they left this cottage, he would prove it to her conclusively.

Chapter Eleven

❧

I now see why you were persuaded to surrender your innocence in a moment of weakness—because passion is so incredible.

—Roslyn to Fanny

Roslyn lay wrapped in his arms, not daring to move. She was conscious of how wildly her heart was thudding, how intensely her senses had sharpened.

The fire threw a welcome heat into the small room, yet the flames had little to do with her increasing warmth. Rather it was because Arden lay so close behind her, his hard-muscled body spooning hers, with only a quilt to separate them.

She'd been a little shocked to find him nearly unclothed. Her admiring eyes had riveted on the broad expanse of his bare chest, on the sinewed torso sculpted by firelight. His body was strong and graceful and even more breathtaking than she had imagined—sleek, golden, beautifully male. Seeing him like that had roused a giddy, fluttery sensation in her stomach, which had only compounded tenfold when he lay down with her before the hearth.

For the longest time they didn't speak. Roslyn stared into the flickering flames, vaguely aware of the hypnotic effect on her taut nerves. The cottage had started to grow cozy, further lulling her. The storm continued to rage outside—rain pounding, wind moaning—but the sounds were muted inside. She could better hear the creaking rafters, the crackling hearth fire, her erratic heartbeats.

Behind her, Arden was nearly still . . . except for sifting a lock of her hair through his fingers. When he leaned closer to press his lips against her hair, Roslyn didn't flinch as she ought, but her pulse raced even harder. Then he eased away from her, and she held her breath.

Moving with a languid grace, he turned her toward him, so that she lay on her back, looking up at him as he braced his weight on one elbow. His blanket had slipped down so that his shoulders and chest gleamed in the firelight, and so did his eyes.

She stared back, transfixed, her heart flipping over in her chest.

Reaching up, he touched her face gently, his hand trailing over her cheek and feathering over her hair. "You tempt me unbearably," he murmured, his gaze locked with hers.

You tempt me unbearably, too, Roslyn thought wildly.

His gaze dropped to rest on her mouth. "I intend to kiss you, sweeting."

"I know," she whispered.

He bent his head to her then, his breath warm on her mouth as he began to kiss her. His lips moved slowly on hers, his pace unhurried, lingering. Even at that slightest pressure, heat kindled inside her. And when he leaned even closer, the heat from his body bathed her heightened senses.

Roslyn nearly moaned as a stabbing rush of longing

assaulted her. Knowing she had to protest, she freed her hands from the quilt and pushed against his shoulders, fighting the dizzying delight he so effortlessly conjured inside her.

She was inexplicably disappointed, however, when his tantalizing kiss unexpectedly ended.

Arden lifted his head, gazing down at her as he peeled back the edges of the quilt that wrapped her body. When she would have pulled it back around her, he gently caught her wrists and drew them closer, pressing her palms against his chest, inviting her hands to explore the hard, tempting expanse. His flesh was smooth and hot; muscles rippled and played beneath satiny skin. She could feel the powerful thud of his heartbeat against his rib cage as well, which made urgent desire flare though her body.

She knew he desired her, too. Her hip rode against his loins, making her aware of his hardness through his damp breeches. There was no mistaking that he was blatantly aroused.

The knowledge made her heart pound harder, even before he began to caress her in turn. His hands moved slowly over her body, roaming from her bare throat down over the thin fabric of her chemise . . . her breasts, her belly, her hips, her thighs, her woman's mound, then back up again to her breasts, his fingers teasing the tight buds of her nipples. He didn't demand her surrender, though; he lured with soft touches, with erotic caresses. His expert, coaxing touch reduced her to shivering need.

Her fingers clenching desperately at the quilt, Roslyn shut her eyes, submitting to those clever, amazing hands.

"No, look at me, love," he urged in a husky whisper.

Helplessly, she obeyed, even though all her instincts screamed danger. She was sinking under his spell again, her reservations obliterated by an intoxicating madness induced by his arousing ministrations. Every nerve came alive with delirious sensation as he deftly touched, explored, discovered. She was no longer shivering with cold but trembling under his hands, melting in a warm tide.

Yet it was his eyes that warmed her the most. The expression in his eyes held great tenderness. The way he looked at her made her feel cherished somehow.

Roslyn drew a shaky breath. This moment seemed like a dream, a fantasy, yet at the same time it felt supremely real. He was her haven from the storm. She felt sheltered in his arms, protected, treasured.

She had never experienced anything like it. Certainly not in the past four years. For so long she and her sisters had had no one to depend on. No man, at any rate. And here Arden was, making her feel infinitely precious.

Her breath faltered entirely when he bent to her again. He took her mouth slowly, thoroughly, his kiss deep and penetrating, as if he was determined to know every secret she had. To steal away every ounce of her willpower. His lips whispered promises of pleasure, of passion beyond her wildest dreams.

Surrendering her last meager defenses, Roslyn reached up and slid her fingers into his silky hair, sighing softly into his mouth upon realizing how completely he'd captured her.

When finally he drew back, she gazed up at him with passion-hazed eyes.

His voice was low and rasping when he said quietly, "I want to make love to you, Roslyn."

She couldn't deny that was what she wanted too. And even if she tried, she knew he wouldn't believe her. His gaze was on her face, too perceptive, too knowing; the tantalizing offer of his body was hard against hers.

She gave up any thought of resisting. She desired him, there was nothing more to understand. He wanted to make love to her, and this time she would welcome it.

Yet he had other things in mind for the moment, it seemed.

He had unfastened his breeches and freed his rampant erection. Letting her gaze drop, Roslyn sucked in a sharp breath at the flagrant virility of his arousal. The thick flesh jutted out, so large, so blatantly rigid, that she could scarcely breathe.

When he brought her hand to his loins, murmuring, "Touch me," she realized that he wanted her to take the lead. Willing to obey, she touched him hesitantly, grazing the swollen head of his member, trailing a finger downward delicately to the heavy sacs below.

"Are you shocked by my anatomy?" he asked.

"Not . . . shocked exactly. Fanny told me something about what to expect."

"Would you like to know more?"

"Yes."

"Then feel free to explore."

Her heart racing, she curled her fingers around the heated shaft, squeezing gently. It was burning-hot against her palm, hard as steel. She realized how arousing just that slight pressure must be for him because his eyes darkened, yet he wanted more.

"Harder. You won't hurt me."

Tightening her hold, she slowly slid her fingers down his great length and up again. He made a sound deep in his throat, like a harsh groan, which inexplicably pleased Roslyn. He throbbed beneath her touch, stirring a similar throb deep in her most secret, feminine places.

Intoxicated by the sensation, she repeated her slow stroking, wanting to pleasure him as he had pleasured her. At the same time, she couldn't help wondering how it would feel to join with him, how her body could absorb his enormous male flesh. She wanted him inside her, filling the hollow ache that had blossomed between her thighs, yet the image of him trying to fit inside her was a little alarming.

When suddenly she drew back her hand, Arden leaned over her, gazing deep into her eyes. "You aren't afraid of me, are you?"

Roslyn couldn't answer. She wanted him with a longing that was new and frightening to her, yet she wasn't afraid. "I . . . I don't know."

"You shouldn't fear me. We have been moving toward this moment since the night we met."

It felt that way to her also. Everything had been leading to this moment.

But he obviously wanted to reassure her, for he resumed caressing her, his tantalizing strokes drifting over her body.

The exquisite, inciting touch of his hands made her shiver and want more. Her skin heated, stoking the fire that was rising inside her.

Her breath was coming in shallow bursts by the time his fingers circled the curve of her shoulder and drew down the bodice of her chemise.

He took her naked breasts in his warm palms, measuring the weight and fullness, then bent his head to suckle her. His tongue swirled over her nipple, tightening it into a knot of aching need, inflaming her nerves all over again.

Gasping, Roslyn arched against the delicious sensation, while a fevered longing filled her. His hot mouth attended her nipples as he pulled the hem of her chemise up to her waist, baring her to the warmth of the fire.

Excitement shimmered through her as Arden raised his head to survey her, his gaze burning. There was hot desire in his eyes, a passion she could feel.

Holding her gaze, he splayed his fingers low on her belly, then skated the flat of his palm downward. As if he knew exactly where she craved his touch, his hand slipped down to tangle in the moist thatch that adorned her mound.

A whimper escaped her as he parted the soaked curls between her thighs with his fingers. With exquisite tenderness he stroked her pulsing flesh, intimately caressing each soft fold until she felt faint with desire. And when he found the secret point that quivered with aching need, her blood turned to liquid fire.

Then he slid two fingers into her drenched cleft, and Roslyn moaned out loud.

Her breath was coming in broken gasps of pleasure when he finally eased over her, holding her captive beneath the sensual weight of his body.

But there Drew hesitated, his hard arousal nestled in the warm folds of her sex.

He drew in a deep, ragged breath as he stared down at Roslyn, searching her exquisite, flushed face. She lay beneath him, silken thighs spread, her bare skin glowing like a pearl in the soft light, her blue eyes hazed with desire. He recognized all the signs of a sexually aroused woman. She was more than ready for him, her body pliant and vibrant in his arms, lush for the taking.

And yet no carnal union had ever seemed this crucial. He'd never before made love to the woman he intended to wed. If he had any doubts whatsoever, this was the point to draw back . . . *before* he claimed her for his wife.

But he wasn't going to change his mind, Drew knew with certainty. Gently he smoothed back pale tendrils of hair from her beautiful face. It bewildered him, the tenderness he felt for Roslyn. His chest was tight with a deep ache, a fierce, elementary need to fill her up with himself. Any regrets he had now would be for causing her pain, for not being able to satisfy her as she deserved. He wanted her pleasure, more than he remembered wanting to pleasure any woman.

Raising himself up enough to kiss her again, he guided the engorged crest of his arousal just inside her pulsing cleft. Her eyes fell shut as he slowly, carefully penetrated her.

She tensed at his invasion, her inhalation sharp and faltering, the resistance of her tight sheath proclaiming her virgin innocence.

Pressing soft kisses over her face, Drew rested there for a long moment, letting her grow accustomed to his male possession. Then he eased deeper inside her, slowly, slowly, slowly pressing in farther.

Eventually her taut body relaxed, softened, and he found himself welcomed by her slickness. Her feminine muscles tightened around him, enclosing him in tantalizing heat.

With infinite care, Drew sank more fully inside her, then withdrew and slowly thrust again . . . long, lingering strokes that stoked the fire building within them both. To his delight, Roslyn began to move beneath him, lifting her hips to match his rhythm. Every time he drove into her, he shook with the pleasure he felt, with the blinding need to claim her.

When the fiery waves of pleasure started to engulf her, he felt them too. Her cry was a sob as the riveting swells flowed in wave after sensational wave. His body shook at the shattering release, with the powerful convulsions of desire that rocked him.

When the turbulence stilled, he collapsed against her, burying his mouth in her hair. His ragged breaths filled with her scent, Drew tried to make sense of what had just happened. They had consummated their union in a stunning explosion that had cemented his claim to her. Roslyn was his now; she had given herself to him.

Fierce satisfaction filled him. She would have to wed him now. The knowledge swelled the emotion that gripped him.

He lifted his head, his burning look surveying her pale, tousled hair, her kiss-swollen mouth, her high firm breasts. Her hair was drying in delicate wisps around her face, which was gilded by firelight, but it was the dreamy wonder in her eyes that made his breath catch anew.

"Are you all right?" Drew rasped hoarsely.

"Yes," she murmured, sounding dazed. "I have never felt anything so . . ."

"So what?"

"Amazing."

Nor had he, Drew thought to himself. This astonishing pleasure was unique in his admittedly extensive experience; the fiery sparks of their passion extraordinary. Nothing in his memory had ever felt this sharp, this intense.

He had never felt euphoria like this, either, along with a whirlpool of other emotions he couldn't even identify. There was tenderness and hunger and possessiveness—

Drew gave up trying to sort them all out. Whatever he felt for Roslyn, he only knew he wasn't letting her go.

Withdrawing from the soft haven between her legs, he eased his weight off her and rolled onto his side, gathering her close, so that her face pressed into the curve of his shoulder, his chin resting on the top of her head.

She lay there in his arms, fitting perfectly.

Drew shut his eyes, his fingers playing in idle circles over the heated silk of her skin as he pondered the remarkable effect she had on him. Surely his softer feelings for her would fade in the cold light of day. Yet he knew his hunger wouldn't easily be sated. His loins were already hardening again, his arousal swelling.

But he couldn't make love to her so soon. Even though he'd unleashed her passion, taking her virginity could not have been entirely pleasant for her.

"Did I hurt you?" he asked.

She gave a soft sigh. "No. Not as much as I expected. Fanny said it might hurt the first time."

He would make it much better for her the next time, Drew vowed. It was a matter of pride with him, pleasing his lovers, but in this case, it was imperative. He intended to keep Roslyn so contented, she would never want to leave his bed.

He didn't like it, therefore, when she gave another sigh that was full of resignation. Drew pulled back to gaze at her. Seeing her grave look, he realized how badly he wanted to soothe away the crease between her eyebrows. "I don't want you to regret this, Roslyn."

Unable to answer, she buried her face in his shoulder again, her body still quivering with lingering bliss, her mind awash with chaotic emotions. She'd been awed by the sheer wonder of his lovemaking. What shocked her, though, was how eagerly she'd surrendered. She'd been gripped by a desire so overwhelming she could have wept for it.

Her throat was tight now. Arden had awakened her to stunning passion, the kind she had never let herself dream of. It was no wonder women fought to share his bed. He was just as magnificent as she'd been warned.

It wasn't his carnal expertise that was so devastating, however; it was his tenderness.

Shutting her eyes, Roslyn savored the feeling of being held in the warm shelter of his arms. The rain had slowed to a patter, while the wind had died down to a low moan, yet she didn't want to leave. Nor did she want to face the enormity of what she had done.

She had given him her innocence.

She ought to have profound regrets, since she had spoiled all her long-held plans for good. She would not be marrying Lord Haviland now. Gentlemen expected to wed virginal brides, and she was no longer virginal.

Strangely, however, she wasn't as devastated as she should be. Perhaps because she had already determined that she didn't want to wed Haviland.

But where she stood with the duke was still very much at issue. She suspected that he intended to renew his marriage proposal. She'd seen the satisfaction that blazed in his face when he was taking her—

A sharp rap on the cottage door made Roslyn give an abrupt start, while Arden tensed. When the pounding knock sounded again, he quickly disengaged himself from their embrace and flicked the quilt over her near nakedness before rolling to his feet.

"Go into the bedchamber," he directed as he buttoned the front placket of his breeches. "I'll send whoever it is away."

But he was too late. As he draped the blanket around his shoulders and turned toward the door, it swung wide open.

The portly gentleman who bustled in froze upon seeing the cottage occupied, his gaze shifting from Arden to Roslyn, who had just stood up.

Recognizing Squire Goodey, one of the largest owners of farmland in the district, Roslyn wanted to sink through the floor. She had managed to pull up the bodice of her chemise to cover her bare breasts and had wrapped the quilt tightly around herself, but her hair was a bedraggled mess and her bare feet were clearly showing, not to mention that most of her clothing hung drying on wall pegs alongside the duke's.

The squire's eyes widened in shock when he recognized her in turn. "Miss Loring! Whatever—"

Arden stepped in front of her to shield her from view, yet Roslyn could see the squire's already florid complexion grow a deeper shade of scarlet upon his comprehending that he'd interrupted a lovers' tryst.

"Your g-grace. . . . Do f-forgive me," he stammered.

"Mr. Goodey, is it not?" the duke said smoothly. "I believe we met at the Haviland ball last evening."

"Aye, sir . . . your grace. I didn't meant to . . . The Missus and I came across a curricle in the road and then saw smoke coming from the chimney, so I came to investigate. She is waiting in the carriage—"

But apparently that wasn't the case, for a plump matron appeared in the doorway, shaking off drops of rain from her cloak. "Ralph, whatever is keeping you—Oh, my word!"

Roslyn wanted to die and to curse at the same time. What a dreadful misfortune, to be discovered by Mrs. Goodey of all people. The squire's wife was the biggest gossip between London and Richmond. She fancied herself a leader of local society and had always looked down her rather large nose at the Loring sisters, not only for the past scandals in their family but for having to earn their daily bread by teaching at an academy for daughters of the lower classes.

Guilty of putting on airs far above her own station, the Goodey woman couldn't even recognize her hypocrisy. She'd been the first to fawn over the new Earl of Danvers, and professed to be glad to welcome his wards back into the fold of the Beau Monde.

Now she seemed gleefully appalled to see Roslyn looking as wantonly disheveled as she did. Her eyebrows rose to her hairline at the titillating ignominy of finding the most reserved and refined of the Loring sisters causing a new scandal. "Miss Loring . . . I cannot believe my eyes."

Roslyn felt her stomach clench into knots as reality returned with a vengeance. The dreamlike moment she had shared with Arden had shattered in a thousand fragments.

Knowing her ruin was inevitable, she decided it was time to stop hiding behind the duke, and so stepped forward, her head held high. "How fortunate that you have come to our rescue, Mrs. Goodey. We were stranded here by the storm when his grace's curricle suffered a broken wheel."

"I can see that," the squire's wife said, her tone gloating.

Arden fixed her with a quelling glance. "You will do me the courtesy of keeping this unfortunate incident to yourself, Mrs. Goodey. Miss Loring has consented to be my wife, and I don't wish my duchess's reputation to suffer. You understand, of course."

His startling pronouncement had the desired effect: The matron's jaw dropped in astonishment.

Even realizing his purpose—to shut up the nosy woman by giving her a more juicy tidbit to chew on— Roslyn froze in dismay and only just managed to keep her own jaw from dropping.

She certainly was in no position to deny the betrothal, however, so she merely forced a smile to her lips. "I admit I was quite surprised by his grace's offer myself," Roslyn murmured. "You are the first to hear of our betrothal, Mrs. Goodey. But perhaps you will be kind enough to keep the news secret until I have had the opportunity to inform my family and close friends."

The squire answered for her. "Of course, Miss Loring. My wife won't mention a word of any of this, will you, dear? We wouldn't want your little mishap to be misconstrued."

His wife looked a little indignant and mulish, but the squire ignored her. "Pray, how may we be of service, your grace?"

Arden offered him a bland smile. "Now that the storm has passed, I would like to take Miss Loring home, so a loan of a vehicle would be welcome. And I must arrange proper care for my horses—they're stabled in the shed—and have a wainwright fetched to repair the wheel."

"Leave everything to me, your grace." The squire bowed deeply. "I will take the Missus home and send our carriage back to you, to use at your leisure. And my servants will see to your curricle wheel and horses."

"Thank you, Goodey," the duke replied. "I will be greatly indebted."

"Think nothing of it, your grace." He took his wife's plump elbow. "Come, dear, we must give this betrothed couple some privacy," the squire insisted, before ushering the sputtering lady out of the cottage and firmly shutting the door behind him.

Chapter Twelve

※

My dearest Fanny, disaster has struck and I fear it is very much my own fault! I am now betrothed to the Duke of Arden.

—Roslyn to Fanny

Roslyn stared speechlessly at Arden, wondering frantically how they could escape this wretched catastrophe.

To her surprise, he didn't seem nearly as dismayed as she was. Indeed, his expression seemed almost nonchalant as he crossed to where her clothing hung. His tone was just as bland when he declared, "We need to dress. The Goodey carriage will be returning for us shortly."

"That is all you have to say?" she demanded in disbelief. "We are facing utter calamity and all you care about is getting dressed?"

He lifted an amused eyebrow at her. "Would you rather remain half naked?"

"No, of course not—"

"Then put on your clothes, love. This is hardly the calamity you think it," he added as he retrieved her still-damp corset and held it out to her. When Roslyn made no move to take the undergarment, he tugged the quilt from around her shoulders. "Don't be so missish," he ordered, tossing the quilt on the chair. "We are betrothed now."

"We are *not* betrothed. You only said that to blunt the disgrace of our being discovered together."

"No, I said it because I have every intention of wedding you. Now turn around so I can hook you up."

"I can dress myself!"

He wasn't listening, however. His hands clasping her upper arms, he spun her so that her back faced him. Roslyn had no desire to don the cold, clammy corset, yet she could hardly leave her lingerie there in the cottage or carry it with her, so she raised her arms and allowed Arden to slide the garment around her torso. She shivered when moisture seeped through her thin chemise, and squirmed when he fitted the bustle beneath her breasts.

"Hold still."

Although gritting her teeth, she dutifully stood as he fastened the hooks, but when she felt his lips caress the bare curve of her shoulder, she whirled and glared at him mutinously. "Will you please leave off your lechery long enough to discuss this predicament seriously?"

"What is there to discuss?"

"Our betrothal, what else! You are purposefully being obtuse."

"No, I fully comprehend your problem. You do also, or you would have refuted my announcement in front of our unexpected guests instead of waiting until we were alone to argue with me."

"It is your problem as well as mine!" Roslyn exclaimed.

"So it is. But I intend to accept my fate gracefully."

She wanted to hit him. When he would have helped her on with her gown, she snatched it from him and struggled into it, wincing when the damp sleeves chilled her arms.

As he started putting on his own clothing, Roslyn clenched her teeth, disgruntled and frustrated that she had landed herself in such a fix. She was furious at herself. She had vowed to keep away from the duke, not to melt in his arms like a perfect wanton.

She was just as angry at him for making her lose her head, for enchanting her so that she'd eagerly abandoned any semblance of common sense. She had planned out her entire future, and now it lay in ruins.

She would not let herself cry, though. In the first place she loathed watering pots. And in the second, she had brought this disaster on herself. Now, somehow, she had to determine what to do about it.

"How could I ever have let this happen?" she lamented in a muttered undertone.

"How could you have resisted?" Arden replied. "I had every intention of taking up where we left off last night."

Roslyn turned to stare at him as he tucked in the tails of his shirt. "You planned my seduction this afternoon?"

He grinned ruefully. "Not exactly. Even I don't have the power to arrange a storm at my convenience. But I was glad for the opportunity to speed up the pace of our courtship."

"Even after I told you I would never marry you?"

"I never intended to let your refusal stand. And having you almost naked in my arms was too great a temptation." He shrugged into his waistcoat and began fastening the buttons. "Did you honestly expect me to keep my hands off you, darling? I may be a gentleman but I'm not a saint."

Roslyn huffed indelicately. "I would say you are not much of a gentleman, either. You promised you wouldn't ravish me."

"And I kept my promise. You were entirely willing."

Her expression contorted into a grimace before she set her jaw. "I won't accept your proposal, your grace."

"You most certainly will accept it," he stated with the cool assurance of a man who inevitably got his own way. "You have no choice."

"There is always a choice," she insisted stubbornly.

"Not for members of our class. Marriage is the only honorable course for a gentleman after taking a lady's virginity. And the lady is even more at the mercy of convention. A betrothal is the only way to keep any shred of your reputation intact."

Roslyn had no immediate response to his declaration. Although indignant at his high-handedness, she knew Arden was set on protecting her reputation. Yet she couldn't stand that he was compelled to offer for her.

"I won't allow you to make such a sacrifice on my account," she finally said through gritted teeth.

"I am not so sure it would be a sacrifice on my part."

"It *will*. You have told me more than once how arduously you try to avoid the grasping females chasing you. If I accept your offer, you will only accuse me of ensnaring you against your will."

Amusement danced in his eyes as he shook his head. "I know better. And it is actually a great comfort to know you won't be marrying me for my title or fortune."

"This is no laughing matter, your grace!"

He suddenly fixed her with those penetrating green eyes. "I agree, but neither is it cause for tears, sweetheart."

Knowing further argument was futile, Roslyn turned away unhappily to fetch her shoes and stockings.

"Don't you think a marriage of convenience preferable to a ruined reputation?" the duke asked.

"No!" she retorted, even though she knew it wasn't true. She sank down into the chair before the hearth to put on her stockings. She wouldn't force Arden into a marriage that was repugnant to him. Nor would she herself be compelled to marry without love.

Confound it all! She had only wanted one critical thing in her marriage: to love and be loved. She'd always vowed she would never settle for less. But if she married the duke, she would have to give up that dream.

"Before you refuse, perhaps you should think of your sisters," he pointed out. "Can they afford another scandal in the family?"

Roslyn's heart sank. Any scandal she caused would certainly reflect on her sisters—just when they had finally gotten out from beneath the cloud of shame that had hovered over them for four long years.

"And what about your academy?" Arden asked. "How will the gossip impact your position there?"

She nearly groaned. She would have to stop teaching when word of her affair with the duke got out. Their pupils' parents would never approve of a scarlet woman tarnishing their precious young daughters, nor should they. Jerking on her stocking, Roslyn muttered an invective that no lady should even know, much less say aloud.

Ignoring her outburst along with his sodden cravat, Arden sat in another chair to don his own stockings and boots. "You must admit," he added congenially, "in the eyes of the Beau Monde, being betrothed to a duke will make up for a multitude of sins."

Roslyn abruptly straightened, her arms crossed defensively over her chest. "Perhaps, but you don't love me, and I don't love you."

"We have friendship at least. We enjoy each other's company. And I expect our married life will rarely be dull."

She couldn't defend against that argument. She did enjoy his company immensely. No doubt life with Arden would be challenging, exhilarating, even exciting.

But for how long? How long before he found another woman to interest him and keep him from the marriage bed?

Their matrimonial goals were vastly different, Roslyn knew. He only wanted a wife so he could beget an heir. She wanted a real family, children to love and cherish. Arden was not the kind of man to put much store in family.

And without love, what kind of marriage could they hope for? Would he expect her to accept his connubial demands, bear his children, run his home, plan his entertainments, and never question his liaisons? Would he leave her languishing in the countryside while he cavorted in London with his latest paramours? Would he continue keeping a mistress after they married?

She couldn't bear having a libertine husband. Her

mother had endured her father's outrageous philandering for most of their twenty-year marriage. Not only hadn't Sir Charles bothered to hide his dalliances and indiscretions, he had flaunted them in his wife's face. It had been a prime source of contention between them.

Would Arden flaunt his affairs and make his duchess an object of gossip and pity?

But the subject was a trifle too embarrassing for Roslyn to argue with him just now.

And then he interrupted her dark thoughts with a casual comment. "Come now, a marriage between us won't be so bad."

"How can you say so?" Roslyn said crossly. "I shouldn't think a determined bachelor is competent to judge the quality of a marital union."

"You must admit we are physically compatible."

"There is a great deal more to marriage than physical compatibility!"

"Perhaps, but that is more than I ever expected with my bride. It's one of your prime attractions—that you act more like a mistress than a wife. Ladies are not supposed to enjoy passion, but you have a healthy appetite for lust."

Roslyn felt her cheeks turn red. "I wish you would not remind me."

He bent to wrestle with his first boot. "Husbands are not expected to pleasure their wives, either," he remarked provocatively. "But I can safely promise that we will find connubial bliss in our marriage bed."

Roslyn's mouth curved without humor. "I have no doubt you would make a splendid lover, your grace, but you would likely be a wretched husband."

"No worse than most any other man."

"I take leave to differ."

Not responding for a or the moment, he pulled on his second boot with difficulty. "I'll wager that Haviland has never aroused you as I do," he said then.

Roslyn fell silent. No man had ever aroused her the way Arden could. Just looking at him now rekindled the delicious sparks between them. She swallowed, aware of her humming nerves, the hollow flip-flopping sensation in her stomach, the tingling warmth between her thighs.

"Isn't that true?" Arden prodded when she wouldn't answer.

"I can't deny that I feel a physical attraction for you," Roslyn replied, her tone grudging.

"But you still hope to marry Haviland."

She looked away. "What I want is no longer the question. I couldn't possibly marry him now."

"Why not?"

"Because of . . . what we just did. Even if Haviland were willing to overlook the fact that I am no longer a maiden, his grandmother never would. She is such a high-stickler, she would be appalled if she were forced to welcome a wanton into the family."

"Which is why you are better off marrying me."

"I cannot agree."

Standing, he strolled over to her chair and bent down. "I intend to change your mind, love."

Before Roslyn could even think to pull away, he kissed her . . . giving her a long, lingering, completely devastating reminder of the sensual power he held over her.

When he straightened, leaving her dazed and longing, his smile was almost smug. "If you won't accept my proposal just yet, you should at least see the wisdom of becoming engaged for the time being. An official betrothal will deter a scandal before it has time to spread."

She knew he was right. The gossip about them would be relentless unless it could be mitigated by a betrothal. The matrimonial capture of one of the most eligible noblemen in the kingdom would be a nine days' wonder.

But it was the duke's choice of words that interested Roslyn most. "What do you mean, 'for the time being'?"

"Our betrothal only needs to be temporary. When the gossip eventually dies down, we can discuss whether to end it or go through with the marriage."

Roslyn's lips parted in surprise. The idea of a temporary betrothal had merit. She was not a total fool. She knew very well she had to at least consider accepting his proposal, even though she hated to admit it.

She didn't reply as she finished putting on her stockings and shoes. When she was done, Roslyn remained in the chair and watched absently as Arden tamped down the fire with ashes, then removed the kettle from the hook and carried it to the kitchen stove.

When a knock sounded on the door, they were both fully dressed and ready to leave.

Roslyn reached the door first. The burly man standing there tugged his forelock. "I'm John Coachman, Miss Loring. I'm to take ye wherever ye wish to go."

Arden answered for her over her shoulder. "We wish to go to Freemantle Park."

"Very good, yer grace."

When the coachman returned to his horses, the

duke ushered Roslyn outside and closed the cottage door behind them. As he escorted her to the carriage, he murmured a low explanation. "We'll return to the Park for now. We need to inform Lady Freemantle about our betrothal so she can help staunch the gossip. And we never did have tea."

Roslyn rolled her eyes in annoyance and exasperation. She couldn't believe he was taking this all so calmly. She couldn't possibly feel the same equanimity.

When he handed her inside the hooded barouche and settled beside her, she felt Arden's thigh press against hers. Instantly a shock of awareness shot through her. She quickly edged away from him, yet she couldn't forget the memory of that hard-muscled male body moving over hers, within her. She knew the image would be forever seared into her memory.

Roslyn swore under her breath. How could she think clearly with Arden so near? She had to order her chaotic thoughts somehow. So serious a decision called for careful, rational analysis.

She didn't want to wed him, or even enter into a temporary betrothal with him. But if she didn't agree, what kind of future would she have? Marriage to any other gentleman was doubtful now. If she refused his offer, she would be condemning herself—and possibly her sisters—to notoriety for the rest of her life.

She shot the duke a sideways glance. There was always the remote possibility that their friendship could grow into something deeper. A formal engagement might miraculously give them a chance to fall in love with each other.

Roslyn bit her lip, trying to convince herself.

Of course, there was always the danger of giving her

heart to him without her love being returned. It would be disastrous to harbor a one-sided ardor like her mother had done with her father in the early days of their marriage. Without mutual love, a husband and wife could so easily degenerate into bitter antagonists.

Did she dare risk it? Roslyn wondered. She would have to keep her own feelings for Arden safely under control. She most certainly could not let herself fall in love with him.

But if she could manage to keep her emotional distance, perhaps a betrothal was the best course.

And it would only be temporary, Roslyn promised herself. She could give their relationship time to blossom. If, however, Arden still hadn't come to love her by the end of summer, then she would break their engagement, regardless of the consequences to her reputation.

September was only two months away. She could keep her heart safe for that long.

"Very well, your grace, you win," she said reluctantly. "We can consider ourselves betrothed for the time being."

"Call me by my given name. If we are betrothed, we should be on a first-name basis."

"Very well . . . Drew."

He offered her a slow smile. "You are showing excellent judgment, my dear Roslyn."

She responded with a barely muffled snort. "It would be the first time today," she muttered. "My judgment thus far has been deplorable."

Leaning back against the squabs, Roslyn shut her eyes. Her head suddenly felt as if it were splitting open, and she still had to face Winifred with the news of their betrothal—heaven forbid. Her resultant shudder had little to do with the damp chill of her gown.

"You will have to inform Lady Freemantle about our engagement," Roslyn told the duke. "No doubt she will be ecstatic, but I don't have the fortitude just now to endure her raptures."

"Leave it to me," Drew said blandly.

He settled back in the carriage seat, yet he was not as nonchalant as he strove to appear. He was honor-bound to marry Roslyn now. He'd chosen her for his bride, and he had every intention of following through—although given her fierce reticence, he'd decided it wiser to conceal his resolve under the guise of a temporary arrangement.

Still, his discomfort was not caused by the parson's noose hanging around his neck, Drew mused. In truth, he didn't feel trapped as he'd expected.

No, the trouble was he was being drawn in too deep. Roslyn made him feel things he'd never felt for a woman. His instinctive reaction was to pull back—doubtless a reflexive response to being considered prey for so long.

Granted, the pleasure of making love to her was so much greater than with any of his previous lovers, even the most skilled of his mistresses. She made passion new and exciting again. Yet Roslyn roused much more than a physical response from him. There was something so unexpectedly natural about the way he felt when he held her. Something so real and right.

A damned dangerous sensation, Drew acknowledged to himself.

He would do better to keep their relationship strictly carnal. And yet some part of him welcomed the change. Until now his life had been rather cold and empty, and yes, passionless. His aristocratic upbringing had left no room for sentiment. He'd been raised to be emotionally detached, to rein in his feelings.

With Roslyn, he couldn't remain detached. Indeed, he'd never felt more alive than when he was with her. She was a delight to be around, whether she was arguing with him or writhing beneath him in ecstasy.

Drew frowned as he gazed out the carriage window. Despite his misgivings, he actually *wanted* marriage with Roslyn now. Or more specifically, he wanted the exhilaration he always felt with her.

Their marriage would not be based merely on convenience or even desire, he knew. He could imagine spending time with her even after they wed, sharing their day-to-day lives in addition to long lustful nights in their marriage bed.

His glance shifted to Roslyn as she sat beside him. His loins tightened when he remembered kissing her a short while ago. She had responded with mutual desire, her lips longing and hungry. . . .

Drew fought the urge to pull her close now and resume where they had left off in the cottage. He didn't want to push his luck.

He had obtained Roslyn's agreement to a temporary betrothal. Now he had the much harder task of securing her hand in marriage for good.

Chapter Thirteen

❧

I confess astonishment that the duke offered for you, dear Roslyn, since he is the most elusive marriage catch in England. I am even more astonished that you agreed, given your distaste for convenient marriages. But I can certainly see your dilemma.

—Fanny to Roslyn

As predicted, Winifred was amazed yet thrilled to learn of the betrothal. The news even overshadowed the distress of having a thief invade her home. When Roslyn reported that they'd lost the culprit's trail but planned to involve Bow Street in the search, Winifred merely nodded distractedly.

"You were brave to follow him, my girl, but I don't like that you endangered yourself again. It is a wonder you didn't break your neck—and it will be even more astonishing if you don't catch the grippe." She turned to the duke. "Your grace, it is so fortunate that you were there to rescue Roslyn from her folly. In any case, my brooch is safe, since I'd hidden it with my stockings instead of my jewel case. But now let us discuss your splendid news! I cannot tell you how happy that makes me. I had hoped you might be forming a *tendre* for Roslyn, but I wouldn't let myself count on it."

When Winifred proposed holding an impromptu dinner two evenings hence to celebrate their betrothal and to invite their closest friends, Roslyn would have politely refused, but the duke—or Drew, as she had to remember to start calling him—accepted with alacrity.

Lacking the energy to argue, Roslyn made her escape from the Park with the excuse that she needed to return home and change into dry clothing. The Goodey coachman drove her in the squire's carriage, while the Freemantle butler arranged to have her gig delivered to Danvers Hall before nightfall.

Drew planned to borrow some dry clothing from her ladyship's late husband's wardrobe and use the Freemantle barouche to return to London, since it would likely be tomorrow at the earliest before his curricle wheel was repaired. But he promised to call on Roslyn the following morning to further discuss their betrothal.

Roslyn arrived home disconsolate and chilled to the bone. Much to her gratitude, the Danvers housekeeper, Mrs. Simpkin, plied her with hot tea and ordered a steaming bath filled for her, then bustled off to the kitchens to supervise the preparation of a special supper with her favorite dishes.

Comforted by the elderly housekeeper's mothering, Roslyn soaked for a long while, so that her body was much warmer and her spirits a little higher by the time she emerged from the tub.

She had sent a message to Tess Blanchard asking her to call at the Hall as soon as possible since she had important news to impart. Roslyn wanted her friend to hear the news directly from her. And even more, she wanted to gain her advice.

Tess arrived in time for supper, and while the two of them ate in the small dining room, Roslyn told her about the disastrous afternoon that had led to her unwanted betrothal, not sparing any of the details, not even the part where she had succumbed to Drew's passion and given him her innocence.

Tess remained thoughtful as she listened, but shook her head wryly at the conclusion. "So Winifred succeeded in her matchmaking after all. She has been trying to pair you with Arden ever since Arabella's wedding."

Roslyn smiled faintly. Tess had no fondness for matchmaking, since she believed matters of the heart were best left to natural courses. "Yes, but I cannot blame Winifred in this instance. My own weakness was at fault. I couldn't resist him. So what do you think?" Roslyn pressed. "Was I right to accept the duke's offer for a temporary betrothal?"

"I think," Tess said slowly, "that under the circumstances, you had no other choice. And your rationale for remaining betrothed for the summer is a good one. You need to allow time for love to develop between you. It's possible that love can blossom given proper encouragement."

Roslyn was not surprised by her friend's cautious optimism. Tess had a more positive view of love and marriage than any of the Loring sisters, since she'd sincerely loved her betrothed before his death at Waterloo two years ago. Her heart was only just now coming out of mourning, and she was debating whether to reenter the lists of the Marriage Mart.

"But," Tess added a qualification, "from everything I have heard about Arden, it won't be easy to make him fall in love with you."

Roslyn made a face. "I don't even mean to try. I would never think of overtly pursuing him. In the first place, he despises being the target for covetous females.

And in the second, he is perfectly aware of the successful techniques of arousing a man's ardor, since he taught me himself. He would know exactly what I was attempting."

"But you could manage a more subtle approach."

She shook her head. "I have no intention of trying to coerce him to love me. If he is truly serious about wedding me, he will have to take responsibility for fostering a love match himself."

Tess looked amused. "You expect him to make all the effort?"

"Precisely. But like you, I doubt he is the least bit interested in a real love match."

Roslyn had little faith that Drew would change his stripes so drastically. She might wonder, wistfully and foolishly, if he could ever come to love her, but she still believed he was too cynical to let himself give his heart to anyone.

"What will you tell your sisters?" Tess asked.

"I'll tell Arabella about the betrothal, of course," Roslyn replied, "but not the rest . . . not about my wantonness. Marcus still considers himself our protector if not our legal guardian, and he wouldn't be pleased to know that I've been intimate with his friend. I'll write Belle tomorrow at Marcus's family seat in Devonshire, although there is no hurry, since they aren't expected to arrive there until next week. They should still be touring the Lake District at present."

"What about Lily? You know she won't be happy to hear you are engaged to wed a man you don't love and who might never love you."

"I know." Roslyn's mouth quirked ruefully. "I think I had best make a trip to London and tell her in person, although I will have to be discreet. Lily wants everyone to think she is visiting our old friends in Hampshire. Only you and Fanny know otherwise."

"That would be wise," Tess agreed. She drank a swallow of wine before speaking again. "Would you mind if I asked a personal question, Roslyn?"

"Of course not."

Tess hesitated, looking oddly embarrassed. "Was . . . passion as remarkable as Fanny says it is?"

Roslyn felt her own complexion warm as she recalled the incredible interlude with Drew in the cottage. "It was better," she said softly. "I can understand now why Fanny forsook all her genteel upbringing and let herself be swept away by desire."

Tess sighed. "I regret that I may never know that kind of passion. I almost envy you. . . ." With a sharp shake of her head, she squared her shoulders. "But I promised myself I wouldn't dwell on the past. And now I feel obliged to play schoolmistress for a moment." She gave Roslyn a stern look, although her eyes held a glint of humor. "If you mean to become intimate with the duke again, you should take precautions."

"Precautions?" Roslyn asked.

"Against becoming enceinte. If you find yourself with child, you will be forced to wed him, regardless of your feelings for him."

Roslyn's cheeks turned a deep shade of pink. "I confess, I had not given the matter any thought. Fanny never worried about such things."

"Some women, like Fanny, cannot conceive easily, but others are more susceptible to breeding. There are ways to prevent a man's seed taking root. You should ask Fanny about them."

Roslyn nodded at the sage advice. For all her romantic sentimentality, Tess had always been rather levelheaded and practical.

"No doubt you are right," Roslyn said. "But my being intimate with the duke should not be a problem in the future. I am determined it won't happen again."

Though looking skeptical, Tess merely sipped her wine.

Roslyn took a swallow of her own wine and silently renewed her vow not to surrender to her wanton desires again. It shouldn't be as difficult as it had been the past two days. Now that she understood what she was up against, she could better guard herself.

She had let passion sway her when what she really wanted was love—and look at the quandary she was in now.

She would certainly *not* make that mistake again, no matter how irresistible the duke—Drew—was.

From the first moment he entered her library the following morning, however, Roslyn realized that Drew's intentions were the very opposite of hers. He strode to the window seat where she was curled up reading, pulled her to her feet, and seized her mouth in an unexpected and unexpectedly gentle kiss that was no less devastating for its tenderness.

Instantly breathless, Roslyn tore herself from his embrace and retreated halfway across the room, her fingers pressed to her burning lips. "Your grace— Drew! You cannot kiss me like that simply because we are betrothed."

He looked unchastened as he moved toward her. "I suspected you were having second thoughts and wanted to remind you why our marriage is still a good idea. Here, this is for you, darling."

For the first time she noticed that he was carrying a flat blue velvet box. When she took it from him and opened the lid, Roslyn nearly gasped to see an incredible sapphire-and-diamond necklace with matching earbobs.

"These are Arden family heirlooms," Drew explained. "I retrieved them this morning from the bank vault in London."

Frowning slightly, Roslyn looked up at him. "They are beautiful but far too expensive for me to accept."

"Nonsense. It's appropriate for me to bring you a betrothal gift. You can wear them tomorrow evening at the dinner Lady Freemantle is giving. It will lend credence to our betrothal."

Roslyn refrained from mentioning that she would likely be returning the jewels to him since she doubted the wedding would ever take place.

"I admit," Drew added when she was silent, "they are something of a bribe, since I must ask you to perform a distasteful task."

"What task?"

"As much as I regret it, I will have to introduce you to my mother."

"The Duchess of Arden?"

"Yes. She spends the summer at Arden Castle in Kent. I'm on my way there now to inform her about our betrothal." His mouth curled. "She would be outraged if I merely sent her a message announcing our engagement, and I would rather not get her back up since I want her to fully support you. I will take you to meet her later this week, if you are free."

"Must I meet her?" Roslyn asked reluctantly.

Drew grinned. "I fear so. If she is seen to give her approval of the match, your acceptance in society will be assured. My mother holds significant sway over her peers."

"I suppose you are right."

Roslyn started to close the lid to the jewel box, but Drew stopped her. "No, try it on."

"Very well," she said after a moment's hesitation. The neckline of her green muslin morning gown was too high and the color wasn't right to do the beautiful piece justice, but it didn't seem polite to refuse.

"Allow me to help," Drew offered, lifting the necklace from the velvet bed.

Roslyn turned so that he could slip the necklace around her throat, but when he fastened the clasp, she found herself recalling yesterday when he'd helped her don her corset. This was much less wicked, yet she felt a tingling shock where his fingers touched the bare skin of her nape.

To distract herself, she asked him about his promise to search for Winifred's thief. "Did you have the chance to speak to Bow Street yet?"

"Yes. I have two Runners investigating the color livery our thief wore. For now we will leave the search to them."

Drew turned her around, his gaze surveying her. "Sapphires look lovely on you," he said softly. "They complement your beautiful eyes."

Roslyn felt her heart warm at his praise, yet she still felt uncomfortable at his flattery. "Drew . . . please—"

"I know you don't care to hear how beautiful you are, but it's true."

His tender look affected her even more than the words. He did make her feel beautiful—

Which no doubt was his calculated intent, Roslyn suddenly realized.

She stiffened with renewed resolve. Pulling back, she managed a light laugh. "I know what you are about, your grace, but your tricks are wasted on me."

"What tricks?"

"You are employing the same techniques of seduction you taught me."

"Is that so?" Drew asked innocently.

"You know it is. You bring me expensive gifts and attempt to flatter me. You look deeply into my eyes and make me the sole focus of your attention. You touch me in order to arouse my senses. . . . Shall I go on?"

Flashing her a slow smile of irresistible charm, he held up his hands. "Guilty as charged. But can you blame me? I know I must use every means at my disposal to convince you to wed me."

"I don't want you to shower me with jewels or empty flattery, Drew."

"My flattery isn't empty. Come here, sweeting. I want to show you how much I desire you."

Reaching for her, he drew her into his arms. Discomfited, Roslyn exclaimed in protest. "I don't want you to kiss me, either."

"Now that I know isn't true." His green gaze intimate, knowing, he smiled softly. "Let me prove it to you, sweet Roslyn. . . ."

Bending his head, he kissed her with controlled expertise while his hands drifted lightly over her body. Every movement was laced with mastery and kindled sparks wherever he touched.

To her dismay, Roslyn soon stopped resisting and surrendered to the clever explorations of his mouth and hands. When he finally pulled back, he left her hot and breathless and dazed.

"The next time we make love," he murmured in a husky voice, "will be much better than the first."

She couldn't imagine how it could be better, but that was hardly the point.

"There will not *be* a next time," Roslyn said shakily, moving over to a chair and sinking down. "Not unless we are actually wed."

"I can see I will have to change your mind."

She narrowed her gaze on him. "That is just what I would expect of you, you grace, using your sexual prowess to try and sway me."

"Why shouldn't I, since it is one of my chief talents?"

"I know." Roslyn sent him a disgruntled look. "Fanny says you can make women weep with rapture."

His eyebrow arched. "How could Fanny possibly know? I have never patronized her."

"She is merely repeating rumor."

Drew shrugged. "My efforts are not entirely calculating. It makes a man swell with pride, knowing he can please his lover."

"Not according to Fanny. She says it is extremely rare for a man to consider his lover's pleasure before his own."

Drew's smile was rueful. "Well, I confess I have cultivated my amorous skills so I would be wanted for something other than my wealth and title."

Roslyn was struck by the odd look in his eyes. It

was almost . . . vulnerable. She found it difficult to believe so powerful nobleman as Drew would have any kind of vulnerability, but she could understand why he wanted to be wanted for himself, not his material assets.

"You certainly succeeded—" Roslyn shook herself abruptly. "How did we stray to this scandalous subject? Yesterday you said you would call on me this morning to further discuss our betrothal."

"And I meant to. But then I realized I would do better to work on my mother, since she could prove to be a thorn in my side. I intend to stay the night at Arden Castle, by the way. While I'm making my duty visit, I have some estate affairs that need tending. But I'll return here in time to escort you to the betrothal dinner tomorrow night."

"You needn't trouble yourself, Drew. I plan to attend with my friend, Miss Blanchard. It would be best if I am not always seen in your company."

"Is that the real reason?"

Roslyn flushed. "To be perfectly honest, I don't want to be alone in a carriage with you."

"Because you don't trust yourself with me."

"Exactly."

His smile was rather smug although still charming. "Very well, love, but I won't allow you to avoid my company altogether. I want the chance to court you properly."

"If you mean to be proper, you will have to abandon your plan to seduce me."

"Now, *that* I won't promise. I will see you tomorrow evening."

Crossing to her chair, he bent and placed a brief kiss

on her lips, then turned and exited the library, leaving Roslyn with her pulse racing wildly.

She pressed her hands to her overheated cheeks and frowned unhappily. She fully comprehended Drew's idea of a courtship. He meant to woo her ruthlessly, using every ounce of charm and every skill at seduction he possessed to overwhelm her senses. And she knew it would be devastatingly effective.

Or would it?

Absently, Roslyn reached up to finger the glittering jewels at her throat. She might be unable to resist Drew's expert physical overtures, but his assault on her senses was not likely to touch her heart. Indeed, knowing the cold, calculating techniques he was employing would make it easier to protect herself from falling in love with him.

Drew Moncrief might be a splendid lover, but he knew almost nothing about real love, and love was the only thing that could convince her to wed him.

The gathering for Winifred's dinner on Monday evening was small and intimate, with only the betrothed couple's closest friends attending.

When Roslyn arrived with Tess and was shown into the drawing room, Winifred welcomed her with a hearty embrace while whispering in her ear, "I'm afraid Fanny could not come, Roslyn dear, since she had a prior engagement. And I did not invite Lord Haviland. I decided it would not be appropriate, considering he is the duke's rival for your hand."

Roslyn refrained from arguing that Haviland was no longer a possible suitor and merely smiled.

Drew was already there before her, but his greeting

was surprisingly tame. He merely took her hand and pressed a chaste kiss to her cheek. "There, are you satisfied? I intend to behave with consummate circumspection tonight."

"Thank you," Roslyn murmured wryly.

Miss Jane Caruthers, a spinster and teacher who managed the day-to-day affairs of the Freemantle Academy, greeted her next, embracing Roslyn with sincere warmth. "Your betrothal is certainly a surprise," Jane said, "but I am very happy for you, my dear."

Marcus's sister, Lady Eleanor Pierce, had also been invited, along with Drew's close friend, the Marquess of Claybourne. Lady Eleanor expressed her delight to Roslyn, while Claybourne offered felicitations. "Marcus thought you might make this old fellow an admirable duchess."

"Did he indeed?" Roslyn responded with skepticism. "I never expected Marcus to be a champion of matrimony."

"He wasn't until he met your sister. He became a convert only then."

As soon as the butler supplied Roslyn with a glass of wine, Lady Eleanor pulled her aside for a private moment. "Drew tells me the announcement of your engagement will be in all the society pages tomorrow. The ton will be astounded to learn he came up to scratch, since he has been so staunchly resistant to marriage, but I am truly delighted by your betrothal, especially for Drew's sake. And I know Marcus will be as well."

Roslyn glanced across the drawing room at the marquess. "How does Lord Claybourne feel about our betrothal?"

"Oh, he is exceedingly amused. Drew always said he wouldn't marry until he had no other choice. When is the wedding to be?"

"We have not set a date yet. Perhaps sometime in the fall. There really is no hurry."

The raven-haired charmer shook her head. "If I know Drew, he would rather get it over with. Once he makes up his mind, he doesn't like to dally. It is his mother who is likely to throw impediments in your way."

"Oh, do you know the duchess?" Roslyn asked curiously.

Eleanor nodded. "I fear so. She is quite the terror. She makes me quake in my slippers every time I encounter her." When Roslyn raised a skeptical eyebrow, Eleanor laughed. "Well, perhaps I don't actually quake, but I have never met anyone colder or haughtier in my life. I suspect she will attempt to persuade Drew to delay the nuptials."

"Why?"

"Because she won't fancy being relegated to dowager after she has lorded it over London social circles for so long."

"She may continue lording as far as I am concerned," Roslyn replied with a laugh. "I have no desire to take her place. And I admit, I am not eager to meet her."

Eleanor gave her a shrewd look. "I suspect you will do very well against the duchess. Just stand up to her. She expects subservience, but I believe she secretly respects women who can speak their mind." She hesitated. "Drew values that quality in women, too. Otherwise, he is nothing like his mother, thank heavens."

"What *is* he like then?"

"Drew? He is the very best of men. I love him like a brother. Indeed, he and Heath were just like older brothers to me when I was growing up. I wish you could see that side of him, Miss Loring. Drew does not open up to many people—he keeps his feelings reserved with all but his closest friends. But you would love him too if you came to know him like I do."

"That is high praise indeed," Roslyn said noncommittally as she sipped her wine. "I have heard others award him accolades. Lady Freemantle says the way he manages his estates is admirable."

"It is indeed," Eleanor agreed. "Drew insists on using all the latest scientific methods on his home farms, and has fought the enclosures of common land. His tenants consider themselves extremely fortunate to have them for his lord. And Drew also is admired for his progressive politics and his efforts in Parliament, as well as his generosity toward his many servants and dependents."

"Does he have many dependents?"

"Heavens yes, a score of them. Aunts, uncles, cousins . . . most have attached themselves to him like barnacles. They take shameless advantage of his largesse, but he provides for them whether they deserve it or not. Drew considers it his obligation. He takes even better care of his old retainers. The duchess would have turned them all off once they had outserved their usefulness, but Drew wouldn't allow her to."

Roslyn frowned. "Is the duchess so very heartless then?"

"Regrettably, yes. But Drew is very different from his mother. Take his old nurse, for instance. Several years ago she became too decrepit to fend for herself, and with no family to care for her, she was likely to wind up in a pauper's grave. Drew heard of her plight and brought her to live at Arden Castle—gave her quarters in the servant hall where she could be nursed back to health. You should speak to her if you visit the castle, Miss Loring. You will see how his servants worship him. I have always believed you can tell a good deal about a person by observing how they treat their servants."

"Are you discussing me, minx?" Drew asked, suddenly appearing at Roslyn's side.

"Of course, what did you expect?" Eleanor dimpled. "I was telling Miss Loring all your secrets."

He gave a mock shudder. "Saints spare me. Don't listen to her, sweeting. She knows too many of my foibles."

"Well, if you will excuse me," Eleanor said brightly, "I wish to speak to Miss Blanchard. I greatly enjoyed meeting her at my brother's wedding and would like to further our acquaintance."

"How long have you known Lady Eleanor?" Roslyn asked Drew once she had left.

"Since she was born. I was shipped off to boarding school at an early age, where I became fast friends with her brother, and Heath as well. I preferred spending all my holidays at their family estates. Arden Castle is a magnificent pile, but it is hardly welcoming to a boy . . . or child of any age."

"She seems quite impressed with you," Roslyn observed.

"As I hope you will be someday," Drew answered with a quick grin.

Feeling her pulse leap, Roslyn eyed him warily. She already *was* impressed with Drew, and tonight Lady Eleanor had given her an even greater respect for his character and accomplishments. It puzzled her, however, how a nobleman who cared so generously for his aging servants could be so thickheaded when it came to romantic love.

Just then the Freemantle butler appeared at the drawing room door in order to announce that dinner was served.

"Very good," Winifred responded. "Oh, and Pointon," she called. "Make certain the champagne is thoroughly chilled."

"Yes, my lady."

Glancing at the guests of honor, Winifred beamed. "I ordered a special champagne from London to toast the happy couple. Your grace, if you will please lead the way to the dining room?"

When Drew offered Roslyn his arm, she found herself frowning thoughtfully up at him. She'd told Tess she had no intention of overtly pursuing him. That he would have to make all the effort if he wanted her to love him enough to actually wed him. And yet, Roslyn reflected, if she truly wished to give their betrothal a fighting chance, perhaps she should attempt to be the kind of woman that appealed to him.

She could be clever and witty if she put her mind to it. She could certainly flirt with him and hang on his every word. Of course she ought not be too flagrant about it in front of Winifred's guests, but she could subtly apply the lessons he'd taught her about captivating a man. She could even touch him. . . .

Summoning a soft smile, Roslyn placed her hand on

his coat sleeve but made a point to brush the skin on the back of his wrist with her fingers. She knew he felt the caress, for he gave her a quick glance of surprise.

"Drew," she murmured in a husky voice. "I hope you will sit beside me during dinner."

"I doubt our hostess would permit anything else," he responded mildly.

Roslyn gave a light, rippling laugh. "No, Winifred would be perfectly delighted if I were to sit in your lap. But I could never be so brazen in public."

She saw heat flare in his green eyes before they narrowed a little in suspicion.

Maintaining a serene smile, Roslyn said little as the company took their places around the dining table, which gleamed with crystal and silver. However, she listened to Drew with bated breath whenever he spoke.

When the footmen had served the soup course, Roslyn picked up her spoon and sipped, but she waited until Drew was looking directly at her before she slowly licked her lower lip. "I find this cream soup quite delicious, don't you . . . ?"

Her voice faded as Pointon, the butler, came hurrying into the dining room. Roslyn had never seen the august servant looking so distraught.

"Forgive me, my lady," he said hoarsely to his mistress, "for intruding this way, but I thought you should know immediately. I went below to the wine cellar to fetch the champagne, and I surprised the thief there. He fled as soon as he spied me."

Roslyn felt her stomach clench at the news, while Winifred turned pale. Before either of them could regain their wits enough to speak, though, Drew demanded, "He broke into the house?"

"It would appear so, your grace. The bolt to the outer cellar door was pried open."

"Did you follow him, Pointon?" Roslyn thought to ask.

"Regrettably I was too late. By the time I recovered from my startlement, he had disappeared."

"What thief?" Lady Eleanor asked curiously.

Her question was ignored as Pointon practically wrung his hands. "In his haste, he left his sling behind. The fabric was bloodied, Miss Loring. Perhaps his wound opened when you and his grace chased him that day."

"What wound?" Eleanor queried. "And why were you and Drew chasing him?"

Miss Jane Caruthers replied for them. "Last week the duke shot a highwayman who was holding up Lady Freemantle's coach."

"You shot a highwayman?" Eleanor asked in astonishment.

Drew's mouth tightened, his ire obvious. "Yes, and I managed to wound him. But he escaped that night and again two days ago after he was caught in her ladyship's bedchamber, rifling through her jewelry case."

The Marquess of Claybourne frowned. "You told me about the shooting last week, old chap, but you never mentioned your latest little adventure. I missed out on all the fun."

Drew threw down his napkin and rose to his feet. "I want to see the cellar, Pointon."

Eleanor gave an exasperated sigh. "Will someone please explain to me why a thief would be lurking in the wine cellar?"

Drew answered tersely. "Most likely he was hiding

until after the household was asleep so he could search without being caught."

Roslyn added more patiently, "We believe he is looking for a particular brooch belonging to Lady Freemantle."

All eyes went to Winifred, who was fingering the enamel brooch pinned to her gown while staring down at her dinner plate. Her normally florid complexion was waxen, her lips pinched and bloodless.

Roslyn was concerned for her friend. No doubt it was terribly distressing to Winifred to have a villain break into her home for the second time after being held up in a highway robbery. She would feel extremely vulnerable, being at the mercy of the elusive villain.

Drew spoke to reassure Winifred. "I'll discover his identity, my lady, if it's the last thing I do."

He started to leave the dining room when Winifred finally found her voice.

"I think I know who the culprit is," she murmured in a barely audible rasp.

Drew halted and glanced down the length of the table at her. "Who is it then?"

Her expression pained, she lifted her gaze to Drew but hesitated to answer. "Perhaps we could discuss this in private, your grace, so as not to spoil everyone else's dinner?"

"Would you like us to leave?" Jane asked quietly.

"No, please," Roslyn interjected. "You needn't leave." Pushing her chair back, she stood. "Winifred, dearest, let us repair to the green parlor for a moment."

"Yes, that would be best."

Clearly disconsolate, Winifred sent an apologetic glance around the dining room, then rose slowly and preceded Roslyn and Drew to the parlor.

When the door closed behind them, Winifred murmured in a hoarse voice, "Thank you, your grace. It is ill-bred to speak of such things in polite company."

At her apparent distress, Roslyn grew even more concerned. "Speak of what things, Winifred? Please tell us what is wrong."

When she didn't immediately reply, Drew rephrased his question. "You said you know the thief's identity, my lady?"

"Yes," she replied, her expression one of misery. "I believe I do. He is my late husband's by-blow. Rupert's natural son by his mistress."

Chapter Fourteen

✤

I have come to realize my strategy is flawed. Seduction and passion may not lead to love after all. Deeper emotions must be involved for the heart to become engaged.

—Roslyn to Fanny

Roslyn felt her breath catch at the startling admission. "Sir Rupert's son, Winifred?"

Wincing, Winifred nodded. "I hoped it wasn't true, but there seems to be no other explanation. I didn't wish to speak of it in front of the others, though. It distresses me to have the world know about my late husband's shameful affair."

"Why don't you sit down, Winifred?"

"Yes, perhaps I should."

When she sank heavily onto a sofa, Roslyn sat beside her and took her hand. "Now tell us why you think the thief is Sir Rupert's son," she urged gently.

"I recognized the resemblance when he ran past me the other day. He's the spitting image of Rupert—both his features and his hair. Rupert's hair was that ginger color before it started turning gray."

"But the thief could be related to him in some other fashion."

"Mayhap, but I don't believe so," Winifred replied, her tone taking on a stubborn edge.

Drew broke in. "I'm curious, my lady. Why did you wait to mention your suspicions until tonight?"

Winifred looked down at her hands. "To be honest, I was ashamed. And the news of your betrothal was so exciting, the thief went entirely out of my mind." She glanced back up at Roslyn. "I didn't want to spoil your happiness, dear, by making you dwell on my troubles."

"But this is not only your trouble, Winifred. His grace and I are deeply involved."

"And I regret that, truly."

"Why don't you let us be the judge? Tell us what you know."

"I will have to explain about my marriage to Rupert so you will understand." Haltingly then, Winifred began to tell the tale. "When Rupert met me, he was nearly penniless, while my father was one of the richest merchants in England. Our union was strictly a business arrangement. Papa . . . bought a baronet for me, so his only daughter could become a lady and move up in the world and have the advantages he was never able to have. Rupert was willing enough, however. He contracted with Papa for my hand, exchanging his title for the security of having a rich wife. But he didn't receive my fortune outright, just an enormous settlement."

"That is unusual, isn't it?" Roslyn asked.

"Yes, but that was the only way Papa would agree to the union. He tied up my inheritance in trust to protect me and any eventual children I might have. Yet Rupert was able to live quite comfortably on the income. And our marriage was amiable enough, even though he never came to love me the way I did him."

Winifred's mouth curled in a humorless smile. "I was hardly his ideal bride. I was rather plump and plain, and a bit coarse in my manner, too. Rupert preferred a more genteel sort of lady, as I discovered later."

"Later?"

"After we were wed, I learned he had taken a mistress. One hears things . . . gossip. Some people are needlessly cruel; the real ladies are the worst. They took glee in telling me of the rumors. Pitying me, laughing at me behind their fans. That was how I learned his paramour was genteel. I never knew her name but she was the love of his life before he was compelled to marry me. It wasn't until Rupert was lost to her as a husband that she gave up her respectability to become his mistress. And then . . . I heard she bore him a child." Pausing, Winifred drew a shuddering breath.

"Are you all right?" Roslyn asked, concerned.

"Yes . . . it's just painful to remember."

"Here, drink this," Drew said, urging a snifter into Winifred's hand. He had poured her a measure of brandy from the side table, Roslyn realized.

The elder lady sipped absently, her thoughts seeming far away.

"Go on," Roslyn said gently after a long moment.

Winifred nodded. "Despite my dismay, I turned a blind eye to Rupert's infidelities. Never acknowledged or let on that I knew. At first I didn't want to face the truth that he was unfaithful. I had my pride, after all. And well . . . I thought he deserved happiness. I *wanted* him to be happy. Rupert never loved me as I loved him, but he was always a very kind and considerate husband, and he shielded me as much possible from the vicious harpies who spurned me for my low origins."

Her jaw locked for a moment before she determinedly drained the rest of the brandy in one long swallow. Then she coughed a little before continuing. "And the thing is . . . I didn't want him to be punished for my failings. You see, even after a number of years of marriage, I was never able to give him children or a legitimate heir to his title. When I realized I was likely barren, I was actually *glad* he had a child by another woman. Gentlemen want sons, you know." Her voice dropped. "His son would be about sixteen years of age now . . . although the thief looked a bit older than that when I glimpsed him."

Her eyes suddenly filled with tears. "I thought I could be indifferent, but it hurts to have blatant proof of his adultery."

Roslyn squeezed her hand comfortingly. "It's still possible you are mistaken about the boy's identity."

"No, dear, I'm not mistaken. I know here. . . ." Her hand covered her heart.

Roslyn felt her own heart go out to her friend. She was sad and angry, knowing how Winifred had suffered from being betrayed by her husband. She was even angrier at the late Sir Rupert for hurting this dear, sweet woman, no matter how frustrating her meddling matchmaking efforts could be.

Hoping to divert Winifred from her pain, Roslyn asked another question entirely. "So why did he hold up your coach and break into your house? Was he after your brooch because it contains a miniature portrait of his father? The brooch was the only thing he seemed to want when he held us up, and he didn't steal your other more valuable jewelry that was lying there in plain sight."

"That seems the most likely reason," Winifred answered unevenly. "And to be truthful, the brooch really isn't mine. Or at least Rupert never gave it to me. It was turned over to me by the jewelers, where it was being cleaned. Rupert died so suddenly—his heart failed him, you know—that he had no time to put his affairs in order. But I think that miniature was his gift to his mistress. . . ."

Pushing the empty snifter at Roslyn, Winifred began crying softly into her hands.

Roslyn put her arms around Winifred in a consoling embrace, which brought her own painful memories rushing back. She'd consoled her mother this way numerous times over the years. Her father's shameless philandering had caused her mother even more pain than Winifred had endured. At least Winifred's husband had been discreet, whereas Sir Charles had flaunted his mistresses just to spite his wife.

When Drew silently provided a handkerchief, Roslyn gave him a grateful glance. Winifred took it and eventually her sobs quieted.

"I am sorry," she murmured, wiping her eyes. "I don't mean to turn into a watering pot. It's just that seeing the boy . . . has dredged up some painful memories."

"I know," Roslyn said softly.

"Rupert had no family relations," Winifred added, sniffing. "He was the last of his line and his title died with him. That is what I regret most."

"You cannot let yourself dwell on the past, Winifred."

"Yes, you're right." Sniffing, she sat up straighter. "I cannot stay here sniveling in this ridiculous fashion. I have dinner guests. It is terribly rude to leave them to their own devices. I may not have been born a lady, but I know that much! You and your sisters taught me all about genteel manners, my dear, and now I am letting you down."

Roslyn managed a smile. "Please don't concern yourself about the thief, Winifred. Don't even think about it. His grace and I will determine what should be done."

Winifred glanced up at Drew with a watery smile. "I didn't expect to involve you so deeply in my troubles, your grace. I only wanted you to see my dear Roslyn's worth."

With a charming smile of his own, he shot Roslyn a glance as he helped Winifred to her feet. "I see her worth quite clearly, my lady. But leave it to me to investigate the boy's identity."

"Leave it to *us*," Roslyn corrected. "We will discuss the matter while you rejoin your guests, Winifred."

"Very well," her ladyship agreed. "I will have Pointon keep your dinner warm."

When she had gone, Roslyn found herself frowning as Drew settled beside her on the sofa. "Do you think she is right?" she asked. "That the thief really is Sir Rupert's natural son?"

"It makes sense. If the brooch came into her possession four years ago, he may want it back. But why now? And what happened to his mother if she was Sir Rupert's mistress?"

"And is the boy really a footman?" Roslyn mused aloud. "If his father failed to provide for him, he may have been forced to seek employment merely to survive. Perhaps he truly is in service in some noble household, and the livery he wore is not a disguise but his regular attire." Roslyn's eyes suddenly widened. "Good heavens . . . what if he served at Danvers Hall last week? We hired numerous extra staff for the wedding celebrations."

Drew nodded. "That would explain why he was able to intercept your coach so readily. If he was acting as a footman that night, he could have kept watch on Lady Freemantle's carriage and slipped out in time to ride after it."

"I should ask the Simpkins if they noticed any of the footmen behaving oddly that evening."

"Good. Meanwhile, Bow Street may develop some leads about the livery soon."

"But isn't there any other avenue we can pursue? I loathe having to sit still and do nothing."

Drew smiled at her impatience. "I won't be sitting still. I plan to interview Sir Rupert's solicitors tomorrow to discover what they know about a former mistress. If we can identify her, it might help us to locate the boy."

Roslyn gave Drew an admiring look. "That is very clever. And if Sir Rupert did keep a mistress for so long, Fanny may know something about her. Fanny makes it her business to know everything about the demimonde, particularly wealthy gentlemen who could potentially become patrons. And even if she can't tell us about Sir Rupert's arrangement, she has acquaintances who may be able to remember his circumstances four years ago."

"She may be a good source," Drew agreed.

"And the jewelers who cleaned the brooch might remember whom it was meant for."

He shook his head at that. "I doubt it. If they returned the brooch to Lady Freemantle, they wouldn't know its rightful owner. In any event, we should keep our inquiries discreet so as to shield her from unwanted gossip."

"True," Roslyn said. "But I want to go with you when you call on the solicitors."

"That won't be necessary, darling."

"It is *very* necessary. Winifred is my friend, and I want to help her. She won't have any peace of mind until we solve the mystery of the thief. And we certainly must stop him from trying to steal from her again."

Drew's eyes glimmered with amusement. "I suppose there is no point in telling you to stay at home and leave the heroics to me?"

Roslyn dimpled. "None whatsoever."

He gave an aggrieved sigh. "I suspected as much. Very well, then, I will call for you early tomorrow morning and we'll visit the solicitors together. You do realize, however, that you will have to ride with me alone in my coach?"

"I am willing to risk it," Roslyn said confidently, remembering her plan to try and arouse Drew's ardor. A trip into the City of London would take the best part of an hour. She might as well use the time to attempt to soften his heart toward her.

During the drive to London the next morning, Roslyn subtly resumed her efforts to captivate Drew, but it seemed to have little effect on him. He parried all of her attempts at flirtation with the skill of an expert, merely lifting an amused eyebrow when her attempts became too blatant.

Roslyn was almost glad when they reached Town and she could abandon her pretense and turn her attention to gaining answers about the late Sir Rupert's affairs.

They called on Fanny first, so they would be sure to find her at home. Not unexpectedly, the courtesan had to be roused from her bed, since in her trade, Fanny often kept late nights.

Even so, she greeted Roslyn with a warm embrace and congratulated the duke on his upcoming nuptials, despite knowing from Roslyn's letters that the wedding might never take place.

"How disturbing for Lady Freemantle," Fanny murmured when she'd heard the entire tale. "Not only having a thief invade her home, but a thief who could be the result of her husband's longtime liaison."

"Yes," Roslyn agreed. "But she wants to know the truth either way, so we intend to find him. We hoped you could help us discover who Sir Rupert's mistress was, Fanny."

Fanny pursed her lips thoughtfully. "I don't recall ever meeting him, so I have no idea who he had in keeping. But I will be happy to make inquiries . . . discreetly, of course."

"Thank you," Roslyn said earnestly. "We want to prevent any more gossip about Winifred. She finds this painful enough already."

"Yes, thank you, Miss Irwin," Drew added.

When he and Roslyn rose to take their leave, Fanny accompanied them to her front door. Roslyn would have liked to speak to Fanny alone about a number of matters—her betrothal to Drew, her interest in making him fall in love with her, the more intimate subject of precautions against getting with child, and most of all, how her sister was faring, since Lily had been in London for nearly a fortnight now, keeping herself out of reach of Winifred's matchmaking.

But there was no opportunity for privacy with Fanny, since Drew ushered Roslyn down the front steps and into his coach after directing his coachman where to find the firm of Crupp and Beasly, the solicitors who oversaw Winifred's fortune.

Regrettably, they had no better luck with the solicitors. They were welcomed obsequiously at the dark, shabby offices on Fleet Street—Drew was a duke, after all. And once he presented a letter of authorization from Lady Freemantle, permitting him to act as her advocate, the nearly ancient Mr. Crupp's stiffness eased and he listened attentively as Drew explained precisely what they wanted.

Despite his age, the elderly lawyer still seemed to possess a keen mind, for he asked several sharp questions to clarify certain points. At the conclusion, however, Mr. Crupp sadly shook his head.

"It is possible, your grace, that Sir Rupert paid an income to a mistress for a good many years, but we would not be privy to the arrangements. Doubtless he contrived for another solicitor to handle his private affairs, since he would not have wished Lady Freemantle to know he was spending part of her fortune thusly. And if he did have a second family, he could not very well provide for them in his will and testament without her ladyship discovering the unsavory truth."

"What other solicitors might he have employed?" Drew asked.

Mr. Crupp responded with a sour smile that showed his false teeth. "The possibilities are numerous, your grace. There are some two hundred solicitors in the City alone, and nearly double that if you count all of England. Even more if you include Scotland. Some of the best legal minds in Britain hail from Edinburgh. But we could inquire of our colleagues, if you wish. It will be rather costly, however. . . ."

"I do wish," Drew replied. "And cost is no object. You will of course keep this confidential."

"Most certainly, your grace. Lady Freemantle has been our esteemed client for many years, and her father before her, and we are privileged to serve her in any way possible."

Roslyn was disappointed to have gathered so little information, but Drew was more optimistic. "I expected as much. If Sir Rupert was considerate enough to shield his wife from learning about his affair during his lifetime, he would have taken pains to hide the knowledge even after his death. But Bow Street may have something to tell us about the livery by now."

The private police service, indeed, had made a measure of progress on the case, for they had identified two noble households that used blue-and-silver livery. However, discovering whether a ginger-haired young man was employed at either place as a footman would require delicate questioning.

Drew instructed them to turn the information over to Crupp and Beasly, who could be trusted to handle the matter with more circumspection than Bow Street. It would raise curiosity, perhaps even alarm, if a Runner began poking his nose into the servant staff of the aristocracy.

The same was true about investigating the temporary staff employed for the Danvers wedding celebrations. When Roslyn had asked the Simpkins about that night, neither could recall any unusual behavior by any of the footmen. And since they had hired nearly two dozen footmen and almost that same number of grooms and cook's helpers, it would be difficult to track the thief through the London employment agency they'd used, even with his distinctive color hair, so Drew decided to pursue that course as a last resort.

On the return drive home, he watched as Roslyn stared despondently out the window. "Don't lose heart yet. We will find our thief eventually."

At his assurance, she sat up straighter, casting him a glance as he sat beside her on the velvet squabs. "I'm certain you are right, Drew. I should have more faith in your abilities. Your ideas have been exceedingly clever thus far." She offered him a smile. "I am very grateful to you for your efforts on Winifred's behalf," she added, her voice soft and low. "Thank you."

"Don't thank me prematurely," he replied. "I haven't accomplished anything yet."

"But you will. I know that once you set your mind to something, you will succeed. Just like when you seduced me in the cottage." Roslyn laughed lightly. "I told Fanny I couldn't resist you, which was true. You were quite irresistible."

"I am flattered you think so," Drew said dryly, wondering at her sincerity.

"It is not flattery, merely honesty. What amazes me,

though, is how easily you made me forget all sense of propriety. I was raised to be a perfect lady, but you made me abandon my principles. But then, what chance did I have against the mastery of such a magnificent lover?"

Drew gave her a sharp glance. "What the devil are you up to, sweetheart?"

Roslyn responded with another musical trill of laughter. "I am only trying to be a good pupil, applying the lessons you taught me. Don't you care for my methods, darling? I was certain you would appreciate them."

When she trailed a forefinger along his arm, teasing him provocatively, Drew grasped her hand and held it away. "Are you purposely trying to seduce me?"

Roslyn eyes widened with innocence. "Well, I admit I am trying to arouse you."

"Why?"

"You said the way to a man's heart is through his lust."

He had indeed said something of the sort when he was advising her how to capture Haviland. But it was her particular choice of words that struck him. Drew studied her warily. "*Are* you after my heart, Roslyn?"

Her smile turned wistful. "Well, to be truthful, I don't think it's even possible to win your heart. But as long as we are betrothed, I thought I should exert the effort to make you enamored of me."

Drew surveyed her silently. Her soft smile tantalized him, as it doubtless was meant to do. Yet he was surprised to acknowledge his disappointment. He had groomed Roslyn to be the ideal mistress, the very kind of enticing female who had once attracted him.

He should be pleased she had become such a good

pupil, yet he'd discovered he didn't like her pretense. And that was all it was, pretense. Her artifice grated on his nerves. Instead, he wanted Roslyn to be herself—charming and warm and frank and honest, rather than cuttingly witty and artificially alluring. He saw qualities in her that were much like Eleanor's. He liked her forthrightness, her independence, her generous nature. . . .

He'd watched her comfort Lady Freemantle last evening, and *this* Roslyn was a very different woman from the warm, compassionate one last evening.

While he pondered, she leaned closer, letting her lips almost touch his. "Am I unnerving you, darling?"

Hell yes, she was unnerving him, Drew reflected. She was playing the role of bewitching temptress to perfection. God help him if she actually tried to seduce him.

When he didn't reply, Roslyn reached up to touch his mouth with her forefinger. "I think I understand what the real problem is, Drew. You like to be the pursuer, and it discomfits you when the roles are reversed. But if you dislike my teasing, I will stop."

Drew frowned. Perhaps that was indeed the trouble. Roslyn seemed to be chasing him. He enjoyed the chase, not feeling like the quarry. But he could always turn the tables on her.

Relaxing back in his seat, he shook his head. "I don't want you to stop. But if you intend to seduce me, then do it properly." Reaching for her hand, he drew it into his lap, letting her feel the swollen hardness at his groin.

As expected, Roslyn quickly snatched her hand back. "I did not mean to arouse you *that* much."

He gave her a wicked smile. "If you mean to play the temptress, love, you must be prepared to see it through."

Putting an arm around her shoulders, he slid his hand downward to her breasts. Due to the warmth inside the coach, she had unbuttoned her spencer, so he had easy access to the bodice of her muslin gown. His hand slipped inside, beneath her chemise and corset, and began to play tantalizingly with her nipples. They jutted out instantly.

"Drew," Roslyn said breathlessly, clutching at his arm to stay his caresses. Yet he saw with satisfaction that her eyes had flared and turned hot.

Using his other hand, he went on fondling her, stroking the taut buds, pinching lightly. "Are you aroused yet?"

"You know I am—and this has gone far enough."

Drew smiled lazily down at her. "But we have only just begun, darling. I intend to make love to you right here. We have ample time before we reach home."

"You cannot—"

"Certainly I can. *We* can . . . and we will."

Her nipples tightening to a hard ache, Roslyn squirmed in her seat, feeling the now familiar quickening between her thighs.

"Be still, love."

How could she possibly be still? Roslyn wondered. In addition to the swaying motion of the coach, Drew was deliberately performing his sensual sorcery on her.

"Drew, you have to stop. . . ." Yet her raspy plea held little conviction, while a reckless excitement uncoiled in her belly at the scandalous notion of making forbidden love to him in a carriage. She didn't want him to stop—and the devil very well knew it. When she lifted her gaze to glance up at him, she saw that he was watching her, his green eyes heavy-lidded and gleaming. He knew exactly the effect he was having on her, deuce take him.

"Drew. . . ." she implored one more time as he tugged at her neckline.

"Hush. I am furthering your education . . . teaching you more about pleasure." Slowly he lowered her bodice so that her breasts spilled out. "And this lesson will benefit me as well. I want to learn your body, so that I never forget the feel of you. . . ." He leaned closer and nipped her earlobe. "I want you to learn mine, so that you never forget the feel of me."

His hot breath burned her ear. Roslyn felt herself melting as the heat inside her burned higher with each seductive word. Drew's eyes sparked with the same heat as he scrutinized her breasts, the pale ripe globes pushed up by the confinement of her corset below, the dark-rose nipples straining and pouting.

His eyes smoldering, intense, he dipped his head to suckle her. Jolting at the touch of his scalding mouth, Roslyn shuddered at the riveting pleasure and fell weakly back against his arm, her fingers sliding into his silken hair.

She could no more resist him than she could fly. Drew knew how to liquify a woman's body, to devastate her willpower, to set all her senses on fire and fill her with longing.

Yet it seemed he was only teasing her. Abandoning the wet, aching crests, he raised his mouth to hers and kissed her with the same potent seductiveness. His lips were hot and restless, moving over hers in sensuous coercion, inflaming her already throbbing senses with the merciless eroticism of a master. Her body and mind were awash with hot-blooded desire by the time he reached down to gather the hem of her gown.

Still kissing her, he slid his hand beneath her skirts and upward, his searching fingers unerringly finding the folds of her sex, feeling how damp she was in the aching hollow of her womanhood.

Roslyn inhaled a sharp breath . . . but he went no further. Instead, Drew broke off his enthralling kisses and, to her bewilderment, left his seat and knelt before her. Then pushing up her skirts to her waist, he parted her legs.

Roslyn tensed, while a flush rose to her cheeks. She looked like a wanton, lounging there with her breasts bare, her pale thighs spread for his blatant sexual perusal—and Drew clearly appreciated what he saw.

At his heated expression, her heart suddenly started pounding. "Drew, what are you doing?"

"Pleasuring you."

Slowly he ran his hands up her inner thighs, stroking upward to the damp verge of her sex. When he began to lower his head, Roslyn gave a small gasp. Yet she wasn't shocked. From the night in the garden, she knew exactly what he intended.

A thrill ran through her, even as her long-ingrained sense of propriety fought against such a brazen act.

When she tried to draw back, though, Drew wouldn't let her move. He slid his hands under her hips, holding her still. Roslyn closed her eyes. He understood her shameful desires. He knew what she wanted better than she did herself.

Giving in to her covetous longings, she remained

mute as he eased her buttocks to the edge of the seat. But then he bent to taste her with his tongue, lightly caressing the bare lips of her sex.

"Oh . . . !" The word strangled in her throat.

Her thigh muscles quivering, she gave a soft moan. The delicate massage of his tongue was deliciously arousing. And then he found the secret point that was the center of her pleasure.

Roslyn clutched at his hair as he ran his tongue along the swollen nub, stroking, laving. "Oh, my . . . sweet . . . heaven. . . ."

Drew only opened his mouth more, his tongue pressing harder against her.

Her hands fisting in his hair, she raised her hips, seeking surcease. She was breathless with need, helplessly drowning in a deep, intoxicating whirlpool of desire.

And Drew just went on arousing her. Draping her knees over his shoulders, he buried his face deeper between her thighs, his lips closing tighter over the throbbing bud as he suckled her with his artful mouth.

Roslyn whimpered at the exquisite torture. The lash of pleasure was almost cruel, yet she couldn't bear for him to stop. Holding his head in place with two tight fists, she arched upward against his mouth as he continued inciting her senses to a fever pitch.

Her head was thrashing now. It was all too much, too overwhelming. A moment later she gave a strangled cry as devastating pleasure flooded her. Her body quaked and quivered with pulsating release, until the blissful spasms finally faded.

Her eyes still shut, Roslyn was dimly aware of the gentle rocking of the carriage, of the exhausted pleasure in her throbbing body.

Her lashes slowly lifting, she opened her eyes to find Drew looking at her with that maddening half smile. He was still on his knees before her, but he had unbuttoned his pantaloons.

His member jutted out from between his well-hewn thighs, and Roslyn found her gaze inexorably drawn to it.

"Touch me," he ordered. The husky command resonated through her.

Fascinated, she reached out and touched his hot skin, her hand trembling as she stroked the beautiful, hard length of him.

"Do you feel how much I want you?"

Yes, she could feel it. He was almost impossibly aroused, while his eyes had darkened with passion.

Roslyn shivered with insatiable longing. She wanted him thick and hot and pulsing inside her. And yet she was unsure what *he* wanted. "Would you like me to . . . pleasure you the way you did me?" she asked softly.

Drew felt his body clench at the erotic question. The thought of Roslyn's luscious mouth on him was nearly enough to make his cock explode. But she was still too virginal for such carnal delights. "Someday soon," he answered, "but not just now. Right now I want to be inside you."

"I want that too."

Her voice was a breathy whisper that fired his blood, and Drew gritted his teeth in response. His own body was betraying him with the intensity of his need, his swollen cock surging up to his belly. He was ravenous for her, his lust primal and urgent. His blood was pumping so hard, he wanted to take her without further wooing or preliminaries.

Yet he knew he had to go carefully so as not to hurt her. Getting up off his knees, Drew returned to his seat and sank back against the cushions. "You can mount me. We haven't yet tried that position."

Her smile was shy and sensual at the same time. "Are you attempting to prove what a creative lover you can be?"

"In part. You can think of it as furthering your education."

His hands going to her waist, he raised her up to straddle him so that her knees were braced on either side of his thighs, his aching shaft nestled in the silken haven between her legs.

When he hesitated, she frowned a little. "Why are you stopping?"

He smiled, gratified by her impatience. "I want to take my time . . . draw out the enjoyment." Which was partly true.

She was incredibly beautiful, Drew thought as he surveyed Roslyn . . . her luminous skin, her hot, pleading eyes. Yet he was more than willing to give her what she wanted.

He lifted her a bit. His erection probing the thatch of golden curls at the apex, he guided the engorged crest into her sleek cleft and eased her down the slightest measure. When she would have sunk faster, he stopped her.

"Slowly," he cautioned. "You can't take all of me just yet."

He could feel the yielding of her flesh, though. Spreading her thighs wider, he slowly thrust into her warm, honeyed interior, his penetration increasing carefully.

Her sex opened and swelled for him until she rode him fully, her body impaled, stretched taut. Now it was Roslyn who hesitated, her breath coming in soft little pants.

Drew clenched his jaw harder. The slick heat of her sheath bathed his throbbing staff, and he thought there was no better feeling on earth. Yet he could feel his control slipping, especially when she started to move her hips.

"Just wait, sweetheart...." His hands curled around the globes of her bottom, holding her still. He felt a wild desperation to bury himself even deeper inside her, to pound into her until there was no breath left in her body or his. The urgency of it burned through him, but he fought the fierce urge.

Instead, he lifted her up a little, then lowered her again . . . and then again . . . until she caught his rhythm. And eventually when Roslyn arched against him and let her head fall back, his mouth dipped to caress her swollen breasts, sucking and pulling at the pebbled crests to heighten her pleasure. He wanted her hot and wet and wanton for him. . . .

Very soon he got his wish. He could feel the urgent need building inside her each time he filled her. And in a few more moments, Roslyn was rocking wildly against him in time with the pitch of the carriage, the inner muscles of her drenched passage clasping him instinctively.

"Drew . . ." she rasped. "I don't think I . . . can wait."

Neither could he. The intoxicating delirium grew like a fever in his blood. He was full, beyond ready to burst.

His hands left her hips, tangled in her hair, as he took her mouth hungrily, his tongue plunging inside the way he wanted to do lower down with his cock. His own breath labored, he tried to shake away the sense of losing control, tried to slow down the pace. But her frenzied abandon was driving him mad.

When fiery waves of pleasure started to engulf him, Drew gave a growl, raw and primitive, and thrust into her one last time, setting off an explosion within them both.

He muffled the sounds with his mouth when she cried out in ecstasy but couldn't contain his own harsh groans when he followed her shattering climax, contracting with the force of his seed spurting from his body.

Afterward, she collapsed against his chest, panting and limp.

Drew held her close, his own breath ragged in her ear, one thought running through his dazed mind: If he'd once presumed that bedding Roslyn would satisfy his hunger for her, he knew now that he was wrong. He would never get enough of her.

Weakly, he raised his head to gaze down at her. Her eyes were half closed, drowsy with languor. She looked utterly delectable with the rosy glow of carnal satiation suffusing her lovely face.

Drew pressed his lips against her hair. Their second mating had been a searing delight, just as he'd expected. It had sapped his strength, left him utterly content.

Amazing, really, considering all the lovers he'd known. But he'd never been so hotly aroused with any other woman, had never relished making love more.

And he was certain Roslyn had experienced it as intensely as he had.

He didn't want to stop now, either. He wanted to learn her body intimately, to discover what pleased her, to teach her what pleased him, to explore the intricacies of desire and passion and carnal bliss.

But they were traveling in his carriage and would be arriving at Danvers Hall in a short while. If they didn't want to scandalize his servants, they would have to erase all evidence of their lovemaking.

With one last kiss to her temple, Drew reluctantly withdrew from her body and eased Roslyn onto the seat beside him.

Recovering her modesty immediately, if not her strength, she fumbled with her bodice. When Drew brushed her hands aside to help her, she flushed a becoming pink. And before she could push down her skirts, he fished in his coat pocket for a handkerchief and dried the traces of his seed from her thighs, then used it to clean his own loins.

"Your handkerchiefs have come in quite handy of late," Roslyn muttered, obviously embarrassed as she reordered her gown. "You offered one to Winifred last night."

"Indeed," Drew agreed. "I seem to need them frequently when I am around you."

He began buttoning his pantaloons, and Roslyn averted her gaze to stare straight ahead. When he glanced at her, he saw her biting her lower lip. "What is the matter, sweeting?"

"I cannot believe I let this happen. I intended to ask Fanny for . . ."

"Ask Fanny for what?" Drew prodded when she broke off.

"Never mind."

"Roslyn, tell me."

"Very well, if you must know . . . I wanted her assistance with something. Fanny has ways for a woman to keep from becoming enceinte."

"And you are worried about that?"

She sent him a look of exasperation. "I should think you would be worried as well. Surely you don't want to father any illegitimate children . . . or perhaps you already have some?"

Drew smiled faintly. He wasn't concerned about fathering an illegitimate child on Roslyn because he had every intention of marrying her. "I have no children at all that I'm aware of."

"Probably because your mistresses have their own methods of preventing pregnancy. But I don't want to end up like Sir Rupert's mistress, bearing a child out of wedlock."

"If you find yourself with child, there will be no question about our marrying."

Her expression turned serious. "Which is exactly what I want to avoid—us being forced to wed for the wrong reasons."

"I will take care of the matter before our next time."

"There will not be a next time," Roslyn stated emphatically.

"I seem to recall you saying that yesterday," Drew replied, his tone amused.

"Will you *please* quit reminding me of how weak I am?"

His amusement grew. "You were the one who tried to seduce me just now, remember?"

"But I never meant to go so far." She shot him a cross look. "You have a deplorable power over me."

"And you affect me similarly, Beauty. You arouse my lust with a mere touch."

Roslyn frowned unhappily. "That is precisely the trouble, Drew. Don't you see?"

"What is the trouble?"

"We feel lust for one another, but nothing deeper. Our hearts are not engaged."

He fell silent, not wanting to discuss the uncomfortable subject of love with her again. But Roslyn clearly wasn't of the same mind.

"You are a magnificent lover, Drew—no one could dispute it. You know exactly how to make my body respond. But that is all."

"That is *all*?" His eyebrow lifted. "You're saying you didn't enjoy what we just did?"

"Of course I enjoyed it. But I want more from marriage than physical pleasure."

"So you've told me."

"But you didn't seem to hear me." She folded her arms over her chest, whether out of defensiveness or mere stubbornness, he wasn't certain. "Becoming betrothed was unavoidable, Drew, but I won't marry you unless we love each other. Only if you can truly say you love me, and I can say the same to you."

He looked at her with hooded eyes. "What happened to your plan to make me enamored of you?"

Her mouth twisted. "I was being naive. I thought I could win a man's heart if I could kindle his desire, but I realize now that I was wrong. Passion won't lead to love. Desire won't make you love me—or make me love you. Nor will these games of seduction we have been playing. I see now how superficial and shallow they are."

"Perhaps, but that has nothing to do with our betrothal, or our eventual marriage."

"It has everything to do with it!" Roslyn insisted.

Stopping, she took a calming breath. There was a quiet plea in her voice when she finally spoke again. "You don't really want to wed me, Drew. You don't want a true wife. Someone who could be more to you than a broodmare for your heirs . . . lover, companion, helpmate, confidante, friend. If you want heirs, any number of women will do."

"I do want to marry you, Roslyn."

"But I don't want to marry *you*. I want love in my marriage, Drew. I *need* it."

His mouth tightened. "I think you put far too much credence in love."

Her voice dropped to a low murmur. "Perhaps, but without it, marriage can too easily lead to heartache. I couldn't bear it if my husband and I battled all the time. Or if he betrayed our marriage vows the way my father betrayed my mother. Love is the only thing that will ensure a good marriage."

Drew responded with an impatient, scoffing sound. "You are confusing love with infatuation."

"No, I am not. Infatuation is merely a powerful physical attraction. True love comes from the heart." Her tone softened. "Heart love is vastly different from physical love."

"Heart love?"

She pressed her palm to her breastbone. "It comes

from here, Drew. It's a feeling of warmth, of caring. Of tenderness. Heart love is when you put someone else's needs above your own. You are eager to be with her, and you miss her when you aren't. Your life is brighter, more joyous because she is in it. You can't imagine living without her." Her gaze searched his. "Have you ever felt that way toward a woman before, Drew?"

He could say without question that he'd never felt any such thing.

When he didn't respond, Roslyn smiled rather bleakly. "I don't believe there is any danger of you feeling heart love for me. To engage your heart, you must first feel real emotion, not merely lust and desire."

"Do you love Haviland?"

For a moment she stared at him, then looked away. "There is no use in my even thinking about Lord Haviland."

Drew felt that fierce stab of jealousy again. Roslyn's emotions were engaged for Haviland, he had little doubt. And he'd taken her away from him.

Just then Drew became aware that the carriage had slowed as it turned onto the gravel drive to Danvers Hall. Shaking off his dark reflections, he reached up to smooth a wild tendril back from her face. Roslyn jerked back quickly, as if his touch burned.

"See," she said quietly. "That is what I mean. Our attraction is purely physical."

He did see her point, since he'd felt the same heated shock. The spark he felt just touching Roslyn was intense enough to burn.

There were other manifestations of his attraction as

well. His heart quickened whenever she was near. He was constantly aware of her. And there certainly was no question that he wanted her in his bed—more than he'd ever wanted any woman.

But those were all physical signs of his growing infatuation. . . .

When the carriage came to a halt, Drew pushed open the door and started to climb out, but Roslyn stopped him. "Please . . . you needn't escort me inside. You have done more than enough already." Her voice was soft as she met his gaze. "I truly thank you for doing so much to help my friend Winifred, Drew. And for trying to protect my reputation by becoming betrothed to me. But I don't believe we are suited for marriage."

He didn't reply as his groom lowered the step for her and helped her down. And he remained sitting there unmoving as he watched Roslyn run lightly up the front steps and into the house.

"Yer grace?" a respectful voice finally interrupted his distracted thoughts.

"Yes?"

"What are yer orders, yer grace?"

"Take me home to Mayfair," Drew answered tersely, wanting to put Roslyn's disturbing conversation out of his mind. But as his coach began moving again, he found himself still dwelling on what she'd said about emotions.

His were rarely engaged, Drew readily admitted. By his very nature, he was dispassionate, reserved, guarded.

But damnation, she was wrong about his feelings for her. How could she say he didn't feel emotion in her

case? For weeks now Roslyn had stirred a riot of emotions in him: amusement, desire, anger, affection, vexation, jealousy, exasperation, passion. Most especially
passion.

She'd brought chaos into his well-ordered life,
warmth to his cold existence—and he found that he
relished it.

It was a startling discovery about himself, Drew realized. All his past liaisons had been based solely on
physical pleasure. But he wanted something deeper.

He wanted real emotion in his life. Real passion
with and for a woman. *With and for Roslyn.*

Drew found himself scowling. But what of her?
What did Roslyn feel for him? Certainly not love. He
could arouse her body but not her emotions. He could
kindle her passion now but nothing more.

As for the games of seduction they'd been playing
with each other . . . she was right about that. Even so,
there was nothing superficial or shallow about what
he felt for her. He might not love her, but he was far
from indifferent toward her.

One thing was clear, though. His courtship wasn't
working thus far. And if he wanted her to wed him, he
would have to change his strategy entirely.

He would have to elicit far more than passion from
Roslyn.

He would have to win her heart.

Chapter Fifteen

❦

It is most puzzling and profoundly disquieting, Fanny. The duke is now romancing me instead of trying to seduce me, which makes him even more irresistible.

—Roslyn to Fanny

When he arrived at his London mansion, Drew unexpectedly found Eleanor waiting on his doorstep . . . or more specifically, sitting in her jaunty little phaeton on the street out in front. As soon as he descended from his carriage, Eleanor tossed the reins to her groom and leapt down to follow Drew up the front steps.

He knew there was no point in scolding her for entering a bachelor's establishment without her maid in attendance. As Marcus's irrepressible younger sister, Eleanor had run tame in his house since she was a very small girl.

"To what do I owe this honor, minx?" Drew asked, allowing her to precede him into the hall.

"I need an escort to ride with me in the park this afternoon, Drew. Marcus is still away on his wedding trip, and it seems Heath had sudden business in Hampshire, of all places."

Drew remained silent as he led the way to his study where he usually entertained his closest friends, although he wondered at the reason for Heath's sudden visit to Hampshire.

"So will you accompany me on a ride, Drew?" Eleanor entreated.

He narrowed his gaze on her. Eleanor was a significant heiress who boasted both remarkable beauty and a lively, engaging personality, so she had no shortage of gentlemen who could take her riding. "Why me? You have a dozen beaux who can escort you."

"But I am weary of them all, and I want you. I sent you a message this morning, but you didn't reply, so I came in person to persuade you. I knew you couldn't resist a personal plea."

Settling in a comfortable leather couch, Drew smiled suspiciously at her. "Why don't I believe you? Coercing me into acting your escort isn't the only reason you called, is it?"

Eleanor dimpled impishly at him as she sank into her favorite chair. "Well, actually . . . I wondered how your betrothal is proceeding. Everyone is quizzing me about it—indeed, all London is talking about it, although the amazement is somewhat lessened since Marcus already wed the eldest Loring sister. But I've had no chance to discuss it with you since I heard the news. You were away from home the past two days visiting your mother, and there was no opportunity for a private word last night at Lady Freemantle's dinner."

His smile ebbed a little. "You know I don't discuss my personal affairs with anyone."

"Except Marcus and Heath, and they are both away. I am offering myself as their surrogate." When he didn't reply, Eleanor studied him. "I was quite astonished that you proposed to Roslyn, particularly since you were railing against the abruptness of

Marcus's marriage barely a fortnight ago. Do you truly want to wed her? Have you developed a *tendre* for her, Drew?"

He kept his expression bland. "My feelings for her are private, minx. I won't share them with anyone, not even you."

"Perhaps you should. I expect I could help you."

"I don't need your help."

"Come now, Drew . . . I have already begun. I sang your praises to Roslyn last night quite fulsomely. But now I feel the need to offer you some sisterly advice."

As the humor of Eleanor's offer struck him, Drew shook his head wryly. "There are too many matchmakers overseeing our courtship as it is. Besides, you are hardly one to advise me on my betrothal. You've had two broken engagements since your comeout, and you are responsible for both."

"But I broke those for good reason. And I think that makes me something of an expert on betrothals. You really should learn from my experience."

"Just what do you think I can I learn from you, minx?"

"I'm sure there is something. If nothing else, I can tell you how Roslyn might think. I am a woman, so I can give you a woman's perspective."

She did have a point, Drew mused. Only a short while ago, he'd concluded that his courtship of Roslyn wasn't working and that he would have to try and win her heart if he wanted her to go through with marriage to him.

Leaning back, he crossed his arms over his chest. "So tell me how I can make her fall in love with me."

Eleanor's eyes widened. "I thought you didn't believe in love."

"I don't. But Roslyn does. And she doesn't want to marry unless it's a love match. Our betrothal will allow me time to court her formally, but I need to do more than that."

"How *does* she feel about you, Drew? She doesn't appear to be in love with you yet, or at least she didn't seem eager to set a date for the wedding."

"She isn't. I suspect she will be happy for any excuse to call off the engagement."

"Do you think you could ever love her?" Eleanor asked curiously.

That wasn't a question he could answer, since he wasn't certain he was even capable of love. "I don't know," he replied finally.

"Hmm," Eleanor murmured, her countenance thoughtful. "So why do you suppose she doesn't love you yet?"

"I don't know the answer to that, either."

"I expect it's because you treat her like one of your highflyers."

That was precisely what he'd done, Drew admitted. His relationship with Roslyn had begun when he'd mistaken her for a Cyprian, and all his tutoring had been designed to teach her how to become an even better one.

Seeing his arrested expression, Eleanor crowed softly. "I am right. You have been trying to seduce her instead of court her."

Drew frowned. "What if I have?"

"Well, it makes all the difference. If you seriously want to woo her, then you are going about it all the wrong way."

His mouth pressed together at the irony. It disgruntled him that he had to woo Roslyn at all when he'd never had to trouble himself with wooing any woman before. But he was at least willing to hear what Eleanor had to say on the subject.

"So what is wrong with my wooing?"

"You are focusing on seduction, not romance. The two are not the same thing."

"Romance?" he echoed. "What the devil are you talking about?"

"Miss Roslyn is not a doxy, Drew. She is a lady with well-bred sensibilities. You cannot rely on physical persuasion to make her love you."

"I realize that."

"So you need to romance her."

His expression turned exasperated. "Very well, how do I romance her?"

"First of all, you must think of her as a person, not a possession or a prize to be won. Not a business transaction, either."

"I think of her as a person."

Eleanor looked skeptical. "Do you?"

When Drew didn't reply, she went on. "You need to be honest with her as well. Honesty shows that you respect her. Along those same lines, you have to at least pretend you are not interested in any other women but her. You can't keep a mistress while you are courting her."

"I haven't had a mistress for months."

"Good. Then remain that way. I would imagine that after Roslyn's experiences, fidelity is very important to her—just as it is to me." Eleanor frowned darkly for a moment before continuing. "Listen to what she has to say."

"I do listen."

"But do you really *hear* what she says?"

Just today Roslyn had accused him of not hearing her, of not taking her complaint to heart. "What else?" Drew asked.

"You should ask about her dreams."

He already knew about Roslyn's dreams—and they didn't include falling in love with him and wedding him. Rather they were all about falling in love with and marrying her neighbor.

"What else?" he repeated.

"Well, you could shower her with kindness. Small, thoughtful acts. It needn't be elaborate. The simplest things are often the most romantic."

"Such as?"

"Stroll with her in a meadow and pick a wildflower for her. She will appreciate a violet more than a hothouse rose. Take her for a drive, just the two of you."

"I already have," Drew said wryly. "We were caught in a ferocious thunderstorm."

"Try something else, then. In romance, it is the tender moments that count most."

"That isn't the advice Fanny Irwin gave her."

Eleanor looked at him in surprise. "I doubt Fanny knows much about romance, since she must earn her living pleasing her patrons." She looked at him earnestly. "*That* is what I mean, Drew. You need to learn how to please Roslyn, but not in a physical way. In fact, I think you should have no physical contact whatsoever. Most assuredly you shouldn't kiss her. Not even her hand. She will see the change in you at once."

"You want me to ignore her?"

"Not ignore. Just don't use your sensual powers to pursue her. It will confuse her if nothing else. She will start to wonder if you intend to make any advances toward her ever again—and she will start to long for it."

"What about gifts?"

Eleanor pursed her lips. "I expect that to someone like Roslyn, the small intimacies mean more than the most extravagant gift. But if you do give her a gift, make certain it has special meaning for her."

"Jewels don't work; I've tried."

"I would think not. You can find out what she likes from her friends."

"I know what she likes. Literature and political treatises."

"So give her a book," Eleanor advised. "You have a priceless library collection. I'm sure you can come up with something that would please her, that shows you are thinking of her." She hesitated. "That is what truly is important, Drew. You have to think more of her than of yourself. Certainly you must be concerned with her welfare. For instance, when you take her to visit your mother, you must do your best to protect her."

"I intend to."

"I hope so," Eleanor said with a shudder. "You know what an icy demeanor and razor-edged tongue the duchess has. If she doesn't freeze you with her stare, she flays you alive."

Drew couldn't help but smile at that description of his illustrious parent.

Eleanor smiled in return. "Actually, I believe it will be good for Roslyn to see you in a different light. It will give you the chance to show her your true self."

"I've shown Roslyn more of myself than any other woman but you—and you aren't really a woman to me."

"Thank you very much!" Eleanor said with mock indignation.

"You know what I mean."

"Yes, I know. You see me as a sister. That should work well with Roslyn. And she needs to understand why you don't readily warm to people. She cannot fall in love with you unless she knows the real you."

"How did you get to be so wise, minx?"

Eleanor made a face. "Wisdom never did me any good. And I am not so wise. I simply know how I want to be courted."

"None of your suitors were clever enough to comprehend what you wanted," Drew remarked.

"Not a one," she said softly, looking as if her thoughts were a million miles away.

"All right," he capitulated. "Go order your horse saddled."

Eleanor seemed to shake herself before offering him an impish smile. "Oh, I didn't really want to ride with you. I did that this morning. I just came to make certain the course of love was running smoothly for you."

"You little baggage," Drew said, laughing. "It's a wonder Marcus didn't bind and gag you as soon as you were old enough to let down your skirts."

"True," she replied, before she rose and sauntered out the door, leaving Drew chuckling.

But his amusement soon faded as his brow knitted in a thoughtful frown. Eleanor was very likely right.

To win Roslyn's heart, he had to romance her rather than rely on his usual methods of wooing.

Roslyn could not understand the change in Drew when he called on her the next morning. Instead of wicked and knowing, his smile was warm and amiable. Instead of sharp and cynical, his conversation was genuinely companionable. And he didn't so much as touch her hand.

His visit then was exceedingly brief, too—only long enough to tell her of the arrangements he'd made for their trip to his ducal family seat in Kent the following Monday to meet his mother, the Duchess of Arden. They would stay overnight at Arden Castle and return the next morning.

When Drew suggested that Roslyn take her abigail with them, her brows drew together. "Because your mother will expect it for propriety's sake?"

"No, because you will be more comfortable traveling with me in my coach. I don't want you to worry about my trying to seduce you again."

His consideration took her aback a little, but Roslyn didn't argue with him, since she would be relieved to have her maid along to act as chaperone and prevent any danger of repeating their shameless passion in his coach.

Nor did she mention her reluctance to make the visit at all. Privately Roslyn thought there was no point in her being presented to his mother for inspection and approval when she didn't intend to wed Drew, yet she realized they needed to keep up the pretense of their betrothal since it was much too soon to break it off.

To her surprise, she saw nothing more of Drew until the day of the journey. Deplorably, Roslyn found herself missing him. And the thought that he'd given up pursuing her was absurdly disappointing, even though she firmly told herself it would be better if he'd finally come to agree with her view that they wouldn't suit.

In the interim, Drew wrote to her twice. Once to send her the latest volume of Cobbett's *Parliamentary History,* which had only just been published. And once to lend her an extremely rare edition of Francis Bacon's *New Atlantis* in the original Latin, which Drew termed merely a loan, since she didn't like receiving expensive gifts from him.

Roslyn couldn't help but smile at his gibe, and repaired immediately to the library to immerse herself in studying the precious little tome.

She was foolishly glad to see Drew when Monday came—and gladder still when she settled in his coach across from him, that her abigail, Nan, was there to help her observe the proprieties. Nan was the lady's maid Marcus had hired to care for the Loring sisters' new wardrobes and help them dress and arrange their hair. Although a bit young, she came from London and was well versed in her duties as chaperone.

In Nan's presence, Drew kept up an easy but impersonal conversation with Roslyn. He spoke less as the morning wore on, though, and as they neared his estate, Roslyn was puzzled to note his near silence. She would have asked him about it, but with Nan listening, she had no opportunity.

The only time Drew spoke was when the carriage slowed to pass through an elaborate stone gate.

"My ancestral home," he said tersely, staring out the window.

The park was immense, Roslyn realized after they had negotiated a winding wooded drive for more than ten minutes. And then she forgot about Drew's silence when Arden Castle came into view.

The magnificent structure of golden stone sat gleaming on a hill in the distance. Built only two centuries before, it was nothing like a medieval castle, but rather a formal palace fit for royalty—clearly a residence belonging to the extremely wealthy aristocracy.

Roslyn saw Nan's eyes widen in awe at the sight, and knew her own expression showed a similar admiration.

A half dozen liveried grooms and footmen rushed to meet their arrival and quickly assumed control of their horses, luggage, and servants. Drew led Roslyn up the sweeping stone steps to the enormous entryway, where they were greeted by a stately butler, then through the majestic house to what he said was the "small" drawing room.

The interior decor was even more splendid than what she'd expected upon seeing the exterior. Every chamber she passed was lavish with brocade and gilt furnishings, gold and crystal chandeliers, and countless paintings, tapestries, and sculptures.

The richness of it all was rather intimidating, Roslyn decided even before she entered a grandiose room occupied by a tall, regal, silver-haired woman.

The duchess rose slowly, her demeanor just as imperious as Roslyn had been warned, and just as daunting. Her pale gray eyes were glacial, and so was the one word she uttered in acknowledgment of her son's arrival: "Arden."

"Mother," Drew responded with equal terseness. His tone was surprisingly bland yet held no warmth, either. The strain between them was palpable, Roslyn realized as he offered his parent a stiff bow and then made the introductions.

Gracefully, but quite deliberately, the duchess raised her lorgnette to one cold gray eye to examine Roslyn.

"Good day, Miss Loring," the noblewoman remarked superciliously. "I understand that you have ensnared my son."

Roslyn couldn't help her amusement at that particular choice of words, but she was careful to keep both her expression and her tone neutral when she replied. "I hardly think ensnare is the proper word, your grace."

"Then what would you call it?"

Doubting she would ever win the duchess's approval, even if she prostrated herself at the disdainful noblewoman's feet, Roslyn smiled coquettishly up at Drew. "I would call it an unexpectedly mutual attraction, your grace."

When he smiled lazily back at her, the duchess immediately stiffened. "You can hardly expect me to welcome your betrothal, Miss Loring, when you had such infamous parents. Your entire family has been under a cloud of scandal for years."

"That was indeed true until recently," Roslyn agreed politely. "But my elder sister married quite respectably."

"Yes, I know. Lord Danvers has long been an acquaintance of my son's. Are you accomplished, Miss Loring?"

"Fairly so. I sing and play the pianoforte well. I am

proficient at needlepoint and watercolors. I am fluent in French and know a smattering of Italian. Oh, and I read and speak Latin."

"*Latin?*" Her tone implied disdain. "Then you have at least one thing in common with Arden."

"Yes, we can enjoy the same books. I consider that a chief qualification for matrimonial bliss, don't you, your grace?"

The duchess's mouth tightened, but Roslyn returned her icy gaze evenly. She fully comprehended the noblewoman's goal in grilling her. The duchess was trying to intimidate her into calling off the betrothal. But she had no intention of giving her satisfaction by complying.

After a moment, the duchess took another tack. "I understand you also teach at an academy for young ladies. You will of course give that up immediately now that you are betrothed."

"Regrettably I must disappoint you, your grace. My elder sister plans to continue teaching at our academy, even though she is now a countess, and I intend to do the same if I become a duchess."

The Duchess of Arden looked angry now. "Do you have any idea, Miss Loring, what obligation you bear if you marry into this family? You have a duty to uphold our consequence."

"I do indeed," Roslyn said, keeping her voice light. "After meeting you, your grace, I have an excellent idea of what to expect. But I shall allow your son to be the arbiter of my proper conduct."

Looking irate and offended, the duchess suddenly turned her attention to Drew, as if dismissing Roslyn from her thoughts altogether. "Your rooms have been prepared, Arden. You may join me in the grand draw-ing room at half past seven for a glass of sherry. You recall that I keep Town hours and dine at eight."

"I recall quite clearly, Mother," Drew said mildly.

"I will expect you to have a word with Mathers. She has been more insolent than usual this week, and she knows I cannot rebuke her."

"Of course, I will speak with her. I intend to visit her shortly."

He gave her another brief bow and ushered Roslyn from the room. As they escaped down the corridor, she let out her breath in relief.

Drew looked amused and perhaps a little relieved himself. "You handled that quite well. You more than held your own with the Dragon."

Roslyn smiled. "She is not so bad, if you like haughty, bloodless sort of people."

"I don't," he said abruptly, curtness returning to his tone. "Come, let me show you the library. I think you will appreciate it."

"Who is Mathers?" Roslyn asked as he led her to an-other wing. "And why can't your mother rebuke her?"

"She was first my nurse, then governess, before I was sent off to Eton."

"Ah, Eleanor mentioned your old nurse. You brought her here to live at the castle when she became too infirm to care for herself. I take it the duchess doesn't approve of your generosity?"

Drew grimaced. "No. It is a running battle between us, but so far I have won."

"How did you manage that?"

"I threatened to make my mother move to the dower house if she couldn't tolerate living under the same roof as Mathers. But of course she doesn't want to reside in a place only a tenth the size of this."

Roslyn laughed softly, and Drew found himself relishing the sweet, musical sound. She seemed to understand his sentiments toward his mother perfectly.

"So what do you think of the Castle?" he asked, pleased that she had emerged unscathed in her verbal parries with the duchess.

"It is very beautiful," Roslyn said carefully.

"But you don't like it."

"It is not particularly . . . welcoming."

"You noticed," Drew said dryly.

"You don't seem to care for it much."

"No."

He'd never liked living here, imprisoned by marble and mahogany. As a home, it was too palatial, too cold, too empty . . . the coldness due in large part to his mother's presence, Drew was well aware.

He'd never thought of this as home, either, not since leaving for Eton at age six. And even after inheriting the title, he'd absented himself as much as possible whenever his mother was in residence, only visiting to spend time with his tenants and oversee his home farms, particularly testing and experimenting with the newest agricultural methods.

"Would you like to see the grounds?" Drew asked. "They are much more appealing than the house."

"Yes, very much."

"Then I will have mounts saddled for a ride this afternoon."

"Does your mother reside here most of the year?"

"Except for each Season, which she spends in London. Otherwise she holds court here."

Roslyn raised an eyebrow. "That must make the Season awkward for you both."

"Oh, we don't share the same abode, God forbid. I bought my own town house and gave her the house in Grosvenor Square. She lives her own life, and I live mine. It works much better that way for both of us."

"I can imagine," Roslyn murmured. "I begin to see why you don't want to marry. You worry that your duchess will turn out to resemble your mother."

Drew shot her a sharp glance before giving her a humorless smile. "How very perceptive you are, darling."

They had reached the library by now, and Drew stood aside to let her enter. The room dwarfed the one at Danvers Hall, and Roslyn showed proper respect.

"Oh, my," she said reverently, moving to the nearest shelf to inspect the various titles.

"The collection in my London library is actually much better. And frankly, so is your late step-uncle's at Danvers Hall. These are only the inferior volumes because I ran out of room at my London house."

"You call *this* inferior?" Pulling out a book at random, she opened it. "I can tell that being obscenely wealthy has quite spoiled you."

He grinned. "Wealth does have its advantages. Now if you will excuse me, sweeting, I want to pay Mathers a visit. She will expect it. I can leave you here or show you to your room so you can change into your riding habit."

Roslyn looked up from the book. "May I meet her?"

Drew felt surprise, yet he saw no reason to refuse her request. "If you wish. Indeed, she has been eager to meet you since my last visit here when I told her of our betrothal."

When Roslyn returned her book to the shelf, he led the way upstairs to the fourth-floor servant hall. At the corridor's end, he knocked softly on a door and opened it when a craggy voice bid entrance.

Immediately his gaze went to the ancient crone who sat in a rocking chair beside the open window, basking in a stream of sunshine as she slowly knitted from a skein of wool yarn. His fondest memories of his early childhood centered around this old woman, and he regretted her pitiful state now—the stooped shoulders, the gnarled hands, the cane resting beside the chair. But it was the cloudy eyes that evidenced her near blindness.

Mathers canted her head, listening intently, then smiled before Drew said a word. "You came."

"Did you expect anything less?" he asked, shepherding Roslyn into the room.

"Not from you, your grace. But I didn't know if your bride-to-be would let you out of her sight."

Drew bent to kiss her age-crinkled cheek and drew Roslyn closer. "Actually my betrothed is here with me. Miss Roslyn Loring, may I introduce you to my former governess, Mrs. Esther Mathers?" Before Roslyn could respond, he added, "Miss Loring asked to meet you, Mathers."

"Did she?" The old woman sounded pleased.

"Yes, it raised her curiosity when I told her how you bullied and beat me when I was a snip of a boy."

Mathers gave him a broad, toothless smile. "And did she believe you?"

"You will have to ask her that yourself."

"So did you, Miss Loring?"

Roslyn laughed. "Truthfully, this is the first I have heard about your cruelty, Mrs. Mathers—but I expect you know that. I am happy to make your acquaintance."

"And I, you." She let her knitting needles fall to her lap. "Come here so that I may see you, Miss Loring."

"Ah, no, Mathers," Drew intervened. "You cannot treat her the way you do me, with no respect." He smiled fondly down at her as he murmured to Roslyn, "I am still six years old in her eyes."

Mathers's rasping laugh was more like a cackle. "I changed his napkins and taught him his manners. 'Tis hard to think of him as a lord, no matter how grand he has become. So, Miss Loring, I hear that you teach at a young ladies' academy. That surprises me greatly."

"Yes, I do, along with my two sisters. Several years ago our finances necessitated that we seek employment, so we opened an academy with the help of a very generous patron."

"And do you despise teaching?"

"On the contrary, I enjoy it very much. We instruct the daughters of tradesmen and merchants on how to deal with society . . . develop their polish and refinement so they won't be quite as disadvantaged if they make genteel marriages."

Mathers nodded in approval. "I hope your pupils are better behaved than this scamp here was."

Her blue eyes dancing with amusement, Roslyn glanced at Drew. "Was he a terror when he was a child?"

"Not a terror, just mischievous, as boys will be. But I encouraged it since the duke and duchess . . ." She shook her head sternly. "Never mind my tongue. It is impolite to speak ill of one's employers."

"I would very much like to hear some of your tales of him," Roslyn said, covering up the awkward moment.

Mathers reached out a shaky hand. "Will you come closer, please? I want to see what manner of woman my lad is marrying, and my old eyes are not what they once were."

"Yes, of course."

When Roslyn complied, bending down, Mathers reached up to gently feel her face. Roslyn stood quite still while the bony fingers inspected her, a little to Drew's surprise.

A look of satisfaction spread over the old governess's face. "You aren't some high and mighty lady, are you?"

"How can you tell?" Roslyn said, smiling.

"Besides the fact that you had to earn your own way in the world? You allowed me to touch you. Some proper ladies would be revolted." She turned her glance toward Drew. "I think she'll do, your grace."

"You can determine that on such short acquaintance?" he replied teasingly.

The old woman cackled. "Yes, indeed. I'll wager it didn't take you long to determine it, either."

"Barely a fortnight."

"She will keep you in line, I have no doubt."

"I expect so," Drew said amiably.

"So, do you love him, Miss Loring?"

Looking taken aback by the question, Roslyn hesitated, as if not wanting to lie. "I am very fond of him."

" 'Twill be good if you come to love him. There's

been no love in this house for years, not since he left it when he was a wee child."

"That will be enough, Mathers," Drew said quickly. "You don't want to bore Miss Loring."

Her cloudy gaze turned toward him. "No, but even if I *am* boring her, she is kind enough to refrain from mentioning it. That warms my heart, dear boy. Only a special woman will do for you, and I have a feeling that this is a special one."

He avoided looking at Roslyn as he lightly touched the old woman's shoulder. "I won't dispute you, love, but if you will you excuse us, I have promised to take Miss Loring riding."

"Excellent! 'Tis a beautiful day with summer full upon us. You will like the grounds, I think, Miss Loring."

"They are indeed magnificent," Roslyn agreed.

With a final kiss to Mathers's withered cheek, Drew took Roslyn's arm to usher her from the room.

Their exchange with his former governess had been discomfiting for him, yet satisfying at the same time. Roslyn's gentleness with the elderly servant was so different from his mother's icy contempt. The contrast made him value her warm nature even more— and in some strange way soothed a little of the sexual frustration he'd experienced for the past five days, when he'd been unable to kiss Roslyn or even touch her. Being forced to bide his time had made him restless and irritable, not to mention aching.

But then, abstinence was not his strong suit, Drew acknowledged. Nor was patience. And he had to summon enough of the latter to get through tonight's dinner with his illustrious mother.

But at least he could enjoy a companionable ride over his lands with Roslyn beforehand. Even so, he was careful to drop her arm as soon as he closed the door behind them, before he succumbed to the fierce temptation to do much, much more than simply savor her company.

Chapter Sixteen

❦

*I would be a fool to lose my heart to him, but I am
tempted more each day.*

—Roslyn to Fanny

In sharp contrast to her icy meeting with the
Duchess of Arden, Roslyn found the lovely summer
afternoon particularly pleasurable, riding with Drew
over the Kentish countryside, viewing his beautiful estate grounds and tenant farms.

He put himself out to be the perfect companion,
even more agreeable and charming than usual. And
yet she noticed a distinct change in him. He seemed
less guarded now. Less practiced. More at ease. More
natural.

And she saw a different side of Drew than she'd ever
seen before—the serious, responsible, generous side.
He took unmistakable pride in his holdings and obviously cared for his tenants, unlike many great landown-
ers in England, who cared only about bleeding the
land and laborers for whatever revenues they could
provide.

As a duke, Drew commanded respect and took it as
his due, yet there was clearly a measure of affection
between him and his people. But then, Roslyn had expected as much after seeing him with Mathers. The

way he cared for his old governess had warmed her heart.

Toward the end of their ride, she learned why he was so fond of the elderly upper-class servant.

They were riding beside a small lake in a meadow when they came to a cottage on the edge of a wood and Drew reined his horse to a halt.

"This was my favorite place as a child," he said a little wistfully. "This cottage belonged to our game-keeper and his wife. Mathers would bring me here to escape the schoolroom. We would make paper sail-boats and float them on the lake and play pirate. Afterward she plied me with hot scones baked by the gamekeeper's wife."

In other words, you were allowed to be a child, Roslyn thought with silent empathy. "It must have been lonely living here as a young boy," she said aloud.

He shrugged. "I rarely saw my parents. And of course I wasn't allowed to associate with other children—certainly not the staff's children, since we had our consequence to uphold. But Mathers made it bearable. And after I met Marcus and Heath at school, I was never lonely." Drew shot her a wry glance. "But you can see why I was glad to leave here."

"Indeed I can."

She would have been glad to leave, too, Roslyn thought with a shudder. The huge house, though magnificent, was cold and intimidating, devoid of life and warmth. She couldn't imagine living in such a house.

Thankfully her own upbringing had been quite different from Drew's. For the first eighteen years of her life she'd had the love of her mother and her sisters, and her father to some extent. Now she had her academy and her friends to provide mutual warmth and affection, in addition to her sisters.

Her own mother was very different from Drew's, as well. Even though Victoria Loring was a noblewoman in her own right, she had sincerely loved her daughters. Thanks to Marcus, they had recently been reunited with Victoria and learned the truth about why she'd been forced to flee the country with her lover. She hadn't wanted to abandon her daughters, and in fact grieved over it.

But clearly the Duchess of Arden bore little love for her son. Instead, Mathers had taken the place of Drew's mother.

Roslyn was glad that he'd had someone to love him when he was such a young child, and disliked the duchess intensely for the emotional barrenness she'd inflicted upon him.

Imagining Drew's loneliness as a boy—and seeing his strained maternal relationship now—brought out Roslyn's protective instincts. Which was absurd, since Drew was a fully grown man, perfectly capable of defending himself against his mother.

"You were fortunate to have Mathers," Roslyn murmured.

"Extremely fortunate. She was one of the few people who treated me as a normal boy and not a duke's son . . . and one of the fewer still whose motives I never had to question." He hesitated, glancing at Roslyn. "By the time I was out of short coats, I had learned that most people want something from me."

"Because of your wealth and consequence?"

"Yes. And when I was sixteen, that lesson was driven home quite painfully."

"What happened when you were sixteen?"

"I let myself be seduced."

Roslyn met his eyes, wondering if he was jesting. But she could tell by the rough shadow of emotion there that he was in earnest. "That seems hard to imagine."

"Regrettably, it's true. She was strikingly beautiful and my first lover . . . a young widow only four years my senior but far more experienced. I should have known better than to trust her professions of love, but I was in the throes of lust, suffering a young man's infatuation. I was heartbroken when I discovered how she'd schemed to ensnare me so she could become my duchess. She had another lover all along, a lover she planned to keep after we were wed."

"So that is what made you so cynical about love?" Roslyn asked quietly.

"I expect so." He gave a short, mirthless laugh. "Truthfully, though, I haven't thought of her in years." Drew suddenly shook his head. "Enough maudlin sentiment for one afternoon. Let me show you my newest drainage ditch. The science can be quite fascinating."

There was a glint of sardonic humor in his eyes as he turned his horse away from the cottage, yet Roslyn was not surprised that he'd deliberately changed the subject.

What did surprise her was how vulnerable those vibrant green eyes had been for a moment. Even more surprising was that Drew had let her see his vulnerability.

She could no longer blame him for his cynicism, though, Roslyn reflected as she urged her horse alongside his. And the fact that he'd been hurt so bitterly as a young man roused even stronger protective instincts in her. She wanted to wrap her arms around him, to kiss away his hurt—

Forcibly quelling the yearning, Roslyn bit her lower lip. She didn't want to see this tender, vulnerable side of Drew. It was far easier to resist the seductive rake, the cynical nobleman.

Which made *her* too vulnerable to him. She could so easily lose her heart to this man. And that could be disastrous.

It would be a tremendous mistake to fall in love with Drew when her love wasn't returned. He wasn't willing to let himself love anyone, to let himself trust, and she would be a fool to let herself hope otherwise.

Drew found his thoughts predictably unsettled as they concluded the tour of his estates. He'd taken Eleanor's advice and risked sharing something of himself with Roslyn, recounting the sordid little tale of how he'd been played for a fool by his first lover, duped by a beautiful widow who'd left his young heart in pieces.

He'd recovered fairly quickly, and the experience no longer caused him pain, but it was still uncomfortable for him to remember.

Fortunately he rarely thought of the widow anymore. He'd determinedly wiped her from his mind long ago. But the lesson she'd taught him had never left him. The wariness was always there, hovering at the back of his consciousness.

His distrust was the reason he'd always shied away from matrimony so resolutely. He didn't want to be locked in a marriage with a woman who only wanted his wealth and title. He wanted to be loved for himself—

The significance of that realization was a little startling, Drew admitted silently. It was the first time in his life he'd ever acknowledged wanting love.

He wanted a wife who could love him for himself.

Could Roslyn possibly be that woman? Unconsciously his gaze went to her as she rode beside him. She would make him an excellent duchess, he knew. Her graciousness, her easy manner with his tenants today, had shown him how effortlessly she could fill the role of lady of Arden Castle.

Unquestionably she would bring warmth to his house. Unlike his brittle, domineering mother, who held her underlings in contempt, who ruled her domain like an ice queen.

Roslyn could be regal in her demeanor, but she was the stark opposite of an ice queen. Rather, she was the very essence of warmth. This afternoon she wore a small shako hat, with her hair knotted simply at her nape. Her golden hair seemed to absorb the sunlight, Drew realized as he watched her, while her smile seemed to rival it.

Her smile was lovely and warm and made him ache inside with longing. A longing that went much deeper than carnal desire, Drew acknowledged.

Roslyn stirred uncomfortable emotions in him that were far more potent—and significantly more disturbing.

Even so, he relished the feeling.

For years he'd striven for emotional detachment. If he didn't feel for people, then he couldn't be betrayed. His two closest friends, Marcus and Heath, had never betrayed him, never disappointed him, and thus had earned his undying trust and loyalty.

But he was in danger of becoming too much like his mother, with the same coldness, the same haughty detachment, the same loneliness.

Until now he'd never thought of himself as lonely, but Roslyn's question a moment ago had made him realize that he was indeed lonely much of the time—or he had been before meeting her. She had roused him from his self-protective shell. Had brought enchantment to his hitherto dispassionate existence. Since coming to know her, his life had been fuller, richer. More passionate.

Drew felt himself frown. Perhaps he'd been unconsciously searching for passion all this time and hadn't even known it. A woman who could make him feel something more profound than mere physical pleasure. Who could shake him out of his cold, emotionless existence.

Regardless, he was very glad Roslyn had come into his life. Despite the danger of the emotions she made him feel. Despite even the supreme sexual frustration that her nearness caused him.

Physical discomfort, though painful, was worth enduring if he could share her warmth.

Drew was not eager to subject Roslyn to his mother again, but dinner turned out to be bearable even with its stiff formality, because the duchess kept her scornful remarks to a minimum, and Roslyn kept up a polite conversation that eased the strain.

After dinner, however, was another question entirely. Proper custom dictated that ladies repair to the drawing room while gentlemen enjoyed their port wine. But Drew had no desire to drink by himself, and absolutely no intention of leaving Roslyn alone with the Dragon, so he accompanied them to the large drawing room.

His refusal to conform to convention roused the duchess's ire even more than he expected; no sooner had they settled in chairs when she launched her first volley. "You disappoint me, Arden. You know I do not tolerate ill-bred behavior in my house."

Drew had to work to keep his reply bland. "Actually, it is my house, Mother."

"Perhaps, but if you expect me to pretend to support this unsuitable betrothal of yours, you will accede to my wishes."

Drew's jaw hardened, but his mother went on stonily.

"You know very well I don't approve of this match. You can do much better in choosing a bride. Miss Loring is so far beneath you—"

He cut off her tirade in midstream. "First, Mother, it is not your place to tell me what bride to choose. And second, I *cannot* do better than Miss Loring."

"Well, you must, because I will not give my blessing to such an unequal arrangement."

He returned his mother's haughty stare measure for measure. "You *will,* or you will remove to the dower house in the morning."

"You wouldn't dare!"

"Certainly I would dare. I'll order your personal belongings carried there and have you barred from the Castle before I return to London. My staff will obey my wishes, you know they will."

The duchess paled, gaping at him in fury.

Throughout their argument, Roslyn had remained silent, but now she intervened.

"Drew," Roslyn said in a low voice. "It doesn't matter. I have never desired to climb any higher in society. I am perfectly content where I am."

"It damn well matters to me."

Nearly quivering with rage, the duchess rose to her feet. "You will not swear in my presence, sirrah, do I make myself clear?"

Rising just as abruptly, Drew held out his hand to Roslyn. "Come, sweetheart, I cannot stay here another moment without succumbing to the urge to do murder."

His mother gasped in outrage, but Drew paid her no attention as he pulled Roslyn from the room. Without stopping, he stalked through the house to the library, Roslyn still in tow.

She made no objection to his rapid pace, but by the time he pushed open the French doors and escaped onto the terrace, she was a trifle breathless. It was only then that Drew realized he had let his wrath get the better of him. Usually he managed to control his fierce urge to throttle his mother by determinedly ignoring her.

Muttering an apology, he dropped Roslyn's hand and crossed the terrace to the stone balustrade, where he stared out at the stately gardens. A full moon had just risen, so the peaceful view was a stark contrast to the anger roiling inside him.

He sensed more than saw Roslyn move to stand beside him.

Her tone was hesitant, wary, when she finally spoke.

"I don't wish to come between you and your mother, Drew."

"You haven't come between us," he said through gritted teeth. "We have been at loggerheads for years. Normally I let her have her way—but not this time."

"I think you are making too much of the matter. I don't want or need her approval. And I should think you wouldn't, either."

"I don't want it for myself, but for you. She can assure your place in society if she chooses to."

"But truly, it doesn't matter to me. And I certainly don't want you to battle over it. It is too distressing. Perhaps I'm craven, but my parents' battles left me with a dread of strife."

Drew felt his heart twist. His ire had reached the boiling point with his mother's implacable view of her consequence and her tyrannical need to govern anyone who came into her realm. But he had no right to take his anger out on Roslyn.

Turning, he reached down to take her hand and bring it to his lips. "Forgive me, sweeting. I should not have let my temper get the best of me."

She smiled up at him tentatively. "Well . . . you *did* have grave provocation. But I doubt the local magistrate would look kindly upon the murder of a duchess. Especially one so closely related to you."

His lips curved faintly at her forced attempt at humor, but all his thoughts faded when his gaze came to rest on Roslyn's upturned face. In the moonlight, her beauty caught him like a sharp blow.

His heart started to pound as he stared at her. As want, need, desire suddenly filled him.

Without conscious thought, he leaned closer. He

wasn't supposed to touch her. He'd promised himself he would employ romance to woo her, not seduction. But he couldn't bear to let another moment pass without tasting her, touching her.

Unable to help himself, Drew lowered his mouth to hers. He kissed her slowly, letting his tongue slide inside, savoring her sweetness, her warmth. After a brief second of shocked stillness, Roslyn opened to him. Swaying weakly against him, she reached up to steady herself, then clutched his upper arms as if to pull him even closer.

At her hungry response, Drew wanted nothing more than to drag her into his embrace, but instead, he summoned every ounce of willpower he possessed to break off. Giving a low groan, he stepped back, putting a safer distance between them.

The kiss had left him raw and aching, left his voice hoarse with need when he spoke. "I didn't mean to succumb to temptation. I meant to keep my hands off you entirely. To show I could woo you the way you want to be wooed."

She searched his face for a long moment, then swallowed before replying. "That *is* the way I want to be wooed, Drew. With tenderness."

His chuckle sounded pained. "I'm afraid I couldn't manage tenderness for long. And I sure as the devil won't be able to stop with a mere kiss."

"I don't want you to stop."

His gaze arrested. "Do you know what you are saying?"

"Yes," she said softly. "I know. I want you to make love to me."

He glanced back at the doors leading to the library. "Not here. Not with my mother in the house."

"Then where?" she asked.

"The cottage," he said after a moment. "The game-keeper's cottage I showed you today. Will you come there with me?"

Roslyn nodded. "Yes," she replied simply.

He felt his heart turn over with elation, felt his loins tighten at the thought of being with her again. This was his chance, Drew reflected, pulling in an uneven breath. Tonight he would make Roslyn feel over-whelming passion for him. The kind of ardent passion he had begun to feel for her.

Stepping closer, he lifted her hand and pressed a kiss to it. "Give me ten minutes. I'll need to saddle a horse . . . and I must fetch something from my room first. Wait for me here, will you?"

Roslyn nodded again silently.

"Are you sure, sweeting?" Drew repeated.

"Yes, I am sure."

Hearing no hesitation in her voice, he gave her fingers one last lingering kiss. "Ten minutes, then."

Roslyn's nerves were taut with anticipation by the time Drew returned. Without speaking, he laced his fingers with hers and led her through the library and down a corridor to a side door, where he had a horse waiting. Lifting her up, he mounted behind her and drew her back against him.

They rode across the grounds in silence. The summer night was beautiful and serene, the darkness awash with silver moonlight, but the ride seemed to last forever. Eagerness strummed inside Roslyn, beating an urgent rhythm in time with her heart. She could feel Drew's warmth at her back, feel the hard muscles of his chest and enveloping arms arousing her senses.

When finally they arrived, Roslyn spoke for the first time. "Your gamekeeper won't mind if we use his cottage?"

"He no longer lives here. I provided him a larger home and kept this for my own because I was fond of it. One of the privileges of having a fortune—being able to indulge my sentimental whims."

She doubted Drew had many sentimental whims, so she was glad he could indulge this one.

Dismounting, he helped her down and preceded her inside. He didn't light a candle but pulled aside the curtains on the front windows instead, letting the moonlight stream in.

This cottage was significantly larger than the one where they had first made love, Roslyn realized at a glance, and much better furnished.

"The bedchambers are upstairs," he said, taking her hand again.

He mounted the wooden stairs with her and guided her to a room that boasted a large, high bed. When Drew opened those curtains as well, moonlight flooded in—bright enough that she could see the wryness in his smile as he turned back to her.

"It's fortunate you decided to put an end to my misery, sweeting. I didn't know how much longer I could endure not making love to you."

Roslyn smiled. "Please don't endure any longer."

He stepped closer and took her face in his hands.

For a long moment he simply gazed at her. "I have missed this . . . just touching you."

"I have missed it, too," Roslyn replied softly.

She raised her face to his, already anticipating the heat of his kisses, but Drew surprised her by reaching into his pocket and drawing out a pouch, which contained several small sponges and a vial of liquid.

"You said you wanted to take precautions against conceiving, so I brought this. Sponges soaked in vinegar should prevent my seed from taking root."

It warmed her that he'd remembered her concern and taken the trouble to alleviate it. "Thank you," Roslyn murmured sincerely.

He laid the pouch on the bedside table, then turned down the covers.

Returning to her, he pulled the pins from her hair and fanned it out over her shoulders. Then he undressed her in the hushed silence, and let her undress him.

When he stood naked before her, Roslyn caught her breath in awe. Moonlight poured over him, highlighting the chiseled planes of his face, the broad expanse of his chest, the virile contours of his body. His form was lean and powerful, sculpted and graceful, like that of a Greek god. And when he took her in his arms, she could feel sleek muscles rippling under taut skin.

The first touch of his lips was warm, intimate, almost sweet, but it kindled a flame in her that she knew would quickly grow. Then all thought fled as she lost herself in the pleasure of touch and taste and need. The tender, openmouthed kisses Drew cherished on her made her whimper, and so did the sensual hands that began to caress her. Her breasts swelled in arousal, while a tremulous pulsing heated her body.

Roslyn almost cried out in disappointment when his mouth left hers, but he only lifted her in his arms and carried her to the bed, where he gently laid her down and then sat beside her.

Holding her gaze then, he made use of the pouch he'd brought . . . wetting a sponge, parting her legs and easing it deep inside her woman's passage. Roslyn trembled at the delicacy of his touch, at the sensual eroticism he was deliberately employing. She was breathless by the time Drew stretched out beside her, bracing his weight on one elbow.

Longing to have him inside her, she reached for him, but he shook his head. "Not yet. We have all night."

He bent his head to suckle her breasts. The touch of his searing mouth sent a streak of fire traveling downward to the heated, throbbing core of her body, making her arch up off the mattress.

"Drew, please . . ." she pleaded.

"What do you want, sweetheart?"

"I want *you*."

He moved closer, pressing his body against hers— his hard belly, his sinewed thighs, and between his legs, his thick arousal—but nothing more. She relished feeling the naked heat and strength of him, but it wasn't enough.

"Hurry," she whispered.

"No. We need to take our time."

Roslyn bit her lip, ready to scream, but she managed to quell her hunger for another few moments as he caressed her.

His fingers trailed down her body to the juncture of her thighs, gliding through the soft curls to find her slick cleft. She was already hot and swollen for him, even before he began stroking her aching flesh with exquisite tenderness.

"Drew, I can't bear it . . . please."

She exhaled a ragged sigh when finally he eased his body over hers, nestling his splendid length in the cradle of her thighs. And she met his first silken penetration with a blissful moan.

Her moans increased as he began to move inside her. Her hands roaming restlessly down his back, Roslyn clutched the taut curves of his flexing buttocks, urging him to quicken his pace. But he wouldn't obey.

Instead he aroused her slowly, gliding in and then withdrawing. Thrusting, penetrating, filling . . . then sliding almost free, leaving her aching with want, gasping with need. He sought her pleasure, courted it, wooed it, whispering soft erotic things in her ear, until she was half wild with passion.

Drew was feeling the same wildness as he reveled in the feel and scent and taste of her. There was urgency in his every heartbeat, yet he forced himself to slow down. He wanted this to last. Wanted her passion to be blazing-hot.

His face taut with concentration, he drew back to watch Roslyn's pleasure . . . and found his gaze captured by her desire-hazed eyes.

Quivering, she wrapped her legs around his hips, locking him close, surrounding him, drawing him in. Gritting his teeth, Drew plunged even deeper into her searing wetness, planting himself to the hilt inside her.

Her harsh gasps becoming frenzied, she bucked against him, surging upward, making him share her helpless shudders as his own frenzy mounted.

She was flame-hot in her arousal; she was liquid fire beneath his aching body. He rode her harder, no longer in control of his response.

The rhythm of their desire turned explosive, and an instant later, Roslyn's entire body clenched. Her keening cry melted his heart, while her convulsive ecstasy propelled his own body to a tempestuous climax.

Drew poured his desire into her, driving with fierce possessiveness, deeper and deeper, as if he couldn't get far enough inside her. Groans tearing from his throat, he pounded into her, quaking, jolting, arching, until finally contracting powerfully and drenching her with his hot, spurting seed.

In the aftermath, they clung to each other with gasping shudders. When the tremors faded, Drew somehow found the energy to shift his weight so that he wasn't crushing her, but their loins were still joined, his mouth buried in her hair.

The harshness of his breathing calmed as the night settled in around them. With a slow, sated exhalation, Drew shut his eyes. Their lovemaking had been a savage explosion of the senses, yet despite the fierceness, he'd never felt such intimacy, such tenderness, as he felt right this moment with Roslyn.

He was pondering what to say when he became aware of the slow evenness of her breathing and realized that she was no longer awake.

Drew smiled ruefully. He had set out to rouse her passion, but instead he'd put her to sleep. Carefully, he eased onto his side while leaving Roslyn still trapped in the shelter of his body. He didn't want to fall asleep, though. He would rather watch her.

Surveying her exquisite beauty in the moonlight, he was hard-pressed to understand why he felt so content in her arms. Why she satisfied him so completely. Why her warmth touched him so.

But the simple truth was, Roslyn filled a need he'd never had a name for until now. It seemed irrational at this point in his life to discover there was this huge need inside him, yet he couldn't deny it. She stanched a loneliness he hadn't even known he was suffering from. She kindled delight and joy in him—

Drew suddenly went very still. He was experiencing some of the same symptoms she had tried to describe. He felt happy in her presence. He felt restless and empty without her. He felt a hunger that went far beyond the physical.

Heart love was what she termed it.

Something clenched in his chest; not pain, but wonder.

Was it possible he was actually falling in love with her? Was he capable of love after all?

How else could he explain the powerful emotions he felt for her? If his yearning for her was only carnal desire, it wouldn't touch his heart and mind.

Drew closed his eyes, testing the theory. Roslyn had slipped beneath his defenses, that was for certain, but the knowledge didn't make him cringe as he expected. Indeed, it was profoundly appealing—the thought of sharing intimacy and love and affection with her for the rest of their days.

He'd never expected to have that with his bride. But now he wouldn't settle for less. He wanted a love match with Roslyn, not just a marriage of convenience. He wanted her to love him, not merely be forced to marry him to avoid scandal.

And if he couldn't make her love him?

His arms tightened reflexively around her. He wouldn't even consider the possibility.

He would never let her go, Drew vowed in the hushed stillness. He would win Roslyn's heart before long. He would wed her and make her his duchess. And he would give her the kind of future she had once envisioned with another man . . . the kind of future he had never envisioned for himself.

Chapter Seventeen

✤

I was right to end it now before the possibility of future pain grows too great.

—Roslyn to Fanny

Roslyn was exceedingly relieved to return to Danvers Hall the following morning, not only because she'd had her fill of the duchess—who continued to treat her with icy disdain at her departure—but so that she could say farewell to Drew. Their night of lovemaking had been magical, Roslyn acknowledged, but such enchanted intimacy wouldn't last forever. And before she sank even more deeply under Drew's spell, it was imperative that she return to reality.

Regrettably, though, when he handed her down from his coach, he gave her a look so intimate, so searing, it made her heart turn over. Fighting the temptation to throw herself back into his arms, Roslyn instead wished him success upon his return to London. He planned to visit Sir Rupert's solicitors again to discover what progress had been made during his absence toward learning the identity of Winifred's ginger-haired thief.

When Drew took his leave, he merely kissed Roslyn's gloved fingers, but she wanted him to do much, much more.

The temptation lingered long after he was gone. At loose ends, Roslyn found herself wandering restlessly through the house, stewing over her quandary. Yesterday had helped her recognize the grave danger she was in with Drew. Seeing that softer, tender side of him had melted her remaining defenses. And dismayingly, her feelings for him were growing stronger every moment she shared with him.

She knew now that she couldn't risk letting him continue to romance her. Most certainly she couldn't indulge in any more forbidden trysts with him. But with their betrothal still standing, she would be forced to share Drew's company to a significant extent. And after their romantic interlude last night, she would find it impossible to keep her emotional distance.

She'd been deluding herself to think she could, Roslyn admitted. Trying to resist an irresistible man bent on wooing her would be impossible. Arabella had been in a similar fix a few short weeks ago. Belle hadn't wanted to fall in love with Marcus, yet she couldn't stop herself.

Roslyn worried her lower lip with her teeth, wondering apprehensively if she was following in her sister's footsteps. Wishing her sisters or Tess were here to talk with, she gave a frustrated sigh. She missed them dreadfully just now and needed their counsel. But Arabella wasn't expected home until late next week. And Tess had gone to London to assist Lily in an unusual undertaking at Fanny's boardinghouse. Without them to rely on, Roslyn knew, she would have to solve her dilemma on her own.

Forcibly shoving her troubled thoughts away, she spun on her heel and headed for her bedchamber to change out of her traveling dress. She would visit the Freemantle Academy this afternoon. There were no classes scheduled for her to teach, since only a handful of pupils had stayed for the summer term and Jane Caruthers had them well in hand. But Roslyn enjoyed the girls' company, and spending time with them would give her something else to focus on besides Drew's disquieting wooing and the resolution of their uncertain future.

Roslyn did enjoy her visit at the academy, so much that she stayed for tea. But when she returned to the Hall, her dilemma was the same: What to do about Drew.

Perhaps she would be wise to end their engagement now. She was wholly convinced that she would be a fool to marry him. Drew had told her—repeatedly— that he would never give his heart to any woman, and she could so easily lose hers to him.

Just look at what had happened to Winifred—all the heartbreak and hurt she'd suffered, loving a husband who didn't love her in return. How difficult it had been for Winifred, struggling with all those painful emotions over the years.

That dreadful experience should be warning enough, Roslyn knew.

To keep her agitated thoughts occupied, she put on an old gown and went out to the gardens. The flower beds were beginning to resemble their former glory since Marcus had spent a fortune refurbishing the Hall and grounds. And they could now afford such wasteful luxury as cutting fresh flowers daily for the drawing room and parlors. Roslyn usually saw to the task to spare Mrs. Simpkin the effort.

She was bending over a rosebush, clipping a particularly thorny yellow rose, when she heard the side gate open and glanced up, expecting to see one of the gardeners. Instead, she saw Lord Haviland striding toward her along the gravel path.

Straightening, Roslyn dropped her rose and shears in the gardening pail at her feet and waited for him to reach her.

"Ah, I hoped I would find you at home, Miss Loring."

Roslyn returned his charming smile as she looked up at him. "To what do I owe this pleasure, my lord?"

"I've come to personally deliver an invitation from my grandmother. She is holding a rout party next week and specifically charged me with persuading you to come."

When Haviland held out an embossed card, Roslyn removed her gardening gloves in order to take it.

"Grandmother would be honored if Arden attended as well," he added as Roslyn perused the invitation.

"I am not certain what his grace's plans are, so I cannot vouch for him, but I would be pleased to come."

"Good, then." Haviland hesitated. "I confess I was surprised to hear of your betrothal to Arden. I didn't expect it, given his avowed distaste for matrimony."

Roslyn felt a blush rise to her cheeks. "I know. It was rather . . . sudden."

"I should like to offer my felicitations, even though I regret that I was so tardy in courting you myself."

Flustered by Haviland's intimation that he'd wanted to court her, Roslyn reflexively clenched her fingers . . . which caused her to drop the card of invitation and one of her gloves.

They both bent down at the same time to retrieve the errant items and wound up bumping their heads together.

Wincing, Roslyn uttered a breathless laugh and clutched her forehead as she straightened, while Haviland muttered a low curse. "Blast it, did I hurt you?"

Roslyn shook her head, still laughing. "No, not at all."

"Let me see." He pulled her hand away so he could inspect the damage he'd inflicted on her forehead.

"Truly, my lord, I am perfectly fine."

"I cannot say the same. I'm abashed at my clumsiness."

"You weren't to blame. I was the clumsy one."

His rough chuckle was warm with rueful humor. "You are being kind, Miss Loring. I know my limitations well enough. I would do better against a French cavalry charge. I'm out of my element when it comes to dealing with beautiful women."

He smiled ruefully down at her, and Roslyn felt her laughter fade. And when he reached up to brush a tendril away from her face, she froze.

"Forgive me, please?" he said warmly.

Before she could gather her wits to reply, an icy voice cut across the garden. "How cozy."

Giving a start, Roslyn glanced over her shoulder to see Drew poised on the terrace steps, staring down at them.

Managing a fleeting smile, she stepped back to set herself apart from Lord Haviland. "Drew . . . I did not expect you to call this afternoon."

"Obviously not. Otherwise you would never have let me interrupt such a charming scene."

Her eyes widened at his savage tone. He had evidently misconstrued an innocent situation, but she couldn't think of what to say in order to clear up his misunderstanding. He was reacting out of male possessiveness, Roslyn was certain. He couldn't possibly be jealous; his emotions weren't engaged strongly enough to warrant jealousy.

Yet the silence became thick and palpable as Drew descended the steps and moved to stand before the earl. "She is betrothed to me, Haviland."

"So I hear," his lordship responded in a much milder tone. "But you can acquit me of poaching on your turf, your grace."

"Can I?"

Haviland raised a dark eyebrow. "I have said so, haven't I?"

Tension vibrated between the two men. Drew looked ready to have the earl's blood, but his tone was low and deceptively controlled when he spoke. "Only touch her again and you won't see another dawn."

At the threat, Roslyn gasped while Haviland's eyes narrowed sharply. "You are laboring under a misapprehension, Arden—"

Drew cut him off. "Spare your breath unless you have a death wish. Now I'll thank you to take your leave."

The earl stiffened, his eyes suddenly snapping with fury. For a moment, Roslyn remained speechless, too stunned and mortified to countermand Drew's order, but then she finally found her voice. "Your grace, that is quite enough!"

Haviland shifted his gaze to glance at her. Although restraining his own wrath, he clearly wasn't inclined to leave her defenseless and alone with the duke. "Will you be all right?"

"Yes . . . I am certain I will. Thank you for the invitation, my lord."

"Very well—but I am just next door if you need me. Good day, Miss Loring."

With a bow, Haviland turned and strode off.

When the earl had let himself out of the gate, leaving Roslyn alone with Drew, she whirled on him. "What, may I ask, brought on that abominable display of manners? You do not have leave to dismiss my guests, or to threaten them!"

"It was no threat. I meant every word."

Roslyn stared at Drew in disbelief. "Have you taken leave of your senses?"

"Not in the least. You're still enamored of him, and I won't stand for it."

His tone was cold, without inflection, but she felt her own ire rise. "You won't stand for *what*, Drew?"

"Your trysts with Haviland."

"My . . . trysts?" Her mouth dropped open. She would have sputtered in indignation except that she was too stunned. "You actually think I might be engaged in an illicit affair with Lord Haviland? When I am betrothed to you?"

"I doubt our betrothal would prove an impediment."

She was shocked that Drew would believe her capable of such betrayal. "You think I could make love to you the way we did last night and then turn around and . . . What kind of cold-blooded woman do you take me for?"

His expression turned hooded. "You wouldn't be

the first to pretend interest in me, only to have another lover waiting in the wings."

"How dare you?" Roslyn whispered. "How dare you accuse me of such perfidy? I have far more honor than that."

"Do you?"

She felt as if he'd slapped her. The breath left her lungs, while a sudden ache burned her throat. "If you have such a poor reading of my character . . ." With effort, she swallowed and turned away. "I refuse to discuss this any further—"

"Don't walk away from me, Roslyn!"

At his fierce explosion, Roslyn jumped and came to a halt. She was suddenly shaking, but she forced herself to glance back at him. "You have no right to command me. I am not your possession, nor am I your mistress whose services you have purchased."

"I do so have a right." Drew took a step toward her, his jaw clenched. "And I want an answer now. Do you love that bastard?"

"I beg your pardon?" Roslyn demanded, flinching at the derogatory label.

"Haviland . . . do you love him?"

"My feelings for him are none of your concern!"

"They bloody well are my concern! We are betrothed, or had you forgotten?"

Her hands curled into fists. "Our betrothal is only temporary, for the sake of appearance."

"There is nothing temporary about it. You *will* wed me, Roslyn."

"You can go to perdition!"

"Then you will damned well join me!"

Roslyn felt the blood drain from her face. Drew had shouted at her, and she had shouted right back at him.

She stared at him, unable to speak. Her chest was tight, while a sick feeling knotted her stomach.

"I have to go. . . ." she rasped finally, turning from him again and making rapidly for the house.

"Roslyn, come back here!"

She clamped her hands over her ears, hearing the echo of her parents' many arguments over the years. She couldn't bear their shouting then, couldn't bear to have Drew shouting at her now. So she simply ran.

"Roslyn!" Drew called after her, his tone harsh with anger.

Roslyn paid him no heed. She ran, couldn't stop running. She sped along the gravel path and stumbled up the stone steps to the terrace, instinctively heading for her sanctuary, the library. Her vision had blurred while a rushing filled her ears.

"Roslyn. . . ." There was an edge of concern to his voice as well as anger, but she didn't stop.

She found the open French door and burst through into the library, pushing it shut behind her.

She stood there quivering, heart pounding. She could still hear voices raised in anger . . . her parents fiercely arguing . . . Mama accusing Papa of infidelity . . . Mama sobbing.

She wouldn't cry, Roslyn vowed. She wouldn't let herself fall apart. Yet the tremors wouldn't stop. Lunging blindly across the library, Roslyn climbed into the window seat and huddled there. She wanted to curl herself into a tiny, invisible ball, just as she had when she was a child.

She was shaking the same way now. She wrapped her arms around herself, but it was hard to pull enough air into her lungs. She couldn't catch her breath. And she kept hearing the echo of her parents' voices.

Eyes shut, she tried to block them out. She held herself tightly, willing them to go away as she battled the ghosts of her childhood.

A sound escaped her throat, half laugh, half sob. How many times had she done this very thing—taken refuge in the library to escape her parents' angry altercations? At home in Hampshire she'd crawled behind the window seat curtains, keeping her hands clasped over her ears until her sisters found her and offered her comfort.

Another shudder wracked her, but Roslyn forced herself to drag in a raw breath, striving for calm. She was an adult now. She didn't need Lily to hold her hand.

She didn't need Lily to tell her she was a fool, either. How could she have ever thought she could wed Drew? If they were fighting this way after being betrothed for barely a fortnight, what would their marriage be like?

It would be her worst fear realized, their union degenerating into the horrible, antagonistic relationship her parents had had.

But what else could she hope for? a voice inside Roslyn cried out. Drew was never going to love her. Not if he could doubt her word so flagrantly as he had a moment ago. Real love meant trusting, and if he couldn't trust her to behave with honor and integrity . . .

A fierce shiver coursed through her. She had to end

their betrothal at once. If she was hurting this intensely now, how much greater would the hurt be if she let it continue? It was frightening to think of battling Drew like this once she came to love him.

No, it was time to sever their relationship before her heart became irrevocably ensnared. His absence in her life would create a huge emptiness inside her, but it was far better to part with him now than later, when it was too late to salvage—

Roslyn froze when she heard the library door slowly open. Drew entered without bidding, then stood for a long moment before his footsteps sounded on the Aubusson carpet as he crossed to where she sat huddled.

"What is wrong, Roslyn?" he asked quietly.

"If you have to ask, then I could not possibly explain it to you."

"I didn't mean to shout at you."

Opening her eyes unwillingly, she looked up at him. "But you *did* shout at me. And you meant to accuse me of duplicity and infidelity."

"No . . . it's just that I saw you laughing with Haviland, smiling up at him. . . ."

His voice trailed off, while hers dropped to a ragged whisper. "I can't bear fighting with you, Drew. I despise fighting."

"We were not fighting."

"What do you call it then?"

"Arguing."

"They are one and the same."

Guilt stabbing him, Drew raked a hand roughly though his hair. He had indeed instigated a fight with Roslyn. He'd acted the worst sort of fool, giving in to his sudden, irrepressible rage of jealousy, and then he'd taken his fear out on her. And Roslyn was pale and trembling now because of it. He could see the tears glittering in her eyes.

When one slid down her cheek, he wanted to brush it away, but he forced himself to keep his hands by his sides. She wouldn't like him touching her just now, he suspected. He wanted to hold her, to offer comfort, but she wouldn't accept his comfort.

"I am sorry," he murmured, knowing he had some serious groveling to do. "I never should have shouted at you, or made such unwarranted accusations. I reacted in the heat of the moment, out of jealousy. I know you have more honor than to tryst with Haviland behind my back."

Her delicate jaw was clenched, as if she was struggling for composure. Finally Roslyn seemed to steel herself and sat up.

"It doesn't matter," she said, determinedly dashing the tears from her eyes. "Regardless of what you meant, our betrothal is at an end."

Not believing what he'd heard, Drew fixed his gaze intently on her face. "You can't be serious."

"I am utterly serious," she replied, her voice low and without inflection.

"You mean to break our betrothal simply because I raised my voice to you?"

"Yes, Drew. I do. I endured such battles for much of my childhood, and I won't suffer them in my own marriage."

Frustration built inside him. "You are overreacting, sweeting . . . blowing our altercation out of proportion."

"I don't believe so. I have known all along a union between us would never work. We don't want the same things out of marriage. And if we're fighting now, what kind of future does it portend?"

Drew felt his jaw hardening against his control. "You are using this contretemps to justify turning to Haviland. You still want him."

Roslyn locked gazes with him. "Whether I want Haviland or not is beside the point. I don't want to marry *you*, Drew. I don't want you for my husband."

He stared at her, a knife edge of alarm twisting inside him.

At his silence, Roslyn forced a bleak smile. "You yourself said that once the first flush of lust has worn off, a couple is left with boredom or worse. It seems clear that the lust has worn off between us. But you should feel relieved that you won't have to wed me. I certainly am."

"Roslyn—" Drew began before she cut him off: "I don't wish to discuss it further."

She had withdrawn completely from him; he could see it in her emotionless expression, in her rigid posture. It was as if Roslyn had erected an impenetrable wall between them.

Frustration filled him, along with a feeling of panic deep in his gut.

Her voice was almost cold when she broke the silence again. "Why did you come here, Drew?"

At her abrupt change in subject, he let out a harsh breath, struggling to remember his reason for calling. "Crupp discovered the identity of Sir Rupert's private solicitor," Drew finally said. "A man by the name of Farnaby. I called on him this afternoon to inquire about

Sir Rupert's former mistress. He knew of her, of course. Her name is Constance Baines. But he claims he lost touch with her four years ago, after his client died. Sir Rupert had maintained a small house on the outskirts of London for Constance and her children, but reportedly the house was sold and they no longer live there."

Roslyn winced at that last revelation. "Children? There is more than one child?"

"There are three. A boy and two younger girls."

Her mouth turned down in sorrow. "Winifred will be heartbroken," Roslyn murmured. "So where are they now?"

"I am endeavoring to find out." Drew paused. "Farnaby seemed extremely nervous about discussing the Baines woman and refused at first even to divulge the address of the house. Frankly, it wouldn't surprise me if he misappropriated the late Sir Rupert's funds four years ago."

"You think Farnaby stole from the estate?"

"It's possible. I think he would have been more forthcoming otherwise. I had to resort to veiled threats to persuade him to cooperate. For now, I've charged Bow Street with locating Constance Baines. They'll interview the house's current occupants as well as her former neighbors about where she and her children might have gone. It may be a dead end, but I hope to know something in the next day or two. If I do discover her whereabouts—and if she is still in London— I thought you might like to accompany me."

"Yes . . . I would."

"Very well. I'll send a footman to let you know when I will come to collect you."

She shook her head. "You needn't go to such trouble,

Drew. I will borrow Winifred's carriage to travel to London."

"Don't be absurd, sweeting. It is no trouble."

Stiffening again, Roslyn returned his gaze directly. "I have no intention of traveling anywhere with you."

That hollow, sickening sensation returned to claw at Drew. He hesitated, debating whether to press her when she was still so upset at him. "Then allow me to send my carriage for you."

"That would be inappropriate since we are no longer betrothed."

"Roslyn. . . ." Drew dragged his fingers through his hair again. "I told you I was sorry."

Her lips pressed together for a moment before she smiled faintly. "Your apologies matter little to me, Drew. Our betrothal is at an end. I trust you will notify the papers?"

"You don't mean it—"

Her gaze turned even cooler. "Pray do me the courtesy of believing my sincerity. I will never wed you. And I won't remain in a sham of a betrothal merely to placate the gossips."

Drew felt his heart lurch, slamming hard against the constricted wall of his chest. He wanted fiercely to argue with her, to make Roslyn change her mind immediately. But remembering her loathing for arguments, he settled for reasoning with her. "You know a broken betrothal will only stain your reputation."

"No doubt. But I will suffer the consequences. For now I want nothing more to do with you."

With great dignity, she stood. "If you find Constance, then please inform me. Otherwise, you are not welcome here at Danvers Hall."

Drew watched as she walked from the room, regal, queenly, dispassionate. Her pronouncement had seemed so final. And so had her declaration that she didn't want him for her husband.

His foremost response was dread; dark and cold, it curled inside him at the thought of losing Roslyn. He couldn't allow their betrothal to end, for how could he convince her to love him?

But no, Drew told himself, willing his feeling of panic to subside. He wasn't admitting defeat. Roslyn was overwrought, upset—and justifiably angry at him. He just had to allow her time to reconsider.

For now he would suspend his efforts to woo her, but he would change her mind about their betrothal, Drew promised himself. Roslyn would wed him in the end, and she would come to love him.

Knotting his jaw, he strode from the library, making for his carriage. Yet he couldn't dismiss the cold, coiling snake of fear in his gut, telling him that he was already too late.

Chapter Eighteen

❧

The sad tale of Sir Rupert and Constance only convinces me further that gentlemen love their mistresses more readily than their wives.

—Roslyn to Fanny

"Fanny!" Roslyn said in surprise two mornings later when her friend swept into the Danvers Hall library. "I didn't expect you to call on me this week. I wrote to you yesterday—"

"I know," Fanny said, waving Roslyn's letter at her. "That is why I have come, my dear—to discover if you have lost your senses."

"Lost my senses?" Roslyn repeated, closing the book she was reading.

"I think perhaps you must have done so if you broke off your betrothal to the Duke of Arden."

Roslyn made no reply, merely waited as Fanny settled herself in a chair and continued.

"I admit I was shocked, Roslyn, that you would throw away the chance to become a duchess and enjoy a lifetime of ease and privilege."

"You know I don't care for such trappings," she said finally as she moved to sit across from Fanny.

"I *do* know. You want to find true love. But it is just as easy to love a rich lord as a poor nobody."

"No, it is not, Fanny. And I expected you of all

people to understand me. You forsook a genteel future for a life of excitement and passion."

Fanny made a face. "What I believed at sixteen and what I know at four-and-twenty are two entirely different things. I am far more mature and experienced now, and much wiser. The life I craved then is not the life I want now."

Roslyn's brows drew together. Never once had she heard Fanny question the choices she'd made in her admittedly colorful life. It was not comfortable, however, Roslyn reflected, to have her own choices questioned, even by her good friend. "Must we discuss this now, Fanny?"

Her friend frowned. "I suppose not, but you don't look well, Rose. There are shadows under your eyes, and your complexion is pale as wax. Hardly the symptoms of a woman happy with her decision."

"I am perfectly fine," Roslyn insisted, despite knowing her assertion was a bald lie. She hadn't slept well since breaking off with Drew, nor had she eaten much.

Absently she pressed a hand to her breastbone, aware of the quiet ache that burned there—and fully aware of the cause.

She felt a profound emptiness without Drew. A feeling similar to the sick, hollow sensation she'd experienced at losing her mother, when Victoria had abandoned her daughters and fled the country with her lover. The same sick feeling as when she'd learned her father had died needlessly, killed in a senseless duel over one of his inamoratas.

But she didn't want to dwell on her problems. "Did you come here merely to scold me about my broken betrothal?"

"No." Her expression softening, Fanny forced a smile. "Scolding you was my prime reason, but I also wanted to report on my inquiries regarding Sir Rupert and Constance Baines. Regrettably I could learn nothing whatsoever about their relationship. If she was his mistress and bore him three children, they were exceedingly discreet about it."

Roslyn pursed her lips. "It doesn't surprise me that they kept their association a close secret. I like to think it was because Sir Rupert was trying to spare Winifred's feelings, not merely to deceive her since she controlled the purse strings."

"Well, if Constance has disappeared, you may never find her. It is the sad fate of mistresses when their protector dies or casts them off, especially if they have children. Their future is dubious at best."

"I can only imagine," Roslyn murmured. "If Sir Rupert loved Constance, as Winifred believes, he would surely have provided an income for his family in the event of his death. But Drew . . . Arden thinks Sir Rupert's solicitor may have been unscrupulous."

Fanny nodded sagely. "Constance would have been completely vulnerable to being swindled, with no legal recourse. So have you heard from Arden yet about Bow Street's investigation?"

"Not yet. I hope to soon."

Hesitating, Fanny searched her face intently before saying, "I won't scold you any further, but are you certain you are making the right decision? It probably isn't too late to change your mind."

Roslyn glanced away, feeling the tightness in her chest intensify. The notice announcing the termination of their betrothal had not appeared in the papers, but that was a very small matter compared to the larger issue. "It is pointless to continue our betrothal, Fanny. I could never marry Arden."

"Because you had a simple argument with him?"

Her gaze snapped back. "It was not merely a simple argument. It was practically a brawl. We *shouted* at each other."

Fanny's mouth curved in a smile. "Not all brawls are bad . . . and most are never as destructive as your parents' were. Sometimes they can serve a useful purpose."

Roslyn eyed her with incredulity. "What purpose?"

"A good brawl now and then makes you feel alive, darling. It spurs the blood, rouses the passions. Brawling has little to do with love, yet even dark emotions are part of loving, Roslyn. Couples fight even if they love each other."

She was silent for a long moment. "Well, Drew and I do *not* love each other. We let passion sway us, nothing more."

"That doesn't mean he can't eventually come to love you."

"But it's highly doubtful," Roslyn retorted. "He certainly never wanted to wed me. I expect he's vastly relieved to be free of our engagement."

"Why do you say so?"

"If he wanted to continue our betrothal, I think he would have made an effort to persuade me. But I have had no word from him in two days, since I ordered him from the house."

Fanny looked skeptical, but at least she didn't press.

"So how is Lily doing?" Roslyn asked, pointedly changing the subject.

Her question brought a genuine smile to Fanny's lips. "Amazingly well. I never expected an academy for courtesans to be so successful. Indeed, when Lily first proposed the idea, I thought she had gone a little daft. But she is so passionate about this endeavor, and Tess seems just as committed—training our boarders to attract a higher-class clientele so they can have better futures. The girls are avid pupils . . . and so enthusiastic about it that several of their colleagues have asked to join in. They spend every afternoon being tutored in elocution, poise and grace, how to serve tea, proper manners. . . ."

Roslyn couldn't help but laugh. "All subjects that Lily deplores. She would much rather teach riding or driving or archery. But it's good that the skills she learned instructing at our young ladies' academy are serving her so well."

Simpkin appeared at the library door just then and waited until Roslyn acknowledged him.

"A message was just delivered for you, Miss Roslyn, from the Duke of Arden."

Deplorably, her heart started beating harder at just the mention of Drew's name, but she tried to quell it as she broke the wax seal and read his bold script.

Constance Baines has been located. I will send my carriage for you at one o'clock this afternoon, if that is convenient.

It was signed merely, *Arden.*

Roslyn glanced up at the butler. "Please reply that the time should present no problem, Simpkin."

"As you wish, Miss Roslyn." With a bow, Simpkin withdrew.

When Roslyn told Fanny about the message, her

friend's expression turned sympathetic again. "Do you want me to accompany you this afternoon?"

Roslyn was very tempted to say yes. It would be much easier to face Drew in Fanny's company. In fact, it would be far easier if she never had to lay eyes on Drew again. But she wanted to solve the mystery of Winifred's thief.

"Thank you, no," Roslyn responded. "I don't know what we will find, but I would rather keep our visit as private as possible, for Winifred's sake." Then she pasted a smile on her lips. "So Fanny, now that you are here, will you stay for luncheon?"

A trill of musical laughter rang out. "I thought you would never ask. I am famished, since I came as soon as I awakened. Only for you, my dear, would I disturb my beauty sleep. So let me tell you about Lily's enterprise. . . ."

When Drew's carriage arrived for her at one o'clock, Roslyn was startled to see that his grooms and footmen were armed with pistols and blunderbusses. But she began to understand the precaution as the vehicle wended its way through London's East End toward the docks, for the streets grew meaner and the signs of squalor were rampant.

Finding it unpleasant to breathe for the rankness, Roslyn viewed the grim conditions with increasing consternation. If Constance Baines lived here in the stews, then her fortunes had indeed fallen desperately.

The carriage turned into a slop-covered cobblestone lane and came to a halt before a dilapidated building. Drew was waiting in front to hand Roslyn down, his expression sober as he gave her a terse greeting.

She responded with a question as he guided her up the entrance steps. "So Bow Street discovered her location?"

"Yes, from her former neighbors. According to the proprietress of these lodgings, Constance has apartments on the third floor, but I haven't approached her yet."

He ushered Roslyn inside to the first door, which was partway open. The proprietress was a heavyset woman with the coarse manners of a Billingsgate fishwife. When Drew handed her a shilling, she grinned widely, showing her rotting teeth.

" 'Tis peculiar ye've come, guv'nor. Missus Baines don't 'ave many visitors. Puts on fancy airs like she was a real lady, she does. But she won't be welcome 'ere much longer if she can't pay 'er rent. It's past due by a fortnight."

The woman climbed the rackety stairs ahead of them and stopped halfway down the dim corridor to bang on the door. Upon receiving no answer, she shouted through the thin wood panel.

"Missus Baines, ye 'ave a fancy toff and his lady 'ere to see you. Unlock this 'ere door or I'll do it meself."

It was another moment before the sound of a key turning in the lock could be heard. When the door cracked open an inch, Drew glanced at the proprietress.

"That will be all," he said dismissively.

Frowning, she spun her bulky body around and stalked away as the door opened another few inches.

Roslyn was taken aback to see a wide-eyed young girl peering out. Perhaps ten years of age, she wore a patched frock that was too small for her thin frame, and she looked wary and frightened. Yet her speech was clearly upper-class when she managed to choke out, "M-May I help you, sir?"

"Yes, child," Drew responded, his tone softening. "I would like to speak to your mother, Constance Baines."

Her expression turned distressed. "My m-mother is ill, sir. She cannot be disturbed."

Drew handed the girl a gilt-embossed calling card. "Then will you give her this and tell her I have questions about her son?"

Appearing indecisive, she looked over her shoulder as if she might bolt for safe refuge. But at last she opened the door fully and beckoned them to enter.

When Roslyn preceded Drew inside, she was surprised to see that, unlike the surrounding squalor of the neighborhood, the room was neat and clean, and held a kitchen of sorts, as well as a sitting area with some threadbare furniture that once had been of good quality.

"If you will please wait here, sir," the girl murmured before she scurried toward the closed door behind her and slipped inside.

Roslyn met Drew's gaze silently as they waited for the child's return but knew her own distress was showing.

Several long moments passed before the girl reappeared. "My mother is too ill to leave her bed, your grace, but if you do not mind, she can receive you there."

The rear room was a bedchamber, Roslyn saw when they followed the girl. Crowded with three beds, it was just as tidy as the outer room but less welcoming, since the windows were open against the warm summer day and foul air reeked in from the lane below.

The woman lying in the largest bed looked gaunt and feverish. There was also another child sitting silently in one corner, a girl of about six who eyed them nervously.

The elder girl went straight to her mother's bed and took her hand. "Mama?" she whispered. "Can you talk now, Mama?"

Constance's eyes fluttered open, and she gazed blankly at her daughter. Then she gave a start as if coming to her senses, and her worried gaze found Drew. She wet her cracked lips before speaking in a rasping, barely audible voice, "Your grace? My son . . . has something happened to Benjamin?"

"Your son's name is Benjamin?" Drew asked quietly.

"Yes. . . ." She tried to sit up, but she was too weak to manage, and at the effort, she fell into a paroxysm of coughing.

Constance was gravely ill, Roslyn realized, hearing the rattle in her chest that was symptomatic of a deadly inflammation of the lungs.

Drew stepped forward with alacrity. "Pray, don't exert yourself, Mrs. Baines. Nothing has happened to your son to my knowledge."

Her daughter leaned closer, obviously distraught to see her mother in such distress, but Constance waved her away. When her coughing fit subsided, she collapsed back on the pillow. "I . . . don't understand . . . what you want with my son, then."

"We have some questions about him that I hope you can answer," Drew said, offering his handkerchief to the ill woman, who took it with a strange mixture of reluctance and gratitude.

"What . . . did you wish . . . to know?"

He started to answer, but Roslyn forestalled him, concerned that the girls were too young to hear about their brother's attempted thievery. "Mrs. Baines, I am Miss Loring. The duke and I are friends of Lady Freemantle. Perhaps it would be best if we spoke in private."

Her expression suddenly growing more apprehensive, Constance nodded weakly and glanced at the eldest girl. "Sarah . . . please take Daisy to the parlor. Don't be alarmed, my love . . . I will be fine with our guests."

"Yes, Mama."

When the girls had left, shutting the bedchamber door behind them, Roslyn moved to stand beside the invalid's bed. "Mrs. Baines," she said gently. "Your children's father was Sir Rupert Freemantle, is that so?"

Constance's fingers plucked at the coverlet. "Yes."

"And your son Benjamin is about sixteen years of age now and has ginger hair?"

"Yes, Carrot-Top is what we call him."

"Tell us, was he wounded recently? In the arm or shoulder, perhaps?"

Constance looked confused. "Yes. A fortnight ago he was helping . . . to harness a team to a carriage . . . when the shaft slipped and gouged his arm. Why do you ask? Is Benjamin in . . . some kind of trouble?"

Roslyn avoided answering directly. "We wish to speak to him, but we've had difficulty locating him—and you as well, Mrs. Baines. We know that you lived in a house in St. John's Wood, but you left with your children several years ago."

"Who told you so?"

"A solicitor named Farnaby."

Constance's eyes darkened. "That evil man . . ."

"*Was* Farnaby evil, Mrs. Baines?"

She set her jaw stubbornly, despite the effort it took. "Perhaps not evil . . . but he was certainly a thief and a swindler."

"Because he was entrusted to care for you?" Roslyn ventured to guess. "But he refused to honor Sir Rupert's wishes after his death?"

"*Yes,*" Constance exclaimed with a surprising show of strength and spirit. But her explanation was halting as she continued. "Rupert bought the house for us . . . although the deed was in his name. He also . . . bequeathed an income sufficient . . . to provide for our upkeep and . . . proper schooling for the children. But . . . there was no proof of his intentions. When he died . . . Farnaby sold the house . . . and forced us to find other lodgings."

"So how did you manage to survive?" Drew asked, his tone sympathetic.

Constance shifted her gaze to him. "To support us . . . my son hired on as a houseboy in a nobleman's household . . . and was later promoted to footman. . . . I found employment in a milliner's shop."

"And how did you come to live here?"

She turned her face away, as if ashamed to answer. "We could not make the rent . . . so we moved to even cheaper lodgings. I abhorred having to bring . . . my children here, but I had no choice. And now we may be evicted even from here. When I fell ill last month . . . my employer let me go—"

Her last words were cut off when she began coughing fiercely into Drew's linen handkerchief.

Seeing a mug of water on the bedside table, Roslyn helped Constance lift her head so she could sip, yet she continued to struggle for breath.

"Has a physician attended you?" Roslyn asked, deeply worried.

Constance swallowed with effort and then fell back weakly, shutting her eyes. "No . . . we cannot afford doctors or medicines . . . on Ben's meager salary." She forcibly opened her eyes again. "Why do you ask about Benjamin, Miss Loring?"

When Roslyn hesitated, wondering how much to divulge, Drew answered for her. "Your son was interested in acquiring a certain brooch in Lady Freemantle's possession, Mrs. Baines."

Constance looked puzzled. "My brooch . . . how did he even know . . ." She fell silent except for her breathless rasping.

"The brooch was yours?" Roslyn gently prodded.

"Yes, it was a gift . . . from Rupert many years ago, at our son's birth. I cherished it because it . . . had Rupert's portrait inside. But when he died, the brooch . . . was at the jeweler's being cleaned, so I never saw it again."

"And you could not legally claim it?"

"No." Her voice lowered to barely a whisper. "Rupert could never publicly acknowledge . . . me as his mistress, out of respect for his wife, so . . . I could not simply demand the brooch back. Lady Freemantle would . . . have learned about me then . . . and Rupert would not have wanted that."

"So why did your son want the brooch?" Drew asked.

"I . . . suppose to return it to me. I remember some

weeks ago . . . when I first became ill and was wracked with fever . . . I told Ben I wished that I still . . . had the miniature portrait of his father. Perhaps I told him it was . . . in Lady Freemantle's possession. I can't recall."

At least that explained why the boy had been so determined to obtain the brooch, Roslyn reflected. He was trying to fulfill what he thought was his mother's deathbed wish.

"Is Benjamin in trouble?" Constance repeated weakly.

Again Drew answered for Roslyn. "That remains to be seen. The evidence against him is very serious, but we wish to speak to him before making any accusations."

"What evidence?" Constance demanded worriedly.

"We believe he attempted to steal the brooch, more than once."

She stared. "You must be mistaken, your grace. Benjamin would never steal. He is a good boy, the best son anyone could hope for."

"Perhaps so, but his arm injury may have been a gunshot wound."

"A gunshot wound! You must be mistaken—"

Just then the door burst open and Winifred's gingerhaired thief rushed into the room, a worried look on his face. He took one look at the visitors, however, and froze in recognition, his expression turning to fear. The parcel he was carrying dropped from his nerveless fingers, while his freckled complexion turned as pale as his sick mother's.

He was no longer wearing a sling, Roslyn noted, although he seemed to favor his right arm by holding it close to his chest.

To his credit, Benjamin recovered quickly and stuck out his chin. He meant to brazen it out, Roslyn realized.

"What do you mean coming here? My mother is too ill for visitors! Please leave at once."

Constance looked appalled by his brusqueness. "Benjamin!" she rasped. "What do you mean . . . being so rude to our guests?"

When she started hacking again, the boy launched himself toward the bed, insinuating himself between the visitors and his mother. Obviously bent on protecting her, he whirled, his fists clenched defensively. "I won't let you hurt her!"

Suspecting his belligerence was caused more by fear than anger, Roslyn would have tempered her reply, but Drew's tone was not so gentle when he responded. "We have no intention of hurting your mother, lad. We are here to discuss your attempted theft of Lady Freemantle's property."

The boy ground his teeth. "It is not *her* property! The brooch belongs to my mother."

"So you thought you had a right to hold up her ladyship's coach at gunpoint, and when that failed, you invaded her home?"

Constance gasped. "No, Benjamin . . . you would never . . . do something so terrible."

He turned to gaze down at her. "I'm sorry, Mama. I thought having Papa's portrait might help you to get better."

He turned back to face the duke, his gaze defiant. "Lady Freemantle won't miss one little trinket with all those diamonds and emeralds she has in her jewel case. She is rich as a nabob." His tone turned bitter with resentment. "It isn't fair that she should be so wealthy while my mother and sisters starve."

"Oh, Benjamin. . . ." his mother murmured in dismay. "I taught you better than to covet other people's possessions."

His tone softened. "I was not coveting your brooch, Mama. It is rightfully yours, and I was only trying to get it back for you."

Drew's gaze remained grim. "You could have injured or killed Lady Freemantle and Miss Loring when you shot at them."

Constance gave a low moan. "Dear heaven, Ben . . . how could you?"

The last fire left the boy's eyes, to be replaced by guilt. "I am truly sorry, Mama. But my pistol discharged by accident. I would never have shot them, your grace. I would never hurt anyone."

Interrupting the uneasy silence, Roslyn spoke up. "I have always found Lady Freemantle to be quite reasonable, Benjamin. Why didn't you simply ask her to return the brooch?"

His gaze shifted to her. "I didn't dare risk it, Miss Loring. Her ladyship didn't know that her husband had another family—and I couldn't tell her. In any case, I was sure she would be outraged if I approached her, enough to have me horsewhipped and driven off her estate or worse. Stealing the brooch was the only possible way I could regain possession of it."

Although his voice remained steady, his chin was trembling, and Roslyn could detect more than a glimmer of remorse in his eyes.

"So you pretended to be a footman and managed to

get hired for my sister's wedding celebrations?" she asked.

"Yes. . . . I mean, it was no pretense. I am in service to Lord Faulkes. But a footman's livery is a good disguise for a thief. The gentry never look at servants—they're invisible."

There was significant truth to his assertion, Roslyn acknowledged as Benjamin turned back to Drew.

This time his voice quivered noticeably when he queried, "D-do you mean to arrest me, your grace?"

Drew's grave expression never changed. "Given the severity of your mother's condition, I understand why you wished to champion her. But when you held up her ladyship's carriage, were you aware that highway robbery is a hanging offense?"

A sob escaped Constance, while Benjamin's face whitened again. "Y-yes, your grace."

"Do you believe you should go unpunished for your crimes?" Drew asked.

The boy swallowed hard. "No, your grace."

"Then what do you think your punishment should be?"

Drew waited, his sharp green gaze steady, while Benjamin remained silent.

Roslyn found herself biting her lip in consternation. The boy didn't deserve to hang, and she couldn't bear the thought of him being locked away in prison, especially when he was the sole provider for his mother and young sisters. But that was what would happen if Winifred brought charges of thievery against him. From the look of fear on his face, Benjamin was aware of the consequences, as well.

"I do not know, your grace," he finally said. "Perhaps I should hang."

With another anguished sob, Constance held out an imploring hand. "No . . . please, I beg you, your grace . . . you cannot hang my son, *I beg you. . . .*"

Drew cast her a softer glance. "He will not hang, Mrs. Baines."

Her sobs arrested. "Then . . . what will you do?"

"I have not yet decided." When he met Roslyn's gaze, she understood his dilemma. They couldn't punish the boy as he deserved, but neither could they simply walk away. Nor could they determine his fate on their own. Winifred would certainly have to be part of the decision.

"I think," Roslyn said quietly, "that we will have to discuss the matter with Lady Freemantle. Perhaps she can be persuaded not to prosecute."

When Drew nodded slightly in agreement, Roslyn let out a relieved breath. It was indeed possible they could persuade the kindhearted Winifred to overlook Benjamin's crimes. And in the meantime, he was unlikely to flee to avoid arrest as long as his mother and sisters needed him so desperately. And if he did flee . . . it would not serve justice, but Roslyn could accept that outcome.

"Thank you, Miss Loring," Constance murmured gratefully as, with an exhausted sigh, she lay back and shut her eyes. The trauma had sapped what little strength she had.

Turning to bend over his mother, Benjamin clasped her hand tightly. "Please, your grace . . . Miss Loring," he said over his shoulder, only this time making it a request. "You need to leave. You can arrest me if you want, but leave my mother alone. She had naught to do with my attempted thefts, and she is too ill to be subjected to further distress."

Knowing he was right, Roslyn reached into her reticule and drew out all the money she had with her—three guineas and several shillings and pence—and held the coins out to Benjamin. "Here, this should allow you to send for a doctor."

"No," Drew intervened, "I will have a physician attend Mrs. Baines this afternoon."

Roslyn nodded in relief, knowing Drew would be able to command the best possible care for the sick woman. But she continued to hold out the money. "Take this, Benjamin. You can use it to buy food for your mother and sisters."

Benjamin's mouth dropped open, but he refused to accept her offering, out of pride, she suspected. "Th-thank you, Miss Loring . . . but we do not want your charity." He glanced down at his mother. "I brought you a mutton pie, Mama, and some bread and cheese for the girls." Then he lifted his gaze again. "I can take care of my family."

Drew stepped in again, taking Roslyn's money and laying it on the bedside table. "You will accept it as a loan then, lad, until you get the funds that rightfully belong to you."

"Funds?" Constance whispered.

"I intend to deal with Farnaby and ensure that Sir Rupert's bequest to you is finally awarded, Mrs. Baines."

Benjamin's jaw dropped open, while Constance burst into tears, much to the alarm of her son. He looked at them frantically, clearly imploring them to leave the room, but his mother managed to find her voice.

"Thank you, your grace . . . I don't care for myself . . . but my girls . . . my children . . ."

"Don't concern yourself any longer, Mrs. Baines," he answered. "You have my word that they will be cared for. For now you need to rest. We will show ourselves out."

When Roslyn and Drew left the bedchamber, they found Constance's young daughters huddled together in a chair, looking fearful. But both girls leapt to their feet and proffered polite curtsies. They had obviously been taught exquisite manners by their mother, despite their dire circumstances.

"Your mama is resting now," Roslyn said softly. "But a doctor will be here shortly to try and help her get well."

Their faces brightened a little before they scurried toward the bedchamber and tiptoed inside.

Sadness tugging at her heart, Roslyn remained silent until she and Drew were alone in the corridor. "We have to tell Winifred," she said then. "As much as I regret having to cause her pain, she will want to know about Benjamin."

"I'll accompany you to Freemantle Park," Drew responded, "and we will tell her together."

When they reached the street, he sent his tiger home with his curricle, along with instructions for his secretary to have his personal physician be brought here at once to attend Mrs. Baines's sickbed. After ordering to his coachman to take them to Chiswick, Drew handed Roslyn inside the carriage and climbed in to sit across from her.

"Did you mean it, Drew?" she asked once they were moving. "You will take on Farnaby and make him pay Mrs. Baines what he owes her?"

Drew's jaw hardened. "It will be my great pleasure."

"I hope it will be soon so she can move to better lodgings. She will die if she continues to suffer those appalling conditions." Roslyn grimaced at the recollection. "I mean to have the Simpkins bring them some nourishing meals, and perhaps clean the lane of that stench."

"Let my servants handle it," Drew said tersely. "Mine are much closer, and it would be inconvenient for yours to come such a distance."

"Thank you. That is very kind of you."

"It isn't kindness. Merely justice."

Roslyn fell awkwardly silent, realizing that this was the first time she had been alone with Drew since their angry parting. But judging from his stony features, she was right to think that he was relieved to be freed from their betrothal.

There was nothing loverlike at all about his demeanor. Indeed his expression was grim, even angry. Perhaps because he was contemplating how he would compel the crooked solicitor to honor his obligations.

Roslyn was grateful to Drew for his involvement and glad he would be there with her to break the distressing news to Winifred, even if she regretted having to make the drive to the country in his company.

When she caught his gaze focused on her, however, Roslyn shifted hers away to stare out the window. She wouldn't think about Drew now. Not when she should be determining what to say to Winifred.

Perhaps she should ask her friend to return the brooch to Constance. She hadn't mentioned the idea earlier, so as not to raise any false hopes. But it would mean a great deal to Constance and provide a small measure of consolation if she was dying of her grave illness.

Roslyn felt her throat tighten as she thought of the woman's terrible plight. Yet it hadn't always been that way. Indeed, some of her past was enviable. Perhaps Constance had not had a legitimate marriage with Sir Rupert, but she had known the joy of true love. And she had three children whom she clearly cherished and who cherished her.

Something Roslyn herself might never have.

Realizing how selfish it was to wallow in self-pity at a time like this, Roslyn forcibly swallowed the ache in her throat. Yet she couldn't help but be reminded of her long-held belief.

Constance's sad story was just more proof that men generally loved their mistresses, not their wives— although she was not about to interrupt Drew's grim silence to point out that distressing truth to him.

Chapter Nineteen

✤

My heart breaks to see Winifred's pain. How agonizing it must be for her to have loved so deeply when her love was never returned. It is the thing I fear most with Arden.

—Roslyn to Fanny

"*Two* daughters?" Lady Freemantle repeated in a stricken voice when she had heard the entire tale. "In addition to a son?"

The size of Sir Rupert's secret family seemed to shock her more than confirmation that his illegitimate son had threatened to steal her jewels at gunpoint.

Drew watched as Roslyn put a comforting arm around her friend. "I am so sorry, Winifred," Roslyn murmured. "But we thought you would wish to know the truth."

"Y-yes . . . I do. But 'tis a blow to know what . . . that woman did for him when I could not. She bore him *three* children. . . ."

Mutely Lady Freemantle bit her lower lip, striving to hold back tears. It was clear she was bitterly hurt to have such blatant proof of her husband's betrayal—and his mistress's fertility. Her hand clutched at her heart. "Faith, how could I not have known all those years?"

Roslyn tightened her arm around the older lady's shoulders. "I'm certain Sir Rupert didn't want to distress you by flaunting the circumstances."

After a long moment, Drew broke the silence. "We need to decide how to deal with the boy, my lady. Do you wish to lay charges against Benjamin Baines for robbery?"

She glanced up at him, still looking dazed. "No . . . I could never . . . he is Rupert's son. I couldn't send him to prison."

Drew gave a faint nod. "I thought you might feel that way, but even so, he must be made to see how wrong he was so that he won't repeat his crimes."

"Indeed he does, your grace, but he shouldn't be punished with prison. I could never be so cruel."

"What about the brooch with Sir Rupert's likeness?" Roslyn asked quietly.

Lady Freemantle shifted her gaze. "You think I should return it to that woman . . . Constance is her name?"

"It would be a great kindness, Winifred. She may not survive her illness, and his portrait may give her consolation in her last days."

Her ladyship drew a shuddering breath. "I fancy it is hers rightfully. She should have it, especially if she is dying."

It had been kind of Roslyn to suggest returning the brooch, Drew reflected to himself—yet one more indication of her compassion. The sharp contrast with his mother struck him anew. He couldn't picture the duchess putting herself out for anyone, certainly not performing a kindness for her late husband's ill mistress and by-blows. The very idea would have been utter anathema.

He was rather surprised, however, that Roslyn's generosity of spirit was shared by Lady Freemantle.

Unexpectedly, her ladyship swallowed her tears and announced, "I'll deliver the brooch to Constance myself. I want to see Benjamin, in any case—and his young sisters also."

Roslyn hesitated. "Are you certain that is a good idea, Winifred?"

Steeling her spine, she sat up straighter. "Yes, I am certain. They are Rupert's flesh and blood . . . all I have left of my husband. I can't turn my back on them. Yes," she argued with herself, "I must see to their welfare. It would be heartless to let Rupert's children starve." Suddenly her brow furrowed. "If Constance dies, what will happen to the children? I will have to care for them myself then," she replied, answering her own question. "Fact is, I should take them in now. . . ."

"Winifred," Roslyn said gently, "if Constance pulls through, I don't believe she could bear to let her children go."

Her ladyship's voice trembled. "But I can provide for them far better than she can."

"You cannot ask her to turn her children over to you. They are all *she* has."

"Yes . . . you are right," Lady Freemantle said sorrowfully before brightening a little. "I know . . . they can *all* come here to live at the Park with me. This house is immense—there is ample room for three children and their mother."

Roslyn continued to withhold her enthusiasm. "You shouldn't rush to make any decisions just now, Winifred. You have only just now learned of their existence. And Constance may have other plans if she recovers the funds due her."

"Yes, of course I should speak to Constance first."
Lady Freemantle's frown deepened. "Then again . . .
if she's a genteel lady, she may not care to associate
with someone of my low origins."

"I don't believe she is like that," Roslyn said
quickly. "And I expect she would be grateful for your
help. But I am thinking of you, dearest. Taking in an
entire family, especially one who may bring you
painful memories, is a large undertaking. You need to
give it careful consideration."

She dashed at her moist eyes. "I *have* considered it,
Roslyn. This is something I must do. I feel sure 'tis
what Rupert would have wanted." Her mouth twisted
ironically. "I should be angry with him for his adultery, I know, but the children aren't to blame for his
sin. And no matter what he did, I loved him."

Roslyn's expression softened. "I'm certain Sir Rupert loved you more than you realize."

Sniffing, Winifred looked wistful. "He might have
loved me if his heart hadn't already been taken." She
smiled bravely. "But now I'll have his children to love.
I always wanted children. I only pray Constance will
be willing to share them with me."

"I think perhaps she might. She will certainly see
the advantages of your support, and she seems to be
the kind of mother who would do anything for her
children."

Lady Freemantle nodded to herself. "Really, there's
no need to wait. Constance should come here at once.
She will recuperate much better here at the Park."

Drew intervened. "She may be too ill to be moved,
my lady. My physician should make that judgment."

"When she recovers, then. Or sooner, if your physician deems it safe. I shall bring Constance and the children here, if she is willing." She glanced imploringly at Drew. "Will you help me arrange it, your grace?"

"If you gain her agreement, then yes, of course. I'll assist in any way I can, my lady. And I will escort you to see Constance now, if you wish."

"I do wish. *Thank you,* your grace. You are prodigiously kind."

Smiling mistily, Roslyn wrapped her arms around the older woman. "It is *you* who is kind, Winifred. You are the best, kindest person I know."

"Pah, you would have done the same, were you in my place—" She faltered, shooting another brief glance at Drew. "But then you would never have found yourself in my place, dear."

Rising abruptly, Lady Freemantle suddenly resumed her usual cheerful, managing style. "If you will give me a moment, your grace, I'll just run up to my rooms and fetch my . . . the brooch. And I must speak to Pointon to arrange rooms in case Constance can be moved. And Cook must prepare a proper supper for the children, of course. . . ."

She trailed out of the parlor, still speaking to herself, leaving Drew alone with Roslyn.

When an awkward silence ensued, he broke it by remarking idly, "The august Pointon may be offended at having to welcome his late master's *fille de joie* and offspring into his domain. Butlers are notorious for their strict adherence to proper rules."

Roslyn smiled faintly. "But he will do so with good grace because he holds Winifred in great affection. All of her servants do, in large part because of how she treats them. Winifred came from the working class and understands that fairness and respect go a long way toward earning their loyalty."

"Unlike my mother," Drew said dryly, "who thinks servants are not human."

Another silence fell between them, but this one Roslyn broke after a moment. "I have no doubt the duchess was pleased that we ended our betrothal."

Feeling his heart constrict at her dispassionate tone, Drew shot her a sharp glance. "I haven't told her yet."

"You should do so at once, your grace. There is no reason to delay."

"Roslyn—"

"Do you intend to send the announcement to the papers, or should I?" she pressed.

He ground his teeth. He had hoped to give Roslyn time to change her mind about ending their betrothal, but it was clear she hadn't—and perhaps never would, judging from her remote expression. The serene, composed, lovely creature gazing coolly back at him could have been a marble statue for all the emotion she showed. Her blue eyes were distant, almost chill, conveying the unmistakable message that she wanted nothing more to do with him.

"I will see to it," Drew bit out grimly.

Roslyn inclined her head regally. "Thank you. I would thank you again for being so generous to my friend, but you have told me you don't desire my gratitude."

"No, I don't."

"Then there is nothing more for us to say. Good day, your grace."

His lungs tight, Drew watched as Roslyn turned and walked gracefully from the room, giving him no chance to say all the things he wanted—needed, yearned—to say to her.

Steeped in his own dark thoughts, Drew remained unusually silent as his coach conveyed Lady Freemantle and himself to London. They had nearly reached the outskirts of the city when she asked him in a small voice, "Was my request for your escort too much of an impertinence, your grace?"

Shaking himself from his distraction, Drew fixed his gaze on her. "I beg your pardon?"

"You are scowling so ferociously, it makes me think I've offended you. I'll wager you disapprove of my decision to invite Constance and her children to live with me."

He managed a wry smile. "On the contrary, my lady, I am all admiration."

She peered at him suspiciously. "Are you making game of me?"

"No. Seriously, I admire what you are doing, although I admit to being a little astonished. Most ladies would be happy to let their husband's other family starve . . . out of revenge, if nothing else. My own mother certainly would never have reacted as you have." Indeed, Drew thought, the duchess would have been outraged and humiliated enough by their mere existence to lash out in anger, not generosity.

"But I am not a true lady, your grace."

"I beg to differ." Winifred Freemantle might have come from the lower orders, but her conduct was more noble than a real noblewoman's. "You are every inch a lady," he said softly.

She flushed with pride and pleasure. "Well . . . my birth and breeding are far from genteel . . . but I have Roslyn and her sisters to thank for setting me a good example."

"You realize that you may suffer unexpected consequences because of your decision?"

Her ladyship sighed. "Yes, I collect so. I'll no doubt be ridiculed and disdained by my fancy neighbors. But I can bear it, since I loved my husband. When you truly love someone, no sacrifice is too great. I think you would do the same if you were in my shoes, your grace."

Drew felt his gut clench at her confident pronouncement. If he'd always questioned the existence of true love, seeing the sacrifice Lady Freemantle was willing to make for love of her late husband, for love of his children, should be proof enough that love was real.

Would he make the same sacrifice for Roslyn if it were *her* children who needed caring for? He suspected he would, since they would be part of her.

Her ladyship was eyeing him intently, and her voice held calm certainty when she said, "You love Roslyn, or I miss my guess."

His heart giving a jolt, he averted his gaze from the shameless matchmaker's prying one, even as he turned the question over in his mind. *Do I love her?*

He knew there was only one answer he could give. Stunning as it was for him to admit, he was deeply in love with Roslyn.

Indeed, he had loved her for some time, although

he'd been furiously resisting his feelings and tenaciously denying the truth to himself. Roslyn had stolen into the guarded regions of his heart and settled there like a quiet fire.

In all truth, he had been missing her all his life; he just hadn't realized it until this moment. He had searched for fulfillment with his countless mistresses but never found it until her. The passion, the emotion, the pleasure, the simple *joy* he felt at being with her filled an undeniable need in him.

He needed her, more than he ever imagined needing any woman. He wanted to have children with her, a family. He wanted her love. The kind of deep, abiding love that Constance had known with Sir Rupert. The kind of love Winifred Freemantle still bore for him four years after his death.

Yet Roslyn didn't return his love, Drew reminded himself, feeling the knife in his gut twist another painful turn. She'd made it abundantly clear that she wanted to cut him out of her life.

It scared the devil out of him to think that he had lost her. But then, he had never really had her, despite their betrothal.

The knife dug deeper. Roslyn could never come to love him the way he did her, Drew reflected. Not when she was in love with Haviland.

Did he have the right to keep pursuing her when her heart belonged to another man? What about *her* wishes, *her* needs? Her dreams? Her happiness?

What was it Roslyn had said to him? *Heart love is when you put someone else's needs over your own.* What did it say about him if he put his own needs, his own happiness, above hers? How could he claim to love her if all he cared about was himself?

If you love her, you fool, you should want her happiness. You should be willing to give her up . . . shouldn't you?

The thought of living without Roslyn for the rest of his life shook Drew to his core. But if he truly loved her, did he have any choice?

The question haunted him for the remainder of the day.

Through Lady Freemantle's awkward yet strangely poignant meeting with Constance, who was pitifully grateful that her children would be provided for in the event of her demise.

Through the interview with his physician, who did indeed determine it advisable to remove the gravely ill patient from the noxious stews of London to healthier surroundings and the clean, fresh air of the country.

Through the painstaking effort to transport the invalid by slow stages to the luxurious mansion at Freemantle Park.

Through the wide-eyed wonder that Constance's children displayed at their new environs; even Ben, whose defiant belligerence and suspicion faded to cautious hope that his mother and sisters might have found salvation in the person of Lady Freemantle, and that the heavy burden of caring for them had been lifted from his thin shoulders.

Through the return journey to London, during which Drew brooded and savagely debated with himself about his course of action.

The hour was late when he finally reached his home. He went straight to his library, where he locked himself inside with two bottles of his best aged Scotch whiskey. If he was going to cut out his heart for Roslyn, he had to be numb enough to do it.

Drew had advanced to the second bottle, however, before he could force himself to relentlessly face the cold, bitter truth: He had to let her go.

He would feel devastatingly incomplete without her, but Roslyn's happiness lay with Haviland—and he wanted her to be happy, even if it meant losing her to another man. His hands were unsteady as he brought the bottle to his lips again.

He wanted her happiness more than anything in his life. More than his life.

"Sho why 're you dallying, you pitiful sod?" he muttered. "No reashon to delay. You 'ave to give her the shance to have her dreams come true."

With effort, Drew rose and made his way over to the bellpull to ring for his majordomo. With even greater effort he remained standing as he haltingly gave instructions for a footman to be dispatched to Brooks Club, where the Earl of Haviland might possibly be found.

Then sinking onto the sofa again, Drew brought the bottle to his lips for another long, mind-numbing dose of fortitude.

He was stretched out on the sofa, half comatose, when a sharp rap came on the library door. Shaking himself awake, Drew hauled himself up to a sitting position and bid entrance.

When a gentleman strode into the room, Drew

narrowed his bleary-eyed gaze. He thought his caller might be Haviland, but his vision was blurred so much that there seemed to be two of him. Drew, however, recognized the curt voice as Haviland's.

"I trust you will explain the urgency of your summons, your grace. I had a winning hand."

Drew tried carefully to enunciate, but his speech still sounded slurred when he replied, "I will reimbursh you for any losh you suffered."

Haviland's eyebrow shot up as he regarded Drew. "You surprise me, Arden. You're three sheets to the wind."

"Four," Drew responded, holding up five fingers.

"So why did you call me here?" the earl demanded impatiently.

Drew grimaced as he tried to gather his courage. "Bloody truth is, I'm sshtepping aside. You can have 'er."

"Have whom?"

"Roshlyn! Who else would I bloody well be talking about?"

"I haven't the faintest idea."

Drew glared balefully. "Y' can't tell me you 'aven't been purshuing her . . . I know better."

"I might have had she not been betrothed to you."

"But *you* made her love you."

"You have a touching but misplaced confidence in my powers of seduction."

"No, I don't. You sheduced 'er before I ever met 'er."

Doubt, suspicion, irritation all tinged the earl's expression. "Just what the devil are you up to, Arden?"

"I'm trying to make 'er happy!" Drew practically shouted and then quickly clamped a hand to his temple.

"You are giving up your claim to her?"

Drew shook his throbbing head. "Thash the trouble . . . never had any real claim to 'er. Sheesh yours and always hash been."

Haviland crossed his arms over his powerful chest. "I wasn't born yesterday, your grace. You'll change your mind when you are sober, and then you'll call me out for daring to woo your lady. I've no desire to meet you over pistols at dawn. If you're half as good a shot as I am, we're likely to end up killing each other."

"Don't be an ash, Havilan'," Drew retorted furiously. "I'm tryin' to be damned noble, givin' her to a man she can love." He took another long swallow of whiskey before saying in a despairing tone, "Roshlyn loves you, you bleedin' idiot."

There was a long pause while Haviland tried to assimilate the announcement. "She never gave any indication that she held me in any special affection."

"Well, shee does. Sheesh been plotting your capture shince I met her . . . and I 'elped her, bloody fool that I am." His slurred laughter was bitter with irony. "Roshlyn will make you"—he took another pull from the bottle—"a bloody fine bride."

"I don't doubt it."

"You should feel damn forshunate, Havilan'."

"I don't doubt that either."

Drew raised his gaze to glare again. "You damned well better make 'er happy when you marry her, or you'll answer to me. Do I make myshelf clear?"

Haviland's mouth curved in an ironic smile. "Perfectly, your grace. And I can promise you that I will give it my best effort."

Haviland turned and walked out, shutting the door softly behind him.

Drew stood and stared for a long moment, feeling as if he had a gaping, burning hole in his chest where his heart should be.

So why then when he threw the bottle against the library door with all his might, shattering the glass, did it seem as if his heart had shattered into fragments at the same time?

From the doorway of Constance's sickroom, Roslyn watched with Winifred as the two young Baines girls tiptoed quietly to their mother's bedside.

After a moment, the invalid's eyes fluttered open. Upon seeing her daughters, Constance gave a wan but beatific smile and murmured a faint greeting. "Good morning, my darlings."

"Are you feeling better, Mama?" whispered the older daughter, Sarah.

"Much better, thankfully," Constance assured them. "The doctor's medicine seems to have helped a good deal. My chest does not hurt as much, and my cough is less frequent."

Winifred's housekeeper had sat with Constance all during the night, applying warm compresses to her chest and helping her sip the doctor's herbal concoction to calm her hacking.

"Oh, Mama," the youngest girl, Daisy, exclaimed in relief. "We were ever so worried for you."

"I know, my love. I was exceedingly worried, too. So tell me . . . how do you like your new home?"

"Mama, it is quite famous," Sarah responded with

awe in her tone. "Our bedchamber is immense, and we each have our own featherbed, so I don't have to endure Daisy's kicking. And you must see the nursery. Aunt Winifred says we are to have our own governess so you won't have to teach us anymore. And Miss Loring has brought us ever so many books to read. Daisy likes the picture books best, but I like the map books that show all the countries you told us about."

"And you, Daisy, my love?" Constance asked her youngest daughter. "Are you pleased to be here?"

Daisy nodded with eager enthusiasm and held up the pretty porcelain doll she had clutched to her chest. "Oh, *yes,* Mama. See how beautiful my new doll is. Auntie Win-fred gave her to me, but I have not chosen a name yet. Auntie Win-fred says I must wait until you are all better and can help me pick one."

Constance raised her gaze to Winifred, her look full of gratitude. "I cannot thank you enough, my lady. I think you must be an angel in disguise."

From the doorway, Winifred flushed with embarrassed pleasure but shook her head. " 'Tis only fitting they should make their home here. And you, too, my dear. You are all very welcome at Freemantle Park."

Tears welled up in Constance's eyes as she returned Winifred's smile.

Watching them, Roslyn felt her heart warm at the bittersweet moment. The two woman shared a common bond, caring for the children of the man they had each loved.

Such love would have to be profoundly strong and deep to be so accepting, Roslyn reflected. The thought brought an ache to her throat. She wondered if she could be as magnanimous were she to learn that Drew had a second family. It would be devastatingly painful, but she believed she could—

But then there was no point in indulging in such distressing speculation, Roslyn scolded herself. Instead she ought simply to feel glad for her friend.

And there was more reason for gladness. This morning it seemed less likely that Constance would die from her grave illness.

Winifred broke the tender moment just then by clearing her throat, as if the display of emotion flustered her. "Now, then," she said with a return of her usual pragmatism as she addressed Constance. "You should have a few moments alone with your daughters, but afterward they must let you rest. I will send a maid to sit with you, but you know to ring the bell if you need anything at all."

"Thank you, my lady," Constance murmured again.

"And you must call me by my given name," Winifred added briskly. "This 'lady' business will not do if we are to be friends."

Constance laughed softly at that. "I should very much like to be friends, Winifred."

"Very well then, Constance. . . ."

Beaming, Winifred turned and left the bedchamber. Roslyn followed her out to the corridor and shut the door quietly behind her.

"It was the right decision to bring them here," Winifred declared, her face suffused with pleasure. "The girls will be happy here, and so will I. They are the children I never had," she added softly.

"And I am very happy *for* you," Roslyn murmured with affection.

Her friend shot her a penetrating glance. "I trust you

and Arden will be blessed with children someday, so you can know the same happiness, my dear."

Roslyn hesitated to reply. With Constance's fate hanging in the balance, she hadn't wanted to burden Winifred with the news of her dissolved engagement to Drew. So she merely smiled and squeezed her friend's hand. "You are indeed an angel, Winifred. Now if only you would cease prying in my affairs, I would be as grateful as Constance."

Winifred gave a raucous laugh, clearly delighted by the remark, but Roslyn couldn't share her laughter. Not when her heart was so heavy. At the moment she felt as if she would never know happiness again.

Yet for the next hour until she took her leave of Winifred and the children, Roslyn hid her despondency well. When she returned to Danvers Hall, however, she was required to continue the charade, for she discovered that Earl of Haviland had just called upon her.

Finding him waiting in the entranceway for her, Roslyn forced herself to paste a welcoming smile on her lips as she moved forward to greet him.

"I beg your pardon?" Roslyn said five minutes later, blinking at her noble caller. Surely she wasn't hearing correctly. Had the earl just proposed marriage to her?

Haviland's handsome mouth curved in a wry grin. "Did I not express myself correctly, Miss Loring? Perhaps not, since this is my first proposal. But regardless of how I should phrase my offer, I would be highly honored if you would grant me your hand in marriage."

Managing to stop staring so impolitely, Roslyn returned an uncertain smile. "Your proposal was entirely correct, my lord. I am just astonished you made it. I had no idea you wished to wed me."

One heavy dark eyebrow rose. "Surely it doesn't come as a total surprise. You know I have long admired you."

"But it is a long step between admiration and suddenly contemplating marriage."

Haviland shrugged his broad shoulders. "It isn't all that sudden. I never wanted the earldom, but when I inherited the title at my father's death last year, I assumed all the obligations of the role. In fact, I returned to England with the intention of settling down with a wife and begetting heirs. I thought I should wait until a proper period of mourning had passed, of course, but now that it is over, my grandmother has been after me to find a bride."

Lowering her gaze to give herself time to think, Roslyn shook her head at the irony of Haviland's timing. What she wouldn't have given to have received his offer three weeks ago, before she had come to know Drew so intimately!

"It is still quite unexpected, my lord," she said lamely, at a loss for words.

"I can see I have caught you off guard," Haviland observed. "But I hold you in very high esteem, Miss Loring, and think you would make an admirable countess. I would have approached you sooner had you not become engaged to Arden. But now that your betrothal is at an end, I thought I would try my luck."

Roslyn's gaze lifted abruptly to meet his. "Where did you hear about our betrothal ending?"

"From Arden himself, last night."

She felt a strange jolt to her heart. Drew had told Lord Haviland about their parting? But she didn't want to think about Drew just now. Especially when the earl was standing before her, awaiting her answer. And now that her initial astonishment had subsided, she could give him one.

Swallowing the dryness in her throat, Roslyn clasped her hands before her as she politely replied, "I am very honored by your offer, my lord, but I fear I must decline."

He hesitated a long moment. "I suppose it would be rude to ask the reason for your refusal. Do you have an objection to me personally?"

"No . . . of course not."

"Then why?"

Roslyn found it hard to meet his searching gaze. She couldn't bring herself to come right out and baldly confess losing her innocence to Drew, but she couldn't marry Haviland without telling him about it. And even if he was willing to accept an unchaste bride, she didn't love him—and she was now less willing than ever to settle for a loveless marriage.

Before she could form a reply, though, Haviland went on. "I think we would deal well together, Miss Loring. We could have very comfortable union of convenience."

"But you see, my lord," Roslyn finally said, "I have never been a fan of convenient marriages. On the contrary, I always hoped I would make a love match someday."

Haviland took a step closer to her. His look was surprisingly gentle, almost tender. "We don't love each other now, true, but there is always the possibility love will grow between us."

"No. I don't believe it *is* possible."

"Because your affections are still engaged by Arden?"

Roslyn found herself flushing. "Why would they be? I was the one who broke our engagement."

"Which seems a very good reason to consider my offer. If you accept, you will have the protection of my name. You know the way of the world as well as I do. A broken engagement to a duke will not be easy for you to overcome."

Roslyn felt herself warm at Lord Haviland's generosity. "I am honored, truly, but I cannot marry you."

"Because you have feelings for Arden," he pressed.

Mutely, Roslyn glanced down at her clasped fingers, not wanting to answer. For days now she'd struggled to deny the truth to herself. She'd tried desperately to keep her heart safe from Drew, to no avail. She *did* harbor feelings for him. Powerful, fervent, irrefutable feelings. She loved him.

A wave of despair washed over her as she acknowledged how utterly foolish she'd been. She loved Drew.

Which made agreeing to Haviland's proposal of marriage impossible. She couldn't marry one man when she loved another.

Her fingers clenched even more tightly. She couldn't pinpoint the first moment when her heart had been irrevocably captured. Perhaps it was at Arden Castle, when she'd seen Drew's devotion to his old governess. Or perhaps it was before that, when he'd shown her the kind of passion most women could only dream of.

Or perhaps even sooner, when he first began instructing her in how to kindle a man's ardor. At the start of their lessons, she had never dreamed she would be opening her heart to unexpected love with her arousing tutor.

"Yes," she murmured finally. "I have feelings for him."

"If so, then why did you end your engagement?"

"Because he could never love me in return."

Haviland gave her an odd look. "Are you sure about that?"

"Quite sure."

"Does Arden know how you feel about him?"

"No," she said despondently.

"Then you should tell him."

Roslyn shook her head. "There would be no point."

"Loath as I am to aid a rival," Haviland said, an edge of amusement lacing his voice, "I suppose I must. I think you're gravely mistaken about Arden's feelings for you, Miss Loring. In fact, I would guess that he loves you a good deal."

She jerked her head up again. "Why would you think so?"

"Because he sent me here to propose to you."

Her heart wrenched, while her stomach suddenly felt filled with lead. Fighting a sick, hollow sensation, Roslyn could barely form a rasping reply. "He told you to propose to me? I should think that would prove just the opposite—that he does *not* love me."

"No, sweetheart," Haviland said gently. "Arden was willing to give you up to ensure your happiness. He's making a noble sacrifice on your behalf. I think that shows exactly how much he loves you." Haviland's mouth curved. "In truth, he threatened my life if I failed to make you happy after we were wed. But I can see now that I never stood a chance. Your happiness lies with Arden, not with me."

She stared at him in disbelief. How could Drew love her if he had given up any claim to her? Was he truly trying to be noble, hoping to make her happy? *Was it possible that Drew loved her?*

"You should tell him how you feel," the earl repeated.

Roslyn could barely hear for her chaotic thoughts. What if she told Drew of her love? What then? Would he still want to marry her? And if so, what would her answer be? Did she dare risk wedding him?

She could wind up facing the same kind of pain Winifred had endured all the years of her marriage. She and Drew could end up battling bitterly with each other, destroying whatever tender feelings they shared now and turning passion to hate.

Yet did she really have a choice? If she hoped to achieve her heart's desire, she had to risk having it shattered. If she hoped to have a chance at happiness with Drew, she had to be willing to give up her impossible notions of a perfect, idealistic marriage for something that was real and honest and strong and lasting.

She had no choice. Because she had no future without Drew. No possibility of happiness. He filled the emptiness inside her, made her feel complete.

She didn't know if she could ever mean that much to him. Didn't know if he could return her love, but she knew she had to take the risk.

The thought that Drew might never love her the way she did him left Roslyn shaken, but she had to try. If he didn't love her yet, she would have to *make* him love her. She could use the tricks of seduction he had taught her, which she had never really employed—

Realizing that Haviland was watching her silent debate, Roslyn suddenly shook herself. It was beyond rude to be plotting her pursuit of Drew when the earl stood before her.

"Thank you, my lord," Roslyn said, her voice uneven. "I will take your advice and tell Arden how I feel."

Haviland's smile held regret as he took her hand and brought it to his lips. "It will be my great loss."

Warmth rose to her cheeks at the compliment. "I'm certain you will find a bride who can make you happy."

"I trust so. I need a wife if I'm to have any hope of stopping my grandmother from hounding me into an early grave."

There was a glimmer of humor in his eyes, which told Roslyn that she hadn't wounded him too deeply with her refusal. But of course, she hadn't, since his heart wasn't engaged—just as hers was not with him.

Haviland gave her a considering look. "I might be more successful if you would aid my search."

"You want my help in finding you a bride?" Roslyn asked in surprise.

He grinned that charming, rueful grin of his. "In all honesty, I do. I obviously haven't managed very well on my own."

She returned a self-conscious laugh. "I will be happy to consider it, Lord Haviland. But now . . . if you will please excuse me? I must go to London at once."

"To see Arden?"

"No, to see a friend."

She had to speak to Fanny immediately and seek her counsel. Fanny would know how she should proceed in trying to win Drew's heart—or so Roslyn tried to reassure herself as she went to the bellpull to order the gig readied.

She only prayed she wasn't too late.

Chapter Twenty

I will do whatever it takes to make Arden love me. I shall begin by employing every trick of seduction I have ever learned.

—Roslyn to Fanny

When Drew woke to find himself sprawled on the sofa, a host of drums pounded inside his skull, while his roiling stomach chimed a chorus of protest at the abuse it had suffered.

Sitting up gingerly, Drew held his throbbing head in his hands. The stench of whiskey permeating the library was no doubt ruining his priceless collection of rare books, but he couldn't bring himself to give a bloody damn.

He had lost Roslyn. Given her up to his rival. Which explained why the agony in his heart pained him even more than the agony in his head.

What an utter imbecile he'd been, encouraging Haviland to go after her. Now that he was marginally sober, he could only lament his insane moment of magnanimity.

Had Haviland proposed to her by now? If so, had she accepted?

Drew clutched his head harder. He couldn't bear to think of it. And yet he could think of nothing else.

What in hell's name was he to do now? If Roslyn

hadn't accepted Haviland's suit, Drew decided, he would go after her himself. He would *make* her wed him, even though she didn't love him. And then he would spend the rest of his life trying to win her love.

Oh, God . . . she didn't love him.

And she didn't believe he could ever love her. He would have to show her that he *did* love her. Rather desperately in fact.

He wouldn't let Haviland have her, even if she loved the bastard. He wasn't ever going to give her up. He couldn't. Not a damn thing in his life made sense without her.

Yet he might be too late. . . .

With a muted groan, Drew pulled out his pocket watch and realized that the time was already past noon. He would have to call on Roslyn to learn his fate—but he had to bathe and change his attire first.

Rising, he dragged himself to the door and emerged carefully from the library, squinting against the brighter light when he reached the grand entrance hall.

His majordomo was standing at attention but appeared not to notice Drew's disheveled appearance and bleary eyes. Advisable, since a wise servant knew better than to show disapproval of his master's foibles.

"May I assist you, your grace?" the butler queried quite properly.

Drew winced at the sound, for it only made his head throb harder. "Yes, Foslett. You can have a bath drawn for me, and then order my curricle made ready in an hour. And have the library cleaned and fumigated at once."

"Very good, your grace. Would you care to see your

messages? Two came for you this morning, but I disliked disturbing you. One is from Lady Freemantle."

Constance, was Drew's first thought. His heart skipping a beat, he sliced through the seal with his forefinger and read the short note.

Her ladyship reported that Constance had rested fairly through the night and seemed a little better this morning. And the physician was more optimistic that his patient would eventually recover.

It was some consolation, Drew thought morosely, that Constance's prognosis was improving, even though his own fate was so precarious.

"Thank you, Foslett. What is the second message?"

"It is from Miss Roslyn Loring, your grace," the butler said, handing Drew a folded sheet of vellum.

His heart somersaulted . . . and then continued beating erratically as he ripped open the missive.

Dear Duke, I would be pleased if you would meet me this evening at eight o'clock at Fanny's special private residence, Number Eleven Crawford Place. I have a proposition to put to you.

Your friend, Roslyn.

Warring emotions of hope and dread battled inside him. What the devil did she mean by inviting him to meet her at Fanny's private house?

Drew glanced at the butler. "You may send a reply to Danvers Hall, confirming my acceptance."

"The message did not come from the Hall, your grace, but from here in London. I believe the footman was employed by a Miss Irwin."

Drew frowned in puzzlement, but he wasn't going

to question what Roslyn was doing in London. He would simply pray that she was giving him a second chance at loving her.

Crawford Place, Drew discovered from his coachman, was situated only a short distance north of Hyde Park and boasted a dozen row houses that appeared elegant and quietly expensive.

It seemed surprising that Fanny Irwin would own a sedate residence in this genteel neighborhood, given her status as one of London's leading Cyprians. Yet it surprised Drew more when he arrived promptly at the appointed time and the front door was opened by a masked woman in a shimmering gold domino.

His heart, which was already thudding with tension, started pounding wildly when he met the glimmering blue eyes behind the glittering mask. The seductive, mysterious beauty was none other than Roslyn.

That she wore her hair down, her pale gold tresses spilling in seductive disarray around her shoulders, surprised Drew most of all.

"Your grace," she murmured in a low, husky voice as she stepped aside to let him enter. "I am delighted you could come. Welcome."

Without waiting for his reply, Roslyn shut the door behind him, then turned and glided toward the nearby staircase. When Drew stood rooted to the floor, staring after her, she glanced over her shoulder at him and crooked her forefinger, beckoning. He hesitated a moment before gathering his wits and following her up the stairs.

He found his tongue as they reached the top landing. "I suppose this is Fanny's secret love nest," he remarked, trying to discipline his apprehension. "Does she entertain her more exclusive clients here?"

"No, never," Roslyn said unexpectedly. "This is her personal hideaway where she can enjoy a few moments of privacy now and then. Fanny conducts business at her main residence and never invites her patrons here. She loaned this house to me for the evening."

Impatiently wishing that Roslyn would tell him the purpose of her invitation, Drew accompanied her down a dimly lit corridor. "I admit I was surprised to receive your message," he prodded. "You said you had a proposition to put to me."

"Indeed, I do." Roslyn sent him an enigmatic glance. "I want to be your mistress for the night."

His eyebrows rose, but before he could reply, she led him into a large bedchamber that glowed softly in the light of myriad candles. Taking in the romantic ambience, Drew nearly found himself speechless again. "I can't say I understand, sweeting," he finally said.

"I want to pretend that I am your mistress and that you are my patron."

Her response made his breath catch and his heart thud. He had no time to ask any of the urgent questions running through his mind, however, for Roslyn took off her concealing mask, then unfastened her domino and let it fall to the carpet.

Drew's mouth went dry. She was dressed like a male sexual fantasy. She wore a red lace corset cunningly shaped to push up her high, ripe breasts and show her bare nipples, and black silk stockings held up by red garters, but nothing else. His cock swelled instantly at the lush sight of her, while his voice turned hoarse.

"What do you think you are doing, Roslyn?" he asked warily as she moved toward him.

Her eyes were dusky pools of temptation as she gazed up at him. "Making love to you, what else?"

"Hold just a moment. . . ."

Her lips, full and wet, pursed provocatively. "You don't want to make love to me, darling?"

"You know damned well I do. But if you intend to wed Haviland . . . Don't torture me like this, Roslyn, playing these wanton games."

"Oh, but I don't intend to wed Haviland," she remarked to his scalding relief. "I turned down his offer."

Drew expelled a long, harsh breath, yet her declaration still couldn't calm his anxiety. "Why did you refuse Haviland?"

"Because I don't love him."

He hesitated a long moment, almost afraid to ask the infinitely more crucial question. Finally he ventured to say even more hoarsely, "And do you think you could ever come to love me?"

When her smile wavered, Drew hardly dared to breathe. Then she laughed softly. "All in good time, darling. I must keep *some* secrets, mustn't I?"

Drew wanted to curse, to argue, to plead, yet he didn't think it would help his cause. Not when Roslyn was so intent on her own inexplicable purpose.

Reaching up to untie his cravat, she slid the fine cambric from around his neck and tossed it to the floor. "You are wearing too many clothes. Let me take them off."

"I can manage." Not trusting his fortitude if Roslyn touched him, Drew forestalled her assistance by stripping off his coat and waistcoat and shirt himself. But when he reached for the buttons on his evening breeches, she smiled. "Please . . . allow me."

Provocatively, Roslyn trailed a finger down his bare chest and over his flat abdomen to the front placket of his breeches. Drew sucked in a sharp breath as the teasing pressure of her fingers made his throbbing erection ache even harder. Yet he forced himself to stand still for her pleasurable torment.

To his growing frustration, she slowly unfastened the buttons, holding his gaze until she finally freed the thick length of his arousal. When she glanced down, irrepressible heat shot through Drew, not only because a beautiful woman was gazing at his burgeoning cock, but because the woman was his lovely Roslyn.

The heat assaulting him turned even hotter when she deliberately closed her hand around his swollen shaft.

Groaning, Drew grasped her wrist. "Roslyn . . . what the devil are you up to, tormenting me this way?"

Her lashes lifted flirtatiously, yet her eyes glimmered with tenderness and something resembling uncertainty. "Can't you tell?"

It was that tender vulnerability that gave him hope. Whatever game she was playing, she wasn't intent on revenge.

"I mean to seduce you, Drew," she murmured, increasing the already erratic pounding of his heart. He recognized her strategy now; Roslyn was using his own lessons in seduction against him. He just didn't know why.

But then, did it really matter? She would not want to make love to him if she believed they had no future together. And she was acting the siren, bewitching and alluring, pulsing with life and sensuality. He couldn't possibly resist her.

"So you mean to play the temptress?" he asked hoarsely.

"Isn't that what a good mistress is supposed to do?"

"I won't argue with that—"

"Excellent, then don't argue, darling."

"—but you needn't pretend to be a Cyprian," Drew finished.

She flashed him a slow, enchanting smile. He forgot everything but the tantalizing promise in her smile . . . until she raised her face to kiss him lightly on the lips.

He reached for her then, desperate to pull her into his arms, but she danced away. "No, Drew, I want to be the one to make love to you. When you have removed the rest of your clothing, come to bed. I will be waiting."

Drew gritted his teeth and stripped off his shoes and stockings and breeches in record time.

She was waiting for him as promised, stretched out naked on the satin sheets. She looked wildly desirable, her magnificent hair falling in a pale mane around her shoulders, her bare breasts enticing, her creamy thighs slightly parted in invitation.

Pure temptation, Drew thought, swallowing hard.

The smile lingered on her lips as she patted the mattress beside her. "Lie here with me, won't you?"

Nothing on earth could have kept him from accepting her invitation. When he had obeyed, lying on his back, Roslyn placed her hands on his chest and rose up on her knees. "Be still, please."

With effort, Drew lay there unmoving as she bent

over him, feeling the warm press of her lips in the hollow of his throat, on his breastbone, over his rib cage, then lower. Sharp sensation shot through him as her hands began stroking in tandem with her soft lips, eliciting shivers of desire deep inside him.

His stomach muscles contracted when she trailed light, tantalizing kisses over his skin. And he found it difficult to breathe when her fingertips traced a sensual pattern down his manhood to the swollen sacs below. Every muscle in his body clenched—and that was before she bent down to his loins, where his aching arousal was thick and straining.

"Roslyn. . . ."

"Hush, Drew. I want to give you pleasure."

Her hands shaped the rampant length of him, making him throb, before she set her lips to the head of his shaft.

At the searing jolt, Drew inhaled against his raging need while his erection surged even higher. She was suckling him now, her tongue gently licking, swirling, making him ravenous for her. Groaning, he sank his fingers into Roslyn's golden hair and surrendered to the gentle sorcery that enthralled him.

In only moments, he was half out of his mind with pleasure, his heart pounding so hard he thought it might come out of his chest, his hips straining against the alluring magic of her hot mouth.

Finally unable to bear her inflaming torment any longer, Drew reached down between her thighs, cupping her slick center, intent on making her as mad with arousal as he was.

"No, be still," she murmured between moist, tantalizing kisses.

"Roslyn . . . I can't wait much longer."

Lifting her head finally, she gazed up at him with blazing-hot eyes, while her tender smile returned. "I cannot wait, either."

To his relief, she shifted one knee over his outspread legs. Letting her damp cleft slide up his thigh, she lay fully on top of him, her silken body covering him, her hot, feminine core brushing against his phallus, caressing him.

Then slowly, she stretched up to kiss him, sliding her tongue slowly into his mouth in a heart-stirring claiming.

Drew kissed her back fervently, drinking of her warmth, cherishing her taste, her touch. When she pressed herself harder into him, the sinuous movements of her body inflamed his blood and the intensity of his longing.

He was nearly wild for her by the time she finally broke off the kiss and sat up to straddle him. Holding his fevered gaze, Roslyn braced her palms against his chest and lowered herself onto his pulsing shaft.

Feeling desperate now, Drew raised his hips and plunged into her waiting sweetness, deep inside her sleek, wet passage, seeking the fire and solace of her. He groaned as joy and pleasure created a riotous explosion of sensation in him.

It only made him hotter when Roslyn uttered a breathy whimper as he filled her. And the flush of heat and desire on her exquisite face told him she was feeling the same ardor for him.

Embracing him with her thighs then, she rocked her hips in a more urgent rhythm, demanding more from him. Drew whispered her name on a harsh breath. He was trembling now, shaking with his need for her, holding on with the last vestiges of willpower. Rasping her name again, he arched his back and thrust upward, his penetration increasing until he was buried as deep as her soul.

His desperation kindled a fierce flame in her. Roslyn began to move on him wildly, riding him, using her hips to stoke his frenzied passion. She was a ravenous temptress, demanding and wanton. She was flame-hot in her desires.

When Drew grasped her buttocks and pulled down hard, impaling her to the hilt, she finally gave in to her need, meeting him thrust for thrust, her moans increasing with the ragged sound of his, their mating raw and primal.

His body surged upward with his powerful climax just as her breathy scream exploded in the hushed room. She fell forward, sinking her teeth into his shoulder as the convulsive waves of passion crashed over them both. The sweet pain of her lover's bite only added to Drew's joyful pleasure.

It was indeed joyful, making love to the woman he loved. His feelings for Roslyn made his passion more intense, more precious, more incredible.

As the feverish urgency ebbed, they lay there exhausted and panting, her cheek resting on the sweat-dampened skin of his shoulder. It wasn't long, though, before Drew's blissful contentment faded and his tension returned.

When the rise and fall of her breathing finally gentled, he repeated his earlier question in a low voice. "What is this all about, Roslyn? Why are you so set on pretending to be my mistress?"

Her eyelids fluttered open, and she shifted her head to

look up at him solemnly, with that same vulnerable, uncertain expression as before. "Because gentlemen love their mistresses, Drew, and I want you to love me."

Just like that, his heart began pounding violently again. His voice was uneven when he managed to rasp, "God, Roslyn, I do love you. More than I ever thought possible."

Her blue eyes riveted on him. Her face was rapt, tense, her eyes wide with uncertainty. "You do?"

"Yes. I've loved you for weeks now."

Shakily, she pushed herself up on one elbow. "You have not."

"I have," Drew insisted. "I just couldn't admit it to myself."

When her mouth parted in awe, he reached up to run his thumb over her lower lip. "Do you remember what you told me about heart love? I know now that is what I feel for you, sweet Roslyn. My passion for you is far more than physical. I want you, yes. My body trembles when I touch you and aches when I can't. But my heart aches more. I miss you when you aren't with me. I long for your smile. And I cannot bear the thought of losing you."

When she continued to stare at him in stunned silence, Drew lowered his voice even further. "These past few days have been utter hell for me. Yet being without you made me realize just how much you mean to me. How much I need you. I need you to fill the emptiness inside me, Roslyn. To banish the loneliness. It's a need that comes from here. . . ." He took her hand, placing her palm over his heart. "Deep inside me."

"You *do* love me," she said wonderingly, searching his face.

"Yes, I do. And I want to marry you." A ghost of a smile touched his mouth. "Until recently, the thought of spending a lifetime shackled in matrimony to one woman seemed a prison sentence. But now the thought of not spending the rest of my days with you is terrifying." His thumb stroked her cheek. "I hope to God you will have me as your husband. I'll grovel if necessary. I will do anything to have you back. I know I have to earn your love, but I want the chance, Roslyn. Please give me that chance."

Her gaze softened and warmed. "You don't have to earn my love, Drew. It is already yours."

Drew squeezed his eyes shut in relief and gratitude; the emotion that rolled through him was so powerful, so deep, he felt weak with it.

"You truly love me?" he asked in that same awed tone.

"Yes, Drew. I tried so hard to resist loving you— because I thought my love would only be one-sided. I feared you would never be able to give me your heart. Even yesterday, when Lord Haviland said he was certain you loved me, I wouldn't dare let myself believe him."

Arching an eyebrow, Drew stared at her. "Haviland said that?"

"Yes, because you were determined to put my happiness before your own."

"I do want your happiness, Roslyn."

She smiled softly. "That is fortunate, because I want it, too. But my happiness lies only with you, Drew. I realized that when you sent Haviland to propose. And I knew that even if you didn't love me, I couldn't let you go without a fight."

Roslyn smiled faintly. "*That* is why I invited you here tonight. I vowed I would try to make you love me. I thought that if there was any chance that my theory was right—that passion can lead to love—I had to try. So Fanny helped me formulate a plan to become your mistress for the evening." Her blue eyes turned vulnerable again. "I am willing to settle for your passion if that is all I can have. I will be your mistress, Drew. But I would far rather be your wife."

His sense of humor returning with the dissolution of his terror, Drew was able to flash her a rakish smile. "Your offer is tempting, sweetheart. I've never had a mistress as enticing and satisfying as you. But I must refuse. I don't want you for my mistress, my lovely, precious Roslyn. I want you for my wife, and I won't settle for less."

"Are you certain?" she asked cautiously. "I don't want you to feel as if I entrapped you."

"I'm certain, Roslyn. You are my only happiness as well." His expression sobered. "I can't believe how barren my life was before I met you."

He'd suffered a cold emotionless existence until Roslyn had come along to warm him. She had touched a part of him no one had ever touched, a part he'd denied existed.

He had wasted so much of his life without love, Drew reflected. Roslyn had taught him that life wasn't worth very much without passion, without emotion, without love.

Emotion welled inside him as he captured her hand, his long fingers twining with her slender ones. "So this means we are resuming our betrothal?"

Holding his gaze, Roslyn shook her head slowly.

"No, Drew. I won't hold you to our former betrothal. If you want to wed me, you will have to offer for me again. And this time it cannot be merely to save my reputation but solely because you love me. Because you want to spend the rest of your life with me."

"Very well, love, will you please, *please* do me the incalculable honor of becoming my wife?"

Her warm smile made him ache with a sweetly intolerable pain. "Yes, my dearest love. I will, and gladly."

Drew slipped his hand behind her head, capturing her nape. "Thank God. . . ."

Bringing her lips down to his, he kissed her fervently, which sent fresh desire coursing through Roslyn's blood. She knew Drew was feeling the same urgency when, with one deft and powerful twist of his body, he rolled her beneath him.

Cradling her thighs in his own, making her feel his swelling hardness, he stared down at her. Roslyn drank in his expression . . . his dark, passion-hazed glance, the blazing possession in his eyes. She saw love there. Hot, possessive, protective, arousing.

"Drew, I love you so much," she whispered in reply, returning his look measure for measure.

"I won't ever tire of hearing those words. . . ."

He rasped her name, then took her mouth again. With the same passionate fire Roslyn opened to him and breathed him in.

Their ardor built as he worshiped her with hands and tongue. It seemed to Roslyn that she could never want more . . . Drew's melting kisses, his hands cherishing her body. But then he fit himself to her, entering her with fierce strong tenderness, thrusting in hard and deep as his lips murmured words of love.

The rapture swelled, mounting, thundering. His wild kisses kept coming, interspersed with fervent declarations of love as he took her body. He wooed her to madness, then healed her again as he poured himself into her, body and heart and soul.

When their passion was finally spent, Drew cradled her in his arms lovingly, his face nestled in her hair, his fingers absently playing with her pale locks.

It was a long while before he spoke, though. "I was terrified that you loved Haviland."

Deliciously sated and weary, Roslyn found the strength to press a kiss against his bare shoulder. "You had nothing to fear, Drew. I couldn't fall in love with him because I was already falling in love with you. There was no reason for you to be jealous."

"Of course there was. You had set your sights on marrying that bastard."

She laughed softly. "You cannot keep calling a belted earl that disparaging word, Drew."

"Very well, he isn't a bastard. But can you blame me if I was insanely jealous? I think you should feel flattered."

"Perhaps so, but you should never have threatened to kill him. I believe you owe Haviland a sincere apology."

"I might give him one, now that I know you don't love him. But if he ever dares look at you again with lust in his eyes. . . ."

Her laughter was exasperated and satisfied at the same time. "He won't look at me that way. He has too much honor. And hopefully, he will soon be occupied with his own romance. I mean to help Lord Haviland find a bride. In fact, he asked for my help."

Raising his head, Drew gazed at her a long moment before finally chuckling. "I knew he wasn't a total imbecile."

"Drew!"

"All right . . . I will become his bosom friend, if it will make you happy. But if I might use him to make a point . . ." Drew gazed deeply into her eyes. "The next time you and I argue—which undoubtedly will happen again—you needn't run and hide in the library. I'll never stop loving you, Roslyn, even if I sometimes lose my temper and you want to throttle me for it."

She winced. "We were not merely arguing. We were shouting at each other, fighting bitterly."

"Even so, that doesn't mean I don't love you with every fiber of my being. And in the future if we fight, we can have the pleasure of making up."

Her mouth slowly quirked. "That is what Fanny said."

"Fanny can be very wise sometimes."

"I know." Roslyn shook her head in amusement.

"What is it, love?"

"I was just thinking that I am not very wise sometimes. It was terribly naive of me to try and decree my own fate. I thought I could arrange my future to my specifications, to avoid the pain and heartache my parents endured. But I was wrong. You cannot apply scientific methods or rules of logic to matters of the heart. You cannot dictate love, any more than you can control fate."

"But I am very glad you tried."

"I, as well," Roslyn said softly.

Drew brought her fingers to his lips for a tender kiss. "I want to have our wedding right away. I'm not letting you change your mind again."

"I won't change my mind."

"I still plan to obtain a special license."

Roslyn frowned a little at that. "Drew . . . Arabella and Marcus are still away on their wedding trip. I want my sisters at our wedding, and Tess and Winifred also. Winifred would be heartbroken if we were to exclude her. And I'm certain my mother will want to return from France to attend. I will write her at once, but it will still take time to arrange her travel. I should think you would want your friends there, too."

"I do. And I suppose we don't want our union to look rushed." Letting his head fall back onto the pillows, Drew sighed. "I generally loathe weddings, but in this instance I suppose it would be best if we call the banns and hold the ceremony at St. George's. Three weeks should give ample time for all your family to return. Is your younger sister still in Hampshire?"

Roslyn hesitated, not liking to lie. "Lily is . . . somewhere else."

"Somewhere else? Do you know where?"

"Honestly? Yes. But she made me promise to keep her location a secret, for fear of Winifred's hounding her to find a husband."

It was Drew's turn to sound amused. "Your sister's secret is safe with me. I'm not about to get mixed up in Winifred's matchmaking for any price."

"I wish Winifred could understand that her efforts are not appreciated. Lily has a severe distaste for matrimony—even stronger than yours. Indeed, I doubt she'll be overly delighted that I am marrying you. But at least I know Arabella and Tess and Winifred will be thrilled for me." Roslyn lifted her head from Drew's shoulder. "Your mother will be disappointed, won't she?"

"What of it? Pleasing my mother is my very last concern."

"I wonder if she will refuse to attend the ceremony."

"Oh, she will attend, I have no doubt. She won't want to be left out and have it said that her son severed all connection with her. She couldn't bear to suffer the social consequences."

Roslyn felt a little sad for the duchess. "I think your mother must be terribly lonely."

"Somehow I can't feel any pity for her. She brought her loneliness on herself—" Drew stopped and slipped his hand behind Roslyn's nape again. "Thank God you saved me from a life like hers."

Smiling, Roslyn traced a finger over his lips. "Drew . . ." she said, returning to the subject of their nuptials, "I know you have your consequence to uphold, but I want Fanny to attend our wedding."

"Of course she should attend. I owe her an enormous debt of gratitude for bringing you to the Cyprians' ball. Otherwise I would have stayed as far away from you as possible."

Her look turned arch. "I think I deserve *some* credit, my lord duke."

"Perhaps you do. You demanded that I teach you how to seduce another man, but my tutoring backfired on me. I fell in love with my pupil instead."

Roslyn brought her face closer to his. "I think I need another lesson in seduction, your grace."

A devilish light of pure happiness glimmered in his eyes. "It will be my sincere pleasure, love."

Capturing her mouth, Drew smothered her laughter against his lips as he obliged.

Epilogue

*How grateful we are for your help, dearest Fanny.
Your plan for Arden's seduction worked to perfection. Indeed, we are agreed that our marriage will be
the most passionate love match ever made. And we
want you to dance at our wedding, just as you did at
Arabella's.*

—Roslyn to Fanny

*I am vastly relieved, dearest Roslyn. I feared I would
run out of tricks for you to try. Now there is only
Lily left . . . although I am not certain her happiness
lies in marriage as yours and Arabella's plainly does.*

—Fanny to Roslyn

Danvers Hall, July 1817

"I am utterly amazed," Arabella said to the company at large, "that so much happened during our absence. We were away for barely a month."

Arabella and Marcus had arrived home an hour ago
from their wedding journey and promptly settled in
the drawing room with refreshments while Drew and
Roslyn detailed their latest marriage plans and re-
counted the story of hunting Winifred's thief and finding Sir Rupert's second family.

Heath had joined them during the recitation, since
Roslyn and Drew had arranged a small dinner this

evening to welcome the newlyweds home and to celebrate their own renewed betrothal.

Sitting across from Roslyn, Drew was content to watch her as she laughed and chatted with her sister. She looked supremely happy, which warmed his heart profoundly.

Arabella looked just as blissful, he noted. And Marcus was watching his wife with that same heart-smitten look that Drew knew was written on his own face.

"But Winifred has no regrets about taking in Constance and the children?" Arabella asked her sister.

"None thus far," Roslyn answered. "The little girls are a delight. And Winifred and Benjamin are beginning to come to terms. He is understandably reluctant to relinquish responsibility for his mother and sisters, even though he's merely a boy himself and should never have had to shoulder such a burden. Moreover, while he is glad to no longer be in service, Benjamin thinks he should earn his own way and prickles at having to suffer Winifred's 'charity,' as he calls it."

With an impish glance at her new husband, Arabella smiled. "I can certainly sympathize, since I was adamant about refusing Marcus's largesse."

Marcus's answering smile was amused. "But you won our wager fairly, my love, so when I was compelled to grant your financial independence, you couldn't consider it charity."

"Fortunately," Roslyn said, continuing her story, "Benjamin no longer requires charity, thanks to Drew." She flashed him a fond look. "He compelled that corrupt solicitor, Farnaby, to return the funds he stole from Constance."

"So their futures are assured," Arabella said approvingly.

"Yes, and it is already arranged that the girls will attend our academy when they are old enough. It is only fitting, considering that Winifred's fortune funded the endeavor. Meanwhile I have started tutoring Sarah and Daisy in sums and reading and supervising Benjamin's studies until Winifred can employ a proper governess and tutor for them."

"That is kind of you, Roslyn," her sister commented. "But you have always put great store in the fundamentals of education."

Roslyn wrinkled her nose. "They are woefully behind, I'm afraid. Working such grueling hours in the milliner's shop, Constance had little time to teach her children much other than their manners, which are frankly exquisite. It doesn't help, however, that Benjamin has a highly stubborn streak. He thinks being a footman was far easier than applying himself to his school lessons, and that at his age he is past the point of needing an education. He and Winifred spar regularly about it, but she seems to relish their disputes."

Drew had to agree on that point, and believed their lively quarrels set a beneficial example for Roslyn. Witnessing good-natured arguments without bitterness and antagonism would only help her deal with any future tiffs they had in their marriage.

He also knew that Winifred was far happier now that she had her late husband's children to care for.

"Will Constance be joining us for dinner this evening?" Arabella asked.

"No," Drew replied. "She's making excellent progress, but she is still too weak to sit up for more than a half hour at a time. My physician expects her to make a full recovery, though."

"So it will be just us and Winifred this evening?"

"Yes," Roslyn replied. "Tess is in London and cannot get away."

"And is Lily still there with Fann—"

"Actually, Arabella, I must speak to you about that," Roslyn interrupted quickly.

Drew noted that Heath was now frowning at the mention of the youngest Loring sister's name, but before they could discuss Lily further, Arabella nodded. "Roslyn, why don't we go abovestairs so that I may wash off my travel dust? And I am certain Marcus would like some time alone with his friends."

"An excellent idea," Roslyn said with a smile.

The gentlemen all rose when the ladies did. When Arabella gave her husband a light kiss on the cheek, Marcus brought her fingers to his lips and held them there for much longer than was proper. The searingly tender look he shared with his bride would have made Drew envious but for his own romance with Roslyn.

But clearly the first flush of love had *not* worn off for the newlyweds. Arabella was positively glowing.

"Matrimony obviously agrees with you, my lady," Drew observed as he gave her a brief bow.

She laughed. "It does indeed. It is beyond wonderful—which I hope you discover for yourself, your grace. I am still amazed that you and my sister are betrothed."

Drew shot Roslyn a tender glance. "I am amazed that I had the remarkable good sense to fall in love with her."

At the warm, radiant smile Roslyn sent him in

response, his heartbeat accelerated and he found himself staring at her, immobilized by the profound affection flowing through him. The emotion he felt for her stole his breath and left him feeling ridiculously weak and powerful at the same time.

When she had left the drawing room with her sister, Drew stood shaking his head in silent amusement. This was what love did to a man . . . made him a witless, drooling hound panting at the feet of his loved one in his eagerness to win her smile.

"More ale, Drew?" Marcus asked, interrupting his wayward thoughts.

"Please," Drew replied, turning back to his friends.

Marcus refilled their mugs from a pitcher as the three of them resumed their seats.

"So, old chap," he said to Drew. "Less than three weeks of freedom left."

"Just so." The banns had been called the previous Sunday for the first time, so it was not long before the wedding. Yet Drew could scarcely wait until the day he could make Roslyn his wife.

"I'm eager to be done with it," he admitted. "I can now understand, Marcus, why you were so impatient to marry Arabella."

Marcus eyed him with good-humored skepticism. "I must say you made an amazing transformation in a very short time. Barely a month ago you were offering me condolences on the demise of my bachelorhood."

"Yes, my fine fellow," Heath prodded jovially, "whatever happened to your vow that you would never be ensnared by any female?"

"I fell in love," Drew replied simply.

"But you don't even believe in love."

"I suppose I will have to eat my words. I am well and truly caught now and wouldn't have it any other way."

Both his friends looked vastly amused that he had succumbed so easily when he'd been so adamantly set against matrimony.

"You will recall," Marcus remarked with a smug grin, "that I predicted your cynicism would vanish if you were fortunate enough to meet the right woman. Funny thing about love—it changes everything."

Drew nodded. "Turns a man inside out. It's brought out feelings in me I didn't even know I could have."

He drank a long swallow of ale, marveling at the change in himself. He could scarcely believe that one woman could make such a profound difference in his life. Roslyn had shattered his legendary dispassion and left him longing to be with her for the rest of his days.

He'd never expected to feel anything so powerful, so deep, for anyone. But he had no doubts that his feelings for Roslyn would last a lifetime. The love inside him was painfully strong; hunger and desire a sweet ache.

"So, Heath, now it is your turn," Marcus commented. "If we must suffer the slings and arrows of matrimony, we should insist on your esteemed company."

"I can't deny the thought has crossed my mind," Heath responded casually.

Both his friends raised sharp eyebrows, but it was Marcus who spoke first. "Do you have a particular target in mind?"

Heath gave a shrug. "There is one woman who

intrigues me, but she clearly has no desire for my company."

"Astonishing," Marcus declared in an amused drawl, "since all the ladies love you for your irresistible charm. Fortunately there are any number who would leap at the chance to become your bride." Marcus grinned. "It would only be fitting if you should wind up falling in love and marrying. We three have been through thick and thin together. Our foray into matrimony shouldn't be any different."

Heath's mouth flickered in an enigmatic smile. "I might have to give it some consideration. You two bleaters are so disgustingly happy, I can scarcely bear to be in your company."

It was Drew's turn to grin as he raised his glass in salute. "To your challenge of finding a bride, then."

Sharing the camaraderie of longtime friends who were as close as brothers, they lifted their glasses to drink.

It was perhaps three-quarters of an hour later when Simpkin appeared with a message for Drew, saying that Miss Roslyn requested his presence in the library. With alacrity, Drew excused himself from his friends. It had been too long since he'd been alone with Roslyn; too long since he had last kissed her and touched her and basked in her nearness.

He found her curled up in the window seat, perusing a thick sheaf of papers in her lap.

Shutting the door firmly behind him, Drew crossed to her. When Roslyn looked up and smiled, the rest of the world faded from his awareness. All his consciousness centered on this one woman. The warmth that flowed through him at just being with her was a reminder of how cold his life had been before coming to love her, how empty his heart.

His heart beat now as if it had finally come alive after a long, lonely sleep. Settling beside her, Drew took her in his arms for a fervent, deeply satisfying kiss.

His passionate embrace left her breathless and sighing in contentment as she rested her head against his shoulder, her forehead nestled beneath his jaw.

"I have missed that far too much," he admitted.

Roslyn laughed softly. "So have I . . . which is absurd, considering that it has barely been two hours since we last kissed."

"But I know we'll be deprived of any more kisses for the rest of the evening, since we don't have the Hall to ourselves anymore. It's a pity we can't send everyone away, love. I would ravish you right here."

"I would like that. But besides being scandalous, we don't have time. Dinner will be announced in a short while."

"Then promise we will be together tonight, afterward."

Lifting her head, she glanced up at Drew coquettishly. "What did you have in mind, darling?"

"A stroll on a moonlit summer evening. We've never made love by the river in the moonlight."

Roslyn laughed again. "I think Arabella and Marcus have. Lily and I once caught them sneaking back into the house, looking flushed and disheveled."

"Fortunately for them, they don't need to sneak around now to enjoy their pleasures, since they're married and they have the master's apartments all to themselves. We, on the other hand, must steal our private moments when we can. So will you accompany me on a moonlit stroll tonight?"

"Yes, gladly."

"I will be counting the moments," Drew murmured. "I think we should set about begetting an heir tonight."

Roslyn's eyebrow arched uncertainly. "Just an heir, Drew?"

Understanding her query, he shook his head. "Not just an heir. I don't want a son merely to carry on the dukedom. I want children because they will be a part of you."

Her enchanting smile returned. "That is a lovely sentiment. And I feel the same way about you. But I hope our children will have happier lives growing up than we did."

Drew lifted their clasped hands to kiss her fingers. "I guarantee I will give it my utmost effort." His eyes smiled down into hers before finally he recalled that she had summoned him to the library. "Why did you wish to speak to me, love?"

Roslyn held up the sheaf of papers. "Besides the chance to kiss you? This just arrived from Fanny. It is her manuscript."

"Manuscript?" he repeated as she handed the pages to him to read.

"Yes. Fanny has written a book on the art of seduction, and she sent it to us to read and suggest improvements."

"Seduction, hmm?" Drew's mouth quirked. "What is it, an instruction manual for courtesans?"

"Not for courtesans. For young ladies who want to marry. She has entitled it, *Advice to Young Ladies on Capturing a Husband*."

His amusement faltered. "This is for scheming husband-hunters? Is Fanny serious about asking for my help? She expects *me* to aid the enemy?"

Roslyn chuckled before her expression turned a little troubled. "It is for a good cause, Drew. Lily told me that some of Fanny's friends are having financial difficulties. And selling this book could help them solve their problems."

"That surprises me. I thought Fanny was highly successful in her trade."

"She is. But she isn't wealthy enough to pay their enormous debts on her own."

Drew glanced down at the manuscript. "I am highly curious to know what Fanny put in her book about seducing a prospective husband."

He thumbed through the pages, reading a passage here and there. "I see that she included a number of my tactics in addition to her own." He smiled wickedly at one particular passage. "Hmm, so that is what you were attempting at Fanny's house when you drove me mad with your tormenting?"

"I will never tell," Roslyn retorted saucily. "We females must have our secrets, remember?"

"You can have all the secrets you want, as long as you use them solely on me."

His gaze skimmed further down the page. "Will this book be published under Fanny's name?"

"No, it will be authored by an anonymous lady."

"I think that wise," Drew said dryly, "since I rather doubt that gently nurtured females of the ton would willingly take advice from a renowned highflyer, even if it *would* help them catch a husband. Ah, here is one we never discussed. 'Never nag or scold, especially when he deserves it. He will be enchanted by your forbearance, and his guilt will act in your favor.' You should heed that particular advice, my sweet."

"*I* should heed it?" Roslyn's blue eyes took on a gleam of laughter. "Have I ever nagged or scolded you, my dearest duke?"

"Occasionally . . . and I found the experience devastating. But scolding or not, you always enchant me."

It was true, Drew thought, gazing down at her upturned face. Roslyn had the kind of enchanting beauty that made him ache just to see it, but it was her inner beauty that had ensnared his heart.

And the loving look in her eyes told him clearly that he had ensnared hers. Caught by that look, Drew reached up to touch her, his fingers wandering with delicacy over her face, her brows, her eyelids.

Roslyn sighed again, then inhaled breathlessly as he cradled her head in his hands and covered her mouth in a long, sublime, heart-stirring kiss.

She could scarcely credit her incredible good fortune, could scarcely credit the feelings she shared with Drew at merely kissing: this passionate need for each other, this hammering of the senses, this exhilarating, endless tenderness. This love. They were lovers, friends . . . and soon husband and wife.

Emotion, pure and powerful, flooded through her whole being. She felt hope and immeasurable joy. And she knew without a doubt that Drew felt similarly when he finally broke off kissing her.

Her dazed, tender look turned wondering as she brought his hand to her cheek and whispered, "I feel an almost fearful happiness, Drew. One I never even dared to dream of. Do you think it will last?"

"I know damned well it will last—if you promise to love and cherish me as I will always do you."

"Of course I promise."

"Good." He grinned. "Now that I have gone to all this trouble to train you properly, I wouldn't care to have to break in a new candidate for my mistress . . . *or* my duchess."

Roslyn's musical laugh rang out in the hush of the library before Drew silenced her for a very long time by capturing her lips again with his own.

Read on for an exciting taste of

To Seduce a Bride

by

Nicole Jordan

Chiswick, England June 1817

"I cannot understand why he flusters me so," Lilian Loring mumbled unevenly to the gray cat. "No man has ever unsettled me that way."

A soft purr was the only reply Lily received to her complaint.

"It is not merely because he is handsome, either. I am not ord'narily attracted to handsome noblemen." If anything she was highly wary of them. "And I care nothing for his rank and consequence."

Giving a woozy sigh, Lily stretched out in the straw as she stroked the cat's fur. She was speaking of Heath Griffin, Marquess of Claybourne, yet she was hard-pressed to explain the deplorable effect he had on her, particularly since she had just met him for the first time this morning at her sister's wedding.

"The trouble is, he is too sharm...*charm*ing." *And virile. And vital. And powerful.*

Whatever his attributes, Lord Claybourne made her absurdly breathless and agitated.

"Devil take 'im...."

Lily bit her lip and fell silent upon registering how slurred her words sounded. No doubt the result of drinking three full glasses of champagne at the wedding—which was at least two glasses too many. But the events of the evening had been dismaying enough to drive her to imbibe.

She wasn't *completely* foxed at the moment, yet it had probably been a mistake to attempt climbing up to the stable loft wearing a ball gown—an exquisite confection of pale-rose silk—and dancing slippers. Weaving her way up the ladder in such narrow skirts while carrying a napkin full of dinner tidbits had challenged her usual athleticism. But she had wanted to bring supper for Boots before she left the wedding celebrations.

Boots, the Danvers Hall stable cat, had recently given birth to a litter of kittens. Currently the family of felines was contentedly curled up in the box Lily had arranged in the loft to protect the mother cat and her new offspring from the home-farm dogs. Lily had left her lantern hanging on a peg below so as not to frighten the youngsters, and the muted golden glow contributed to the tranquility of the loft, as did the warmth of the night, since it was nearly summer.

The three kittens were little balls of fluff, their eyes barely open, but they were beginning to show their own unique personalities—much like the three Loring sisters, Lily thought. If she was honest with herself she would admit that she'd sought refuge in the stable loft as much to escape Lord Claybourne as to feed the estate cat and indulge in a bout of self-pity.

While Boots was nibbling delicately on breast of

roast pheasant, Lily carefully reached inside the box and picked up one of the adorable kittens.

"Do you re'lize how precious you are?" she murmured, pressing her nose into its soft ebony fur. The black kitten was the rambunctious one, like Lily herself, and it swatted at her nose playfully.

Lily gave a low laugh, which helped staunch the ache in her throat at the poignant memories she was trying to hold at bay.

It was extremely hard for Lily to bear, losing her sister Arabella to marriage, but the evening had been made even more difficult by the meddlesome matchmaking efforts of their kindly patron, Winifred, Lady Freemantle. Four years ago, when the Loring sisters had been penniless and in desperate need of earning their own livings, Winifred had supplied the funds to start their Academy for Young Ladies for the daughters of the wealthy merchant class. Yet all during the ball, Winifred had kept pushing Lily in the path of Marcus's close friend, the Marquess of Claybourne.

Eventually, much to her chagrin and dismay, Winifred cornered her and practically *forced* his lordship to dance with her.

As soon as the waltz was over, Lily had extricated herself from his unnerving company.

It was blessedly quiet here, set away from the rest of the yard.

Her head was still swimming from the overindulgence of wine, along with her potent memories of Lord Claybourne. The feel of him as they'd waltzed—sinewy and powerful, all lithe grace—had uncustomarily flustered her.

"But I trust I will never see him again after t'night," Lily muttered as she returned the black kitten to the box. "Or at least that I will never again be the victim of Winifred's humiliating mash...*match*making schemes."

It was then that Lily heard a faint noise from below, like a throat being cleared.

Wondering who had entered the stable, she shifted her position to look over the loft's edge. Her heart skipped a violent beat when she spied the broad-shouldered Marquess of Claybourne leaning against a post, his arms folded, his head cocked to one side.

When her head suddenly started spinning dizzily, Lily drew back in haste. *Oh, dear heaven.* Had he overheard her lament that he was too charming? What other incriminating observations had she made about him?

Holding a hand to her throbbing temple, Lily slowly peered over the side again. "M-My lord, what are you doing here?"

"I saw you leave the ball and wondered why you would visit the stables."

"You followed me?" Lily asked blankly.

Claybourne gave a bland nod. "Guilty as charged."

Her eyes narrowed. "So you were shamelessly eavesdropping?"

"I was curious. Do you always talk to yourself, Miss Loring?"

"Sometimes. But in this case I am speaking to the cat.... Actually *cats*. Boots the stable cat recently had kittens."

"Would you care to explain what you are doing up there in the loft?"

"If you mush...*must* know...I am feeding her."

"You came here to feed the stable cat?" His tone held surprise and a hint of disbelief.

"Should I have let her starve?" Lily asked rhetorically. "Boots is an excellent mouser, but at the moment she has more important tasks to occupy her, namely taking care of her kittens."

His handsome mouth quirked. "Do you mean to remain there with the cats?"

"No. I will come down as soon as my head clears. I seem...to have drunk a bit too much champagne." To her chagrin, she was too dizzy just now to climb safely down the ladder to escape Lord Claybourne's unwanted presence.

"Then you won't mind if I join you," he said, moving across the isle to put a foot on the lowest wooden rung.

Yes, she minded! Lily sat up abruptly, wondering how she could prevent him from imposing his company upon her. "You cannot climb up here, my lord!" she exclaimed, yet her protest obviously had no effect, since his head soon appeared above the edge of the loft.

"I believe I can. I plan to keep you company."

With his torso in view, he paused to survey her with interest.

"You will get your coat dusty," Lily said lamely, eyeing his elegantly tailored evening coat of burgundy superfine—Weston, no doubt—that fitted those magnificent shoulders to perfection.

"My coat will survive." His gaze raked over her own attire. "What about you? You are wearing a ball gown."

"That is different. I don't care about clothing."

When his eyebrow shot up, Lily realized that her retort could have two meanings. "I d-don't mean that I like to go *naked*. . . ." she stammered, feeling scalding heat flood her cheeks. "I only meant that I don't care about *fancy clothing* . . . ball gowns and such."

"How novel." His tone turned wry as he climbed the last few rungs and settled a hip on the loft's edge. "It strains the imagination. You must be the first female I've ever met who isn't interested in fancy gowns."

"But you see, I am not normal, my lord. I am very *abnormal*."

"Is that so?" he replied, easing himself closer to sit beside her.

Even in the dim light, she could see that his hazel eyes were dancing. He was laughing at her!

Stiffening her spine, Lily opened her mouth to remonstrate, but he spoke first. "What is so abnormal about you, angel? You look exceedingly normal to me."

When his gaze drifted downward again over her body, Lily pressed her hands to her flaming cheeks and willed herself to calm down—which was deplorably difficult considering the fluttery, flustered sensations that were racing through her at his lordship's close proximity.

Stretching up to her full sitting height, she tried to appear regal and made her tone dampening as she replied. "I *meant* that I am not usual for a *female*."

"I have little doubt about that."

She shot him an exasperated look. "The thing is, I should have been born male. I would have been much happier."

"Oh, and are you so unhappy now?"

In her slightly inebriated state, her thoughts were

more sluggish than usual, and she had to consider his question for a moment. "Well...no. I like my life quite well. But women have little of the freedom that men enjoy."

"What freedom would you like to enjoy, love?"

Lily bit her lower lip, abashed at how her tongue was running away from her. Yet she couldn't seem to help herself; the champagne had loosened her tongue deplorably. "Never mind. Don't listen to me, my lord. I don't hold my liquor at all well."

"So it would seem. What made you drink so much then?"

"I was drowning my sorrows, if you insist on knowing."

"What sorrows?"

"At losing my sister to matrimony. I was indulging in a bout of melancholy. But it was supposed to be *private*." When he didn't respond, Lily added pointedly, "That is a veiled hint for you to leave, my lord."

Instead of retreating down the loft ladder, he smiled and leaned back, casually resting his weight on his palms and crossing his long, satin-clad legs in front of him, as if settling in for a long stay.

Lily exhaled in a huff. "I don't think you comprehend the danger you are in, Lord Claybourne. It is a grave mistake for you to be alone with me. If Winifred knew, she would be ecstatic."

"Winifred?"

"Lady Freemantle. She is the main reason I left the ball early—to escape her machinations. She is trying to match me with you. You must have noticed."

Her allegation didn't seem to alarm him as it

should. "Perhaps, but her machinations are no worse than usual. I'm well accustomed to eager mamas throwing their daughters at my head."

Lily grimaced in disgruntlement. "Perhaps *you* can dismiss her scheming, but I cannot. It is mortifying to the extreme. I am not a prize heifer to be exhibited before an eligible gentleman and judged for my defects and qualifications."

His eyes were dancing again. "I should think not."

At his blithe reply, exasperation welled up in Lily full force. "Do you not *understand*? Winifred wants me to set my cap at you."

"But you don't intend to."

"Certainly not! I have no interest in marriage."

"That is quite a unique perspective for a young lady. Most women have made it their mission in life to find a husband."

"True. But you needn't worry about me hounding you, Lord Claybourne. Oh, I know you are a prime catch. You are disgustingly rich, you have a vaunted title, you aren't so shabby in appearance, and you are said to be irresistibly charming."

"But you aren't swayed by this delightful catalog of my attributes."

"Not in the least." Lily smiled faintly to soften the harshness of her observation. "No doubt you have a bevy of lovestruck admirers, but I will never join their ranks. And I have no intention of behaving like all the other flagrant husband-hunters you know. I won't chase after you."

"You relieve my mind, Miss Loring. I don't enjoy being chased." From the provocative laughter in his voice, he seemed to be enjoying himself far too much.

"But I am quite curious to know why you have such a profound distaste for marriage."

Lily drew a deep breath. Hoyden or not, she normally would never dream of discussing her personal affairs with a perfect stranger. But in this case, she was eager to be rid of him, so a liberal dose of frankness might stand her in good stead.

"In my experience marriage usually leads to unhappiness for a woman," she said honestly.

"You speak from personal experience?"

Lily made a face. "Unfortunately, yes. My parents' union was hostile enough to give me an aversion to matrimony for life."

The gleaming light in Claybourne's eyes faded as he studied her. His searching perusal was more unsettling than his amusement, however.

"I don't need a husband," she hurried to add, "despite what proper society decrees for young ladies. I am financially independent now, thanks to the generous settlement Marcus made me. So I can have a fulfilling life without having to marry. I mean to use the funds to travel the world and explore new and exciting places."

"Alone?"

"I am one and twenty, old enough to take care of myself."

"So...you won't marry because men often make their wives unhappy," Claybourne said slowly, as if testing the theory in his mind.

"Yes. First you make us too infatuated to think clearly, so we give over all control to you, and then you make our lives a misery. I am not about to give any man that power over me."

To her surprise, Claybourne leaned forward and

raised a hand to touch her cheek. "Who hurt you, angel?" he asked quietly.

Discomfited, Lily drew back. "No one hurt *me*. It was my mother and my sister who were hurt."

He was silent for a moment. "I understand your father was a champion philanderer."

Lily looked away, not wanting to recall the painful memories. "He was indeed. He flaunted his mistresses before my mother at every opportunity. It hurt her terribly. And Arabella's first betrothed betrayed her almost as badly. She *loved* him, but when the scandal broke, he ended their engagement out of hand."

"Is that why you didn't want Marcus marrying your sister?"

"In large part."

"You seem to harbor a strong prejudice against noblemen."

"I won't deny it. Noblemen can make the worst sort of husbands."

"Then I can take heart from the fact that your aversion is not directed at me personally."

Her brows drew together. "No, I have nothing against you *personally*, my lord. I don't even know you." *Thankfully*, she added to herself.

Claybourne remained silent for another dozen heartbeats before shifting his position to study the box's inhabitants. "I take it this is Boots," he murmured, reaching down to scratch the mother cat behind one ear. Surprisingly Boots didn't object but started purring at once, rubbing her head sensuously against his fingers.

Lily found her gaze riveted on his lordship's hands as he stroked the silky gray fur. He had strong, graceful hands, surprising in such a bold, masculine man.

"I think you are forgetting one important fact," he said finally.

She didn't immediately realize Lord Claybourne was speaking to her. "What fact?"

"It is true that some men can be hurtful, but they can also give women great pleasure."

Warmth rose to her face. "Perhaps some men can, but that is beside the point."

Just then the black kitten pounced on the lace of his cuff and started chewing his knuckle.

"Hungry little fellow, aren't you?" he murmured with a smile. "And you as well," he added as the gray kitten attacked his thumb.

He drew out the tiny creatures, settling them in his lap. Almost at once the black kitten crawled up his chest, digging its claws into the gold brocade of his waistcoat.

"I am sorry, my lord," Lily said regretfully.

"It is no matter." When the black one scampered higher, Claybourne gave a soft laugh. The low, husky sound raked across her nerve endings with undeniable potency.

"Here, let me help...." she hastened to say.

Leaning forward, Lily reached out to pluck the kitten off his chest, but the curling claws clung to the priceless lace of his cravat. She tried to extricate it without damaging the fine fabric and somehow wound up pushing the marquess back in the straw.

He lay there, looking up at her. Leaning over him, Lily froze at the expression on his face. He had gone quite still, but there was a soft fire in his eyes that made her heart beat faster.

"I am sorry," she repeated, suddenly breathless.

"I am not."

His fingers closing gently around the tiny black paws, he managed to free his cravat and set the kitten in the straw beside him. Immediately it bounded off toward the box, and the gray went scrambling after its litter mate.

Even so, Lily couldn't look away from Lord Claybourne. When he reached up and slid his fingers behind her nape, her breathing faltered altogether. Then shockingly, he drew her mouth down to meet his in a featherlight contact.

She was unprepared for the rush of sensation that shot through her at that unexpected caress; his lips were warm and firm yet enticingly soft—and much too tempting.

Stifling a gasp, Lily pressed her palms against his chest and lifted her reeling head. "W-Why did you do that?" she asked, her voice suddenly hoarse.

"I wanted to see if your lips were as inviting as they look."

His reply was not what she expected. "And were they?"

"More so."

Lily stared down at him, unable to move. Her gaze was riveted on his face. It was a strong face, arresting and beautiful in the muted glow of lamplight. His lips were chiseled and generous, and they curved now in a faint smile as he returned her regard.

"I expect you have no idea what you are missing, sweetheart. Passion between a man and a woman can be quite remarkable."

Lily cleared her suddenly dry throat, fighting her enchanted stupor. "Even so, I don't care to have anything to do with passion."

"What do you know about it? Have you ever even been properly kissed?"

Her brow furrowed cautiously. "What do you mean by 'properly'?"

His quiet chuckle was soft, husky, as he drew her face down to his again. "If you have to ask, the answer must be no. I think we should rectify the deficiency at once...."

As the warm mist of his breath caressed her mouth, Lily braced herself for the renewed shock, but when his lips began to play over hers with exquisite pressure, she felt her resistance melting.

The effect of his kiss was spellbinding. The heady sensation he roused made her lightheaded and giddy, much like the effect of the champagne.

When he left off this time, he reached up and stroked her cheek with a finger. "Did you find that pleasurable, sweeting?"

She couldn't utter a denial for it would be a lie. His kiss had left her breathless and dazed, and she felt a strange quivering between her thighs, an restless ache low and deep in her feminine center. "Y-Yes."

"You sound unsure."

"It was...quite pleasant."

His mouth curved wryly. "Merely pleasant? I think I should be insulted."

"You know you needn't be. You are said to be a devil with the ladies, and you have countless conquests—" She paused, shaking her head in a futile effort to clear it. "At least now I can understand why everyone says women adore you."

Somehow she was sprawled all over Lord Claybourne, pressed against his hard, muscular body. Warmth radiated up from his chest, infusing her breasts with a delicious heaviness.

And that was *before* he raised a finger to the hollow of her throat and lightly stroked. "I think I should demonstrate."

"Demonstrate what?" she asked unsteadily.

His eyes smiled into hers. "The kind of pleasure a man can give a woman."